PIGEONS DO TALK

PIGEONS DO TALK

To Robin

1ˢᵗ Edition

TONY WILSON

Tony Wilson

*we do not see enough of
each other.*

First paperback edition

978-1-80227-711-1 (paperback)
978-1-80227-731-9 (ebook)

To Nigel and Helen for letting me and Cathy stay in their beautiful Chateau near Limoges. It inspired me.

To Mr Sharma for a successful hip operation. I took time off work December 2016. Then a month delay (no beds) and time after I did the first ten chapters. The second lockdown 2021, Debz instructed me to finish it. 6 years a slave to my dream.

To Debz Hobbs-Wyatt (author and literary advisor for her guidance and patience.)

To Alan Marsden who sadly lost his wife but lived in Tremolat. This beautiful French village has a Michelin star hotel with a helicopter landing area. The Pizzeria has tables where you can watch the world go by. I stayed at "Lou Cantou" in Tremolat. My imagination wandered.

To anyone who has felt trapped, not knowing what the future might hold, hope is eternal.

To all my friends who smile, laugh, socialize , discuss randomly, and spread the love of life.

To Cathy who has put up with me for many years and my rock and help.

I hope one day this might be a film.

When I ache to live, my mind loves to stay with the peaceful
whiteness
of a pigeon's care... in boundless amity.

– Munia Khan

Chapter 1

Northern Tunisia
Wednesday, November 9th, 2016

The Tunisian guard had a machine gun.

It's the first thing Rochine saw.

It was her governess, Francesca, who first woke her. As Rochine's hands moved over tired eyes she'd seen the guard, who was frantically telling her to get up – they needed to get away.

She stumbled over her slippers as Francesca grabbed two small bags. The gunfire and explosions were far too close. Rochine instinctively threw on sweatpants and found her favourite Nike trainers, pushing her feet in as she grabbed a warm sweater for over her nightdress. The guard left her to move to the upstairs landing, holding the machine gun, wearing a belt of hand grenades. He was there to protect them. *What normal families needed protection?*

Her parents were now in her room frantically throwing items into the bags. Rochine saw Francesca trembling, tears wet on her cheeks as she followed Rochine's father down the emergency chute that lead to the outside. *And what normal families needed emergency chutes?*

It was built for times such as these; but in the hope it would never be used.

On the beach, Rochine clasped onto her mother's hand and they moved quickly... the *rat tat tat* of machine gun fire behind them; from the garden and now from the house. The boat was anchored next to

1

their private beach. They had to get away. Rochine looked up; at least the full moon made it easier to see. A cold breeze came off the ocean. When she looked back, she could see whoever was after them now had control of the house.

Rochine's father was armed. She saw him trip as he ran towards the moored boat. Next thing there were men gagging him and tying his hands. She tried to call out, but it was too late. Now more men were doing the same to her mother and governess. She felt a hand close around her throat. Her hands were bound together, as she was pushed with force towards the boat.

No. This was not happening.

But it was.

Stay calm, Rochine. Do as they say...

Dear God. Two of their trusted crew were dead, one lying near the boat with his throat cut; the other in the water. Was this to do with her father? He worked for the Exxon Corporation and had just come back from America. Trump nonsense. Her mother was to be the new French ambassador in Tunis, was it to do with her? Surely not. Rochine looked at her governess sobbing as the rest of the raiding party came down the chute. Two were injured but okay to join them on the boat, dinghies on tow as they set a course out to sea.

Rochine had always felt a prisoner in her own home, now she really was a prisoner.

Her eyes were drawn to a soldier. He had released two pigeons. For a moment, she watched transfixed as they flew up, silhouetted in the lunar glow; flying a full circle before heading in different directions over the ocean. A sense of strange irony mixed with the fear.

The boat slowed down, and everyone transferred to the two dinghies. She watched the soldier give instructions as he put their family boat onto autopilot. She watched the boat drift on the moonlit water, until it disappeared. Rochine shivered; her governess sat trembling. She felt her mother's heart beating and saw fear in her father's eyes for the first time.

All Rochine could think was those lovely innocent pigeons flying to freedom.

| Chapter 2 | **RAID HQ (Research, Assistance, Intervention, Dissuasion) Tuesday November 8th, 2016 (1 day before)** |

Danielle Bousquet approached the barrier just before midnight.

On the outside, the board said 'Horticultural College'. It was located amongst the dormant volcanoes of Clermont Ferrand, France. A mere forty-minute drive from the city. But this was no college.

She parked her Peugeot 606 next to the accommodation unit; helicopters in the distance next to the hangars, across from the medical centre. She walked past the building with YMCA inscribed at the front. Of course, that was its pet name. Everything about this building was a façade.

Nestled off the D145 it was an ideal location; south of Le Lot D'Aydat. The area boasted hiking routes around the extinct volcanoes; hilly areas good for farming and industry. The 'college' was well hidden, two concealed entry points. Who would ever guess what really went on there? Or what Danielle did. Or any of the two hundred personnel for that matter.

The park, with its littering of benches, was to her left and the library and gym/pool complex to her right. The medical centre was by the hangars, the ambulance parked out front. She was on speaking terms with some of the nurses, not all sixteen, though she knew the four doctors, but not well. The short walk took her to the entrance of the RAID building. She was greeted as usual by the serious stares of Margaret Thatcher and President Mitterand in the framed pictures on the foyer walls. Underneath a plaque that reminded all of their function: Research, Assistance, Intervention, Dissuasion.

Yvonne, the Polish receptionist with her blonde hair neatly in a ponytail, raised her hand. "Evening, Danielle, not often you work nights, wonder how the big election in America is going?"

English was the chosen language for all.

With a short movement of her head, and without stopping, Danielle said, "Hillary is going to win."

If Trump won it would have massive consequences for RAID. Since the Brexit talk, Britain had reduced staffing levels. Annual budgets were always agreed on February 1st to coincide with the American President's inauguration. Danielle's status and earnings would be seriously compromised if the unthinkable happened and Trump won. So it couldn't happen. Wouldn't. Mustn't.

Danielle knew what they all thought of her; the girl who excelled in everything and at forty-eight she knew she was a force to be reckoned with. It didn't always make her popular but this was no popularity contest. She was the designated *unofficial* 'Boss' at RAID.

Danielle moved hastily to the French booth. There were forty such small booths all with their own computers and soundproofed. A master board of the world was on view to them all with two rows of seats in a semi-circle in front of it. People could congregate in front like a cinema and openly discuss it if they wanted to. Lights and numbers would distinguish where an incident or abduction had taken place, the countries involved and a colour-coded grading of the *state* of that incident. To an outsider it looked like a stock market floor.

The staffing levels varied from country to country but it was imperative most were manned every day of the year, twenty-four/seven. Some countries shared one room to reduce costs and staffing levels. Great Britain had two booths to include all of the British empire.

Danielle was well versed in its inception, its function and how important it was. It was her job to know it all, from when it was started by just four countries: France, the UK, Germany and America to its present status with thirty countries. The Russians were always in their booths, as were the Israelis, Tunisians and the founding members. If a country couldn't man its booth for the full twenty-four hours they would at least always be on standby.

The role of RAID was to see and respond to any act of terrorism and abduction for member countries. They were busy every day.

It was only when you had to go to the Mole rooms at a lower level that the work became *deadly* serious. It became life or death for someone somewhere.

Norway had flagged up red on the map. The team in the Mole section had transcribed an action plan to the negotiators in Norway. Danielle reviewed the information on the abduction in progress.

```
Act immediately. Father has daughter; unlikely to
kill as would have been done by now. Remove petrol
from requested car so only a few miles in the tank.
Take car to him and swap for daughter. Intercept
when he runs out of petrol.
```

It looked to be in order so Danielle left the booth; she needed to look at her own French news. Of course, she could not help but be drawn to the American election. 2 am was the key time in America; 9 am French time. The counting would only start at 5 am French time but felt she was better at work as sleep would be difficult for such a major event.

An hour later: applause. Thumbs-up signs everywhere, some rushing to the Norwegian booth as the main board came up green for success.

Daughter back with Mother. No need for aerial support. Details to follow.

Another crisis averted. For now, the Norwegian team was top dog and celebrating with coffees, chocolates and, of course, fish. Smiles everywhere, even Danielle when a cheeky Norwegian blew her a kiss. He got no response from her.

Danielle was thinking of her stomach. A long corridor led to the ground-floor dining room. It reminded her of a college refectory with a self-service area of hot and cold dishes, salad bar and breakfast bar.

Armed with a latte and a croissant, she sought a table.

There were by now a few Norwegians at the long table. It was natural to join the group and ask for more details of their success.

Danielle was still listening when one of the Russians joined them. "I was sorry to hear about your husband, my sincerest condolences."

At first Danielle did not look up, it wasn't as if she was in mourning.

The whole marriage had been a sham. Even her son had left home and refused to have any contact with them. Last she heard he was living with his grandmother in Marseille.

Husband Pierre had been the other boss at RAID. They kept together because of their high-powered jobs and the hefty income. He was the second of the French committee members along with the American/British/German that was the select committee that ran it. They met at her chateau.

With Pierre dead, a vacancy was open and the French government were sending a new member that weekend. Pierre had died of AIDS and his Tunisian lover, Cas, still worked on the premises. It was well known by the main committee that there were two ISIL infiltrators working in the village, one was Cas. Mobile phone trails and classified information deliberately leaked to him, was a necessary part of counter espionage and helped negotiations. Cas came from Casablanca, hence his name. He was

8

not on duty that night and Danielle had noticed his paler complexion recently and hoped he would not be on this planet for much longer.

Danielle despised her husband, but because of her own failings, and the need to maintain her chateau and lifestyle near Limoges, she'd accepted his dalliances with Cas. He only returned to the chateau for committee meetings. Danielle had not made herself popular with the French government. She had joined protest marches against Francois Hollande in the failed effort to stop same-sex marriages. She feared the threatened divorce proceedings would lead to her humiliation with his marriage to Cas. On top of that she was a fierce supporter of the thousands of entrepreneurs that had been hit with a 60% tax. The movement in France was labelled 'Les Pigeons'. Francois Hollande's administration was under attack and his ratings were at a record low along with high unemployment. Against this backdrop she felt the implications of the American election along with Theresa May's rise to power as a brexiteer did not bode well for RAID, but who would win, Hillary or Trump?

It was no surprise that ISIL or any other organisation with inside information had levels of reward expectancy for the 'type of person' up for ransom. This simply was not a level playing field. Insiders could relay the amount expected to save an ambassador as against a banker or a politician. These people at RAID secretly scaled those abducted from one to ten on a level of importance. What was finally agreed was down to 'the five' on the committee to decide. Saving the abducted was still the number one objective, irrespective of that person's status.

Danielle sat with her hand cupped around a tall bottle of the local water: Volvic, when she saw Doc, one of the Germans. So named because he claimed to have a doctorate. Most people did not believe him, but it was well known he was Merkel's man at the YMCA, reporting to her on a regular basis. Germans had now become a target because Mrs

Merkel's policy of allowing many immigrants into Germany was not popular. Hostage demands got higher as funds from other sources were hit; targeting more selective, so fewer demands but for a few dollars more. Danielle exchanged greetings with Doc as she left to return to her booth. She was not one for small talk. She had far more important things to attend to.

It was now well into the early hours and she had already decided to sleep in the quarters provided when her shift finished at 8 am. A bedsit had been allocated for her. She picked up a phone in her room and pressed 2.

"Flight HQ."

"It's Danielle, I shall not be flying back till this evening now."

"OK."

The phone went dead, it was a simple courtesy call. Flight HQ had several helicopters, two of which were the Westpac Rescue Helicopter BK 117-B2 and two smaller ones available for emergency calls and use by Danielle; the best and fastest way to get to her secluded chateau. These two older helicopters were called "Maggie" and "Mitter." She was allowed this taxi service as they had regular summit meetings at the chateau, and it was also good for the aircraft to have regular outings. They were used by the RAID equivalent of the SAS to help collect/deliver the hostages in case fire power was needed or even just as a deterrent. Most of the time, a smaller helicopter was for her own use. The two Westpac helicopters were not standard by any means. They were always in action. It was a condition of all countries that at least one of their employees should have a helicopter licence.

Danielle also used Mari as a pilot on an emergency contract basis in case the helicopters were already on "live" exercises. Mari lived near Tremolat in the Dordogne. Mari had all the features to be a cover girl. Her steely approach to life embossed in her for ever due to the civil war in her native land. Her dominant father educated her in ways she never expected.

Incredibly fit, Mari was a survivor, a marksman, a woman extraordinaire. One phone call from Danielle and Mari would fly anywhere, anytime. The contract for doing nothing or something was too lucrative to turn down. Mari's other contract was a fortnightly trip to the Auvergne, a monastery called St Agatha.

Danielle wandered back to her booth concerned the American election was too close for comfort.

Chapter 3

Northern Tunisia
Wednesday, November 9ᵗʰ

Rochine sat on the boat looking out at the ocean, a coating of salty spray on her lips; on all of the occupants being bounced in the dinghy. Rochine, in her helpless state, surveyed the scene. The victorious soldiers armed and with concentrated smiles. Her parents and governess, cold, shivering with frightened anticipation just like Rochine. She wondered what the hell was going on and who would save them all from this nightmare.

* * *

In Tunis not far from where he worked at the French embassy, Mohammed Aqbal studied the note a pigeon had brought before he went to work.

"At 5 pm send this demand for 15 million dollars and a helicopter for the exchange of the Houston family and their governess to the French booth at RAID HQ France. Acknowledge within forty-eight hours or one dies."

Mohammed told his wife he would be back by 5 pm and wished his daughter, Elena, a good day at the primary school where she taught.

* * *

Captain Gerald Menzies of the American army reconnaissance training group had his small platoon of five vehicles on night patrol in North Africa. They had been sent to the Algerian/Tunisian border to monitor and look out for any ISIL movements. This mountainous region of Algeria, Kabylie near the provinces of Boumerdes and Bouira was homeland for an ISIL unit led by the legendary Tariq. Communication was a problem, given the terrain, so they stayed close to the coastline to easily report to land or sea. His role was to observe, note and report the instructions. Soft introductory work as a grounding for future operations. The vehicles kept within four miles of each other. The Americans were welcomed for the income and the added security they gave, especially after the killings in Tunisia was affecting tourism. They were well armed, but Captain Menzies was itching for a battle after his demotion for suspicious killings in the Iraqi war weighed unfairly on his shoulders. They were close to the border when his phone crackled into life.

"HQ here, suspected ISIL attack near Bizerte, attackers have hostages and may be heading your way by sea. Observe and report regularly as they are well armed, hostages of high importance, do not engage if sighted."

"Received and understood."

Captain Menzies smiled and stopped his vehicle. Other vehicles radioed and told to rendezvous. He checked the map. A team operation was required. He ordered each vehicle to be a maximum of three miles apart and check the coastline for any activity. The lead vehicle to go eighteen miles ahead immediately and each one three behind. He had trained these men and they obeyed willingly, action at last. They were on red alert. It was 5 am when all lookouts reported no sightings.

"What about the mountains behind us?" one cadet said.

Menzies was quick to advise using the heat-seeking equipment to check any movements on the mountain. Three vehicles replied, reporting something small; animal-sized, high up. Menzies had a look and agreed it was possibly a wild boar. Then excitement as one of them reported a dinghy-type boat off the coast in the distance but too far to see clearly. Menzies ordered all vehicles to be switched off. Leave one to guard the first and last vehicles and the rest go on foot and look for any possible landing site. He was supposed to contact HQ and observe. He sensed his advantage as the dinghy neared a possible landing area. An open beach and terrain where he could hide and prepare.

"Two more small contacts up the mountain." Menzies checked again but they all concurred: still looked like rabbits or wild boar. Menzies prepared his ambush meticulously. Ordering marksmen to take them out from left to right as they finished alighting the dinghy. He told his men they would not be able to stand easily after time at sea. Two from each group would go for the hostages as soon as the shooting started and take them to safety. As he gave his instructions a second dinghy appeared.

"Shit!" he said, "Hostages all on the first dinghy, prepare smoke bombs to distract the second dinghy."

He then instructed two of his men to rapid fire at the other boat as soon as the action started.

* * *

Rochine lay back, her back ached, she felt nauseous. The dinghy was approaching the shore. Francesca had thrown up several times into the sea. The soldiers were preparing their machine guns and looking out to land with binoculars. One had a rocket-type launcher on his shoulders, aimed at the beach. She saw the other dinghy closing in on them fast as they slowed down to wade out. A strong arm held each of them, so the soldiers were all behind them as they struggled to get out, especially Francesca.

Rochine felt a soldier behind her, guiding her to stand and exit the dinghy. The cold water covered her trainers and soaked the bottom of her sweatpants. It was difficult with hands bound, the soldier's hands holding her, so she did not fall. Gazing down at the water to feel the solid beach and safety of land. Then the soldier released his grip and she saw the others in front of her with a soldier behind each one; guns raised and aiming at a sand dune.

Rochine sensed danger; moments later there were explosions in front of her. Some dived, some fell onto the sand or into the sea; waves beating against them. Rochine stood firm; watching bodies flying into the air in their sandy brown uniforms; human carnage dispersed all around the beach and from where they had been hiding. Missiles and bullets smashing into the overgrowth in front of them. She heard Francesca shouting "I am going to die" then saw her father trying to kick a soldier, but he was no match with his hands tied and he was hit hard twice. She was helpless as she stared at the dead bodies. She saw people charging down the mountain chanting "Death to the Americans!" followed by "Tariq, Tariq, Tariq." Rochine was fluent in three languages, having had a governess with forced learning and virtually no contact with the outside world… she knew what they were saying, but had no intention of revealing her skills. She chose to speak French and a little English. She heard soldiers celebrating Tariq's battle plan and his ambush site. Rochine saw men, women and boys with weapons. She watched as soldiers took two jeeps going in the opposite direction. She heard them pray for a pigeon that had brought them the news. She guessed it was one she saw released earlier… but why were they using pigeons?

There were two stretchers to help the wounded soldiers. Rochine watched as the dead, and remaining jeeps, were stripped of anything valuable or useful. Rochine looked up at the formidable mountains above the beach and knew it would be a long hard walk to wherever they intended to take them; they were hostages now. But why? It had to be connected to her father. Not her mother. She hated him. She tried to look at him, but he always wore the same look of hate when she was in his company; like she was a bad smell. Earlier he had looked away from her questioning gaze. She was scum to him; she knew it. She heard the crackle of fire, felt the heat of flames, as the remaining jeeps were burnt.

Rochine looked at the weather-beaten but proud commander, contemplating her fate. Francesca had warned her of men like this. She noticed her now with her parents; hoods being forced over them and now shackled by ropes to one of the other soldiers. Rochine then felt a rope being tied around her and a hood with air vents near the nose and mouth. She could hear birds, people close by, muffled voices and feet. The smell of the clear mountain air the only relief as they began their march uphill. She heard the panting of two men and the words, "Only one got away, all jeeps burnt." She knew the commander was close to her.

The pigeon is an important symbol in the traditions of many different cultures from around the world. In religious symbolism the pigeon features in Hinduism, Buddhism, and Christianity. The pigeon has a long history of association with gods, goddesses, and spiritual teachers of many traditions

Chapter 4   Wednesday, November 9th

Mari woke just before the alarm. It was 6:30 am and the AW009 helicopter with its Rolls Royce M250-C20R/2 SP engine was waiting with its rich cargo and her favourite pigeon, Zag. Mari was to fly to St Agatha Monastery in the Auvergne. She'd leave Zag there for a few days until they needed to send the next message. She suspected it was an all-female commune, she had seen the young women wearing hoods. Her suspicion was they were coming from war-torn countries like Yugoslavia and Syria, she knew something about that, of course… but what happened at St Agatha was speculation… protection? Trafficking?

Take the money, don't ask questions.

She had been lured to France to a property in the Dordogne with a helicopter and work included in the price. It was a far cry from her old life, having escaped war-torn Yugoslavia in the 1990s.

It was while taking clients from all over France mainly to and from the Vieux Logis at Tremolat that she had met Danielle. They were dining at Le Vieux Logis in 2012 just after Danielle had been appointed with her then-alive-husband as part of the famous five to "run" YMCA. She spoke to Danielle about her past and how she loved to fly. Danielle offered her the contact; which meant Mari could spend more time at

Le Vieux Logis. She was a happy single bunny with a healthy bank balance.

By midday Mari had flown for two hours. She was surprised to see Zag flying back into the loft after such a short time at St Agatha. She carefully opened the message attached to the bird's foot. *Please collect two passengers this afternoon and take to Bergerac Airport for 6 pm.*

Time for a long lunch and a siesta.

Arriving at 5 pm at St Agatha, Mari saw Sister Edith in her long blue habit, a small but formidable woman, though to the world she looked like an innocent nun. Her broad shoulders underneath her gown disguised her muscles that gave her the advantage over her flock. She was with the two girls waiting to board. One young lady looked Syrian, but seemed happy as the other girls and staff were taking it in turns to kiss her goodbye. She had a small piece of luggage and Edith had several small bags. Edith looked focussed on whatever her tasks were. The other Spanish-looking lady was also saying her goodbyes... for whatever fate awaited them. That was not for Mari to know.

Mari took off to Bergerac Airport keeping below the flight path and height that many airlines used to approach Bergerac, especially Ryanair. The two girls were blindfolded until they landed near the hangars out of sight of the main public buildings. This was her normal landing zone. Mari was asked to wait as she would need to return to St Agatha. Her regular local trips to the airport meant she avoided any customs checks. She waited in the small coffee shop as they went to the car park. They approached a large Mercedes and a van. Edith collected two bags as the young girls got into one vehicle each. A good half hour later she appeared with a big smile on her face and two more bags in her hand.

"Business concluded," she said and gave Mari one bag. "This one is for you."

Mari returned to her helicopter to the smiles and lurid looks from a few tourists and a custom's official.

In two hours, she would be sipping wine back home and an extra 2000 euros in cash in her secret place in her bungalow.

* * *

At St Agatha, Mother Superior Angela was counting nearly 160,000 euros in cash. Despite the harsh realities of this monastery-type environment, her policies had given hope, happiness and a reason to enjoy the strict routine that all the girls now endured. With one extra staff member and ladies awaiting new homes at the rate of six to eight a year, business was good.

Angela felt on a high. She rang a bell, and an African lady entered.

"Send in Misha," she demanded.

Five minutes later, seventeen-year-old Misha arrived to stand in front of Angela.

"You are to learn obedience." She used her menacing look: stern with obvious intention.

"Yes," replied Misha in a submissive tone.

"Come round the table and kneel down in front of me."

Misha was mixed-race: blue eyes and blond. She had been an excellent addition to St Agatha, and they expected good money for her in the future. A willing worker and obedient, she had also accepted punishments of varying degrees and degradation. Angela pulled back her long skirt till her silk pants was showing. She pointed and simply said, "You know what to do."

It had been a good day for her cash flow. St Agatha was well run with rota systems in place for all sorts of duties. The atmosphere was one of acceptance and togetherness. Many on the outside world would think these places did not deserve to exist. To those in it, this was a way of life with a purpose based on DOLLAR. It was a simple code that worked for those who followed it. Alternative avenues of life could be much worse than this secluded monastery near the village of Aubrac an area on the perimeter of three communes on the southern edge of the Auvergne. 1000 square miles of almost virgin volcanic wasteland. A remote area in pristine condition due to lack of people; a forgotten part of France. A perfect place not to be discovered.

It was here in 1120 the Pilgrim Adalard was on his way from Puy-en-Velay to Compostela that he was attacked by villains. He was injured and survived the ordeal but nursed back to good health by a local girl called Agatha. He was so impressed by their help he built two monasteries in the area. One he named the Domerie of Aubrac, after the head monk called Dom. The other he built in a secret place, so few knew about. The first monastery was destroyed during the French revolution, but St Agatha had survived; a foreboding place inhabited by nuns. A landslide had made the journey virtually impossible to this remote hidden retreat. Dracula would have loved this place. A steep drop on one side with a thick forest on the other made it virtually impossible to access unless you were an experienced mountaineer or prepared to fly in by helicopter. It was hidden from view unless you were high above and travelling to another airport like Claremont Ferrand, or on another route path.

It was here that Sister Angela and Sister Edith now managed an exclusive business. They had started by advertising in adult only magazines – mainly gay ones. The advert would simply read *"Meet first and discuss your role at our secluded retreat. Exclusive pick up by helicopter for up to three ladies only in choice of several designated areas in the south of France.*

Day and overnight rates available. 500 euros or 700 with overnight stay. Either Sister Angela or Edith will interview you first. Outfits provided for your convent experience. Sisterly discipline with love and education the order of the day. Cash paid up front, no refunds if no show. Reply to P.O. box 44 Bergerac allow 14 days for response, dates to suit."

They had no electricity and never used mobile phones. They did not need the internet. The business had been run successfully since the late 1990s.

Sister Angela was now in her early fifties; Edith was three years younger than her. They had met as teachers at another convent school near Bergerac in 1988. They enjoyed each other's company to such an extent that when this monastery was advertised for lease in the 1990s at a ridiculously low price, they could not resist the challenge.

* * *

Danielle sat in her booth all alone. It was still only 5 am and another three hours before the busy dayshift arrived. People of all colours and races would descend on YMCA and go to their respective booths or duties for whichever country, or indeed countries, they now represented. Her mind wandered back to when, after several months of deciding, do I or do I not reply to the advert she saw in her husband's gay magazine. Her life was a sham and somehow, she felt she wanted to reinvent her childhood. The pressure of her work in the immigration section was now ending and her new job at the YMCA with Pierre beckoned.

This was not a good time for a divorce. He spent most of his life in Paris, and he could now stay at the YMCA. He only came to the chateau for RAID meetings. Her mind wandered and thought of unimaginable pleasures and situations.

It was with trepidation and excitement that she sat outside the pizzeria in the beautiful Tremolat square four years earlier. The old school and church created a scenic backdrop with two old trees resplendent with age. She had long trousers, a simple buttoned white blouse and a blue scarf as instructed. Sister Angela sat down opposite her. It was 11 am.

"You must be Danielle."

"Yes."

They looked each other over. Angela continued. "Have you got the 700 euros for this weekend?"

Danielle hadn't expected an instant demand for the money.

"Do you have more information?" she replied with nervousness.

Angela looked at her with her piercing eyes. "I understand you have not done your homework and you have been a naughty girl."

Danielle felt a sudden unexplained glow as she answered meekly, "Yes, Miss."

Angela clearly knew she had won. "Mother Superior to you."

Quietly responding in case anyone else could hear, "Yes, Mother Superior."

"You will report here on Saturday morning at 8 am, simply walk round the corner. There is a helicopter pad opposite the Vieux Logis. The pilot will wait till 8:30am at the latest and then take off."

A waitress came to the table and Angela ordered two coffees.

Angela continued, "Only a small suitcase, we have uniforms for you, and I want a brief report on all of the following subjects."

She handed her a written note with the motto of DOLLAR. Discipline-Obedience-Learning-Love-Absolution-Reward.

"A good convent has to have rules, I want your interpretation, do you understand, young lady?"

Before Danielle could reply Angela said, "Money please."

Danielle felt almost in a trance as she felt in her handbag for the envelope with 700 euros. *Why was she doing this?* But it was all too late, the money was taken from her and she looked into Mother Superior's eyes. The triumphant look back said it all. Danielle felt a sudden urge to go to the toilet. She felt more moist than normal and her heavy breathing of future anticipation meant she was on a road of no return. She excused herself, returned a little later. Angela had gone and now it was only two days till Saturday morning.

Danielle remembered being surprised to find a lady pilot. Even more surprised that there would be two other ladies on the same journey. One lady lived in Marmande, south of Bergerac, who had an agency business for *ladies only*. Cecilia would become an integral part of the new venture. The other lady from Italy would be "girls at the convent" putty in the hands of two sisters who might show no mercy. All were staying till Sunday morning. Being blindfolded in the helicopter added to the adventure.

Danielle drank some water in her booth and then thought of her experiences that weekend. The initial assembly after changing into suitable clothing. Long blue trousers, blouses with ties and no bra with a jumper if cold. White socks and gym shoes. The luxury was silk underwear that felt sexy. Matron inspected all three girls in turn. Personal questions to answer and a report sheet to take to Mother Superior when Matron had finished her intrusive examination. Sister Edith enjoyed her matron role play.

Angela would interview them one at a time. Each failing to be good and receiving punishment to suit her taste and desire. If they were seriously bad, they might be tied up and thrashed till they begged for mercy by Edith while Angela watched. It did not happen to her on that visit and she was not aware if anyone else did either. They had bands on their wrists to indicate their position at the monastery. They had green ones as we were newcomers. During the day if they were good, there reward was a white one. They could then indulge with any activity with any of the girls except the sisters. They had to go to the food tables hand in hand with someone and not the same girl twice. They sat next to that girl. If Mother Superior decided to punish them in front of everyone, it was her prerogative.

Sometimes she made them kiss before eating. They had to chop wood and keep the fires burning. Cleaning and making sure hot water was available. With no electricity and using natural water from a spring this was a bleak existence. They had goats and a greenhouse that backed onto a wall where on the other side was a large fire. The fire was never allowed to go out, nor two others as the monastery was a cold place to live in. In the morning they did one lesson in English. They had a short PE session. They fed the pigeons and talked to them, cleaning out where they rested.

They chopped down a tree from the large forest and cut up some wood which was great for group therapy. It took all afternoon to put the wood in a shed. A warm bath in front of a fire was humiliating and exciting as they drank hot punch as a reward for their efforts. They washed each other as Edith watched and waited with a warm towel to dry each one in turn. The three slave girls helped with the washing. The floor was covered with rugs and eventually they all finished on them. Warm oils were rubbed into their skins as they somehow got into pairs. Edith still watched. Slowly she moved round each pair and they all became embroiled in caressing and kissing, and Edith forced her fingers into areas she had not experienced for a long time. She checked all the couples were happy. Danielle was beginning to understand the meaning of DOLLAR.

Beds made of local wood with blankets and duvets. In their reports they had to give marks out of ten to the three resident slaves and the sisters. Danielle chose Angela simply because she had been her initial contact and she felt slightly safer with her than the unpredictable Edith. This gave them an insight into who they would share a bed with to keep warm. Danielle was chosen to sleep with Cecilia from Marmande, or it might have been the other way round. They did engage and explore but they knew they were not meant for each other.

They all left the next morning, glad to leave but in a strange way glad they had come. Cecilia and Danielle both agreed that a female slave at their houses was a good idea. On the helicopter back she jokingly said to the other two girls 80,000 Euros and there are three slave girls to choose from. No questions asked and they will have no identity, simply they do not exist. For your eyes only, not a bond film she joked.

"Send me three photos," said the Italian lady. Cecilia looked at Danielle.

"OK, give us your email and I will send you the photos."

Emails were exchanged. Cecilia and Danielle then met up. Many refugee girls needed housing. She had been in Immigration so knew the problems. Surely this is better than that. 80,000 euros at least four times a year makes a tidy profit. She questioned Cecilia about her agency in Bordeaux. They talked and discussed that as she had only ladies on her books there might be potential clients for female slaves.

They agreed to get one each and see if it worked. It would be their business and they could send them to St Agatha first then enrol them if they passed the test.

Danielle looked at the clock, her mind now focussed on the present.

They had come a long way since then. Cecilia and she had a female slave each. St Agatha had one more like-minded sister. They have a prep school near Bergerac for twelve to fifteen-year-olds before they can go to St Agatha. Now there are eighteen girls at St Agatha, two more of which are moving out soon and more to arrive from those prep schools. Danielle smiled to herself. No one in the world outside St Agatha, except Cecilia and Mari, knew about this lucrative business. Cecilia did not even know that Danielle had a second prep school off the D906 near Portes in the Gard department of the Occitaine region. It is a quiet location and handy for all the big southern ports and migrants coming from Eastern Europe or North Africa as well as local girls who may have fled to this area of France to escape abuse. A local helicopter pilot was used independently so that nobody knew the other prep school existed. This reserve supply of ladies and supplies was used less but an important safety net for the business. The pilot was paid handsomely and the set-up ran smoothly. Edith the only visitor from St Agatha. The same rules existed and girls when ready simply went to the secret location that was St Agatha, a different type of abuse than what they might have expected. This was purely insurance if the school near Bergerac had to close. Paying clients never knew where these girls came from. Danielle gave herself a slap on the back for the selective way these girls were brought into the system. There was the simple way of girls having no family, loners who had escaped their own problems and wanted a new start. Then there was this new breed of refugees that needed housing from war-torn countries like the Middle East. Countries did not know how to handle this huge problem. Refugees were transported from Calais but where did they go?

Danielle knew that by taking them in small numbers the authorities allowed them to be given a French passport with a simple R at the end of their number. This meant they could travel anywhere as they were officially refugees.

People who took them on could not claim state benefit and they had to be sponsored for school or jobs. Cecilia's business was the perfect disguise for this new problem. Only taking on a select few girls and they were sent to the special school near Bergerac.

Sometimes older girls could qualify and go direct to St Agatha. A safe house on the outskirts of Bergerac was deemed suitable for testing first. All paperwork would go to this address, so the paper trail ended there. These girls officially did not exist – they were all itinerants.

The implementation of DOLLAR was not open for discussion. Obey DOLLAR and survive was the simple message.

Anyone who attended Angela's study had to repeat the motto and were asked which one or two of the letters they wished to discuss.

The theory that "Hell has no fury like a woman scorned" did not exist at St Agatha. This was never allowed to happen. Even Sister Angela and Edith accepted each other's behaviour for the better good. Up to 2012 little changed.

It was only when Sister Angela met Danielle Bousquet in May 2012 at the pizzeria in Tremolat Square that their lives changed forever.

The first images of pigeons were found in Mesopotania (modern Iraq) by archaeologists dating back to 3000BC

Chapter 5

Wednesday, November 9th

Danielle visited the helicopter hangars on the way to her room as her shift was almost over. There she came across Cas's brother. They were complete opposites and he had no idea his brother was working as an ISIL infiltrator. He had changed his name to Jacques Cousteau after the intrepid explorer. Strong and resourceful, he loved his job on the hostage rescue team. He never spoke to his brother and he lived happily with his French wife, Suzette, in a nearby village. Attractive to the eye, slim, anorexic looking, they had the one nine-year-old daughter Lorna. Jack had no idea Cas had been the lover of Danielle's late husband. The YMCA simply called him 'Jack'.

"Any action?" Danielle asked.

"Oh yes, just got back from the Greek islands."

Danielle saw the immigrant problem from Syria and North Africa as causing havoc in Europe, much to Putin's delight. Saving properties has become RAID's new role as some belonged to senior politicians. Rules bent to help *who* you knew, not always *what* you knew. Jack had served in the French Army and left to be nearer Suzette. Headstrong but brave he was YMCA's top marksman with six hits from the helicopter. He practised shooting, parachuting, keeping fit; a professional you wanted on your side. Only 'Greco the Greek' was close to him as a marksman. Single and without a care in the world with no humour he had four hits with YMCA but was available as an independent hit man. The Russians had used him, and he sometimes went on missions with Jack. Greco would kill anybody at any age and work for anyone. Jack had principles and stuck to them, he did not like Greco. Some would call him a psychopath. A dangerous introvert, a clinical killer; his gun polished and oiled daily. He was also in the hangar. The other helicopter having been deployed in Italy for the same reasons. He was like a coiled viper wanting to sting someone rather than immigrant house duty. Danielle was talking to Jack, but Greco clearly overheard.

"Off this weekend?"

Greco was quick to respond. "I am off till Tuesday."

"Make the most of it, situation could get worse if Trump wins." Rumours that it was a close election in America did not stop Danielle retiring to her quarters to sleep before her last shift at 2 pm.

She woke at 1:30, much to her surprise. No time for a shower, quick wash, teeth cleaned, casual clothes and left to go the short distance to her booth. As soon as she walked into the open and across the campus to the main building the atmosphere told her something was wrong.

She entered the main auditorium.

Trump had won. He'd actually done it.

People who had finished their shifts had stayed behind and congregated. Everyone wanted to make a comment. It was like a gaggle of geese or a gathering of penguins. Noise level high, intelligent conversation low.

She checked the main board. Greece and Italy with problems and one in Germany, and a Russian Aircraft Carrier in the Bering Sea, otherwise quiet. Nearly every booth manned.

Danielle had her booth manned twenty-four seven every day of the year. Her new young recruit had arrived for his shift with her. They stared at the screens in disbelief. What the hell would it mean for them, for her and for

YMCA? He tried to reason with her that all governments need information and methods of reasoning with abductors that seemed independent. Her late husband left her position precarious and she could try for a new job. The thought of being too qualified and getting older not in her favour. It was 5 pm when the email flashed up from Tunisia. Danielle froze, her mind racing as fast as a formula one driver.

"Four hostages taken: Gerald, Cherie and Rochine Houston, and Francesca the governess included, 15 million dollars and a helicopter, forty-eight hours to respond or one dies."

This was it. The opportunity she needed in light of the election news – a way out.

She felt her heart rate hitch up a notch. Her job was in danger; she'd been tipped off by the Polish receptionist that the Paris connection had been wanting information about her and the expenses incurred at the chateau. Danielle feared she was going to be moved sideways and replaced, especially now her husband was dead. The lifestyle she knew and loved was now in jeopardy. She needed to act. This email might be the answer but she had to act fast.

Danielle sent her recruit to the canteen with a food and drink order. She also gave him her apartment key to fetch a jumper. This gave her time to delete the email and replace the hard drive after copying the files to the new one. A spare hard drive was always available. The few minutes might never be missed by the hackers and support staff that were supposed to check every few months. Danielle then asked him to hold the fort in the booth while she went outside in the new jumper. She went to her car and used her private phone to text Mari "*Meet me at 9 pm at the chateau, urgent task will take eighteen hours at least, passport required.*" It showed successfully transmitted and shortly after a simple response "*OK.*" She ate her food and the hot drink calmed her down. It was nearing the end of her shift. She put her purse in a drawer making sure her recruit didn't notice.

She checked the internet and found no details of this Rochine Houston. The governess came from the agency in Bordeaux, Cecilia's business. That intrigued her. It was 7 pm when her pay-as-you go phone bleeped. Using three phones for security reasons. The text message was clear. It came from the headmistress of the prep school near Bergerac.

"Crisis, Matron's throat cut by one of the girls… Girl claims raped by Spanish man who took her to ecole. Girl out of control – she is 'spoiled goods'."

Danielle felt her life was in free fall. The young recruit was shocked when she said, "Fucking hell." Composing herself she lied, "My dog has died."

Events had changed her life forever.

The relief shift had come early to talk about the American result. This gave Danielle time to change and fly the helicopter herself to her chateau. Her next official meeting was Sunday with the replacement for her late husband and three others, the five that were in control of RAID.

Philippa, Danielle's in-house slave from central Europe, opened the door. Normally a kiss, but now she was in fast-forward mode. She went straight to her pigeon loft and sent out two pigeons, one to St Agatha and the other to the prep school near Bergerac.

"Mari will be here at 9 pm, send her straight to my computer room."

It was not long after that Mari arrived in her shiny red Porsche. It was rare for Mari to go in the chateau and Danielle sensed her uncomfortable mood.

"10,000 euros now and a bonus if successful."

That worked wonders on Mari now very attentive. "Take the 7:45 am flight from Bordeaux to Tunis. Go to this café near the embassy and tell the owner to contact Mohammed Aqbal. He will come within fifteen minutes. Tell him to send an email at exactly 1 pm tomorrow asking for 'twenty-five' million dollars; a helicopter as before. Give him 10,000 euros deposit and 40,000 when he returns before 2 pm. Insist he tells no one. He is the ISIL contact in Tunis. We have known about him for years. He might pretend he is not an ISIL contact but tell him to send a message that we will pay a deposit of 5 million dollars on Monday on condition we see the hostages and the girls have not been violated. Wait for a place and time for the meet on Monday. He will know this as it would have been told him already. Only pay the balance when you get this information. Tell him there will be a further 50,000 euros if the deal is successful. Mohammed will agree as money talks. You are booked on the 6:15pm flight back to Bordeaux. Your bonus is 20,000 euros."

Danielle had to repeat the instructions several times. Her thoughts shifted to that email. Her intervention, the new instructions. If it went as planned, she would be better off to the tune of ten million. But no paper trail – only her and Mohammad Aqbal would know of the deception, hence the need to pay him well.

Mari listened intently. She seemed happier when Danielle explained a pre-meet was the new normal for exchanges and had proved beneficial to both parties on several difficult abductions.

Cash was no problem at the chateau, and she knew her late husband's code as two were required to open the safe. In it was slush money of many different currencies, mainly dollars, euros and pounds. Only the five committee members knew about this extra 30 million funded by the UK/France/Germany and the USA. Danielle's position allowed Mari to travel with cash as a RAID worker with first-class access, no security checks

35

and for transport by whatever means. A hotel was booked with parking at the airport.

Mari's trip to Tunis was successful. Mohammed was lured in by the large amount of cash that Mari offered him. He dutifully returned to his private computer in his home and sent the email with the new demand for twenty-five million and the helicopter. He had sent pigeons to Tariq's HQ to confirm there would be a five million deposit and no violation of those abducted. Mohammed returned to the café and confirmed to Mari that the new email had been sent to YMCA.

Mari met him at 2 pm in the café. She had received confirmation from Danielle regarding the new email, so was pleased to pay him the balance of the money. She was about to leave when Aqbal's daughter appeared. She went straight to the food bar saying she was starving. As she ordered her food Mari noticed her nervously almost scratching the back of her right ear. Mohammed pre-empted any questions "My daughter, Elena, has always done that when ordering anything in public, like a nervous disorder." Mari did not see his daughter and she left before she could recognise her as well.

The pre-meet and the final exchanges of the abductors would take place at the ambush site on Monday and Thursday. Monday at 5 pm; Thursday at 8 am. This avoided the midday sun. Danielle knew how brutal abductors were and expected the large deal would be a deterrent for their sordid entertainment desires, rewards to key soldiers who had performed in the field. Danielle hoped they would have no idea of the altered demands.

* * *

36

Rochine smiled in relief when the soldier she had come to know as Tariq came into the cabin and declared they were worth more alive than dead. It stopped Francesca crying and shaking. Hot soup and the wood-burning stove a relief after the torturous walk, blindfolded and carried on stretchers or with a rope by someone unknown depending on the terrain. The wooden beds better than nothing. An armed lady guard watched them eat. No father in this room. A basic hole in the corner and a curtain gave some decency as Rochine needed to relieve herself. Rochine finished her food first and was tied to the bed as were her mother – Cherie, and Francesca. Soiled clothes would be replaced later. *They were alive at least but what the hell was happening to them? Would she ever see her home again?* Tariq came in and told them they would not see Mr Houston again till a deal was done. His next comment created an icy chill.

"If you want to stay alive you will obey me and anyone who I send."

Her mother became the spokesman. "What exactly do you mean?"

Tariq eyed her up and glanced over at Rochine, where a wicked smile played in his lips before he turned around and left.

Chapter 6　　　　　**Thursday, November 10th**

It was just after midday. At the YMCA, Doc the German, the Englishman and the American met for dinner in the canteen. They and Danielle were the four remaining on the main committee; their role to decide what demands should be paid and how much. They speculated who the new French member would be, expecting him or her to come from the government very soon. They preferred to meet at Danielle's chateau, but now there were rumours the government were going to replace Danielle as well.

They talked quietly about the money at the chateau they used for deals and what changes might occur. The receptionist said that Danielle would be coming soon to pick up her purse. The three of them wondered if she'd heard the rumours about her reassignment.

Danielle arrived just before 1 pm in time for the email to arrive from Tunis. She had heard the rumours but gave the impression to everyone that all was normal. The tactic she had put into place to keep the disparity in the ransom would be her own leaving present. The main problem she had now was Cas, who was in the Tunisian booth. She did not want this leaking back to ISIL about the 25 million ransom when they were expecting only 15 million and a helicopter. She went to the Mole room with Cas, representing Tunisia, two Americans and the two on duty for the French.

"Geoffrey and Cherie Houston are top priority," said the American from the committee.

"What about the mother, and the daughter, Rochine?" Danielle said.

They all searched their computers and bemused faces told the story. No records of Rochine and no photos. The French thought she had been registered in Tunisia and the Tunisians believed she had been registered in France. Rochine did not officially exist.

"The governess?" Cas said.

Two minutes later they all had the same information. Francesca Lorenz was recruited from "Work for ladies only" based in Bordeaux. Employed for four years full time, living in with languages her speciality. Danielle spoke knowing she would lose.

"Too big a demand."

The Americans as usual said, "Pay the lot and then blast hell out of them."

It was later they learned that an American submarine had found the Houston boat. No fuel and no one on board. It was identified at 4 am, when two sailors went on board, they saw no obvious danger. Only when they walked down into the cabin it triggered a massive explosion that sent the two sailors and the Houston boat to the bottom of the ocean. If that was bad enough, losing nineteen more men was too embarrassing to admit just yet. Danielle put her plan into action.

"I can take Cas on Monday with the five-million-dollar deposit as a pre-deal, no point in taking you, Americans."

It was logical especially with them knowing Cas was an ISIL informer. They all agreed. Danielle went to the Tunisian booth alone with Cas. An email was sent back to Tunis. It would take till Saturday for confirmation from Mohammed who was probably seeing his own dollar signs. He never had to send any confirmation to Tariq as Mari had already set the deal up.

Danielle spoke to Cas. "Just one problem with this deal is we have agreed but Germany, UK and the new member have to ratify on Sunday when we meet." Cas now seemed suspicious.

"You will vote against?"

Danielle was thinking quickly. "If you can get me the red pilot case for me nicknamed 'Cyanide' I will vote for it."

"Why?" Cas responded.

"Simply insurance for me. If there is a problem I do not want to be around at the mercy of these abductors, do you?"

Danielle had made her point. Success for the hostages was paramount and Cas saw the logic, except how to get this insurance exploding bomb without anyone knowing. It looked like the red cases stored at the chateau used for money exchanges. He thought his cover was not known and would get brownie points for delivering the best ransom deal ever to the cause. Danielle was aware lots of ammunitions, rockets etc. had been mislaid and a black market existed in-house. Secret cameras had caught a Russian, but he had not been arrested yet as they thought more were involved. He was being watched. Danielle had taken money from the safe in the chateau. She gave Cas 30,000 euros.

"See what you can do with this, we do not have time to wait for approval on Sunday. You will come with me with the five million on Monday. Thursday you fly one and I will fly the six-seater. We do the exchange and return with the four hostages. They only need a small helicopter for the mountain and local use. If you want to keep some of that 30,000 it is okay by me. I will not mention it on Sunday if you have managed to get one. Just text me by 3 pm Sunday so I know, then I do not have to beg for it at the meeting."

Cas seemed ecstatic with his role and possible bonus. He knew the Russian was working Saturday and he could keep some of the euros for himself. ISIL would honour him, and he had no need to tell them. The French and the Americans would vote for, so it was a done deal.

Danielle left the helicopter at YMCA. She drove back and thought about Philippa and what she had planned for her. She needed to let off steam and relax. When she arrived at the chateau, she had tea on her own – made by Philippa. She ordered Philippa to dress in a school uniform and report back to her at seven. She obeyed with shirt and tie, trousers, black shoes and a jacket for inspection. Danielle asked her to fetch the cane from behind the curtain and find her leather slippers. The special chair with straps would expose her for Danielle's pleasure. She would feel the full force of a lady in trouble and turmoil.

The first recorded network of Pigeon messengers was by Cyrus the Great in 5ᵗʰ Century BC in Assyria and Persia. Dovecotes in Palestine and Egypt found from 44BC

Chapter 7

Sunday, November 13th

Jack took off from the YMCA with Doc, the Englishman and the American.

After an hour he spotted the chateau. It was on the D13 between St Junien and Morterolles, a village called Brandiol, Limoges the nearest big city. Gates and low walls, an indiscreet place, in a quiet village but with lots of land and a wood. There was space for three helicopters to land if necessary. Houses up the hill opposite could see part of the garden as large trees and bushes gave some privacy. A fountain on the lawn with borders of shrubs and flowers gave the imposing property a feeling of luxury inside. The lane called "Rue De La Fontaine" named after it.

The new French RAID representative, Henri Sami, arrived by car after Jack had landed. Phillipa welcomed them in, this time in a normal French maid's outfit. Henri introduced himself to everyone. He was the new committee man, Pierre's replacement.

They were shown around the chateau with the old furniture and pictures from La Vie Parisienne. Young ladies in various forms of dress and undress. Sur La Plage De Deauville dated 1st Octobre particularly eye catching. Henri was impressed. They descended to the large room near the outside pool. Covered over for winter but used a lot in the summer. Phillipa served coffees first with snacks.

Philippa returned to the kitchen where Jack was waiting. Jack helped her put jugs of water and wine with suitable glasses on the large table in the dining room. It had a special cover over it so Jack could not see the type of wood but guessed oak. He was impressed by the baby grand in one corner, with a bay window to the left and another behind the piano gave it enough light to play, without putting on one of the chandeliers. They had two over the dining table where eight high-backed chairs were placed. Jack noticed pens, paper and folders and knew they would come back up soon for the big meet after snacks downstairs. Two King Louis chairs and another round table with two relaxing chairs in the bay window matched the opulence of a room he would have loved to dine in.

Jack returned to the kitchen to talk to Phillipa. He had a coffee before taking a walk around the village.

It was on his walk he met a local lady with a dog who was carrying a fancy camera. It was late afternoon and the French love to go out at this time. He stroked the dog and she explained she liked to walk around the estate and the woodlands. She took photos of birds. Jack mapped out the village mentally, it was a habit of his. There was nothing unusual about this quaint rural village and the residents out in force, no idea of the big meet in the chateau.

* * *

It was 4 pm. Committee now sat ready around the dining table with pens poised and files ready. Agenda in front of each of them. Danielle looked up at the nearest chandelier, then she glanced at her phone, no one was watching; pleased that Cas had texted her to simply say "OK." The 'Cyanide' case was available for the journey.

Business soon started… first up, problems in Greece then the Somalian pirates. They made good progress; of course, they were saving the biggest problem till last – number 7 on the agenda. The ransom demand from

ISIL for hostages held in Algeria. They wanted twenty-five million and a helicopter.

Henri opened the conversation looking at Danielle in particular. "Since July 14th, after the Tunisian Mohammed Lahouaiej-Bouhlel, killed eighty-six on the promenade with his 19-ton cargo truck in Nice and wounded 458, the expected lifting of the national guard has not yet happened. We should inform the military chief of staff Benoit Puga and let him deal with this."

Danielle was on the attack looking straight back at him. "We have a limited time scale here. If we let this go to them, delay will cost lives. The national guard is for internal matters. This is on foreign territory. This is what we were formed for. This is our specialist area. It is a Sunday, when will they meet and how would they deal with this problem?"

Doc acknowledged Danielle's comments as did the Englishman with a nod of agreement on Danielle's immediate response. The American was waiting, fidgeting with his pen for his turn. It did not take long when Doc stated. "Too expensive a demand especially with a helicopter."

This time Henri agreed.

The Englishman simply observed, "And exactly how are we going to express our reduced offer in such a short time scale they have given us?"

The American stood from his chair and banged the table so hard glasses shook and papers bounced in the air. The startled committee members looked as he pointed vaguely in the direction of America through the bay window, "There is a new no nonsense president over there. Pay up or Trump will definitely pull out of this RAID agreement."

Danielle had to negate the unforeseen problem that Henri had brought to the table. "We need to vote first on the motion from Henri that we inform the military chief of staff to take over or do we get on with our job?"

Tension was mounting as the American glared at Henri and then at anyone who dare vote with him. Luckily for Danielle only Doc joined Henri even though he had acknowledged her earlier comments, and it was 3–2 to proceed as RAID.

Danielle argued the small helicopter in reserve and hardly used called Maggie was ideal to give away. It was old and not up to modern standards. The other in mothballs was called Mitter.

The table went through all points of interest and delayed the vote on this problem to check if Mitter was still airworthy. Wine was brought in by Phillipa and then an enormous bowl of mussels cooked in white wine and garlic, with baguettes. The mood improved as eating and drinking took over. The reply came back from YMCA. *Mitter fine for duty, can remove rocket launchers, needs servicing will be ready by Wednesday.*

Doc the German asked to see the money. This was normal practice at every chateau RAID meeting. Danielle was worried now as she had taken amounts out. A large metal door led down to a basement where all the money was stored. She asked for someone else to input their code to open the door, pretending she never knew her late husband's code. Danielle then presented them with twelve more red cases from the secret storage cupboard that only they knew about. She opened six of them with 2.5 million in each. If you have tried to count such a large amount of money it would take days. Danielle had gambled on that.

"Shall I open the other six cases and check each case?"

She thought Henri was going to insist but she filled his glass with wine and joked, "Have you got the muscles to lift all that money?"

The UK came to the rescue by saying using Cas was a good idea. The American concurred and asked Danielle to lift one. She just managed it and they all accepted that Cas would carry the money for her. The vote was taken 4-1 only Doc going against. The UK needed the friendship of America whoever was in power. Danielle sighed with relief. Everyone seemed happy and the meeting closed. An hour later Jack flew them back to YMCA and Henri drove back to Paris. Danielle retired to bed early. Cas would fly over and pick her up at 4 am. They would need four fuel stops to get to North Africa.

Chapter 8   Monday, November 14th

Cas landed at the chateau at 4 am. Danielle was waiting with two red cases with 2.5 million dollars in each. She noticed the 'Cyanide' red case identical to hers in the hold. Too early for chit chat they went towards Spain. They stopped for the third time in Gibraltar to fill up with fuel. They crossed over to North Africa and did one more fill before they were due at 5 pm at the agreed meeting point.

* * *

Rochine at least had some clean clothes for the next journey. What did seem strange was how the other night, she'd her head hooded. Her mother was next to her and she heard someone enter. The three of them were tied to their beds and Francesca was in the corner. She heard her mother groaning and swearing that she would kill him. All she could hear was her mother's moans and then there was a hand over her breasts. They were soft hands and that gently explored her; nothing more than gentle massaging. Then it stopped and the two of them left the room. Her mother still tugging at her ropes; swear words muffled by her gagged mouth.

They were blindfolded when taken to the beach; on stretchers or with ropes; dragged by their captors. They stopped after several hours and were rewarded with their masks being removed. Rochine saw three pigeons in cages left behind at what seemed to be an outpost. The sea was visible and the road that lead to Tunisia. She knew this area. She had not seen her father for a while. He looked broken. He had difficulty standing up. He did not speak as they ate and drank. Francesca was as so pale; her mother had the look of a woman about to commit murder.

Slowly they descended the mountain towards the beach as four soldiers were left behind including two known as Pinky and Perky, which made Rochine smile. They sat near the beach and her hopes lifted when she heard a helicopter. It approached slowly before landing on the large expanse of beach. The blades slowed down and then stopped. A man clambered out of the helicopter, followed by a woman who had flown it. Rochine was impressed by her skill. They moved towards her with two red cases. The pilot spoke to her first, then her mother and father. She eventually spoke to Francesca. The Tunisian man was with Tariq looking inside the red cases. She watched Tariq approach and speak to the pilot. Rochine felt the pilot's gaze on her, surprised by her authoritive handling of the situation. All she heard her say was, "So long as she is intact, I will replace her with another; and the rest of the money."

Rochine was wise enough to know what she meant. Francesca had nurtured her and gave her lessons not only on languages but why to avoid men. Rochine was young; she wanted to explore the real world. Rochine wondered why the pilot had looked at her so intently. That was when she realised what was in the red cases – they were being traded. She looked at them as they took off in the helicopter, praying they would come back and take her home. She remembered the pigeons circling and then disappearing and the helicopter did exactly the same.

| Chapter 9 | ArudyPolice Station |
| | Monday, November 14th |

Arudy Police Station was nestled between Pau and the Pyrenees. Dan Rowbottom (known to all as Yorkie) worked for ageing station commander, Rene, who was sat at his desk, ready to start his day. A Lay Abbey sign still sat over the entrance from years ago. The only two patrol cars were on duty and Lisa was about to put the kettle on. Nothing much happened in his sleepy town. Yorkie watched Rene flick through the day's paper, waiting for his brew.

Yorkie originated from Robin Hood's Bay in North Yorkshire (hence his nickname); he was a long way from what he used to call home. Tomorrow was to be a big day – he would sit his final exams to qualify as the new bobby. He knew his parents would be proud; they'd both died in a motorway crash near Bordeaux three years ago. They'd been on their way to their second home in Arudy. Yorkie had joined the local rock-climbing school as a teenager, during one of their many visits to the Arudy home. Single and with no job, Rene had given him a part-time job for two years helping with the translations as so many incidents involved English-speaking tourists. He always arrived five minutes late.

"Morning, Yorkie," said Rene, "Lisa has the teas made, time for our morning debrief."

Lisa threw a Yorkshire tea bag away. "Good luck for tomorrow, I think he is giving you the rest of today off to revise."

Rene looked at Yorkie. "You need to check your mountain gear, as if you need telling, winter is on the way. Your job today is to get the snow grips for my patrol cars. Do not want them floundering if they go off-piste."

Lisa, being all motherly as usual, brought the drinks over and the three of them sat at the regular informal meeting. The patrol men attended rarely as they had fixed rotas on the roads.

"Well, Lisa, anything to report?"

"No, should be quiet till December. We went to Pau Saturday for the Pigeon releases. Two competitions, one to England and one to Malaga, the last of the season. Yorkie says his friend from Doncaster has sent some pigeons down via the special vehicles."

Rene looked over. "I am not really bothered about someone from Doncaster and Pigeon races."

Lisa continued. "Well, we did accidentally help your friends at Pau Police Station."

"Oh, do I have to listen to this?"

Yorkie noted Rene's lack of enthusiasm, especially as there was often little to talk about at these debriefs. "Just be patient and I will fill your cup up. Have you got anything to report?" Lisa said.

Rene mumbled "no" as he sunk back in his chair and surrendered to her enthusiasm for a trivial matter.

"They released them for the last race of the year from Pau at 7 am. I have heard about this, people video them flying off so thought it would be nice to see it. Yorkie says last year his friend sent twelve, four came back and then a week later the other eight arrived within twenty minutes. He thinks the people did not release the birds at the same time. Then there was another going off at 8 am on what is called the Malaga flight back. The Pau Police were there as well. I took my camera which helped as Yorkie will explain."

Rene shook his head. "So you like birds of the feather variety as well, they leave as big a mess as the human variety." He laughed at his own joke, but Yorkie was not to be denied his comments.

"Thanks, Lisa, I was simply trying to help my friend who thought the previous year some pigeons were not released till days later so others had a better chance of winning. Well, seeing 2000 pigeons being released from several transporters was a sight to behold. I spoke to two transporter personnel who had travelled from the UK. These transporters are amazing. One came from Northern Ireland something called alucrate lightweight, state-of-the-art for these pigeons. They talked about a pigeon called 'Son of Forest Gump' that had bred many good pigeons. Says only the top 2% get merits. Timed yards per minute. They always lose a few, some terrible losses if they get the weather forecast wrong. The vehicles had to move away to let the Spanish transporters line up for their release. That was when Lisa spotted something on her camera. Looked like an envelope being given to a driver from someone. We took it to the Pau patrol car and showed him it. Your turn, Lisa."

"We got a text the next day, they said they found the bribe was from an English pigeon fancier and he had not released a few pigeons. He is being reported but we are not sure what will happen."

Rene smiled, looking more impressed now and less dismissive of their actions. "Okay, good work you two, not a bad start to your career, Yorkie, but let us get on with the real work."

Lisa coughed so Rene continued, "And you, Lisa."

Lisa smiled. "We watched open mouthed when they all flew out. They travel over 500 miles, and all competitors have to be registered, birds tagged with mobile phone numbers on in case they stray."

"They do look after those pigeons. I thought it was a legitimate release at first, a cacophony of fluttering feathers, difficult to check. The Spanish were just as enthusiastic as the English but this time a lot less than 2000. I prefer the mountains but pleased we went. Lisa makes good sandwiches."

Lisa poured more teas as Rene reminded Yorkie, "Do not forget the snow chains?"

"Yes, I can get them in my Lada, I will leave them in the compound later today."

"Then revise?" Lisa asked.

"Yes, I had better get off, see you Wednesday."

Rene closed the meeting. "Give my regards to the team, we will get the results by early Thursday morning. I need you for all those problems in the Pyrenees, good luck."

Yorkie left and Lisa checked her photos before doing a few errands for Rene. Sometimes, it seemed, she was treated like a secretary and not a qualified policewoman. Something Rene would often joke with Yorkie about. Her 'secretarial' work included reports for Rene on stray cats, minor thefts, but most important of all the arrival of legendary rugby player Jonny Wilkinson on Sunday morning at the local bar. Lisa was a Toulon supporter and had won a raffle to have breakfast with him on a day to suit. As she worked during the week and teams sometimes played on Saturdays, Sunday had been agreed. The village of Arudy had a buzz of expectancy and joy for the arrival of one of the world's greatest rugby players.

Chapter 10   Tuesday, November 15th

Danielle and Cas arrived back at YMCA early Tuesday morning; Cas had done most of the flying. Before going to sleep Danielle checked the main auditorium. She enquired about the alert in the middle of the North Sea. It turned out it was the Russian Aircraft Carrier on the way to the Middle East. The British government were keeping tabs on it and the Russians and UK representatives exchanged one and two finger gestures through the booths as tension mounted. They all saw it as one big joke and ate together to discuss the situation much to the amusement of everyone else. Putin had retaken the Crimea and his actions in Syria were a distraction for his expansion hopes in the Ukraine. The EU had sent soldiers and equipment to this area much to the annoyance of Putin. The sad point is that some of the Ukrainians saw themselves as Russian. Stalemate existed and would for a long time, like a game of chess.

Danielle slept till 1 pm. She had organised the rota, so she was free all week to take care of this ransom deal. She rang Cecilia at the Bordeaux Agency.

"Hi, been a long time need your assistance."

"Oh, what can I do for you?" Cecilia replied.

"One of our packages is to be returned. Can you collect from the prep school and I will take her back in my helicopter early Wednesday evening?"

"Why can't you go straight there, I am very busy?"

Danielle had never been to the prep school. Edith was the contact and Cecilia had been several times. She decided it was time to warn her about the incident in North Africa.

"You have an employee that has been kidnapped at the Houston house in Tunisia. This is inside information, please do not let anyone know just yet. I am up to my eyes in this problem, I have not time to prepare the package. I will land at 8 pm so it does not interfere with your work. It is handy you living near Marmande, it is on my flight path."

Cecilia agreed as she could pick her up Wednesday after work. It was a big detour as the prep school was in the rural area of St Remy, north of Bergerac and she lived south of it. Cecilia was even happier when Danielle confirmed two packages had been delivered so her dividend was due soon. Danielle said she would sort it out.

She checked her watch and decided it was time to go to the hangar and see Greco before flying to her chateau. She was focussed on her next move as she left the main building, vaguely aware a polite goodbye from the receptionist who always noted her time of departure from the building. Danielle could see Greco's helicopter in the distance as she walked towards the hangars. She stopped for a polite hello to Jack's wife and daughter wishing them a nice swim as they headed towards the leisure centre with the swimming gear spilling out of a supermarket bag. She wondered if Suzette had calmed down. It was common knowledge she was a nervous wreck every time husband Jack went on a mission.

Danielle walked on with purpose. She entered the hangar and saw mechanics busy servicing Mitter; preparing it for his last sortie. Jack came past her, and they acknowledged each other. Danielle was relieved as his next stop was the leisure centre as well, intent on his swim and no chit chat. She saw Greco alone in the canteen area cleaning his pride and joy. This was a lucky break for her. "Still on four hits?" she said as she sauntered in.

Greco looked on, almost ignoring her but he paid more attention when she continued "I have a job for you."

Greco twitched with anticipation, he clearly needed real action. Danielle checked no one was coming into the canteen through the windows. She turned to him and smiled. "I will have 200,000 for you by tomorrow night, the balance on a successful outcome."

"What is my mission?"

Danielle produced a photograph and an address with one further instruction.

"No mights, just a simple yes or no will do."

"Just had my helicopter serviced, they have put the prices up and I needed a new rotor."

"The balance of 400,000 is the norm." Danielle was not going to raise her offer. She took the instructions off him. "I did give you the first chance."

"Hey, wait a minute, I had better do it, I have heard rumours your time here is limited." His wry smile annoyed Danielle intently but just like her favourite helicopter Maggie she was not for turning.

Danielle looked around again to check no one could hear or see them. Greco gave a nod that no one else would have noticed even if they were in the room. Danielle gave him the instructions back. "I will go and see those mechanics first before I fly back." She left and talked to the staff. Danielle had to change first, before she got all clear from the mechanics to take Maggie. It was protocol to get their approval every time a helicopter went out.

They had standard procedures, enough fuel the priority. Before changing into her pilot's gear, Danielle headed to the main desk. Her arrival duly monitored by the receptionist who did not want to make conversation or eye contact as speculation mounted, she was to be old news. She proceeded to her own French booth first making polite conversation as it was an informal visit. Just filling in time till Maggie was ready. Danielle decided to visit the Russian booth. She spent fifteen minutes, occasionally looking up at the main board and all the ongoing incidents that had different-coloured flags. She left without going back to say goodbye to her own colleagues, and without any acknowledgement of the receptionist who entered her time of leaving. She felt abandoned and alone as she approached the hangars. The mechanics were now drinking teas or coffees and giving her the thumbs-up. It did not take her long to change into her pilot's specialised gear. Time had moved on and she was a lady with her own mission, her plan of action now in overdrive.

Danielle flew Maggie with extra verve arriving at the chateau in record time skimming the trees, and then shuddering to a halt as if she was a doctor in *Mash*, running to the chateau; her mind focussed. Phillipa just watched her go straight to the stairs and down to where the money was kept. She was grateful for the milk and a biscuit that Phillipa had waiting for her when she returned to the kitchen. She went to the pigeon loft and released one which would not take too long to get to St Agatha. She had taken the necessary money from the safe area. She drew breath and told Phillipa she would be back at 8 pm. She gave her a friendly peck on the cheeks then it was back to Maggie and on to St Agatha.

It was 5.30 pm when Danielle landed at St Agatha, three times as fast as the roads. As soon as the helicopter landed, there was a new pigeon in a basket waiting for when she left. She felt relief she had arrived safely.

60

Danielle was held in high regard by Sister Angela and Edith. As the entrepreneurial genius Danielle had delivered them ladies for the monastery and money. Danielle believed the wine merchant from Spain was a liability now, and this should be the last time to use him. They told Danielle Juan Rodriguez was bringing a refugee and would need paying. Danielle explained about the fatal incident at the prep school, the matron killed by the girl. Juan had transported her so it was likely he was responsible for her being 'spoiled goods': the girl had been interfered with and had lashed out. It was agreed to send a pigeon to Mari with instructions to be at St Agatha at 9 am the next day, also to be available Thursday and Sunday. The response as usual was OK. Angela was pleased to tell Danielle two more ladies were going out on Thursday. One to drop off at Le Vieux Logis, the other at Bergerac Airport. Danielle had a word with Edith in private to discuss the situation with Juan. "I do think Juan needs to be told."

"Yes, I will be checking the new girl thoroughly as well," Edith concluded with a hint of anticipated enjoyment. Danielle pondered for a while.

"There is a note in this envelope and some extra money for the coroner."

Edith opened the envelope, her smile said it all. "I will see to it."

"Good, I will be back soon and hope all goes as planned." Danielle finished the conversation, said her goodbyes to Mother Superior, as well as acknowledging a couple of girls walking hand in hand. It was getting cold and dark now as she walked towards Maggie, checking her watch, she was pleased to note she would be back in the chateau by 8 pm. The pigeon was on a seat observing her as she strapped herself in and used a blanket to cover the basket. The engine purred into action and dutifully took off, only a few watching from the monastery. Her lights flashed on her helicopter as a warning to any other aircraft. She did not see any others on her route to Brandiol. She flew over several small villages and wondered what was on the menu tonight for those eating in this part of rural France.

Landing safely at the chateau, she entered through the kitchen. Philippa had the door open for her and the smell of beef Bourguignon was so welcome and much needed. The dining table was set just for the two of them. No wine as Danielle had to be fit for the long journey in the morning. They drank Volvic water. Little was said; Philippa knew Danielle's moods well enough.

"I have the massage table out downstairs and the log fire is burning bright."

Danielle eyed her up as she finished with a Creme Brulé. "Thank you. I need a long slow massage."

They retired to the room where Philippa now lit several large candles. An hour and a half later Danielle drank another small bottle of Volvic. Her oiled body warmed up from head to toe. Gentle caressing of every inch of her body, Danielle felt Philippa's hands expertly arousing her to a loving and gentle climax.

They kissed and Danielle reciprocated before retiring; preferring to sleep on her own in preparation for another big day. She wondered how many more big days were on the horizon, but drifted to a deep sleep as she counted pigeons not sheep.

* * *

On Wednesday morning Doc had been up early. His BMW Series 5 with Munich plates his choice of comfort, class and style. He enjoyed the meandering drive to this quaint village and the chateau. He normally came by helicopter. It had been a long time since he had to drive this route. He was lost in thought and had to do a sudden stop when a tractor came into view unexpectedly around one corner. He felt proud he could stop in time and not stall the engine. He arrived to find Philippa had a coffee for him, the chateau gates already open in anticipation of his arrival. Danielle was having breakfast on the dining room table alone perusing a book called *The Mating Behaviour of Pigeons*. Doc took his coffee and sat near her. He was finding it difficult to make conversation as he too had heard Danielle was going to be redirected. Instead, they just got down to business after polite hellos. They descended the stairs and used the codes to access the money required. There was not enough time to check the balance. The committee could do that at a later date. Doc waited for Danielle to board Maggie and watched it take off; heading back in the direction he had come from. He felt happier to be driving on this crisp sunny morning. He thanked Philippa for another top-up of coffee and as he drove out the gates, he nodded to a lady with a dog about to go on their morning walk.

* * *

Danielle was in cruise-control mode. She would have time to do the business with Greco without Doc's suspicions, should he have seen her talking to him. Flying at a sensible speed and admiring the views from her vantage point. She loved the volcanic mysteries of the terrain after the lush valleys and forests she had flown over. She would be at least one and a half hours in front of the Doc, even with his fast car. This she knew was an advantage as one person less to worry about while she found Greco. Cas and a few of the servicemen were waiting for her as now Maggie was going to be checked over while they used Mitter and a six-seater helicopter for the big mission.

She left them to check her over and asked Cas to help transfer the red cases to the waiting helicopter. Cas had a broad smile and so he should have. About to embark on a mission of this importance was a red-letter day for him. It was several hours before the big depart so Danielle looked around the hangar anxiously for Greco. No sign of him and she did not want to arouse any suspicion and ask for him. There were very few people around now and they were busy. This was ideal for the business she needed to do with Greco. Luckily for her he appeared from the sleeping quarters, and they could meet privately in the canteen again. The maintenance staff were firing up the two helicopters, making final checks. It was noisy but easy for Danielle to hand over the 200,000 to Greco. Greco smiled and walked back to his bed, no doubt to clean and polish his trusty rifle. Only time would tell if the hit was going to be successful and Danielle had to find the other 400,000.

Danielle and Cas each rested for a while, eating in the restaurant together and going over final details. She deliberately did not talk about the cyanide red case or any money back from the deal he would have done.

It was early evening when they set off in two helicopters as agreed. Cas was in Mitter and Danielle in a six-seater. Danielle said she needed to pick something up near Bergerac and would meet Cas later.

Danielle flew to Cecilia's house in Marmande. She was waiting with the 'spoiled goods', easily strapped in and drugged, a present for Tariq. Nobody noticed Cecilia's live-in slave peering through the window as anybody would when a helicopter lands in the back garden. The changeover only took minutes and she continued on her way to catch up with Cas.

Cas was clearly impressed by Danielle's tactical brilliance to reward Tariq and guarantee the changeover. They then followed the same flight path as before. When they landed in Tangier, Danielle asked Cas to check the camera on her helicopter as she took a toilet break. The spoiled goods from Spain asleep, drugged and inconsequential to Cas.

The first biblical reference to a pigeon is in the Old Testament Noah and the dove of peace

Chapter 11

Tari HQ North Afric
Thursday, November 17th

Rochine was sick of being handcuffed to a bed and unable to see around her. She heard Francesca screaming as she was taken from the room. Only allowed to unmask to eat and go to the toilet, Rochine felt resigned to her fate. They had all been marched back the same route as when they had been captured and landed on the beach. Again, not allowed to see where they were. She was intelligent enough to know why and hoped that it meant an exchange was imminent.

She felt the soft sensations of oils over her whole body each night. Rochine thought she could sense the smell of an African lady but simply surrendered, opening her legs willingly.

Then she heard the same muffled noises of her mother and the creaking of the bed, not knowing who it was enjoying her. At least by the loud groans it was the sort made by men she guessed. The words of the lady pilot gave her a feeling of relief and hope she would not receive the same fate as her mother.

Rochine had no idea of the day; just that they were all led, still unable to see, to the outpost that overlooked the ocean. It was even more basic than HQ sleeping rough in sleeping bags but handcuffed to wooden posts. She could see at last but was aghast at her father who was unshaven, gaunt, a completely broken man. Her mother wore a stern look of revenge. Francesca was speechless, white with shock, a trembling wreck.

The sun was up when they were gathered together and released from their handcuffs. She saw Pinky and Perky stationed with what looked like powerful rifles overlooking the beach not far from the outpost. Two soldiers had guns pointing at them as Tariq, with another soldier, led them all down the steep path to the beach. Rochine recognised it as the same spot as before. But when was that? She was tired of the uncertainty and the abuse her parents and Francesca must have received. Would the trade still go ahead? Her confused mind focussed on the horizon as they all sat on the sand.

The sound of a helicopter raised her hopes.

* * *

It was Cas who landed first. Danielle was three minutes behind deciding to land a good distance from Cas and where Tariq and all were congregating. Cas showed the helicopter to his counterpart, explaining a few features. Tariq waited for Danielle to bring over the first case. It was too heavy for her and she asked one of his soldiers to fetch the first one as Cas was busy. Tariq, forever the commander, insisted on one exchange at a time.

Danielle knew this was normal protocol with ISIL. He did not disappoint. The first red case had 2.5 million in. He insisted on a second one before the first exchange of girls. Danielle went back to the helicopter and Cas this time took the second case. Another 2.5 million and all smiles. While Cas took the second case and as Danielle unstrapped the drugged girl, she switched a red bag for the Cyanide one. Identical in looks. Danielle walked over with the girl now more awake. Danielle's heart sank for a minute as Tariq said, "Stop." Thankfully, he checked her to make sure she was not a human time bomb. This he did with relish. No problem and all smiles again.

Danielle felt the sweat dripping from her forehead. It was a warm clear morning; hardly a cloud in the sky. She looked at the desperate but hopeful eyes of the remaining captives. She turned and walked nonchalantly with Rochine past Tariq holding her hand for comfort. Cas was smiling the smile of a victorious spy, the red case with more goods for his imperious commander. She knew he had the case as she checked he had not disturbed the others as she had organised.

Danielle felt for her handkerchief as she helped Rochine into the helicopter. With the rotor blades switched off, there was an eerie silence. The secret compartment used for sniper duty already open with the last six red cases. Danielle had done this before and using the chloroformed handkerchief expertly on Rochine, the hapless girl guided into the area and a deep sleep.

Danielle picked up a small gun and two smoke bombs from a compartment. She put her headgear back on, turned and faced the exchange area about one hundred yards away. The distance just far enough away for them not to see what she had just done. Cas was about to open the case with a soldier in attendance. She noticed the commander had walked back to a boulder where he was drinking water. Francesca was just in front of him. She saw the commander looking up at the hillside and then to the helicopter where his pilot was helping the new girl into it. Geoffrey and Cherie Houston had walked closer to the exchange in anticipation one would then be allowed to go to the helicopter and freedom. The pilot was now outside Mitter, the new prize and waiting for the deals to be completed.

Danielle walked two steps; it was lucky the commander was not taking notice of her. She fell to the ground, looking through her protective visor. She saw Cas click the switches on the red case. It was primed and ready to explode. Cas's body was shredded to a hundred or more pieces of bloodstained parts as was the soldier checking its contents. Two heads blasted into the air of the humid Algerian sky, no longer attached to their owners. Danielle saw Cherie and Geoffrey take the full impact as well. Parts of their bodies, limbs, arms, face going for a short spin before landing on the sand. She saw what was left of the large governess, her misery now at an end. The commander had fallen onto the boulder, trapped by the governess, neither were moving. To the right she saw the pilot drop to the ground as body parts hit the helicopter. Danielle rose with purpose to her feet, now unable to see clearly as the bomb had caused a cloud of sand. She had her camera and started to take pictures as she moved towards the carnage. Then she threw two smoke bombs beyond the dead bodies to act as a screen between her, the helicopter and anyone who might be watching from the mountain behind. She noticed the pilot staggering to his feet and fired several shots at the area she thought he might be as the smoke bombs made visibility impossible. Then she heard the whine of bullets hitting the sand near her helicopter, her only avenue of escape. No time to hang around now, she sprinted back to her helicopter as bullets rained down around her, hitting the side of her helicopter. She knew whoever was on guard duty would have instructions if anything went wrong. She was unscathed, she had danced between the bullets. Relief as the helicopter purred into life, the rotor blades whining triumphantly, quickly gaining ground and heading out to sea. She smiled to herself sighing heavily. It took seconds to be out of range. She opened the sniper compartment to check on Rochine, oblivious to all that had just happened, an orphan and destined surely for St Agatha.

Danielle skipped the waves and was relieved to see the Russian Aircraft Carrier in the distance as her fuel was at zero. When she landed on the carrier, it was fill up and go. She had told the Russians at YMCA she would need this fuel stop and they happily agreed. She saw Greco's helicopter as well. The visit to the captain's stateroom was nerve racking but essential. He gave her the steely look of a dictator intent on having his way with her. Danielle felt nervous as he looked out of the window. He used his finger to tell her to come to the window. They could see the helicopter being refuelled and sniffer dogs smelling the underbelly. "I hope you have nothing to hide in there." The comment of a man who clearly hoped there would be so she could be detained and interrogated. "You are full of sand and dirt, perhaps you have time for a shower?"

She could not refuse but only had forty-five minutes as the carrier was heading in the wrong direction and she wanted to get out of his stateroom.

"That would be much appreciated."

The captain pressed a number on his phone on his desk. A knock on the door almost immediately. The captain told a crew member to show her the appropriate washroom for guests. She followed him down a corridor. It did not take long before he opened a door to a room with a single bed. He showed her in and left. Danielle stripped and strolled into the wet room. The soapy hands caressed everywhere till she could no longer stop herself. The trouble with missions like this the adrenalin gives out relief hormones that need satisfying. She felt washed, clean and refreshed. Danielle lay down on the bed, spreading her legs, gently fingering herself. The thought of one of her conquests screwing her at the Vieux Logis was too much for her. She shuddered with relief and gave a loud exclamation as the orgasm engulfed her. She dried any wet areas, dressed, checked the time and went back to his stateroom.

71

"Pity you do not have more time," said the commander, grinning, as he showed her on screen in the shower room, then her antics on the bed. She hated the fact that he had allowed Greco to watch as well. "I believe you two know each other, how did your mission go? I see no passengers."

"Disaster I'm afraid. I will report to YMCA later."

Danielle observed the Russian commander; traces of a smirk on his lips... this disaster would clearly work to Russia's advantage. More trouble in North Africa and Europe was better for Putin's expansion plans elsewhere. "I had better get off," Danielle said.

Greco gave the thumbs-up as the commander looked out of his window. Mohammad Aqbal was no more, the Tunis trail destroyed. Greco followed her to the deck. Danielle paid him the balance, using a red case out of view of the watching commander, as he gave her Aqbal's hard drive. She fired up her helicopter, relieved Rochine was still asleep. She watched Greco put the case in his own helicopter. The engine purred as she climbed off the aircraft carrier. The figures on the deck became smaller and smaller as she continued to her next stop, Bergerac Airport to meet Mari. Danielle's mind fluttered with anguished anticipation of what the future might hold.

Greco went back to see the commander.

* * *

Sister Edith spotted the helicopter approaching St Agatha. She was prepared for her regular visit to Bergerac. Two more girls were ready to depart. This time they stopped at Le Vieux Logis. Edith saw a car in the hotel's private parking spaces that had blacked-out rear windows with Swiss plates as they approached the landing site. The helicopter landed on the grassy area not far from a school and properties that backed onto this area. The village of Tremolat serene, almost magical, from olden times. Mari shut the engine down. Edith and the girl with her suitcase walked over to the car while Mari waited in her cockpit. Edith knocked on a car window first. The girl went into the front seat and Edith got in the back. Edith got out after a short time. She walked down to the Dordogne river, a short distance away near a cemetery. She returned ten minutes later. The large lady climbed out and put the suitcase, that had been left near the boot, into it. She gave another bag to Edith who went back into the rear of the car. The girl stayed in the front seat as Edith got out after another ten minutes and walked back to the helicopter with the same bag the lady had given her. Edith was beaming as she got into the helicopter and instructed Mari to go on to Bergerac Airport. As they ascended into the clear sky Edith saw the car leaving Tremolat over a beautiful old bridge, the innocent Dordogne river beneath it, but could never reveal it's mysteries.

It was a very short ride to Bergerac Airport. Mari parked in her usual place away near a hangar but away from the main building and went to the café and waited for Danielle as instructed. Edith repeated the same procedure as at Le Vieux Logis except it was a van this time. There was no river nearby, so Edith walked past the car-hire parking area into the fields. After a few minutes, collected a bag from another lady driver. This time she walked into the main car park and found her own Renault diesel estate car which had arrived from the prep school. Edith spoke to her and put the new bag in the boot. Edith let her drive the short distance to a small ecole on the outskirts of Bergerac, Rue D'Airport. This was the safe house and used occasionally for lessons for up to four girls. Edith checked her bedroom, put her bags in there. She had time to amble the short distance with another smaller shopping bag into Bergerac and find the coroner's office. The secretary asked her to make an appointment. Edith smiled and in her blue habit and submissive manner begged to see him as she had to return to the monastery and would not be around for a long time. Edith produced a gift from Mother Superior for the secretary. Fifty euros to jump the queue. It was in a large envelope.

"I think if you check the records, we did book an appointment on an ad hoc arrangement because of necessity of my work."

Edith turned around and smiled innocently at those waiting. They looked at Edith with a mixture of resignation and annoyance. She turned back to the receptionist. "It will only take a few minutes." That certainly helped the atmosphere as waiting in a coroner's office was not everyone's idea of a good time. The receptionist opened her gift, checked the computer and her diary. "Oh yes, sorry I missed those notes."

It was five minutes later when a couple came out of the coroner's room. The receptionist buzzed him, and he appeared apologising to those waiting and ushered Edith in.

Edith did not have to say much. It had been a long time since the last need to finance a false story to keep their business away from the public eye. People who are well paid for this do not forget.

The matron from the prep school was duly certified dead from natural causes after a road accident. The coroner happy to be 10,000 euros better off. It took twenty minutes to conclude and check all was as said. Edith smiled at the receptionist and those waiting on her way out. Edith stopped for a few provisions on her walk back to the ecole. All they had to do now was wait till Juan arrived with a new girl and his van full of wine.

Juan parked at the rear as he had done before; out of sight from the main road. Sister Edith and the headmistress greeted him and walked to the side door of the van. Juan opened the sliding door and removed several crates of wine. The cries of a young girl curled up against other

74

cases of wine. The small skylight let in enough light for the young girl to see Edith in her nun's attire.

"Do not be afraid, child, I am here to welcome you to a new life, schooling and love." The innocent and warm smile hid Edith's true intentions for her.

Juan waited behind Edith with the headmistress but wanted his say, "I have brought you to a safe place of sanctuary, you are better here than your previous existence."

Edith decided it was better for her to enter the van, holding out her hand, the girl slowly got up. It had been over five hours in the van. There were empty water bottles on the floor and crumbs and the smell of urine, but Sister Edith guided her out hands together.

"Come into our ecole where there are fresh clothes and a warm bath for you. Then some food and a drink afterwards."

The girl obeyed, blinking at the brightness of the sunlight as Edith took her inside and led her up the stairs to a bedroom. Edith from the top of the stairs shouted down to the headmistress, "Mop the floor in Juan's van and check the four cases of rioja he has brought. I will come down soon and see Juan off before I bless our new recruit."

Edith started to fill the bath as she asked her to undress. "I will need to measure you for your new school uniform. We have them here but the main school we will have to drive to where you will stay. This is just an outlet we use sometimes for teaching."

Hesitantly, watched by Edith, the girl stripped and walked towards the bath. Edith had a tape measure and she slowly used it to decide what size garments she needed. She deliberately moved her hands over her breasts with the tape. The girl did not flinch or object, so Edith left her to bath on her own.

Downstairs Juan was showing the headmistress the bill for the four cases of rioja. Then she continued cleaning the utensils she had used to clean his van. Edith picked the bill up and eyed up Juan. "I am just going back upstairs to help her dress. Then I will come straight down and discuss your payment."

Edith went upstairs before Juan could answer. The girl was still in the bath, a luxury for her. Edith found suitably-sized clothes and put them on the bed. Edith went into the bathroom. The girl walked in with just a towel; Edith was standing. "Now, my child, before I dress you, it's time for confession."

She made her kneel in front of her. "Confess your sins, tell me all." The girl said she had not sinned, but others had by taking her. She had no family and asked why she was there.

"I am your salvation, stand up, child."

The girl obeyed.

"You must obey me and tell the truth."

"Yes, Sister."

"I am Sister Edith."

"Yes, Sister Edith."

"Hands on your head." The girl obeyed as Sister Edith removed the towel. "Now confess, did that man fondle you here and here." Edith expertly fondled and touched her till her nipples stood erect and the girl started to breathe heavily.

"No, no one has done that, you are the first."

Edith stopped her examination and intrusion and went to the bed to show her the new uniform. Edith helped her dress and they returned to the room downstairs.

* * *

Juan was waiting for his money and wanting to get to Bordeaux now. Edith gave him a drink of the monastery's special honey brew first as she opened a bag with some money in. Edith explained that for various reasons she had not been able to get to the bank in Bergerac. They did not open till 3.30 pm and Juan was impatient to get off. He was angry but reluctantly accepted the 1000 Euro payment for now. Edith explained she was going to Lourdes the next day to pray and seek redemption. She would go to the bank later and meet Juan at an agreed spot near the Pyrenees. They checked the maps and settled on a layby near Arudy at 7.30 pm. It suited Juan as he preferred this scenic route home. Edith concurred the girl was of good quality, and he would be paid in full the extra 9000 euros. They walked back to Juan's vehicle as Edith asked why he had so many pigeons in his van? He explained that he brought eight pigeons with him and sent one back at regular intervals to let his mother know all was well. He said there was just the two of them and it gave his pigeons some exercise as well. He was off to Bordeaux next followed by an overnight stay. Then to St Emilion and home by late evening on the Friday. They exchanged pleasantries as Juan continued his journey. Edith felt relieved this girl had not been interfered with; they did not need more spoiled goods. As soon as Juan had left, and the new girl had been fed and watered the three of them left for the prep school north of Bergerac. They went via the Credit Agricole where Edith made a withdrawal.

It took less than an hour to reach the school. Edith decided not to stay. She drove back alone in her car to the safe house, the ecole, on Rue D'Airport. Edith opened a bottle of Juan's rioja; she had bought four cases, and some would go to St Agatha on the helicopter where space was limited. It had been a successful day for Edith who only drank half the bottle. She retired earlier than normal. Edith needed a good rest before her long journey to Lourdes and back as well as paying

Juan the balance. She wondered if Juan had released another pigeon to let his mother know all was well.

Chapter 12

The sniffer dogs could only find the stale meat Danielle had left behind. She had closed the air vents and used air freshener to put off the dogs. As soon as she was in the cockpit, she reopened the air vents, probably still an hour's supply, the drugged Rochine still asleep. Refuelled, she dropped Aqbal's hard drive into the ocean, next stop Bergerac Airport

Danielle was pleased to see the reliable Mari. She handed over a sleepy Rochine. She gave her a bag containing the camera, the gun she'd used, ammunition, two spare smoke bombs and all the red cases except two. "Go to St Agatha, tell them I will be there soon, I am taking next week off."

She noticed the pigeon, smiled at the innocent nodding of the head, "Pick me up Monday morning from the chateau at 9." She shrugged and hurried over to her waiting helicopter. Finally alone, stomach flipping over, she realised she'd have to face the music soon. Danielle flew slowly back to base, all the time thinking and rethinking, she just hoped to God she had covered every angle. She questioned her own strategy, had she made a mistake? What is the weak link? All she had to do was survive until Monday when Mari would arrive. She was still thinking when she saw the old volcanoes and the buildings that she knew all too well.

Danielle arrived at YMCA at 3 pm. When she landed, there were people waiting for her.

She had never seen them before. Handcuffed immediately, the helicopter quarantined, people in white uniforms and gloves, blue tape around the helicopter within seconds of stopping. Force-marched down to a Mole room, she knew how interrogation teams worked. She looked at the faces, only two she recognised: Henri and the American. They sat either side of two more government agents: one gentleman and a lady. At the back were two more in army uniform; an obese but strong-looking man and a tough-looking woman perhaps a prison warden. The questions came thick and fast from the agents.

"Why did you not have back-up?"

"Why were the missile launchers removed?"

"Why did you not put a tracer on Mitter?"

"Why did you come back via a carrier and not through Spain?"

"Why did you come back via Bergerac and not Rodez, the natural flight path from the carrier?"

"What the hell happened?"

Danielle began her defence, explaining it was a done deal and no foreseeable problems. She had the missile launchers removed so ISIL would feel safe with the exchange. The same reason she did not want a tracer. The job was to get the hostages back. With her rank it gave natural importance for her to do the transfer. She said it was easier and quicker to use the Russian Aircraft Carrier. She felt it was safer than a potential missile attack going along the coast to Gibraltar. She had booked a refuelling stop at Bergerac as initially she was going to come back via Spain. When she heard about the carrier, she changed her plans but used Bergerac in case the carrier altered their plans.

It was only forty minutes' difference. She looked and pleaded total innocence. The first crunch question.

"We have ransacked Cas's apartment, found cash and a hospital letter, dying from AIDS basically. You did not check his health report, this is a potential suicide bomber in our own back yard."

Danielle had no idea, her lips gaped open. "Sorry my mistake." She noticed the others twitching as the barrage continued.

"You, the great Danielle, has rushed out to do a deal, not checked health records, no back-up, no tracer, a botched-up job. Why not take Mari on sniper duty?"

"Not much fun for anyone to be couped up in the sniper hold, it is only a six-seater. The main reason is that Cas would have warned them about my sniper. I wanted a clean deal and all six back here. I thought it more important for Mari to be on call for another emergency."

Danielle's reply was met with emphatic disgust from the American. "So getting my man and your ambassador back was not an emergency?"

The phone went. Danielle watched as he lifted the phone to his ear.

"More bad news, Danielle, the cameras were not working. You failed to check them."

"Sorry."

"A red cyanide bomb bag is also missing. The same as those used for the money transfer, any ideas?

"I know nothing about that, sorry."

Danielle froze as she looked at them. The American was furious. "A top American, and your Tunisian ambassador killed. All you can say is sorry."

Danielle felt the anger growing. "I have returned 5 million."

The American said what they were all thinking. "You can shove that up your tight arse when we take you back to your chateau, you are finished."

The two agents corrected him: "Fired with immediate effect, here you are guilty till proved innocent. We do not use recordings unless you want this public."

"You Americans dive in and think you can take out the Somalian pirates and rescue two American couples on their boat 'Quest'. The retired Admiral John Stufflebeem has to announce they were dead before you killed two and then captured the remainder of the pirates. We negotiate here, and I hope we have just saved the couple from New Zealand. Cooperation with South Africa and Italy should bring success today. I thought I had negotiated successfully with ISIL; we all make mistakes."

The American had his final word. "We are dealing with the present not the past."

Danielle simply nodded; just as she suspected. "You will be driven back to your chateau. The two at the back here will escort you, help gather your belongings here. Your car will be impounded. We will need to see you again. We will take your passport and driving licence. We will bring back all the money at the chateau, the American has the code so he will go as well."

Danielle deployed her best acting skills, even feigning tears, and hoped to be out of there as soon as possible. It was a relief that the money would balance as she had taken less for her cut that was now at St Agatha, delivered unknowingly by Mari.

"Can you take my cuffs off?"

She then heard a scuffle outside the Mole room. That's when she spotted Jack; face red, seething gasps. "My brother is dead, I want the bitch, what the hell happened, get me to Algeria now."

The guards did their job. Danielle watched the two agents approach him. They spoke and whatever they said seemed to calm Jack down. The agents returned a few moments later.

"He is taking Maggie to Algeria. We have no spare helicopters."

He then asked the American for back-up. He made a phone call and said a Black Hawk would meet him at Algiers at 5 am. The phone went again. The agent responded, "Not enough time to put the missile launchers back on, just use the two new decoy anti-missile attack ones, we do not want any more deaths."

"About the hand cuffs, when you are at the chateau and we have checked more information," one of the agents remarked.

Danielle felt the enjoyment of their power and her hopelessness as the army pair followed her to get her things. She handed in her identity badges, passport and driving licence. She took a bag of items from her bedsit, the two agents carefully monitoring. Danielle smiled to herself and wondered if they would ever find her at St Agatha. She felt the suspicious eyes of all the staff at YMCA that could see her as they deliberately paraded her one last time.

It was 10 pm when the four of them arrived at the chateau. Danielle looked at the confused expression on Phillipa's face. It was late and obvious to Phillipa that there was a serious problem. Danielle tried to comfort her by telling her not to worry. She watched her asking them all if they wanted a drink. Phillipa served teas and coffees, and Danielle went with the American to open the coded locks to get to the rest of the money. The other two made Phillipa show them around the chateau. Danielle heard her scream then silence as she showed them every room including the private chamber. Danielle smiled in relief when they all returned and Phillipa was none the worse for whatever they had done to her. Danielle sucked in a deep breath when the American told them to take her and inspect the rooms as well. Phillipa was ordered to stay with the American. Danielle heard Phillipa's cries as she was about to leave. The American demanded answers about

Danielle. Danielle pleaded, still handcuffed. "She knows nothing, she is just my maid."

It was then that Danielle felt several punches from the woman she thought was a prison guard. She was held by the fat man and punched again in front of Phillipa. The American asked Phillipa again, "What do you know?" He then pushed her onto a chair and roped her so she could not move. They left the American to count the money. Danielle was paraded around her chateau by the other two until they found the dungeon room.

"If you want your maid to work again, we need answers," said the fat man. Danielle was trapped. They used the equipment that Danielle had enjoyed using on Phillipa when she liked. She looked at the prison guard and knew she was in for a rough time. They could not hear what was happening to Philippa. Danielle winced as her pain level receded. The questions kept coming. "What happened?"

Danielle recounted the same story. She knew they did not believe her. The woman had the experience to break Danielle as the torture reached an unbearable level, much to the amusement of the fat man.

"I will tell you," Danielle continued. "We have planted a secret camera at the stores, we think the Russian and an insider is running a black market. Just ring and ask your men to get it, I did not mention it before because it might be the American."

They looked astonished at that news. These were French government agents, and their job was to get the truth. Danielle watched her leave the room to get a signal to ring YMCA. The fat man had five minutes alone with her. Danielle just accepted his wandering hands and was pleased when she returned. Danielle saw her looking at her exposed breasts. Luckily for Danielle she had left the phone where it could be heard. The prison lady went to fetch a leather strap, but the phone rang. She dashed upstairs and came down very quickly. She felt the full force of the strap across her breasts.

"Cas's fingerprints found on the camera in your helicopter. How do you explain that?" She stood there in control, the fat man just watching.

The whipping stopped.

Danielle had been waiting for this question. "At Algiers I took a toilet break, he must have done whatever he did then."

She watched her hand over the strap to the fat man. She held her neck as he used it again on her breasts. It was becoming too much for Danielle.

"I have told you everything, why would I risk my job, it is all I have. This chateau is mine. I like it here. Did they find the camera?"

Danielle knew that whatever had happened in the chateau would not get out. It was the untold rule, and each would back the other. She was still at their mercy and she needed to buy time. "I need the toilet."

It was a waste of time. They both left Danielle strapped to a chair and went to see the American. He had finished counting the money in red cases as best he could. Phillipa was waiting to be untied, untouched. The agent's phone went again. She left the room and came back very quickly. "We have a problem. They have checked the camera and it has shown Cas leaving the stores with a red bag."

The American sighed. "What did they say?"

"Come back, tell her the enquiry is ongoing. No change with the decision, she is fired and no extra pension, neglect of duty, intolerant handling of a crisis."

Danielle was relieved to be untied and see Phillipa was unharmed. Danielle watched them leave with her car and all that money. She knew how the system worked. She had expected the torture. She had waited for the prime time to surrender the whereabouts of the camera. She had given them time to find the fingerprints. She had framed a dead man and now had over nine million waiting for her at St Agatha. This, she knew, was the reason she's regarded as one of France's top female operatives. All she had to do now was lay low until Monday 9 am.

Chapter 13

Jack was on a mission. He'd deployed two helpers: a cool Swede navigator and a Pole who'd volunteered for the sortie to Algiers. They armed themselves as best they could and waited for the two new decoy anti-missile units to be put on. As they ate in the canteen, Jack told them the grim news. They were to meet up with a Black Hawk at Algiers and proceed to the beach where the incident occurred. Mission simply to land, check the area and return immediately. Engagement with the enemy was not on the agenda.

It was 6 am when they arrived at Algiers. The Black Hawk with huge armoury: the insurance back-up was arriving at 6:30 am due to a delay. It was only an hour to the beach.

"YMCA here, just a note the Russian Aircraft Carrier has changed course. Heading now south west towards you 800 nautical miles away, no immediate threat, but at high speed."

The message intrigued the experienced Jack. He knew the carrier was heading in his direction, but why? He knew the Mig's limit range at 770 nautical miles. By the time Jack got to the beach, any Mig could be there at the same time. Any helicopter was no match for a Mig. As soon as the Black Hawk arrived, they set off for the beach on red alert for any ISIL or Russian attack.

It was the Black Hawk that told them two Migs had left the carrier, showing on the powerful radar and heading towards them. Jack stayed on course, the Black Hawk on point duty facing the mountain. Jack had done a full circle and climbed higher than normal so the Migs were behind him. They were not at war with Russia, and he saw it as a training exercise for the Russians. He could have had a Russian on his helicopter. It was normal practice for countries to shadow and observe.

"Closing fast," said the alert Swede. "Missile launched."

Jack swore and continued his flight path. Black Hawk was not the target as it was facing the mountain but was aware of the problem.

"Sixty seconds to impact," the cool Swede said; and all facing certain death.

Jack pressed the first anti-decoy button, no response, failure coming up. He pressed the second button.

"Decoy released," the Swede uttered as Jack dived at speed then steadied as the Swede continued. "Parachute on decoy opened." He was watching a screen as if on a game.

Jack held his height in line with the decoy and went full throttle. Twenty seconds later the decoy exploded on impact by the Russian missile, Jack's helicopter shuddered but were lucky to be able to head straight for the beach. Black Hawk sent a message almost immediately "Mig 2 has sent Mig 1 to the bottom of the Ocean. Mig 2 returning to Carrier."

"Decoy destroyed, no imminent danger." The cool Swede a good choice for the mission. Jack gave himself a pat on the back for getting him on board.

Jack's training had saved them. The new decoys built by the Barnes Wallis Institute in the UK were nicknamed PE1 and PE2. They were programmed to burn out within sixty seconds. This had been their first live test. One thankfully had worked. PE was the nickname everyone had given to this new programmed decoy "premature ejaculation" not the inventor Peter Edwards.

When Jack landed on the beach, the first thing he saw were the vultures circling, as he got closer, he could see buzzards and seagulls had joined them, drawn by the smell of human meat. His eyes were drawn unwittingly to the carnage, he felt sick. Body parts scattered on the sand some gently bobbing in the water. Amongst them, somewhere was his brother and for a moment he wanted to search every damn limb torn from its body… but then he imagined he might find his head bobbing with the tide like a buoy. He imagined his hands turning it over … looking into those familiar eyes and that's when he was on his knees puking. As he looked up, he saw a hand amongst the fragments; male and female bodies, tatters of bloodstained clothes. There was no way to identify anyone. Small mercy – or was it?

The crew did not want to stay.

Duty made them dig a hole and they placed whatever remnants of bodies they could find into a makeshift grave while Jack watched and reluctantly took pictures; in some way it was a relief he did not see his brother; but another part of him wanted something, anything that had been his, that was him. He stared into the grave and uttered his goodbye; then he ambled back to his helicopter as Black Hawk radioed unidentified helicopter approaching from the mountain. As they took off and headed back to Algiers, the Black Hawk headed in a different direction and out of sight.

Jack swore he would kill Danielle Bousquet.

In the New Testament during the baptism of Christ a dove descended as the holy spirit, an image used extensively in Christian art

Chapter 14

Friday, November 18th

Tariq woke from his concussion to be advised that the governess had taken the full brunt of the bomb, which had saved his life. He had a few scars and minor wounds and a headache from landing on the boulder. Tariq was alive; angrily asking for Pinky and Perky and his pilot to report immediately. He had no idea it had been Pinky and Perky who had stretchered him all the way back as the wounded pilot made repairs to the helicopter to make it airworthy again. It was now back at HQ after a quick sortie to the beach again. This was all getting too dangerous. Cas was the reason he was involved in all of this in the first place – extra cash in exchange for girls. Until it got more personal. Cas was his contact in RAID, only now it seemed he was dead. He'd need someone to fill his place. And soon.

Pinky and Perky listened as the pilot told Tariq the story.

"A pigeon brought a message to say two helicopters were in the area, one on the beach. By the time I got there they were heading out to sea, so I returned."

Perky relayed the same story about the beach. "All we saw was a bomb going off, total carnage and so much sand and bad visibility. We had the big helicopter in our sights and after we saw two more smoke bombs go off and what sounded like shots fired, we both decided to fire at the big helicopter. We could not see what, if any damage was done but soon saw the big helicopter heading out to sea. We scrambled down with a stretcher that we always keep handy and brought you back. We followed your orders to aim for the big helicopter and the pilot if anything went wrong."

Tariq thought for a long time, assessed the information. Cas his main contact was dead. He only had ten million and he had lost more of his men. He needed to check his trafficking trail was still okay that Cas had set up. He wanted revenge. He looked straight at Pinky and Perky and gave them new instructions.

"Go in the helicopter to our contact in southern Spain. She will drive you to France. Pick up the money from Juan, the wine merchant, on the way. By the time you get to her house in Spain, I will send her pigeon to give you further instructions. When you return bring another of her pigeons. Go to France to this chateau at Brandiol. Kill Danielle and anyone else in the chateau, I only want the girl that we had here. Make your own way home, I cannot leave the helicopter in Spain."

Tariq checked the time and sent a pigeon with a message to his Russian contact. He produced a picture from his pocket of a much younger Cherie Houston with her husband. The photograph was sixteen years old, and Cherie was heavily pregnant. He muttered, "Wherever you are, I am going to find you."

* * *

The Russian Aircraft Carrier had received orders to observe the events unfolding on the Algerian beach that Jack was heading for. The orders from Moscow were clear. The commander gave the new recruit a chance to show his capabilities. The Migs took off and the leader let this recruit take the lead. As the two Migs approached the helicopters, the captain was informed of an American nuclear submarine on the radar. Seconds later, a British submarine was on the opposite side. He gave orders for the Migs to return to base. The rogue pilot thought otherwise and sent his missile straight for the first helicopter in sight. The Russian Mig pilot would normally be at the front, sent the information to his commander and was instantly told to take him out to avoid a naval battle at sea and the possibility of World War three. Moscow was hoping yet again to create unrest and insecurity to the western powers by sending a rogue pilot. The new decoy system PE2 saved the day.

At 5 pm the Russian commander received a message. He asked to see Greco.

"Your mission to Greece has been cancelled."

Greco said nothing as he had heard the news that after the election defeat of Hillary Clinton, Obama was now not going to visit Greece.

"There is a new one for you, an extra 100,000 for this assignment. You are to meet at the 24hr service station in Eymoutiers on the D940 at 2:30 pm this Sunday. You will put your flask on the roof. You will join forces and go to the chateau at Brandiol and assassinate Danielle Bousquet. He gave Greco the recent photo of her in the shower.

"In case you need reminding, here is your deposit payment, balance on completion."

Greco was looking forward to this mission and took his time to gather his goods. He cleaned his gun and oiled it yet again. He would fly back via Greece and be home sometime on Saturday, plenty of time to drive on Sunday for his appointment at the service station.

* * *

It was late Friday evening when a pigeon returned to Tariq's HQ. He immediately sent a pigeon to his contact in Spain where Pinky and Perky were about to arrive. The message simply said "Collect money for the girl we sent to Juan first. Then go to the service station for 2:30 pm this Sunday in Eymoutiers on the D940. Find the car with a flask on the roof and take orders from him." Tariq was confident now that he was going to get even with that bitch, Danielle Bousquet.

Pinky and Perky had been at Paula's country home near Turre, just outside Mojacar for a good hour before the pigeon arrived. The helicopter roared into life and sped back to Tariq's HQ after they read the message. Paula found the soldiers a room for the night. She made no comment when they slept together. She had learnt to hold her tongue, collect her commission and enjoy her passion which was cycling and watching the tours. After breakfast, the three of them set off at 10:30 am, refreshed with little luggage. They would not have that luxury till they returned. Paula was the driver and insisted they stayed in the back. The windows were blacked out and only her visible. She loved to tap her large rings on the wheel, listening to music of her choice. They would stop several times before arriving at a small but secluded farmhouse and a large barn on the outskirts of Pamplona.

* * *

Sister Edith drove to Lourdes on that Friday morning. She had not checked the weather forecast. Rain turned to snow the nearer she got to Lourdes. She spent the day at Lourdes before leaving to meet Juan at a layby on the mountain pass between Arudy and Izeste. It had been arranged to meet there as it would be quiet and en route for them.

Spain was close and the preferred road back for Juan. She left earlier to allow for the snow.

Juan had left Bordeaux that morning with French wine and drove to St Emilion. He filled up his van with local wines and stayed for lunch and afternoon tea while business was concluded. The drive to Arudy was slow and tedious. He liked to go this way as the scenery was spectacular. He always stopped north of Pau at the Aire de L'Adour Total service station for a break. He sent one of his pigeons off to say: *back for 10 pm.* It was 6 pm and the rendezvous was scheduled for 7:30 pm. He had one pigeon left to release after his business with Edith.

Edith arrived at the layby. The road works sign 'road closed' that she had seen near the D36 fitted in her boot. She arrived at 7:15 pm and placed the sign further down the road so no vehicles could come from Arudy. Juan would not have seen that sign as he came from the other direction. He turned off the D934 onto the D918. Two inches of snow made it difficult to turn around in the layby, but he managed it and parked behind her Renault. Both vehicles were facing the same way. Edith looked in her mirror and observed Juan with his happy expression as she knew he expected a good pay day.

The flask next to her contained the monastery's homemade honey drink. She added an extra special ingredient before opening her door, her gloves a defence against the wintry conditions. Edith could not see the usual impressive Pyrenees due to the snow and darkness. She carefully moved over the snow to the side of his van, smiling at him with her flask in full view and her carrier bag full of money. Juan leaned over the other side of his van and moved his last pigeon closer to him which allowed Edith to sit near the passenger door. "Here is a quick drink for you before I pay you the balance and some extra for the usual four cases of champagne and St Emilion red." Edith showed off the money as she opened her flask and gave him a large cup of the sweet-tasting drink.

"You might as well have this before we brave the snow and put those cases of wine in my boot."

"Good idea, I will be off straight away as the weather is not good." Juan half checked the large amount of money Edith had brought. He removed one glove to grip the cup easier and drank slowly with an air of satisfaction as if he was tasting a rare wine.

"Just the job, that was beautiful. I will have one more after I have put the wine in your boot." They both got out, but it did not take long to load up the eight cases of wine into Edith's boot. Edith had deliberately waited to pay him the extra money for the wine. What with him having an extra drink as well, it was the ideal time for Edith's plan to work. They were soon back in the van; Edith filled his cup again. "I will be off in a few minutes, just enough time for me to count out this extra cash for the wine." She slowly counted the 1150 euros as Juan finished his drink. She saw Juan's eyes starting to roll, moving the basket with the pigeon towards her as she put the money nearer him. Edith smirked and took the money back as Juan grasped his throat and tried to cry out for water. She watched his body fighting to stay awake, but he was losing his battle.

His croaking voice and eyes that were now closing, his hands going in all directions failed to stop him collapsing over the steering wheel. Edith simply watched before she placed a spare plastic bag she had in her pocket over his head. His face went whiter and whiter as the lack of oxygen denied him life. She put the money back in her bag and found the 1000 deposit.

Sister Edith kept her own gloves on as she strapped the belt back over Juan's body and just managed to find the catch to secure it. She went back to her car and moved it onto the road, still no traffic anywhere. She went back to the van. She started the engine and removed the plastic bag from his head. She took off the hand brake and put it into second gear, then steered the vehicle towards the edge and the ravine below. She managed to trap his foot on the accelerator and then shut the door. She watched the van crash down the steep ravine. The van crumpled; wine bottles smashing inside, the door opening and more cases careering into the overgrowth, along with the squawks of a pigeon that might or might not survive. She did not care. She wandered to her car, retrieved the 'road closed' sign and headed back to Bergerac. In her thoughts she had now taken revenge for the way Juan had abused the north African girl and caused the death of her matron. No one crossed Edith; a force to be reckoned with.

Edith was prepared for the arrival of Constant the next day. She left the gates open so she could have the first glimpse of her as she pulled up in a taxi. She watched a small lady get out and take her overnight bag out of the boot. Edith listened for the bell and opened the door.

"Good morning, it is a good thing you are on time, young lady. Put the bag down and go and shut the gate. Make sure it is locked." Edith waited and when she returned, she continued, "Follow me to the office first, leave your bag at the bottom of the stairs."

Edith walked into her office and sat behind her desk. "Now then, Constant, you passed your first test with Cecilia I hear, let us see if you pass this one. Do not speak unless you are spoken to is that understood?" Edith felt her own body heaving with anticipation. Constant eventually murmured "Yes, Miss"

"Yes, Matron," demanded Edith.

"Yes, Matron."

"That's better, now stand up and come round next to me."

Constant obeyed, Edith continued. "You know why you are here? We need a new matron at our prep school and I will show what I expect of you. You will take the part of a new girl and after tea we will change roles. You will stay the night and leave in the morning. I will decide if you are suitable. You can leave when you like if this is not for you."

Edith sensed her nervousness, which prompted her to move her hand over the back of one leg and towards her bottom. "The first thing I to do is check you over." Edith lingered on her bottom. "I am going to undress you and inspect you for any health issues or worries, I have a special room for that."

Edith held her hand and guided her to another room with a massage table. Slowly Edith undressed her then ordered her to lay face down. Edith found some warm oil and rubbed it gently onto the back of her neck and shoulders. "Tonight, young lady you will sleep with me."

Edith was on a high, she introduced Constant to the meaning of DOLLAR. After lunch Constant had a school lesson wearing her uniform. She did not do very well in one subject. Constant felt her punishment was too severe but accepted it. In the evening Constant got her own back on Edith as they switched roles. Wine from Juan gleefully drunk when Edith said she had passed her test. The night in bed of orgasmic pleasure for Edith who needed it after her visit to Lourdes. Constant would start work immediately. Her new address, the same as Edith would be L'Ecole, Rue De L'Airport, Bergerac. All her mail would now come here, and her employee was still the agency.

"Constant, drop me off at the airport please and use my car. Take my car to the prep school on Monday morning when you will start your new job."

Chapter 15   Friday, November 18th

It was Friday night when Yorkie heard the phone ring. He whipped the phone from the table and glanced at Rene's name on the screen. He was *just* relaxing too. Without so much as *a hello, how are you?* he heard Rene say, "A lady has rung in to ask why the road was closed going out of Arudy and then another phone call to say they heard a strange noise but went quiet afterwards. They live on the road to Izeste."

Yorkie looked at the weather outside and knew instantly why he had rung him. If it had been a domestic or bar problem, Rene would have gone. "I will take my 4 x 4 Lada and check it out," responded Yorkie.

"Thanks... oh and well done for passing your test, see you in the morning, Gendarme Rowbottom, ring me back only if urgent."

The Lada was reliable, perfect for a night like this. It had pulled many Mercedes, BMWs and other cars stranded in waterlogged fields at music festivals when they could not cope. He drove down the snowy road very slowly looking for the road sign. After several passes and no sign of it, he cussed at it being a waste of time, drove back home to a glass of wine and his bed.

On Saturday they only worked till midday. Yorkie walked in, to a big hug and kiss on both cheeks from the 'motherly' Lisa – *his partner in crime…* of sorts. She congratulated his passing his exams. She was a godsend for Yorkie. A bright easy-going but meticulous officer cum 'secretary' – rugby Toulon supporter as well as a keen photographer. She was in a buoyant mood as her raffle prize – the great Jonny Wilkinson – was flying to Pau airport the next morning. A bus with forty from the supporter's club were picking him up and all coming to the main Arudy café/bar for breakfast. It was big news for the locals. Lisa was in a teasing mood.

"Hear you had your first case last night, a missing sign and a bang from outer space." She laughed.

"Ha, ha, snowing like mad, wild goose chase," Yorkie said, "could not see anything, no signs and too much snow, do you fancy a quick run in my Lada and double check?"

"Why not, I will bring my camera just in case, should be back in twenty minutes, Rene, where did the phone calls come from?"

Rene passed them on to Lisa who promptly asked Yorkie, "Did you go to the house that called about the bang?"

"No, did not see any sign, so thought a waste of time."

"Let's go to that one first then."

They both put their police caps on as they left the station. It was a relief the snow had stopped and only a short walk past the old houses on the high street to Yorkie's property. The side garage had space in front to park his Lada, so he hardly had it in the garage, which was full of climbing gear. They spoke to a couple walking by as they approached his car. They made an enquiry if they were on a new case. They certainly looked on official business. The drive past the quaint old houses onto the rural road with the Pyrenees now visible was breathtaking in its natural raw environment. They made a statement – we have been here for centuries, and we are not moving. Some families in the villages locally could claim the same.

Yorkie slowed down as Lisa pointed out the house standing back a little was the one that had phoned in. She knew all the locals by name and many in the nearby villages. They parked on the verge in clear view of any traffic that might appear but time to avoid the police car. Hardly space for two vehicles to pass but who would care? Lisa opened the gate as Yorkie followed, both aware the curtains had moved when the dog started barking. Lisa knocked once and the door was opened immediately by an elderly gentleman who launched straight into Yorkie. "Are you the new rookie then?"

Yorkie did not reply as Lisa responded, "Yes he sure is, and we need your help." She had paper and pen in hand. "Now tell us about this noise you heard last night."

He turned to his wife as the dog was still barking. "Can you remember that noise we heard, come here, Napoleon, and have a sniff." The dog obeyed and a voice from the room came over. "Sounded like a screeching noise and then a rumble and a clonking noise, you told the police a bang, but my hearing is better than yours even if I am in a wheelchair."

Yorkie was impressed by her description so asked politely, "Why did you think it sounded like a bang, was it a single bang?"

"Eh, lad, it was an awful night and by the time I rung you I just remember some sort of bang."

"It was more than one bang, I am sure there was some sort of crashing noises, certainly not a gun." His wife had wheeled over, and the dog was still sniffing around, tail wagging, waiting for a pat. Lisa asked, "Where did this noise come from?" She patted the dog.

They both pointed in the direction of the next village and shrugged. "Do you want a drink?" she enquired as though company was a relief for her.

Lisa knew it was good politics to stay for a quick drink. They eyed up Yorkie and he joked, "I think he is a bit young for you, Lisa."

"It is none of your business, they are colleagues on a job, you old rascal." His wife slapped his legs as she moved past in her wheelchair. They all laughed and waited for a hot drink even though they offered wine. They discussed the recent events with the couple who warmed to Yorkie even though he said virtually nothing.

"Thanks for the drinks," Lisa had taken control; this was her territory. "Okay. Yorkie, you drive slowly out of here towards the next village."

They went at a crawl as any noise had to be close for them to have heard. They had only just got into fourth gear when Lisa saw the layby.

"Better park over there and we will have a look around." There was plenty of snow on the ground as they got out for a stretch and a walk. Yorkie had a habit of looking for any climbing opportunities. It was no surprise that as he wandered around and looked down the ravine his good eyes spotted a van at the bottom.

"Come over here, Lisa, I have seen a vehicle down there and it looks like wine cases all over the place, some broken."

"Bloody hell, Yorkie, you had better get your ropes out. I will ring Rene and get my camera out."

Yorkie had his climbing equipment in his car at this time of the year and his special boots. Lisa was on the phone to Rene in seconds.

"We need heavy haulage and tape to cordon off, serious incident, van at bottom of ravine, suspected deaths but cannot see yet, Yorkie going down."

Lisa helped Yorkie with the ropes, securing one end to a tree. It took him several minutes to secure himself and then drop himself into the deep ravine. By the time he got to the bottom, a siren could be heard. Rene arrived and confirmed to the recovery company who were available twenty-four-seven to come immediately. Yorkie shouted up,

"Driver dead, just the one casualty." Many crates and boxes of wine scattered everywhere.

Yorkie hauled himself back up. They surveyed the scene. Rene surmised that he must have been tired and skidded as he left the layby, accidentally going over and bingo! Yorkie went back down with some special bags.

"There is a pigeon, shall I let it go?" Yorkie said.

"Not yet, can you bring it up and any paperwork or items of interest that can fit in those bags."

Yorkie's task was more difficult than it looked from the top. The smell of wine was obvious. He eventually made it back to the top. The pigeon in a distressed state and best left in the basket. Rene found a blanket to put over the basket to calm it down. Lisa took more pictures of the van even though it was far away. The man's identity was confirmed by the name and telephone number on the van. *Juan Rodriguez – it looked like a Spanish area* code...

Rene concluded, "Not much more we can do till the recovery wagon gets here. I will take the documents and pigeon back to the station. Yorkie, you stay here. This can be your first case and make sure the van is in our compound. The body will go to forensics, I have just rung them. Lisa will help you with the paperwork. Lisa will come back with me as a phone call might be necessary to his wife or whoever. I will also contact his local police station in Spain and seek help for counselling, if required."

Yorkie waited two hours for the specialist heavy-duty recovery wagon. The driver and assistant were tired from being out all night on other recovery missions due to the unexpected snowstorm. They drank coffee and worked out a plan of action. It took nearly three hours before they even started to haul the vehicle out. The forensics waited patiently near the layby. The village had very few residents, but everyone seemed to have heard about it. People were talking and guessing what had happened. The blue tape and Yorkie stopping them getting any nearer. Dogs on leashes and cries of "There is a dead body" echoing amongst them. The forensics van a giveaway as well. They were used to accidents but not always this close to the village. "Told them I heard a bang" repeated many times. "You should be in nappies," joked one old lady to Yorkie. Then an even older lady: "Told them the road was blocked." Somebody else laughed and replied, "How would you know? You are always drunk and forget everything."

Yorkie was learning crowd control but decided to ask them questions.

"Anyone else see the road closed sign?" Nods in total agreement. "Too bad to go outside" was the general response, nobody concurred with the mad old lady. Someone else had the final word before the road was blocked to allow the recovery wagon to do its job.

"She said it was blocked so she could go back to the bar." They all laughed as the winches pulled the van up to gasps from everyone as the dead body came into view on the driver's side. The cabin was crushed so badly, Yorkie wondered how he had got the pigeon out and the few items.

Forensics took the body and Yorkie followed the recovery vehicle to the police compound. It was now Saturday afternoon and no other policeman to stop the crowd against a tape. As soon as they were out of site many of them rushed to the edge to look down. It is a sad fact people behave in strange and wondrous ways. The van had gone, just overgrowth flattened, shrubs devastated, glass and debris but people just had to witness and walk over an area that should have been out of bounds. It was too deep a ravine for people to speculate if there were any full bottles of wine for salvage. The local bar would be busier than normal for the next few nights. The two coffee shops will be full as well. The village a cauldron of speculation and gossip on top of the anticipated visit of one of the world's great rugby players.

Yorkie went to the station, but it was closed. He walked round to Lisa's house to get the latest news.

"Rene contacted the police station in Pamplona who confirmed he was single, living with his mother south of the city. It is very rural near Olcoz. Nothing on file and a wine merchant, business at the same address."

"What about the items I put in bags and does his mother know yet?"

"Yes, I rang her as agreed with the Spanish Police, just before they arrived. I told her about the accident. She broke down, it was unbearable to hear her. I tried to calm her. We were on the phone for ages, she begged me to be a hoax or wrong. I heard the doorbell go and then I hung up when I realised a local policewoman had arrived."

"Well done, it must have been awful, can I have a drink as well." Yorkie noticed her wine glass and a bottle nearly empty. Lisa, despite her experience had found it difficult to tell the mother the sad news. Yorkie continued, "The forensics have taken the body and the van is in the compound. We will check that on Monday and arrange to take it to her with the body once forensics have finished."

Lisa nodded in acceptance of Yorkie's report. "Looks like we are partners of the layby incident. An old battle axe and a young rookie."

"A secretary in a police uniform, multi-tasking and young at heart with an active brain, you have had a difficult day, especially telling his mother her only son had died."

Yorkie could see that Lisa was at breaking point. The trembling lips; the shaking hands. Yorkie moved over to her and put his arms around her. "I am lucky to have a local knowledgeable lady to help me. Hey ho, I always fancied being someone's toy boy."

Lisa smiled and tears slowly escaped onto her cheeks as they both tried to laugh at the same time. Yorkie found his clean handkerchief and gave it to her as he removed his arms and sat back in his chair. "Sorry, I am a bit of a softy," Lisa continued. "I will wash this and give it back to you, that poor mother."

"Whenever – it is not important." Yorkie looked at her, he needed a new distraction. "Bit peckish, any food in the house, I do not fancy the local tonight, too many questions and I have no answers."

Lisa blew her nose and wiped the tears away, standing up and moving to the kitchen. "Yes, yes, I'll bring something out, I have some pizza, will not take long to heat up."

Yorkie filled his wine glass and did the same for Lisa as he walked into her kitchen. He put his arms around her again and gave her a gentle kiss on one cheek. He then retreated to his chair and waited for the pizzas to cook. They split the two in half, a margherita and a pepperoni. She found some garlic bread. It had been a long day. They ate and said little as the meal was washed down with the wine.

Lisa reminded him of Jonny Wilkinson's morning visit. Cue to leave, so he staggered the short distance home, having drunk quicker than normal. He laughed to himself about the sign that was never there and all the comments by the locals. Then he thought about the bang from outer space that Lisa mentioned. So, was the mad old alcoholic woman with Alzheimer's telling the truth or not? Had she used that as an excuse to drink more. He thought *time to be a detective*, he would check on Monday what time she left the bar and what time she came back and why. He questioned himself as to why he was in Southern France and not in Robin Hoods Bay where he learnt to climb the cliffs. Why did his parents die? Yorkie fell into a deep sleep and just thought: *destiny*.

Chapter 16

Saturday, November 19th

Paula knew the way to Juan's barn. She had delivered another young girl on Tuesday and returned the next day. She also took two pigeons and kept them quiet with Tariq's by putting a blanket over them in the boot. They arrived at the barn and parked out of sight from Juan's mother's farmhouse at 9 pm. She told them to stay in the car while she tried the barn entrance bell. It was dark and no response. Paula went to the farmhouse and found Martina Rodriguez, Juan's mother, in tears and talking to herself about her poor boy. She had often talked to her when she came up. She had no idea about her son's secret trade as he slept in the barn and she hardly ever went in. She only went to the outside stairs to the loft to attend the pigeons. A string went from the height of the barn to the farmhouse, so when a pigeon returned her bell would sound and she would check the message.

Juan would eat in the farmhouse and take food to his barn to store in his fridge. As far as she was concerned, he had his own reputable business. Juan did all the paperwork himself, buying and delivery service only to his clients.

Paula was stunned by the news. The police said initially no suspicious circumstances, bad weather the cause, worn tyres. Martina knew her son only had the van serviced when necessary. She willingly gave Paula some keys for the barn. It took her some time to find them as he told her to use them only in an emergency. Juan's barn was his castle. His barn reflected his untidiness. Wine stored all over and some with names on waiting to be delivered. Paula went in alone with Martina.

"I am on my own, it is a bit of a mess, but can I rest here for a while before my long drive back? I have come for some cases of champagne he was bringing from France and some St Emilion. That is not possible now, so here is some money for four cases of rioja."

Martina wanted her to stay in her farmhouse, but Paula was insistent as she had enough to contend with and might need to contact any relatives. Martina said no living relatives, her husband long since dead.

"I will be off before dawn. I will lock the barn and drop the keys off when I leave."

Martina agreed as she trusted Paula. As soon as Martina returned to the farmhouse, she let in Pinky and Perky through the back door where the car was parked. They discussed the situation. They were not computer savvy, nor was Juan who had all his paperwork trail in a book system. Year planners had all the information. The three of them checked for any clues about the slave trade. There were none. Paula knew where his secret room was. She had helped him carry girls on more than one occasion into the soundproofed room. A skylight the only place for air to penetrate. Loads of cobwebs high up. A pulldown chord that could block the skylight and act as a sound barrier. A wooden bar around the small room with a rope attached. The bed in the middle and metal containers. Various cuffs and specialist items to control or punish. A cupboard out of reach, unless you had a step ladder, had drugs to administer to sedate or put to sleep accordingly. She had a similar room where she lived. The slave market was lucrative, and this could be hell for anyone who did not agree with the system.

They agreed to remove all items in this den, except the bed, which was too bulky. It might never be discovered as it was so well disguised. They found a saw and cut up the bar and cupboard into wood. Contents except the bowls put in the boot of the car. By the time they had finished it was a secret room with a bed. The sheets were removed and stuffed in the boot of the car as well. His main bed was in a corner of the barn next to a shower and toilet. As an afterthought they sawed up the bed and that became firewood. Now it was an empty room, perhaps ideal for special cases of wine. They decided to put some in that looked old and not sold. They felt much happier about their efforts. Pinky wrote a message and released a pigeon. They decided that killing the mother would be too suspicious after the son's death.

Paula locked up the back door. She looked round one more time, turned the lights off, locked the main door and dropped the keys off at the farmhouse.

It was 5:30 am when she drove out and headed for Arudy. Near the Pyrenees they fly tipped the items. It was 8:30 am Sunday morning when they turned on to the D934 drove past the layby and into Arudy.

There were crowds gathering and no place to park as they drove through the traffic lights to the edge of the village. A bus was parked in the small car park which was full. She told Pinky and Perky to lie low, even though the windows were blackened for privacy. They found a turning point and Paula stopped the car behind another parked on the verge.

"Wait here, I will find out what is going on."

Paula stopped a couple; her French was poor but adequate. They said Jonny Wilkinson had arrived and was in the bar on the left. Paula told them her Spanish friend had died somewhere here and had they heard anything. She asked another old lady the same question. She was told the same information: "It was in a layby as you leave the village on the right about four kilometres away. Van skidded off into a ravine, no other vehicle involved, terrible night, lots of snow."

Paula returned to the car. "Sounds like a victim of the weather. We will stop at the layby and then move on."

As she drove to the lights, they turned to red. Paula had the window down to look at the scene. She saw an elegant oldish lady in a rugby top with her hands around Jonny Wilkinson at the entrance. She admired him from the rear at his wide shoulders and strong thighs. There was joviality and pictures being taken. She wanted to stop and join in, but urgent matters took precedence. They stopped in the layby, but the blue tape had gone. They saw the destruction down the ravine and the marks of the recovery vehicle. They saw nothing suspicious. Paula decided to move on as it was a long drive ahead of them. She was thankful it was a Sunday and no HGVS on the road to slow her down. It was 2:30 pm when they arrived at the service station in Eymoutiers.

Pigeons mate for life and can start breeding from six months old. Given a warm climate and abundance of food can breed up to eight times a year

Chapter 17   **YMCA – Evening**
                 Friday, November 18ᵗʰ

Jack had landed at YMCA with his crew. The agents from Paris were waiting as were the German Doc and Henri. This time the cameras on Maggie were working. All the crew went to a Mole room separately to see the video and report. They each gave the same explanation about the Mig fighters. The Swede told them one decoy failed but the other saved them. The Pole remarked he could not fire at the missile because the angle was wrong. It was a fault with this old helicopter it could not fire directly behind. Jack explained as mission commander he had ordered the Black Hawk to face the mountain while he gained height for the video. This put him between him and the Mig. He was not expecting an attack but neither helicopter was a match for a Mig and he had the new decoy defence that Black Hawk did not have. He had followed guidelines to be at 4000 feet to give the decoy a chance of working. Jack noticed nods of respect and admiration from his interrogators. He had become the most admired member of the village. His standing now enhanced where some of his colleagues would want to be in his team. A legend in his own lifetime.

The video and some of Jack's pictures made horrific viewing. There were no bank notes scattered around. They concluded the red cases must have been on the helicopter at the transfer. The photos showed evidence of the destructive capabilities of Cyanide, the red bomb case.

It was the same as another incident that they compared with from ten months earlier. They saw the destroyed American trucks. The American when he came back from the chateau would be updated.

The crew were dismissed and asked to be on standby for duty on Saturday. There were several incidents on the main map. Jack got permission to take Sunday off. They agreed to give him Saturday off as well as he was in shock over his brother's death. Jack rang home to say he was on call all weekend, would try and get over during the week. Suzette was used to this; she would have Sunday with her parents. Jack checked a French map and concluded about 3 pm Sunday was a good time to arrive at the chateau and kill Danielle Bousquet.

Chapter 18   Sunday, November 20th

It was sunny but cold as Jack drove along the D940 and stopped to refill at Eymoutiers. It was thirty minutes to the chateau. His experienced eye noticed a car with a Spanish plate leaving as he pulled in. It was the blackened windows that made him do a vehicle check on his computer. By the time he had filled up and moved on, two key points hit him. The station had no cameras, and the Spanish plate was not recognised. He decided to do what he always did when on such a mission. Jack parked less than a mile from the chateau in an entrance to a field. He locked his car and walked to the chateau, armed with two guns, a knife and binoculars. Four spare rounds for his guns tucked in his belt and three hand grenades. He had been before so knew the lay of the land. The drink and walk when he met Phillipa not wasted.

The binoculars showed nothing unusual. He saw Danielle in the front room through the bay window at the piano. The door to the kitchen at the rear was ajar. This was the entrance he used from the helicopter. He circled the chateau and went into the kitchen where Phillipa was tidying up after lunch. The music was on loud and the door to the other rooms closed.

"Hi, never heard you come." Phillipa was surprised but knew him as a friendly associate. Jack's armoury not in view.

"Just popped in to surprise her and say goodbye." Jack was slick and grabbed a bit of leftover meat to chew. "Got some presents from work for her in the car, just making sure all fine first."

"I will just go and have a word."

Jack moved forward and opened the door to a corridor that led to the front room. As he did so he turned the music back to loud and shut the door. Phillipa was happy to continue her work. Jack entered the room; gun in hand.

Jack saw the tense face of Danielle with the gun pointing at her. He ordered her to stand next to the piano and sat in front of her in a King Louis chair. Danielle was struggling to speak, "Been getting my things together to move out." Jack sensed her nervousness as he looked at some old photos on the piano. One in particular caught his eye.

"You got my brother killed, now it is your turn." Jack's gun ready to fire.

"Please you have got it all wrong, you see he had AIDS, but I did not know. He was on a suicide mission, he worked for ISIL, and you had no idea. It was only the few of us on the committee that had that information."

Jack's mind was now in overdrive. He thought of the Mig attack, the burnt army vehicles, parts of his dead brother and then the Spanish car plates. He looked again at the photos on the piano. Jack stood up as the sun shone, it reflected on some steel at the bay window, Jack fired three shots rapidly. Jack saw her freeze; the pee trickle along her bare legs. He barked out an order.

"Check outside, grab any guns and come round the back to the kitchen." Jack slowly went behind the door to the corridor as Danielle ran to another door. As she stepped outside, she saw Greco – dead – three holes in her bay window, two implanted in his head. The blood oozed out onto the stone. She picked up his rifle. Perky was in the corridor after hearing the shots, as he peered around the door, Jack smashed the door on to his arm, swung round the door like a monkey, forcing his arms behind his back, calmly putting two bullets in his head. Parts of his brain and blood staining the wood where pictures of young ladies hung. Some blood and tissue splashed back against Jack, alive and pondering his next move. He then walked on tip toe to the kitchen door, the loud music still on. He heard shots and walked in to see Danielle at the kitchen door. Pinky was stretchered over a meat table, more blood dripping onto the floor with Phillipa under him a knife in her neck, her trousers and pants removed and faces frozen with fear and ecstasy. As Pinky fell, his erection became visible after he crashed onto the stone floor, Jack instinctively thought *smaller than his*. The girl following her knickers and trousers tangled around her ankles as she careered against him and both lay there motionless, his gun catapulting over the kitchen floor. Jack winced for only a second and refocussed. They were dead.

"Stay here, there is at least one more." Jack crept up to the road, using the bushes for cover. The car was parked in a small layby next to the other side entrance to the chateau, which was ideal for a quick getaway. A woman was in a parked car. Jack crawled around. He was far too quick for her, by the time she had picked up her gun one bullet was enough, the silencer causing no alarms in the village through the open window. He opened the side gate and drove the car down to the kitchen entrance in front of a large barn.

It was only 3:30 pm, the villagers might be out soon. Jack dragged Greco into the chateau to be out of sight. Danielle was shaking as Jack moved over to her and sat her down in the King Louis chair. He went outside to inspect the car after putting the kettle on. He took out the four cases of rioja. He left two pigeons in the boot. He had only seen one person in the front of the car when it left the service station. He knew

Greco was a loner so was confident of no more attackers. He made two teas and went back to give one to the shaking Danielle.

"Why did you not kill me?"

"Too many unanswered coincidences and I saw the photo of your husband with a younger man. When I saw the inscription *with love from Papillon*, I had to look closer and confirm it was my brother, that was his nickname. I was angry and not thinking logically. We have one hell of a mess to clean up here."

"Top shooting, how did you know he was there?"

"I had no idea who it was, the sun came out and I saw the barrel reflecting, lucky for you, I just used instinct. I did not like him."

Jack sat there with Danielle as they both realised this was an ISIL attack and they would still be after Danielle.

"I cannot go back to work. I am sacked and if I did there is still another ISIL infiltrator we have not found." Jack pondered on Danielle's comment.

"We have five dead bodies, an untraceable car and Greco's car to find. He will have parked it within a mile of here the same as I did. What about your maid?"

Danielle was in survivor mode now. "I was in Immigration, I saved her and officially she does not exist. She has an R on her passport."

Jack knew about this method of accounting for the endless wave of refugees coming into Europe. He sensed Danielle needed him to solve the crisis.

"I need to disappear." Danielle stated the obvious. "I have Mari coming at 9 am tomorrow, I will think of somewhere."

"Fine, I do not want to know where. I need to get a team in from YMCA we can trust. It will be classified as an ISIL attack. We need a glazier for the window. Two more to make this spotless. We will get the car to an accident hot spot. The lady will have her teeth removed. All four will be burnt to hell. The car will be crushed. It will be reported by us that you were assassinated but a surveillance squad took them out. How does that sound?"

Jack had to think again when Danielle was quick to point out the squad had not been authorised. He solved the problem. "I will say I came to say goodbye and interrupted the attack, unfortunately I could not stop your death. In accordance with YMCA procedure the whole incident had to be put to bed to avoid any suspicions locally and abroad. I have my bullets to prove it was me. The three men will be found so if checked it all stacks up. I killed them. Rather than four burnt to death just you and the lady driver. Your maid can take your place. The two women will be cremated by Wednesday and untraceable. I will inform YMCA officially on that day. I will plead due to the sensitive nature of recent circumstances it was best to delay common knowledge while I investigated further. Given my recent exploits and no Greco, they need me more than ever."

Jack saw from her expression that Danielle liked his plan. He rang the Swede with a coded message. It would be over five hours before his YMCA team arrived. It was going to be a long night and Danielle was leaving at 9 am.

Jack found Greco's car keys on him. As he walked out of the chateau, he saw the same lady with her dog. He patted the dog and spoke to her, the lady naturally oblivious to what had happened. When he returned, he had a large bag which he dropped in front of Danielle. They opened it and nearly a million in notes were visible.

Jack was not surprised to find the money. Hit men like Greco liked to have hot money close to them all the time. Assassinations came at a price, he thought he might have more hidden at home. He saw Danielle studying the bag. "That money will be unaccountable, and I need some to live on if I am officially dead. I have to leave my house, credit cards, everything with no income for the rest of my life."

Jack saw the logic in that but responded, "I have a team coming later, working nights and this will help keep us all happy."

Danielle had an eye for business and a quick brain. "If you take too much, they will spend, and suspicion will be raised. You might be more careful. We need to be sensible, 500,000 will do for me and you pay the others what you like."

There was an awful lot of money. "No good, we need to be in this together, you go and change, have a bath, in the morning you will be travelling light. No cards, phones, nothing – just what you're wearing: one old bag/clothes etc., that would not be missed and your share when we agree." This chateau will be spotless. When the vultures arrive on Wednesday, they will be thorough. I will only pay those coming tonight in stages. It will be hard work, and some may have to come back another night. You cannot even sleep in your bed... you are officially dead now."

Jack sat in the chair as Danielle went for her final bath in her chateau. The glazier came first at 10 pm. It was 10:30 when the Swede arrived in a special van with two more already dressed for the job of clearing the mess. He called the glazier in for a meeting with the three that had arrived. Danielle sat at the piano. All the curtains were closed. Jack explained the situation that Danielle had to disappear for her own safety. They knew Danielle had been sacked but trusted him. They did not have the same regard for Greco. Jack told them here might be another ISIL contact that could turn up, he was confident of his loyal men. Jack explained that there was some dirty money he had been paid to kill Danielle. When he opened the bag, they all gasped at the amount.

"I want a thorough job done. There is over 800,000." Some of that money will be from other jobs over the years. He explained the plan and came to the crunch. Danielle needs more than us as she will have nothing. We could have kept it for just the two of us, but we are a team. We must decide how much to give her then divide the rest by five. Any suggestions?" He knew they would want him to decide but allowed them to think for a while. He looked at their faces. These were professional people and sensible. They all looked at the pitiful Danielle but still had lingering doubts about her. It was unanimous, they all muttered "100,000 each and give her the rest."

Surprisingly, it was the Swede that came up with a safer solution. "When the team from Paris turn up on Wednesday, they find 200,000 in the bag which Jack has left in the boot. I believe that is a standard deposit for him. You took out a bit for the girl who you let go. Another young refugee on the run is not their problem. I suggest we take 70,000 each clean money, the rest for Danielle. Jack, you need to sleep around here till Wednesday when you come back to work. Tell them you have been staking out the property in case the other ISIL contact no one knows about turns up to find out what has gone off."

Jack watched Danielle's expression. She made no objections; it was clear she was impressed with the plan. Thinking caps were on. It was logical and much safer. The deal was done. Jack insisted the Swede took all the money to a safe place in case their houses/apartments were searched by the Paris team. Dividends could wait a while and be drip fed. He told them to take cases of rioja from the Spanish car he had taken out and save some for him. Jack would take the bag and 170,000 euros back to Greco's car, which will be brought to the barn. He would say he gave 30,000 to the refugee girl who left with a bag and some of her clothes.

Danielle apportioned the money accordingly while the team went to work. She could not use her computer, but it was clean with no links to her private life. The business phone she left next to the computer also clean. The other two she removed the chips and would then dispose of at St Agatha. The large barn at the rear was ideal for the cars and the dead bodies. The Swede found fuel and prepared the Spanish car for the inferno after carefully placing the two pigeons back in the chateau kitchen

The two in special boiler suits cleared any bloodstains inside the chateau and near the window. The kitchen and corridor particularly bad. They hoovered up with high performance equipment. It was 4 am when the inferno in the car did the job on the two female occupants. Jack picked up Greco's rifle, cleaned it and then made sure his prints were on it. The glazier had expertise with wood, removing and filling holes where bullets had lodged. He was the first to leave at 6 am. It took two hours to get back to YMCA for the Swede and his two cleaners. They had a shift to do and had agreed to go back on Tuesday evening to double check their work.

Jack rang in sick, which was understandable for the secretary who received the call. He rang Suzette to say he had an undercover job and would be back Wednesday evening. Jack had to sleep rough in the wood so when the Paris team came, they would see where he had camped out. He went back to his car and got out his camping 'requirements' – things he always kept in the boot. He left the car out of sight. He walked to Greco's car and drove it back, parking it in the barn. If the unknown ISIL spy turned up, he was ready to see who it was. It would be Wednesday morning when he would go back to work and report his unauthorised mission.

Chapter 19

Monday, November 21th

Mari put Sebastian into the basket this time. One of her new pigeons and going out for the first time. It would take an hour to the chateau and nearly two hours to St Agatha from there where she would leave Sebastian. She spoke to him. "Now you be a good pigeon, I will see you soon."

Mari landed at the chateau at 9 am as instructed. She was surprised to see Jack coming over and asking her to shut off the engine. She followed him to the kitchen and then into the front room. Mari had never been in this room before. She saw Danielle on the piano stool with three bags. Jack explained why he was there. "Danielle is an ISIL target, and you will take her wherever she says, I do not want to know. The maid has left for her own safety. I will leave you with Danielle. I need some fresh air."

Mari was handed a pen and some chateau-headed notepaper. Danielle paused, took a deep breath and began. "I was sacked on Friday, your job at YMCA needs terminating as a reserve. I need to hide out at St Agatha with no one ever knowing, that is why Jack has gone for a walk. I am going to pay you a lump sum and an improved contract for your regular trips to/from St Agatha. I have a list of items here for your first return. You will be the only one that knows where I am, I trust you. It will always be cash as normal, one of these bags is for you."

Mari smiled in the knowledge that whatever amount of money was in that bag, it was always a good pay day. She pondered before accepting the bag. Her mind quick to acknowledge she would not be on standby for RAID at the YMCA HQ. The thought of more leisure time and trips to Le Vieux Logis a big plus in her desire of quality of life. The need to fly and have a contract to earn was still very evident from Danielle's comments. She was back to her original contract with better pay and less danger compared to some of her journeys with Jack and others at RAID. Mari felt a weight lift off her shoulders. Without showing her happiness at her proposed new contract, she restrained herself before responding, "Good to do business with you, Danielle, you know I have always been available for you. I only have one proviso."

"What is that?"

"If Jack ever required my services, I would help him and his family in an emergency."

"Sounds reasonable as I would do the same."

"Good, what do you want me to write?"

"Saturday November 19th. Due to the sacking of my friend Danielle, I no longer wish to be considered for any work at your Horticultural College. This is with immediate effect. Yours Mari."

Mari wrote as instructed, signed and placed it in a chateau envelope. Mari then walked into the village to the post box. The collection time was 3 pm. Sunday no collection. It would arrive Wednesday morning at the latest. Mari returned to the front room. The curtains were still closed. Danielle had put a coat over her head to hide herself as they walked to the helicopter with the three bags. Mari was used to people being blindfolded or kept from prying eyes. They walked quickly across the open land to the helicopter. The bushes and trees making it difficult for anyone to see. Mari only visible as Danielle kept her cloak over her. Danielle kept her head down as she put the safety belt on after sitting in a rear seat of the helicopter. Then she lowered her head as if in the crash position in an aeroplane about to make a forced landing. Mari powered up her partner, looking longingly at the chateau, knowing she would probably never be here again. She noticed a lady with a dog emerging from a house as she took off. Then Jack walking towards her, stopping to talk. They were all looking up at her including the dog as Mari swung the helicopter around and climbed above the trees and on her way to St Agatha. She knew it would be difficult to notice anyone but herself in the helicopter from the ground below. She smiled to herself and thought if there was one man she would like to invite in for tea, it would be Jack.

* * *

It was a straightforward journey. Danielle sighed with relief and thought about her future. They were expecting her for a week. She had no intention of telling them anything differently just yet. There was a 50,000 bonus for Mari and more money for her regular trips. Danielle worked it out she had enough money to live all her life at St Agatha. She had convinced everyone Cas was the guilty party. Her aching body from the beating would be soothed soon by willing gentle hands. Phillipa was in the past, her only thought now was Rochine. With these thoughts she waved goodbye, but more in gratitude, to Mari for getting her to St Agatha.

Edith walked with an air of expectancy with her to her room, pleased with her recent completed tasks. Mari had brought her back on Sunday afternoon as planned. Danielle waited for the instructions from Edith to visit Mother Superior in an hour's time. This was normal for her week's visit. She would have to select two from DOLLAR and await her fate. Danielle's bruised body wanted rest and Rochine's company.

She was not ready for anything else but the feeling of success and all that money in her red cases gave her the advantage. She checked the contents that were protected from prying eyes by a secret code. She checked her camera and found the gun she had used from the trip to the beach. She had three spare bullets in the gun along with three rounds of ammunition and two smoke bombs. They might come in handy one day. Danielle was in no mood to let Mother Superior have it all her own way.

An hour later, one of the girls came to escort her to Mother Superior's study. Edith was in attendance. Danielle eyed them up. "I will come back for my DOLLAR inquisition once we have cleared up some business."

They sat smiling as they knew money was in the air. "Four good sales, funds excellent, wine and food in abundance." Mother Superior started the informal meeting.

"Good, was your trip to the prep school successful?" Danielle enquired of Edith.

"It will be the last Spanish vintage as Juan has retired, but we have a new matron."

"That is a surprise, he did have good contacts until the last one," Mother Superior noted, not aware of what Danielle had instructed Sister Edith to do. "Did you break the new matron in gently?" Edith smiled but did not reply.

Danielle got to the point as she opened her bag. "I am going to give you a bonus each." They smiled and Edith opened a bottle of champagne to celebrate. They toasted to success and liberation of their flock. Danielle gave a large wad of money to them and declared, "I want to rest tonight with Rochine. Tomorrow, Mother Superior, I want a personal tour of the whole complex and check the conditions inside and out. I will then report to you on Wednesday as we will have a lot to discuss and where to spend some of this money. Thursday will be DOLLAR day now. I am not going back till Sunday."

Danielle saw the pleasure on their faces, beaming with the taste of champagne and a great year. Rochine was sent for. Danielle took her back to her allocated room. The camera she had given to Mari showed the pictures of the carnage on the beach. "I am sorry, Rochine, but one of our operatives working for ISIL became a suicide bomber. He killed all those in the picture. He had AIDS and I did not see the hospital report. He seduced my husband who died of the same disease. We both have had disasters."

Danielle watched the tears wet her cheeks and put her arms around her to comfort her. "I was so upset I have given up my job and want to be a recluse. ISIL are now after me as the blast killed some of them. Mother Superior says you can sleep with me. I will look after you until you are ready to leave here, please tell no one."

"It is my sixteenth birthday soon and I am an orphan."

Danielle had gained her confidence as they held hands and kissed. Danielle could not help noticing her soft olive skin with her large brown come-to-bed eyes. She kissed her again gently, sighing inside her tortured mind, knowing St Agatha was surely just a waypoint.

* * *

Juan's van looked a sorry sight as Yorkie and Lisa unpadlocked the compound's metal gate. It was 9:30 am on that cold Monday. She had her camera and took a few photos from all sides. Forensics had turned up and a mechanic who got his blow torch to cut the cab open to allow better access. Forensics did not stay long, taking a few swabs inside and outside the cabin and the sliding side and broken rear doors. The mechanic took a little longer and left. A glove was found on the floor behind an empty pigeon basket. Lisa started to make an inventory, counting the number of wine cases. A few had survived but were left in situ. Over half full of diesel, hand brake off and in second gear. Lisa commented that they will have to travel in the large recovery vehicle with the body to Spain when the coroner is happy, and forensics had finished the report. They went back to the police station to find Rene was sat in his chair, having just put the phone down.

"Spoke to the coroner, agreed the cheap option, cannot see any point in wasting money for a Spanish wine merchant with nearly bald tyres. Should have the body ready to go to Spain by Thursday. Lisa, you are fluent in Spanish, you can go with Yorkie. It is better we send a woman to console his mother. Yorkie, you can be her chaperone, these people do not respect our weather."

Lisa knew better than make a case for an expensive autopsy report, but Yorkie was keen to start his new career. "I have to go and find out about this lady who said the road was blocked. If it was blocked, it would be suspicious."

"I can always ring the coroner back. You have till tomorrow morning for me to change my mind," Rene concluded and asked Lisa about Jonny Wilkinson's visit.

"Fantastic, he stopped all morning got a picture of him and me. Sending it to my sister who will be jealous even though she supports Clermont Ferrand."

Lisa was showing them some photos and then the van ones which reminded her. "Yorkie, you had better get down that ravine again and count any loose cases. We need numbers for any insurance claim the poor woman will have to make. We need to put as many as possible on the truck when we go to Spain."

Yorkie did not need telling twice. He called at the bar, but the lady usually came at 4 pm on a Monday. He went back to the station for a sandwich and tea. Lisa walked with him to his house to go in the Lada to the layby and keep eye on him.

"Lesson number one. When you get a lead, never assume and take notes and/or pictures. You must have been taught that?"

"Yes."

"Why did you not go to the house that heard the strange noise? Big mistake. If you had gone and found the layby, you might have seen more tyre marks. You did not and by the morning they would be covered with fresh snow. Also, exactly where did she say the road blocked sign was? You did not get out the car and look for indentations in the snow! Heavy signs leave fingerprints, another big mistake and I am not the detective."

Yorkie protested he was not an official detective just a routine bobby. He was learning from a *secretary*, though probably best not to say that; now was not the time to use one of Rene's jokes. Besides, Lisa had not stopped. "Now get down that ravine and count properly, look everywhere, put it on your phone so we can look later. Rene and I left you at the scene with the blue tape to keep people away from spoiling any evidence. So, what did you do? You did not designate a local to stop them. Remember the public can be your friend, if you had given anyone responsibility, except the mad old woman, the blue tape would still be intact."

Yorkie was beginning to realise he had a lot to learn. He did as he was told. It took longer than he thought to count and retrieve whatever was possible. It was 5 pm when he met the old lady in the bar. She was on her second wine and he wondered why no one had ever taken the car keys off her. The barman confirmed her story. "She left in the evening and was back before 8 pm. She stopped for two more then left. I got her some food to soak up the drink. She only lives in the next village. No one else reported it, but the bar was quiet, due to the weather." Yorkie bought her a drink and thought *what the hell*. He called at a few houses near where the sign might have been, but no one had seen a 'road closed' sign. The next morning, he told Rene she was the only one that had seen it. He did not ring back to forensics. The next morning forensics sent a basic report. Traces of alcohol but not over the limit. Head damaged on steering wheel. Possible asphyxiation or mini stroke. No conclusive evidence due to freezing conditions and state of the deceased.

Rene rang the recovery company about a vehicle to take the van to Spain with Lisa and Yorkie. Friday was the best day and he confirmed that with the Spanish Police and the deceased's mother. Yorkie and Lisa were listening to the conversations and made their plans. It was a long time since anyone from this rural police station had done such a journey with a dead body and a van the insurance company would write off. Before the Friday departure, Lisa bought two used tyres and got the local garage to replace the illegal ones. They wondered what sort of farmhouse they were going to and would they find any interesting information. Yorkie could not understand why Lisa had bought the tyres.

Chapter 20

Wednesday, November 23rd

Jack had driven to YMCA for his midday shift. He went to the main reception and asked to see one of the directors. It was Doc who he saw and informed of the deaths and carnage at the chateau. The American and Henri joined the discussion. A phone call to Paris followed and by 2 pm the team had arrived by helicopter. The interrogation in the Mole room followed. The same agents that interviewed Danielle, but two different armed combat men he had never seen before. Doc, Henri and the American made it seven v one. Jack was not fazed. He had been in much worse situations. The questions came thick and fast, but he was prepared.

"I went to question Danielle about my brother's death. I was armed as I might have killed her myself. I was annoyed to find her dead in a burnt-out car with another woman. I guessed it was ISIL and I was angry, so I took the three attackers out. I was lucky not to be injured. I used Greco's rifle to kill one of them. I called in a team without you knowing as I wanted to find this other ISIL infiltrator. I staked out the chateau for three nights. You do have two pigeons you can put a tracker on, one should finish up in North Africa if my hunch is right."

He knew they would send a team to the chateau. They interviewed the glazier, the Swede and the two cleaners individually. They all had the same story and knew nothing about how Jack had taken out three armed ISIL attackers. They also did not know why the two women had been burnt to death.

Jack was not Mr Popular with the Paris team. He was called back in for further interrogation after they had interviewed his chateau team. It was Henri who asked the question, "How and where did you kill them?"

Jack was in no mood to talk now. He looked slowly around each individual in the room eyeball to eyeball. "I am a pro and I am alive. Goodbye."

Jack got up and walked out. The YMCA needed him. They had all seen Mari's letter of resignation and Greco was dead. The officials in the room were gobsmacked – no one had ever walked out on them. There was shrugging of shoulders, no one sure what to say or do next. The phone rang which relieved the growing tension even though no one had spoken. The news was that a task force was on the way to the chateau. This was the cue for the Paris team to go back to their helicopter and head for the chateau to meet up with them. They gave one instruction to the remaining three committee men. "Can someone drive over with a vehicle to collect the dead bodies after we have examined them?"

This was not a duty they were accustomed to doing themselves. They rang the hangar and organised their request. By the time a van would reach the chateau the specialist task force would allow them to take them away. The two helicopters arrived at the chateau ten minutes apart. These were professionals and they got stuck into the work required, some bringing overnight bags. They took her computer, phone and ransacked every inch of every room. Some stayed overnight. They found where Jack had been lying low. They took the bag of money from Greco's car. The chateau was spotless. They took all the rifles and guns and the three male dead bodies for further examination. Nosy villagers wandered around. The two heavies patrolled the chateau. The lady with a dog and camera gave them tea and cakes. They never answered any of her questions. They concluded Jack was a dangerous man to argue with and Danielle was better dead and out of the way. The bullets matched Jack's story.

It was late that evening when the four on the committee had an emergency meeting to discuss the information that had been forwarded to them from the chateau. They agreed that it was most likely the Russians had paid Greco on behalf of ISIL but thought no action was a diplomatic move. They had no option but to accept the information sent to them. They were not qualified or experienced in forensics and investigative work. They were thankful that Jack was alive and still working for them.

It was Doc who asked the question, "Where is the lost son of Danielle Bousquet? The chateau is now in his name as the only surviving relative." There was silence as a computer search revealed Philip had left home at fourteen to live with his grandmother in Marseille. No further records and she had died four years ago, when he was twenty-four. They shrugged, they didn't care, it wasn't their problem.

* * *

It was Saturday morning when Tariq received the message from the pigeon released at Juan's farmhouse. He stared at the handwritten note – *he was dead? How? What the hell happened?* He had no means of contacting them now. He would have to wait for another message. He hoped to get the next message after the successful visit to the chateau. The pigeons for security all went to the outpost that looked out over the beach and ocean. Then another pigeon took the message to HQ, safeguarding his whereabouts.

Late Monday afternoon Tariq got another message. His contact in Tunis, Aqbal had been murdered and his hard drive taken. Tariq pondered for some time then called in two of his female operatives. He was worried, no news from France was also bad news.

"Go to Tunis and contact Aqbal's daughter. She is a qualified teacher at a primary school. When the holidays start, bring her here. She is single. Inform the mother all is well, we need the daughter to help us find her husband's killer. Give the mother this money with our blessings. While you are there find another lady of similar age and looks from a respectable background with no current passport. Tell her we will pay her a substantial amount to change identities until told otherwise."

He needed to replace his informant; he had a plan.

Tariq dismissed them. The seasonal Christmas holiday was not far away. He was in no rush to plant another Tunisian at YMCA. Cas had to be replaced but because of Trump's victory, they might wait till another in the team retired or left. Countries were not expanding at YMCA, they were descaling. He had lost Cas, and within a year he planned to have another. It was logical that if Aqbal's daughter applied for the new job, her family history might prevent her employment by the committee. Planting a respectable female was far better. It could take six months to a year. Tariq was in no rush; he was a commander with vision and patience. He smiled to himself. He wondered when he would get a message from his other current contact at YMCA. He decided to send a message to that contact, it simply read: "Tunisian replacement will be sent within nine months, details next year. Find Philip Bousquet born 25/04/1988, last known address with his grandma in Marseille, confirm if mother alive or dead."

Chapter 21   Friday, November 25th

The recovery vehicle company near Arudy had no spare driver. There were no paying passengers and the gross vehicle weight allowed Yorkie and Lisa to take the van back to Juan's home.

Yorkie put his ropes in as a precaution along with the snow chains. They had all the invoices and contents of the van in the front so they could study them during the journey. The pigeon that had survived the ordeal was in a basket covered with a blanket. The weather had improved slightly. It was a cold crisp winter's morning, so Lisa decided to drive first while Yorkie woke up. She had her soft warm black leather gloves on that matched the steering wheel. The meandering roads slowed them down and frustrated drivers trying to overtake did not bother them. Eventually Lisa would pull over and then receive grateful hoots and waves especially when they saw them in police uniforms. The slow start did not bother them as they took in the spectacular scenery, ignoring the signs for the yellow train. They could see hardened hikers and skiers aiming for the cable cars.

Yorkie concentrated on the paperwork as the scenery became monotonous. Pulling over again and again Lisa eventually stopped at a roadside café. Here they could stretch their legs, have a drink and a toilet break. Yorkie took over the driving, much more alert now. They estimated another two hours at least. Lisa started her perusal of the evidence but could see nothing interesting. She had been up early and as she focussed more on the horizon, the drone of the engine was sending her to sleep or was it a nap. Yorkie had been very quiet so far, but his next comment made her realise she had to focus on the job.

"It does not make sense that he took eighty cases of wine to France but came back with one hundred and ten."

"Maybe the champagne cases are larger and why was he wearing one glove?" Lisa said.

"If it had been a local man, I bet Rene would have paid for the proper autopsy report," Yorkie said.

"Yes, but the weather did make it impossible for them. They do not have the same expensive equipment as Bordeaux."

They arrived at the farmhouse at 1 pm. A hearse as arranged by the local police was waiting and his mother had one last look, sobbing uncontrollably. They offloaded the van with all the broken bottles and cases/boxes in no fit state for resale. They gave her the pigeon that had survived the crash and she took it up the outside metal staircase to the hutch. Lisa went around the barn taking pictures. Yorkie waited for the mother to calm down and fetch the keys to the barn and Juan's workplace. They all entered and put items from the van on his desk, mainly paperwork. They asked her about his business, but she knew nothing.

"He did it all, I kept away. Look in the corner he even slept there." They had to put the lights on as it was a dark barn with two small windows higher than if in a house. They found his year planners and brochures for exotic holidays to Barbados.

He went nearly every year in January, business very quiet after Christmas."

They looked through the year planners and saw details for local deliveries. Then the entries for Bordeaux and St Emilion. A bed and breakfast receipt for the overnight stay outside Bordeaux. Lisa took more photos of receipts for fuel in Bordeaux, St Emilion and one for Bergerac. There seemed nothing wrong, so they walked outside as a car turned up. It was a gentleman from the insurance company. It was 3 pm and he scoured the vehicle. Lisa checked if all okay as she spoke Spanish and acted as though on the mother's behalf. He went round the vehicle, went back in the barn and checked the invoices to and from France.

"Got all the information, I will get back in touch with an offer. You will get all the money for the wine. There is some death benefit as well as he was not over the limit. The police did ask us to check the tyres and they are just legal as well. You are fortunate, Mrs Rodriguez, as bald tyres would invalidate all the claim. The vehicle is covered for replacement value less the salvage worth. We will write to you within fourteen days with the total value."

Yorkie took it all in and smiled in admiration of Lisa. The insurance man left, and the mother went back in the house. They sat in the recovery vehicle and thought about the whole event surrounding his death and his workplace. They concluded she was not in a fit state to interview.

"We have lots of photographic evidence to sift through next week. If we find anything worth coming back for, we will ask her then, I will drive the first bit. It should be quicker with less weight, and you can do the bit over the Pyrenees."

Lisa stopped at a service station for the toilet. She waited for Yorkie to fetch some coffees. He came back to the driver's side as Lisa had gone to the other. He handed her a coffee, "Wait a minute; I will take my glove off." It dropped on the floor and they both looked at each other, mouths open, remembering the single glove found in Juan's van.

* * *

Danielle had done a tour of the monastery with Mother Superior. It took a day and half to check all aspects. Pointing required, deforestation, pigeons breeding too quickly, mountain goats had stopped producing the normal quantities of milk. Greenhouse panes to fix. Many problems. The inventory they did meticulously. Mother Superior seemed to be annoyed with Danielle's authoritarian and inquisitive attitude. She was looking forward to Danielle being paraded in front of her and finding fault. Edith would administer as she too disliked her interfering methods. They were both upset that Rochine was with her. They had designs on her and planned together to give the new girl a proper introduction to life at the monastery starting on Monday when Danielle had left. Danielle was friendly with the other girls but sleeping every night with Rochine. It was Wednesday evening when the mother superior told Danielle to report to her at 7 am the next morning in her nun's outfit. She gave her the code that was DOLLAR.

"You only have a few days left so I will select one and you will have a choice." The small booklet gave examples of Discipline, Obedience, Love, Learning, Absolution, Reward. Danielle put on her innocent expression. "Yes, Mother Superior, perhaps I should bring you cocoa in the early hours. I have been such a naughty girl. I deserve to be thrashed before I see you. I do not want anyone else to know, I would be embarrassed."

Mother Superior normally left such disciplinary measures to Edith but now this was her opportunity to give this bossy lady what she deserved. Mother Superior thought for a moment. "The girls on duty will be in other wings between 2 am and 3 am. Bring me some cocoa at 2 am. I will deal with you in my chamber."

At dinner Mother Superior announced Danielle would be reporting for her DOLLAR lessons the next day. She then announced three more names for Friday/Saturday/Sunday. She had put Rochine between her and Edith at the head table deliberately to annoy Danielle who was at the other end. On Monday it will be our new Sister Rochine who will be introduced to DOLLAR. Danielle smiled. She was watching Sister Edith holding her hand under the table and moving it onto her thigh, then forcing it between her legs, gentle fingers probing. Edith too strong for her to stop the seductive intrusion and Rochine knowing it might be bad to resist. Edith withdrew her hand slowly, knowing Rochine had got the message. It had been Edith who walked hand in hand with her before dinner. Mother Superior had made everyone kiss the girl next to them as part of the L in DOLLAR before dinner. Mother Superior had therefore kissed Rochine. Grace was said every time before eating, they let Rochine do it as an honour. On Monday Rochine would have to choose Edith or the mother superior to sleep with. This was St Agatha and rules were rules. Danielle was losing out to the two sisters that controlled St Agatha. They insisted Rochine slept with another of the girls that night as was the code. That is why she was at the head table.

Rochine surveyed the sixteen girls of different nationalities and selected a tall girl who had washed her when she first came. She had been alone till Danielle came and now it was time to understand what life here entailed. There was clapping as they left together after kissing in front of all in the room. Hand in hand they departed for readings, prayers and bed. No locks on any doors so the sisters had access when they liked. Mother Superior eyed up Danielle, she had decided to give Danielle a lesson she would never forget, just the two of them and solid walls would hide her screams.

* * *

139

Danielle could not sleep. They did have old fashioned battery clocks. It was 2:50 am when she got up and dressed accordingly. Making a cocoa was easy with no one around and a big jug of hot water on a wood-burning stove always available. She walked to Mother Superior's chamber. She was lying in bed waiting for her.

"You are five minutes late." Danielle noticed the clock deliberately fast. "Put the cocoa on my table and stand in the corner, face the wall."

One minute later another order. "Lift up your gown and stay facing the wall." She felt her eyes on her bottom. She waited several minutes then, "Turn round and do not drop your gown."

Danielle did as she was told. "You have been a very naughty girl. You can move your hands. There is a crop behind the curtain, bring it over; I have finished my cocoa."

Danielle obeyed. As Mother Superior put the mug down, Danielle moved slowly to the side of her bed. She could see her face full of intent and revenge. Danielle felt her hands moving up her leg, she looked into her eyes showing false submission. Her next move took the mother superior totally by surprise as Danielle grabbed the second pillow from the bed. Expertly she smothered it over her face and jumped onto her head. Her strong knees held the pillow over her mouth. Mother Superior flayed and struggled to stop her. Danielle's strength gained from work and the gym at YMCA disguised her frame. Screams and gasping to breathe were smothered and negated by the pillow and the walls. Danielle imagined her face going whiter and whiter, the legs and arms tiring as she held her so tight, she could not open her mouth or use her nose to breathe. Danielle's thighs dug into her neck, the life and soul slowly drained from Mother Superior. She was probably dead for a minute before Danielle removed her thighs from around her neck. With relief she saw the pillow only had saliva marks but a slight tear. She composed herself, putting Mother Superior on her side in the bed. She put the crop back behind the curtain.

She took the mug back to the kitchen, washed it and put it back in its rightful place. She went to her room and exchanged one pillow, identical to hers. The bed sheets up to her chin, a peaceful pose. Danielle admired her handiwork and went to her own room unnoticed. She heard two girls talking in the main hall and the crackling of the fire they had put more logs on. She shut the door gently, no locks to do. Danielle lay in bed and soon slept, her tired and bruised body still suffering but her mind buzzing with excitement for whatever the future might hold.

One of the girls on night duty sounded the alarm at 7 am. Screaming and begging for help. Danielle kept her cool and was on the scene with Edith and the new Sister Helen. Girls were ushered out of the room, distressed at what they saw. For most it was the first time they had seen a dead body. Danielle took over as she had the experience. She analysed the situation and asked for confirmation from the two sisters. "Looks like a brain clot or a massive stroke." She knew they were not qualified to argue. Sister Edith had basic nursing qualifications she just enjoyed her matron role play. Sister Helen was new to St Agatha, been there a year, languages her specialist subject.

Danielle decided to hold a meeting with them in Mother Superior's office. She had the upper hand now as Edith had lost her ally, lover and was in shock. Danielle sat in her chair behind the desk. "We will have three days of mourning and then bury her in the monastery's graveyard. This is such a shock to me I have decided I will stay until a replacement can be found. We will inform the necessary people by post via Mari, the next time she comes. Died of natural causes unless you can see any other reason. The authorities will not journey here as this is a place of sanctuary and this is such a rare event. They will not question the death. It is best no one travels here as the girls might talk."

This hit an instant nerve with the two sisters. They had an existence here with power, control and gratification to suit. They could hear wailing in abundance as the girls gathered outside the office. Danielle opened the office door to confront her new flock. She told them absolution and love now the order for three days. She organised everyone into pairs, holding hands and to go for prayers immediately. She put on Mother Superior's spare gown, and walked into the chapel with Rochine. She asked for silent prayer and for Edith to prepare a speech after the funeral. She asked the girls to make a coffin from wood in the forest. She said there would be three days of fasting. On the day after the funeral, we will have a celebration to honour her life. The wine will be opened, and a feast prepared. She gave tasks to all the girls including the sisters. Death had brought grief but hope and a new regime beckoned. Young girls had jobs to do, a new dawn on the horizon and their spirits were raised.

She sent a pigeon to Mari with a list of more requirements and smiled as she sat in her new office and surveyed her kingdom as the new "Boss" of St Agatha. The wine cellar was healthy but decided it was best to wait and celebrate at the wake.

*Pigeons were shot down in wars to stop
the relay of messages*

Chapter 22   Monday, November 28th

It was 9.05am when Yorkie arrived at the station. Rene was sat with his feet on the table reading the report from Spain that Lisa had given him. Lisa had brewed the tea and put a mug on Rene's coaster with two marmots trying to look intelligent. The small table in front of Rene's desk was sufficient for Yorkie and Lisa to be seated at. The coasters on that one of the red and yellow train in the Pyrenees, the flavour of the day.

Lisa, pleased she had spotted them on their recent journey. Lisa had her notebook at the ready, having put down two more mugs of tea. Lisa had to make sure that Rene had seen the new acquisition.

"Nice new coasters, Rene, those marmots look alert and ready for action, just like you," she smirked and turned her gaze to Yorkie to start the proceedings.

"We took the vehicle back, but his mother was in no fit state to interview. Lisa took photographs as usual and saw the hearse and the insurance man turn up. We saw nothing suspicious at his barn, it was bit of a tip. Just one question, Rene, for you. If you were offered a drink by your wife in a car, would you take one glove off or both to hold it?"

"I do not wear gloves."

"Please ask your wife then or the postman when he comes."

"Come on, get to the point."

Yorkie told him about the coffee incident with Lisa who nodded to confirm. "So, you think someone offered him a drink?"

Lisa and Yorkie looked at the figures: eighty-six cases from Spain but only eighty-two invoiced to the Bordeaux wine company which means four cases sold en route. Then 110 invoiced in total from Bordeaux and St Emilion but only 102 found and claimed for insurance purposes.

"So eight cases sold on the way back, four champagne and four St Emilion Grand Cru, Expensive tastes," Yorkie concluded.

Rene pondered. "Champagne takes up more space and maybe fewer orders?"

Yorkie agreed but asked, "Can we go to Bordeaux and St Emilion and check?"

"We can go through the photographs as we travel," Lisa said. "It is a long way, but we do not need an overnight payment. We will make appointments with the wine merchants. We can take my car; it's faster and more comfortable than his Lada."

The postman turned up and they asked him the question about taking gloves off to have a hot drink. He responded that he would take both off. Rene looked quizzically at his new intrepid pair of rookie detectives. "One condition, I want six bottles of St Emilion Grand Cru between you for my Christmas present."

"I am going to my sisters before Christmas, I will get her some champagne from Bordeaux, what about you, Yorkie?"

"I am hoping to go to see my auntie in Robin Hood's Bay. I will get some cheap wine on the ferry. They think a Grand Cru are better sailors."

They all laughed and decided Wednesday.

Lisa picked up Yorkie at 7 am to get to Bordeaux for the 11 am appointment. It was exactly as the invoices said. Seventy-six cases

146

dropped off. He took thirty-four cases of champagne and forty of various white and reds. Lisa bought two cases of champagne. Yorkie got one case. They went to the bed and breakfast where he stayed. They remembered watching the pigeon fly off before he left. All as per the invoice. The journey to St Emilion on the back roads added to the day out. Lisa was driving.

"Bergerac filling station, Rue D'Airport, why the hell did he go so far out of his way, maybe an order?" Yorkie said.

"Not that far, after we have checked here, we will go and fill up there, I am enjoying myself."

The St Emilion wine merchant was upset at the news. "He was a lovely man. He bought quality wine, thirty-six cases, mainly red. We never bought off him, the wine merchant in Bordeaux did, we never drink Spanish wine but some like it."

Yorkie confirmed; looking at his notes and numbers. "He did not use a mobile phone how did he communicate with you?"

"His mother had a phone in her house, and we agreed a date every time he came, let me see now, yes here it is, next visit Friday April 7th, fortnight before Easter. He always sent one of his pigeons from the front of his van before he left. I think he spoke to his pigeons while he was driving."

They arrived at the filling station on Rue D'Airport an hour later. Lisa filled up while Yorkie stretched his legs. She asked the lady behind the counter if she remembered the van or the driver. "No, dear, but I will check the rota, see who was on."

After serving a customer, she told her, "It was me, how silly, it is a busy station, we have good prices and a mini market."

They decided to walk the whole length of the street while they enjoyed a snack from the service station. It was getting cold. They walked past an ecole, but it was padlocked near several large houses. Smaller houses on both sides towards the city centre. They tried the larger houses first. They showed photographs of the van and Juan. Nobody had bought from a van and they could not remember seeing a van or him. Yorkie knocked on the row of houses. "You told me off last time for not getting out and looking." He reminded Lisa of his previous failing. He got the same result. It was a dead end, time to head back. It had been a long day, but the change of scenery was welcome. They arrived late after a coffee stop, wine safely waiting the Christmas paper.

The next morning, they reported to Rene. "Can we go back to Spain and interview the mother?"

"No, I do not like Spanish wine, and it is a wasted journey, we have a stolen car, a grabbed handbag and some hikers missing. Off you go, Yorkie, try and find these hikers, I will investigate the car, Lisa, you go and see the lady."

It was the following morning, they met as usual for the 9 am debrief. Yorkie reported he had found the hikers resting overnight in a disused sheep hut up the mountain. Bad weather and no signal, he had joined the mountain rescue volunteers. Four youngsters had learned a lucky lesson, they had forgot to take some flares with them and no blankets. The hospital checked them over and let them go.

Lisa did not have far to walk to the home of the lady who reported a car with Spanish plates that had pulled up and asked for directions. They'd grabbed her handbag and pushed her over. She was too shocked; her arms grazed, to take down any number plates. She said the last time someone stopped her, a woman asked about her friend who had died in a van. She told her where the layby was. It was the day Jonny Wilkinson came because she was walking towards the café. She remembered her because she had lots of big rings on her fingers and a nice bangle, and she got back into a car also with Spanish plates.

Rene sipped his tea and said, "No leads for a stolen car from the car park. It might be in Spain by now along with the handbag. We are getting a lot of this happening now as the season is just starting for us. I will tell our two patrol men to do spot checks. We only have those two and us here nowadays with cutbacks. Pau Police should patrol more now, and neighbours Laruns Police station are feeling the cutbacks as well. I have asked again for more help."

They were still sipping tea when Yorkie remarked, "Jonny Wilkinson came Sunday morning. Juan's mother only found out Saturday afternoon. I will make a note if we go back, we must ask her who she told. I know we were closed, but we had no other enquiries, did we?"

"Good point, not as far as I'm concerned." Lisa smiled at Yorkie for his observation. Rene concurred and Lisa added them to her diary of events. "I have booked Thursday December 8th to 11th off, back for Monday, going to my sisters to exchange Christmas presents."

"I will be away in England for Christmas going on the 22nd and back for the 28th, the rock-climbing group in Arudy are deciding between Auvergne and Andorra for the New Year climb. I will be on that," Yorkie said. They all knew Rene would be around with his two officers that patrol together. They were all planning for the festive season.

* * *

Danielle was reading the papers that Mari had brought. She liked *The Bugle*, which was the English version and free at airports, and the papers from Bordeaux or Bergerac. She did not mind if they were out of date. She was pleased to be able to use Mari's address for her written demands. Mari paid for them and then brought them to St Agatha and was reimbursed with cash and a tip every time she came.

Life had settled down at St Agatha. Mari brought back news that the council were sorry to hear the news about Mother Superior. The registrar had entered the necessary details. The rates for St Agatha were going up 5% from January 2017, which were extremely low anyway. Danielle was pleased with her regime. She used the proven DOLLAR method and Sister Helen was proving an asset, as was Rochine, with their combined language skills. Edith had calmed down and was not allowed to inflict as much pain on any of her subjects as she had done before. The girls were enjoying the new rotas. It would be in March when more would leave. It was the quiet time and with winter approaching Mari would only visit fortnightly when the weather conditions allowed.

* * *

Tariq had received the news about the loss of his team. The pigeon that had returned to the outpost was discovered to have a tracer on it. He immediately put that lookout to a new position and had another outpost manned on the opposite side of the mountain pass. He knew the Americans could take that out when they liked. There was nothing else he could do. He was now waiting for his two female operatives to bring Aqbal's daughter. He was planning to get the information over time and then – his revenge. It was time to stay alert, be quiet and invite one of his girls into his room. He looked at the five names from his source at YMCA that were at the chateau with their addresses as the girl walked in. There was Jack, the Swede, two cleaners and the glazier.

* * *

At the YMCA Jack was on patrol as usual. Henri was the new 'Boss' of RAID along with Doc, the American, the Englishman and a new French lady, Jean, who had been there several years. The glazier, Jack and the two cleaners had all received bonuses from the vigilant Swede who kept the balance of the money in a safe place. Staffing levels had been lowered and Trump had announced he would be pulling out and no more money from March 1st, 2017. Other countries were considering what to do. The Tunisians had not replaced Cas as they had a second pilot in their team. He was due to retire in August and they felt a single replacement then would be sufficient given the uncertainty Trump's victory had created. The hostage rescue team led by Jack had upgraded the Swede and formed a new team from existing staff. Helicopter trips to the chateau not required. The hostage demands still controlled by the committee, headed by Henri. The Americans now knew where this outpost was in Algeria near the beach. For now, no action but see if that information would be useful in the future. The incident and deaths at the chateau were history, the Russians denying any involvement. Danielle was not the topic of any conversation. Christmas looked likely to be a farewell party for many.

Chapter 23   Thursday, December 8th

Lisa arrived at her sister's house at 4 pm after a long drive. She had luggage and Christmas presents to exchange. It was Rufus who got the cuddles first and strokes as Jennifer's dog jumped up as soon as he saw her. The paws found a puddle which left marks on her skirt. Lisa did not mind. She adored her older sister who had retired early and found a lovely quiet village on a hill overlooking a chateau. Property prices here were some of the cheapest in France. The quaint village of Brandiol is where she found herself and Rufus who loved the walks in the fields and especially around the church and chateau. Kisses on both cheeks as was the custom, followed by tea and cakes from the local patisserie. So much to catch up on. The big topic was of course Jonny Wilkinson and there it was all framed above the mantlepiece a picture of them both at the entrance to the café/bar. Lisa admired it and asked if Jennifer had taken any rugby photographs as she was as keen as Lisa, a family addiction.

"Not recently, I have taken more photographs around here. So much activity, the owner of the chateau committed suicide with her maid, big scandal. I met a few of the guards, must have been important, she was cremated three days after the incident."

"Gosh, you have more action than we do in Arudy."

"Yes, might show you some of my photographs later."

After tea Jennifer took Rufus for a short walk while Lisa rested for an hour and had a bath before supper. Food and drink, then relaxing in front of the log fire, slippers off, this was bliss for Lisa. "It was a Sunday afternoon. I was upstairs thinking about taking the dog for a walk when I looked out the curtain. There it was a Spanish number plate near the side gate of the chateau. You know me, I just took the one picture, thought it very unusual."

She showed it to Lisa who was taking more interest. "Have you got any more?"

"Yes, but not of that car, I take them of helicopters, they have enough room for three to land. I just find the place fascinating. Posh cars as well, here is a BMW top of the range at the gates and some in the driveway. Those bushes spoil some photos, I am a bit nosey."

"Blimey!" Lisa looked again at the photograph of the Spanish-plated car outside the chateau and the picture on the wall. "That is the same car that was seen at Arudy the same day that Jonny Wilkinson came."

"What you talking about?"

"And it's the same woman who asked where the wine merchant was killed?"

"What wine merchant?"

"And I recognise her rings and that bangle."

Jennifer patted Rufus. "Hope you're following this?"

"This is work, Jen. I need to ring Rene and Yorkie. I'll explain later."

Lisa got her mobile out and rang Yorkie first and then Rene with the same facts. "There has been suicides here and a wine merchant from Spain found dead. This is the same woman who asked where the layby was."

Rene told Yorkie to fly to Limoges on Saturday and come back with Lisa on Sunday. Jennifer said he could sleep on the sofa. Rene was adamant about Monday morning meet insisting, "Do not go looking without

154

permission, we are a small rural station, we could be out of our depth and very unpopular. We need to do our investigation first."

Lisa picked up Yorkie from Limoges Airport at 2 pm and introduced him to Jennifer who was pleased to have a young man in the house. Teas and cakes again the usual late afternoon delight. Yorkie asked, "Who lives in the chateau now?"

"Nobody it is has been empty, rumour has it they are looking for a lost son. The lady at the patisserie said if they do not find him within six years it goes to the state."

They viewed the chateau better from the upstairs window. No lights on.

"There is a church behind and a large wall, on the other side is the outside swimming pool. A big barn adjoins the house. That was where the car was found, suicide, they say she had lost her job." Jennifer seemed pleased to give the facts.

Lisa guessed what Yorkie was thinking. They decided to let Jennifer in on the idea.

The village was silent at 2 am as Lisa and Yorkie, wearing dark clothing, scaled the wall and found themselves in front of the ground patio doors next to the covered pool. Yorkie's recent training was more than useful as he found a way to open the doors. They slid open and no alarm went off. They had a torch each and moved slowly up the stairs to the kitchen. They walked along the corridor to the kitchen and the front room. They went up the stairs past all the erotic paintings of ladies 1920's style. They returned downstairs and found the basement with stocks of wine and items of restraint with equipment to match that form of desire. Everywhere they looked the chateau was as expected with no obvious clues. Lisa took several photos in every room. They left the chateau, climbed over the church yard wall and returned unnoticed. They had plenty to think about before the meeting with Rene.

Chapter 24   Monday, December 12ᵗʰ

Rene was at in his chair as usual. Yorkie had already presented the facts while Lisa sat quiet. A pin-drop silence filled the room as they sipped their tea. Rene had a serious look.

"Okay," he finally said. "I need you to listen to what I have to say, and before you tell me it's not protocol... hear me out..."

Lisa cast a furtive glance in Yorkie's direction.

"I am going to start a Narcotics Division."

Lisa felt her lips gape open, Yorkie simply shrugged. It was a tiny sub-station, why the hell did they need a Narcotics Division? She was about to speak when he lifted his hands.

"Or at least that's what we're going to call it."

"I don't—"

"Hear me out, Yorkie."

"If you guys go investigating these deaths, you'll hit a brick wall and I'll tell you why... there's more to this but you go sticking your noses in – Lisa..." he looked at her, "not really seen much action other than paperwork... and you, Yorkie..." Yorkie looked at Lisa before turning his head to Rene. "Newly qualified. Even your firearms' licenses, some might say is wasted skill out here... but for this assignment it might be useful. This is our cover, we must be savvy."

"But why Narcotics, how will you get approval?"

"Lisa, leave that to me. Drugs were found in the van, that's what we say. We did not disclose it because we want to find the trail. You two will be on that trail. No other police force will accept you otherwise. That's the story. If they ring me, I simply confirm. Undercover operations for drugs are acceptable. Helicopters, fancy cars and this Danielle Bousquet cremated within four days. This is Interpol territory. I do not like them they can be so corrupt. It is time to step up. Do you want to continue, this could get complicated and dangerous?"

Lisa and Yorkie sat there as Rene fetched two 38 special calibre revolvers from his cupboard and three rounds each. "You might need these. So now there is call for guns and you know what to do."

Rene then said he would phone his printer friend and order two badges for them with the necessary wording on.

"So we get to play proper cops," Yorkie smirked.

Rene's expression said this was no time for joking. "These are real guns... we might be going undercover but this is no game."

"Of course. No. Sorry, sir." He wasn't sure what he saw on Lisa's face.

"You need to go back to the farmhouse and check again. Yorkie you think those photos of rings and the bangle is Whitby Jet?"

"Yes, I remember buying one for my first girlfriend when I was in love at seventeen. It is just down the road from Robin Hood's Bay."

"You go back there for Christmas, could be useful if they were bought from Whitby?" Rene was in overdrive for the first time in a long time. "You can go to Spain tomorrow, take your time and report Wednesday 9 am, best you take your Lada with all that snow, I will find out where this Danielle Bousquet worked."

Lisa and Yorkie thought they had been offered a chance to get out of the investigation. They looked at each other and Yorkie said he would check the tyres on the Lada and fill it up. They left early in order to get to the farmhouse before lunch. They had rung Juan's mother to confirm she would be in. After a pit stop, they arrived before midday.

"Any joy with the insurance company?" Lisa enquired.

"Made me an offer but I refused it. I rang an insurance expert and he said hang in till they give you it all."

"We had reports of a woman asking about Juan's death on the Sunday morning after the accident. Who did you tell after you found out on the Saturday afternoon?"

"I told no one. I was in shock and I only have my boy. There was just that woman that comes who asked about him. She left with some wine. She went to look at the pigeons."

Yorkie was looking at the rickety exterior stairs leading up to the pigeon loft and asked Lisa, "Did you go up last time?"

"Not likely, those stairs are dangerous."

Yorkie borrowed her camera, bounded up to the top and took a few photographs of the building. By the time he got down, Juan's mother was waiting with the keys. Lisa took her camera back and looked at the few photos he had taken. It was dark in the barn and they had to put the lights on. Lisa looked up "Where is the skylight?"

Yorkie and Juan's mother looked at each other to a chorus of "What skylight?"

"Well, there is one here that you just took Yorkie. It will be out of sight on top of the building unless you knew about it. Better get your climbing gear out of the Lada."

Yorkie tentatively moved across the roof and smashed in the skylight. It was the only way he could descend with a rope and a torch on his helmet. Lisa was in the barn now. Yorkie banged on the walls. It took ten minutes to find the secret to opening it up. There were some cases of wine and nothing else. They got as much light in as possible. They both spotted less dust where a cupboard had been. Then in the centre as Yorkie lay on the floor, he found small traces of wood shavings in the cracks. The area the size of a bed became more obvious as dust levels had left a different mark on the floor. The walls had faint scratch marks. They went back into the barn and found the wood waiting to be burnt. The sawn-up slats indicated that they had been used for a base of a bed once. It was obvious Juan's mother knew nothing about this secret room.

It was Lisa's turn to ask about this woman who had called to buy some wine. "Did you notice anything unusual about this lady that stopped for the wine and was she alone?"

"I told her he had died in Arudy. She stopped a bit in the barn before driving home. She had a lovely bangle and some big rings. I did not see anyone else. She slept in the barn."

"Did you do any paperwork, post his letters, do the banking or any deliveries?"

"No just posted all his invoices and letters. He did any banking and all the deliveries. Very few came here. That woman came about twice a year, nice lady."

"Was it all local mail, any to France?"

"Nearly all local except two, one to Bordeaux and St Emilion." She seemed proud to have remembered those two. "Oh yes, there was another to France somewhere in Bergerac, I remember because of the name Cyrano De Bergerac."

"Have you got the address?"

"No, it will be in his year planners."

They went through every year planner and documents they could find. No address in Bergerac. Lisa asked again "Does Rue D'Airport ring any bells or a name on the envelope?"

"I am sure there was no name. If I remember I will tell you. He is not in trouble, is he?"

It is strange that even though Juan had been dead a couple of weeks she did not want him to have been a bad boy. It was getting late. They rang Rene to tell him the news. Yorkie bought six bottles of rioja with cash, noticing the "JUAN" stamped on the bottle. When he asked about the label, she said it was to remind customers where to rebuy. Yorkie drove most of the way back as Lisa checked all her photos again.

"The van, look there, it has a skylight in the middle, why would you need that?"

"For his pigeons," Yorkie replied as the wipers washed away the snow and he slowed down.

"They were in the front, remember we had to rescue one. The merchant at St Emilion said the same, so what do you need air for and a secret compartment in a barn with possibly a bed? If someone was hidden in the van that explains why he had less wine going and more coming back." Lisa looked at Yorkie and both said the same word in unison "Trafficking."

The next morning Rene had the new badges. He was pleased to announce he had found out where Danielle Bousquet worked: the Horticultural College near Clermont Ferrand, you two had better go there and make some subtle enquiries, remember it's a drugs' ring we're after."

Yorkie looked at the map. "Can we fly to Clermont Ferrand, hire a car for the day and get the evening flight back to Pau?"

Lisa could see the problem of cost so intervened. "That chateau was too spotless to be true, we are up against professionals we need to be at our best. A long car journey and overnight stop with two rooms, it sounds cheaper to fly. We will claim just the 100 euros each, will that help?"

She could see Rene relax, happier at the budget proposal. He looked for agreement with Yorkie, but Lisa was the organiser. They were on the computer within seconds and booked the 7:40am flight and 6:50 pm return. Narcotics agents having firearms would be acceptable on the plane, along with fast access.

Chapter 25

Thursday, December 15ᵗʰ

They arrived at the gatehouse to the Horticultural College at 11 am.

Lisa had decided to act as the driver and had taken off her badge. The uniformed gateman advanced to the car. Yorkie showed him his narcotics badge. "I am following up enquiries about a drugs cell that has links to this establishment. We do not want to have a full squad here of thirty plus, we prefer to see a director first and just ask a few informal questions."

He went back into his booth and rang Henri. Henri then informed the others on the committee and they agreed to meet this narcotics agent in a Mole room. Yorkie and Lisa went into the booth to get the badges. They were behind the door on hooks. Yorkie was given a VIP badge and asked to put down his name and address. He used the police station in Arudy.

"Your driver will have a standard pass and can park over there next to the apartments. There is a park with benches for her to use."

"If you are going into that warm building, Yorkie, you will not need your big overcoat." Lisa took it off him and hung it up behind the door taking a spare VIP badge without the guard noticing. "Are there any toilets I can use?" Lisa asked as she was about to leave.

"Yes, there is that outside block between the apartments and the food hall."

Yorkie was escorted via outside steps to a Mole room. The American, the Englishman, Doc, Henri and the new girl Jean were seated. Yorkie had photos to show them.

"We believe there is a drugs ring linked to this man, Juan, in northern Spain and this chateau at Brandiol. Our agents have been tailing them for some time. Juan died when his van went down a ravine near our police station. The lady driver, you see here with the rings is believed to have gone to this chateau. We have lost contact with her, but my intrepid superior discovered the owner of this chateau works here, can I speak to Danielle Bousquet?"

It was Henri who spoke. "I am sorry, but Danielle Bousquet and her maid committed suicide. She lost her job it was too much for her. You can see we are a government organisation, and we are on the same side. We can assure you if drugs had been found, the authorities would have been informed. We have the keys, and you are welcome to go to the chateau and see for yourself, it is empty and clean."

They all nodded in agreement.

The phone went. Doc answered, "Your Rene has confirmed your position carry on."

Yorkie continued giving the impression he had already been. "So, that is why no one answered and there are locks on the gate at the chateau. Do you know who this woman is with the rings? I want to know Danielle's movements before she committed suicide."

The American was more brash. "You look a bit young and green for this job, there are no drugs here, you can tell your boss to send us a pretty young lady next time. Piss off back to where you came from."

Yorkie could feel the resentment about being challenged by him and his sexist remark annoyed him. "Are you from the backwoods of America where inbreeding is common in bringing up arseholes like you?"

164

Yorkie thought he was going to hit him but instead with an air of smugness. "You smell like you came from a pig farm, the door is over there, do you want to go out as you or bacon?"

Yorkie would not stop now. "You are right, I worked on a farm in North Yorkshire, and I can smell good manure. For a horticultural college there is no such smell here except from your backside."

The Englishman tried to calm things down. "Hey, just give the boy a chance; he is just doing his job."

The Doc joined in. "Go back and tell your boss this is a clean outfit."

Yorkie surrendered. "You know what you are right." He packed his papers away in his briefcase. "I will just leave and speak to my boss in the nearest layby when I leave. You see we are just a small team on the Pyrenees border. We try and stop the flow of drugs from Spain mainly via other countries. I am a junior officer of a much larger organisation covering the whole of Spain, France and Andorra. When I tell my boss that you would not show me around your college it is like a red rag to a bull. I know what happens. He makes a few phone calls and within an hour the first ones will arrive. No one in or out. Within three hours he will have more than thirty people sniffing every crack of your fat arse, Mr America, then we will decide if you are clean or not."

It was Jean who spoke. "Do you mind waiting in the corridor while we talk?"

Yorkie obeyed. He returned and they made him sign a secret's act before showing him the role of RAID and the maps. He was impressed with the helicopter hangars and saw a strong-looking man who was giving orders. They all returned to the Mole room where the American had decided to stay. Henri spoke.

"You can get who you like in, there are no drugs here. We cannot give you classified information and we have never seen that lady. We wish you good luck in your quest."

Yorkie thought about any alternative questions. He looked at them all, slowly, directly into their eyes. The icy look back and his inside knowledge there were no drugs resigned him to accepting the evidence given. Yorkie noted their pompous looks of victory, we told you so. "Thanks, it is obvious there is no drug connection here, we will have to look elsewhere."

Yorkie was escorted back to the car park by Doc, the German. Lisa was waiting inside the car. They drove up to the barrier. Lisa got out and fetched Yorkie's coat putting both VIP badges back behind the door. They had to get to the airport, give the car back and fly to Pau. They spotted a car following them all the way to the airport. They were on time.

The next morning Rene asked for a report. "I got nowhere, it is a Hostage Rescue Operation under the guise of a Horticultural College, how about you, Lisa?"

"I did not tell you yesterday, but I managed to get into the canteen. It is surprising what you learn from the kitchen staff. Someone called Cas was killed on a mission and Danielle Bousquet was responsible. It happened in North Africa, a beach in Algeria Thursday November, 17th. The Tunisian cook knew the exact day because it was her birthday. It was a good thing I went in as a driver."

They all studied the new information. "Yorkie you must do some digging in Whitby. That sort of jewellery is not bought on the internet. It is bought as you see it on a holiday or whatever. Come on, guys, think. Why would a Spanish lady be in Whitby or North Yorkshire and when did she buy it?"

They did not have any answers. "I will only have a day and half as it is Christmas eve Saturday, early closing. Lots will then close till the New Year."

"OK, gang, meet tomorrow, Lisa can you get some Tunisian/Algerian papers from November 18th to 25th, homework required."

It took a while to get the newspapers. It was December 21st and Yorkie was driving to the UK the next day. They found a headline about a Russian Mig that had been lost on a routine training exercise. They scoured the papers until Lisa saw a two-liner. *Due to the sudden death of Cherie Houston, her husband, daughter and governess in a speed boat accident the new French ambassador in Tunis is to be Andria Rousseau.* "Maybe you can check this, Rene, you have amazing contacts due to your length of service." Lisa teased her ageing boss.

Yorkie was in a good mood and had cycled in as he sometimes used it to go around the local villages. As he left the building a local spotted him. "You will not get far on that old thing on the Tour De Yorkshire."

He rushed back into the station. "2014 the Tour De France started in Yorkshire, that might be the connection." Rene smiled at his recruit and responded,

"Ee by gum Dan Rowbottom tha better get off." He did not know that in Robin Hood's Bay the accent was so strong people in the same county ten miles away could not understand them. It was a blessing that Yorkie could speak French *and* Yorkshire.

Pigeons are used as messengers on ships

Chapter 26

Thursday, December 22nd

Yorkie had taken the overnight sailing from Zeebrugge to Hull arriving early Thursday morning. His Lada was still a reliable vehicle, but he had taken out breakdown cover just in case. The journey from Hull up along past the signs for Hornsea, Bridlington and Scarborough made him feel slightly homesick. He arrived late morning at his cousin's house in Robin Hood's Bay.

They drank in the local pub and walked along the beach despite its bitter coldness. A hearty dinner and the next day he went, as arranged to Whitby. He showed the picture of the bangle and rings to many shops. It was 3 pm when he called in at RFH Wilson & Sons and asked if she had sold that ring. The woman behind the counter looked at it long and hard.

"It does look familiar, did you say 2014 – June, I think July the race started."

She checked her invoices that were filed and on the computer. "No, it does not look like it. A bangle like that would be £80 and I can see no sale for the week before or that weekend."

Yorkie was about to leave when a pregnant lady, with a little girl came in.

"Hi, Mum, Phil is parking the car. Busy out there he will be a few minutes."

"This gentleman is asking about a Spanish lady who might have bought a bangle from here in June, 2014 just before the Tour De France started. I

169

have been checking my invoices. You had finished college, remember and you ran off to follow the Tour with that refugee girl you mentioned?"

Yorkie noticed how uneasy she had become so decided on an alternative way to proceed with his enquiry.

"Hope you do not mind me saying how healthy you three look."

The lady smiled back. "Thank you."

"Just asking your mum about this bangle, I did not mention it might be part of several robberies we are investigating near the Spanish border in France. I am from Yorkshire as you can tell with my accent. Perhaps you can help me?"

"I am Sarah, and I cannot help, Mum is always here."

Yorkie took out his card, "Ring me if you think of something."

When it was clear they had other things to talk about Yorkie left. He had two more shops to visit. He watched the seagulls over the harbour squawking in the cold winter air. The Christmas lights a joy to look at as evening beckoned. He thought about having fish and chips, but dinner would be waiting at his cousin's house. His phone rang.

"It is Sarah, are you still nearby – I can give you ten minutes."

"Just on the harbour wall near where the jetty for the pleasure boats go in summer."

"Great get me a coffee at the harbour café, it closes in thirty minutes."

Yorkie did not have to wait long. They sat with the two coffees. Sarah gave her account.

"She was Spanish, and I was looking after the shop on the Thursday afternoon July 3rd while Mum had her hair done. She had a girl bit younger than me. They had met at Calais. They looked for ages and she chose three rings and one bangle and two earrings. It was closing time, so she said she was staying at the Raven Hotel at Ravenscar. She said she had the cash at the hotel. I went back with them and told my mum I was staying with a friend in Scarborough. I was young and naïve. Things happened and I went back to see my mum. They said they were following the Tour into France. I joined them and had a wild time for a week. My dad was furious, I did not tell them about the sale. I kept the money for my holiday. Mum knew, she had been a hippy, and just said be careful. Luckily, I met Philip on the tour, I got cold feet with the Spanish lady. The car smelt rotten with the pigeons. I was pleased when she let one fly back. She had a favourite that had some diplomas for races. She invited me to her place in Spain. I think I have the address somewhere. If I find it, I will text it to you. Please do not tell Philip, it was a bad experience I want to forget. I told him I was seeing some more friends in the south of France. It was a lie. I simply dumped them and tagged on with Philip."

She massaged her lump and Yorkie said, "It will remain a secret with me."

Yorkie watched her leave and drove to the hotel at Ravenscar. The records showed no Spanish lady staying. The receptionist winked at him on the way out. "We do accept cash for rooms, no receipts."

Yorkie fancied his chances, but she did not finish till midnight and he was hungry. He drove back for dinner and wished he had rung them and said he was staying at Ravenscar. The next morning the text came from Sarah saying sorry no address found.

Chapter 27

Thursday, December 22nd

It was Jack's last shift for five days.

The hangars were quiet as the Swede and his crew had gone on a mission at short notice. He had spoken to his trusted two cleaners and wished them a *Merry Christmas*. The glazier he would call on as he lived close to Jack and he worked mainly from home in his workshop. It was late morning when his phone rang.

"Help us, Daddy." Sobbing; his daughter in deep distress.

"They have us Jack, they are taking us to a chateau at Brandiol, why?" Suzette in stammering mode.

"Be there on your own in your helicopter by 2 pm, no tricks, no guns or they die a slow death." The foreign accent obvious and full of intent. "We will have fun if you do not turn up."

The phone went dead.

Jack sat back in his chair, there was just Maggie available. He had coached Suzette for this event, though he never expected it for real. He had no knowledge as to why they wanted him. He could only guess it was linked to the previous incident at the chateau. Jack made one phone call and set off alone unarmed.

Jack was the toughest guy around, but now his tears flowed like the river he flew over. He clenched his fists on the helicopter's rudder and wondered what the hell he was flying into. His hands shook and his breathing became laboured. He could see the chateau as he approached over the small forest next to it. The clear sky a relief as he saw figures near the kitchen door. He manoeuvred the helicopter, facing the village but at an angle that was not perfect on the target that was painted in circles to help the pilot. By any standards it was a poor landing. The blades whined until they stopped. He looked across at two armed men one with a gun at Suzette's head with his daughter hand cuffed to her. Their mouths were taped over so they could not speak. The other had a gun aimed at the helicopter. On the floor was a can of petrol. He could not see anyone else. The one with the gun at his wife's head spoke.

"Come over here slowly, remove all your uniform to show us you have no weapons."

Jack took off his helmet and leather jacket. He placed them at the front of the helicopter with his shirt and trousers stripped down to his underwear and socks and started walking towards them. He was a beaten man, his legs wobbling with fear, then stumbling, falling on the floor at the mercy of the abductors. "What do you want with me? Please let them live."

His daughter was pulling at the hand cuffs, terrified, but luckily Mummy stoically holding her. Jack could see in their eyes the look of finality. Their bodies wriggling and shaking like an octopus trying to escape from a trap.

"Stand here." Jack stood in front of them all. He watched the other gunman take his wife and daughter towards the helicopter. He had some rope.

"Do not turn round." Jack stood motionless and begged again. "Please, what do you want?"

French people do not come out till after 3 pm, some houses were close and these abductors knew what they were doing. The village was quiet.

His abductor put cuffs on Jack, and he did not resist, falling on his knees for mercy.

"Turn around." Jack turned and saw his loved ones. The other man had stopped, putting his rifle on the ground. He opened the petrol can and poured some over them. He left the can about fifty yards from the helicopter so he could put the rope around them both and pushed them into the back seat of the helicopter, wiping his hands on her covered breasts now pushed higher by the rope. As the man started to walk back to the petrol can, he could see the wickedness in his eyes. Jack looked around. The tree branches he could see clearly through at this time of the year and very few bird sounds. He wondered if there was anyone else but could see no one. The man picked his rifle waiting for his order. The one that seemed to be in charge put his gun to Jack's head. "Stand up so I can hear."

Jack slowly got up. "This will be the last time you will see them alive, unless you tell me where Danielle Bousquet and the girl are?" He spoke to the other man. "I think under the fuel tank, just wait a moment."

The other man was grinning as he picked up the petrol can. Jack had to respond. "They died together in that barn, suicide."

Jack felt the full force of the butt of his gun, his hands and cuffs protecting his face. "Liar."

Jack had his hands below his chin. "Where are they?" Then looking to his associate, "Take the can and we will let him watch it all go up in smoke, they will frazzle in the heat of the confined cockpit." Like a cornered rattlesnake, but with his sting removed, Jack had lost.

Jack lowered his hands to protect himself in case he was kicked or butted in his privates. "I will tell you if he stops." The man with the can stopped about ten paces from the helicopter. Jack slowly muttered his words "Danielle went with a helicopter pilot called Mari. The girl was killed."

The flare that came from behind the helicopter, simultaneously came with a shot that sent the man with the gun to Jack's head reeling backwards. As the gun fell from his grasp, Jack was splashed with parts of his bloodstained scalp and brains. The flare took the attention of the man with the petrol can long enough for a second shot to go through his heart. The next shot came from the barn and caught Jack on his shoulder as he sought shelter with his dead abductor. Jack felt for his gun and with difficulty gripped it with his cuffed hands. Shots came from the barn that sunk into the already dead abductor with Jack underneath. One grazed his leg. More shots now came from the helicopter towards the barn. Jack joined in but he did not need to. Mari had been in her special sniper hold and when the shots came from the barn, it gave away his position. She had clearly guessed it would be a good spot for another abductor. He fell from the barn door where he had concealed himself behind some straw bales. He and a bale hit the floor in a photo finish.

* * *

Mari pulled herself out of her hold and untied Jack's wife and daughter who were hysterical once the tapes were removed. Mari shouted to Jack, "It is only water."

The three of them ran to Jack jumping over one dead body to get to him. There were kisses and hugs, relief for all, but all Jack really wanted now it was over were his clothes back on. It was winter and cold. The kitchen door to the chateau was open, they had somehow got some chateau keys. Jack was so grateful for Mari. They found the keys for his cuffs on the dead abductors. They all went inside after Jack even with his injured shoulder moved the dead bodies to the barn with Mari's help.

"I would have been lost without you. Good thing you were available, there was no one at YMCA. You must have driven fast to get to the agreed rendezvous point when I picked you up. That Porsche was a life saver, and your bloody good shooting. I have been here before so parked at an angle to give you a better chance in case they were near the back door. It was logical that is where they would be."

"Took longer to get the one in the barn, I am not so good these days over 800 yards. Liked the new flare plot. The switch was next to my foot so I could aim at the same time. Waited for your signal, hands over the crotch, whatever you said to them, no one else will know. I remembered that trick from that one in Sicily we did."

Jack was impressed with Suzette. "Got the message we agreed on, it is difficult under pressure, your why at the end of our conversation told me why=3 letters=3 abductors, never thought I would need that code." He then spoke to Mari.

"Someone knows or thinks Danielle is alive and they wanted the girl, but she died in the house. These are ISIL with inside information."

Mari said nothing.

They were sat in the kitchen when Jack searched for his phone and said, "My phone is in the front compartment near the controls."

When a ten-year-old girl, fleet of foot and wanting to help Daddy, no one was quick enough to stop her. As his daughter glided into the open air and ran up the meadow type land towards the helicopter Jack and Mari burst into action despite his pain. Mari picked up her trusted rifle and scampered outside to hide near a bush and scour the landscape. Jack shouted at his wife. "Take a gun upstairs and look out, there might be a second unit around as back-up." He saw the panic in her reaction and her speed. Jack heaved himself to the kitchen window, a captured gun in his left hand, his right shoulder making that side out of order. His daughter had found the phone, triumphantly holding it up without a care in the world, except to be useful.

"I am coming, Daddy." Her mother now at the window, looking with hope there was no one else around, a gun she had never used pointing at the open landscape. Jack watched Mari moving her gun from left to right and then right to left into the forest, a natural place to hide. Something caught her attention and for a moment, she prepared to fire; but it was only a rabbit. Jack saw the happy face of his daughter draw nearer, his phone in her hand tripping over a slight uprising in the ground. With agility she regained her footing and then it happened. The church bells sounded, the village came to life, cars came from all angles, lots of hooting and sounds of happy voices. This was a small but noisy local wedding, just before Christmas. They congregated back in the front room, opened the curtains and watched the procession go by the side of the chateau and to the church at the rear. Relief for all in the chateau, some people looking at the procession and the activity with a helicopter at the chateau yet again. It was a happy day so there was no need for them to be suspicious, it was not an unusual occurrence.

Jack continued his own mission briefing and made a phone call to the Swede. They found a tourniquet and plasters for Jack. The water was still on so they could have a drink. They wiped some of the blood and human gunge from Jack's face and arms. Mari came back in and reminded Jack it was water in the petrol can. Jack smiled. "They were going to use the helicopter for the escape, we were expendable once they got the information. We will wait a while here."

Jack watched Mari check around the perimeter of the chateau. As a friend of Danielle, she clearly knew it well. On her return she said, "They are singing in the church. A few walkers now, one nice lady with a dog and a camera." Jack insisted she kept watch with her rifle handy.

178

The Swede had returned to RAID after a fruitless hoax to save a property allegedly being broken into by refugees. He received Jack's phone call and went into action.

He went to the hangar and called a meeting of his hostage rescue team. "We have a serious security breach. Jack is injured. He says at least one in the committee is an informer. We need to secure the base, no one in or out. I will report the hostage crisis in fifteen minutes, everyone check watches and we need our comms on. There might be more informers. One helicopter will be leaving soon. It should have three on board, we will send a pilot to the chateau with another as back-up on board in case there is a second cell near them. Jack is too bad to fly his. There are only eight of us left to control the main entrance, the goods entrance, and the hamlet with the single track, and arrest five committee personnel."

The Swede paused for a second.

"Jack says one has to stay inside the armoury, once we are armed. It is no good outside as if he is taken out, they have access. That leaves seven, we need two on the main gate doing maintenance on the barrier as cover. Use the vehicle to block any forced entry or departure. Two more on the goods in/out barrier. Tie up the duty men in the booths and only untie if we are overwhelmed, and risk they are with us. One can do the single-track block. That means me and one other will secure the Mole room with the outside steps. We can lock out anyone else in the main building from getting inside that Mole room. I am taking control and responsibility. There are over two hundred personnel in this village, and we are not certain where the five on the committee are. We do not apprehend them till we find out who tries to do what or to get out the village. One by one, after they have made any moves, we arrest each one and secure them in that Mole room. When we bring Jack back, he will be in the first helicopter. The other needs to be ten minutes behind so they do not know we are bringing back three dead ISIL men until they are secured in that Mole room. One final message is codenamed Jack. That means all hands even tied up ones or the one in the armoury go to that point for support."

They all understood, and the armoury was raided and locked with the married one inside who was on maintenance. They went to their positions. The Swede left his guns with his support man on the steps out of sight, but in view of the main entrance. He informed his trusted associates in the Swedish booth of the problem at Brandiol. The main board flagged up accordingly. The committee were contacted wherever they were in the village. They had to respond and go to a Mole room. It was not the same Mole room that the Swede was going to use later.

The Swedish representative, Stephan, then reported to the committee that in return for Jack's safe return with his family, three abductors wanted safe passage back to Algeria in Maggie from the chateau at Brandiol. Please send a helicopter to pick them up. They had used the Swedish embassy for their demand as it was deemed neutral. They all met in a Mole room that Stephan had requisitioned. Henri, Doc, the Englishman, the American and Jean. The five of them had to decide quickly. Several points were made before they accepted. Some wanted more time to try and get a ground force to reconnoitre the chateau first. It was agreed Jack was too important. The green light was given for another helicopter to be sent and the ransom accepted. The committee left the building unaware of the Swede's team strategically placed. It was not long before they came across them as four of them tried to leave the village. Jean simply went to her booth and made three phone calls, drank her tea. She went up to the reception but saw two of her committee men being escorted to a Mole room. There was no easy escape for her, so she went back to her booth. She answered the phone twice. "Yes, you need to see them now, it is urgent."

The Swede's defence system was holding firm. They had asked each one on the intercom via the normal guard who spoke, where they wanted to go and why. One down the single track was the Englishman. He was frogmarched under armed guard by the Swede's man to the Mole room. He was the first to be secured. Doc had tried to get out the goods entrance, he was the second. Henri had approached the main entrance; he was the third. The American was more aggressive at the main gate after Henri had tried, saying he was in command and get the hell out of his way. His car was damaged as he hit the truck before he was arrested at gunpoint and sent to the Mole room. All was going well, but Jean was not seen outside at all. She was accompanied to the Mole room after the first helicopter landed with Jack, his wife and daughter.

It was a good two hours' flight to the chateau and back. The other helicopter arrived back ten minutes later having dropped off Mari for her car. The committee could not understand the false information and three dead bodies. It was time for a debriefing and interrogation in the Mole room. There was the bandaged Jack, the Swede, the American, the Englishman, Henri, Doc and Jean. The American was always the brash one. "What the hell is going on?"

Jack took over. "In this room is the second ISIL contact." Silence followed. All five members sat nervously. They knew individually who was and who was not but had Jack got the evidence? Who could play poker best? The guilty party had the background to remain aloof and not be found out, surely. Suspicion was hanging over the committee like the sword of Damacles. The Swede got up and stood in a corner watching. Jack continued.

181

"You see you were the only ones who knew the five of us that cleaned up the chateau. Someone sent the Swede on a hoax mission to leave me isolated. The glazier's wife rang here at 1 pm. It was not logged till 2 pm. She went to his workshop to give him his lunch. What she saw I would not wish on anyone. The cleaners went to the house and found a dead body tortured and cut to pieces with his own equipment. If he had talked, they would not have gone for my family. The job had to be done with one hit within hours or we would get suspicious. This is an inside job and I know who did it. There was only one person here who could have changed that log entry, the one person who sent out the Swede on that hoax. One person who keeps pigeons. One who tried to leave the compound. Your movements were monitored on our own internal cameras. Too many mistakes."

"Doc, you tried to leave to get the Christmas present for Markle perhaps, going out the goods entrance was logical as the shop is on that side of the city. Jean, as the new member but you did not leave because you were busy getting counsellors for me and my family, thank you. The Englishman going for his lunchtime snack with the Polish receptionist who lives in the hamlet. Some will be jealous, but you are no traitor. As for you, Mr America, where you going to report back to Trump still begging him to change his mind. You have a cushy number here. That leaves you, Henri, the mistake you made was telling the gateman, you were going home to feed your pigeons. Might have been a harmless statement but that was the final part of the jigsaw, you are the bastard informer."

Tension was mounting in the Mole room. The facts were too much for Henri who produced his gun with alacrity and fired in quick succession at all in the room. The other committee members dived for cover, chairs falling over as dud bullets hit most of them. Jack and the Swede moved with the swiftness and clinical training that prepared them for such an event. As they overpowered Henri, the two cleaners who had been waiting outside dashed in and rained punches on him. Mumblings of "another for the glazier and for his wife and children." The rest of the committee did nothing, relieved they had caught the infiltrator, and there were no holes and blood all over the room. Henri meanwhile was in agony and bleeding from his nose and mouth, punched and kicked into a heap on the floor. The Swede produced cartridges he had removed from all the guns owned by the committee members. The ones he had replaced all duds. he spoke to the dishevelled lot as they put their chairs back upright. "We had to be sure it was only one of you."

The cleaners were given hand cuffs by Jack as they attached them to the frightened, trembling and groaning Henri. Jack gave the final order to his cleaners and the Swede. "Take him to the chateau, you three. Ring me when you have more information." Jack stayed motionless, looking at Henri's eyes.

"We took precautions and searched all your rooms. Please check your guns; they all need loading with real bullets."

Jack looked on as the helpless Henri was escorted roughly to the hangars. He knew his two cleaners and the Swede would use whatever was necessary, including drugs, to get vital information. Jack pondered on how he would have to report the demise of Henri. Maybe they'd claim he was on a raid against the Somalian pirates. The cleaners and the Swede had enough information to take out two terrorist cells and find out the name of the Algerian leader responsible for the American deaths at the beach. Tariq was now high on the American hit list.

Tariq had lost his contacts at YMCA for now. Jack, the Swede and the two cleaners found discreet homes close together in case their new security was breached. 2017 was just around the corner and Aqbal's daughter was in Tunisia at Tariq's HQ learning a new trade.

It was the next day when Jack got a phone call from the Swede. "Those cleaners have ways of making a man talk. I do not think he will survive the night mind you."

"No problem, he was due to go on a dangerous mission."

"He could only confirm that Cas was the other infiltrator, but we knew that. Tariq is the commander in North Africa. When we ransacked his house before we went to the chateau, we let his tagged pigeons off. One went to that same beach area in Algeria. Another went to a cell which we have now taken out. We had to move fast before they did. The others came back to his own loft. The bad news is the pigeons in the cell house they killed."

Jack listened before he spoke.

"Great job, it proves my theory they are using pigeons for communication."

"Yes," said the Swede. "Pigeons do talk."

Chapter 28   **Thursday, December 29ᵗʰ**

Rene was sat in his chair while Lisa had put the kettle on waiting for Yorkie who was due back. On cue he came in at 9.05 and took the mug of Yorkshire tea that Lisa pushed into his gloved hands. They thanked each other for the Christmas presents, then Rene began the debrief. "Well, Yorkie, no luck in England with your enquiries?"

"The girl could not find any address and spent a week with them in a car full of pigeons. The Spanish woman did say she had one good pigeon."

Lisa was taking notes and having a drink. "Did she actually get any merits?"

"Well remember when we went to Pau, all owners of pigeons have to register their proper address in case a pigeon gets a merit. It has to be in the top 2% that return with the best times."

Rene nodded. "You went to the Pau one where they sent some to southern Spain."

"The Malaga run." Lisa checked her notes.

"It is worth a shot, ring the organisers and get all the addresses of those with merits. Female-only entrants and then I will decide if you two are heading off to Spain and or Portugal to check."

"I will try, they might be closed till the New Year."

"Good point, write and send an email we will meet again Wednesday 4th. Yorkie, you are on duty on the 3rd after your New Year's jolly with the climbing club, so leave that to Lisa."

Reliable Lisa checked her emails and rang several times but got no reply.

It was Thursday afternoon when an email finally came through with only sixteen female entrants who had got merits in the entire year. It covered all Spain and Portugal. She put a map up for the Friday debrief with pins of locations.

"You are not going all over," insisted Rene as he sipped his tea. "I need you two here."

"With all due respect, this could be a murder investigation linked to trafficking, just think what that would look like on your retirement CV," Lisa said; she fancied a trip to Spain.

"Yorkie, what do you say?"

"We think there is a link to North Africa, so why not concentrate on Central and Eastern Spain for one trip over two days. It is a long way we all find this case intriguing."

Lisa was in the mood. "Go with your gut, Rene, it is big enough after all the festivities."

"Cheeky buggers, go and practise your Spanish, Yorkie, one night only please."

The morning briefing finished; Yorkie decided to take his Lada down to the local garage on the outskirts of the town. It was off a roundabout on a very small industrial estate but clearly visible from the road. The sign local garage and the name of Charles Lacoste; the owner, in capitals. The small office adjoined the repair shop with a second unit probably for vehicles waiting to be repaired. Yorkie parked in one of

186

the three vacant bays and walked into the office where Charles was sat looking at his computer. He knew him as he had his brake pads done recently but he felt they were still not up to standard.

"Morning, Charles, can you please give a quick check on my brakes again, take it for a spin if you like." He saw the other mechanic changing a tyre but apart from that the garage was quiet.

"Okay, but will be better to get it up on the ramp when Germaine has finished changing that tyre."

Yorkie handed him the keys but decided to let him take his Lada out while he spoke to the other mechanic. Charles continued but speaking to Germaine. "Put the kettle on when you've finished that tyre and put the car outside so when I get back, we can double check with the old Lada on the ramp."

Yorkie knew they had no respect for his Lada, but it didn't bother him. He waited in the reception room spotting the remnants of pot smoking in the metal waste bin. He found bottles of alcohol in a cupboard while Germaine reversed the car to park up. Yorkie was simply in an inquisitive mood. Germaine dishevelled, unshaven, joined Yorkie and flicked the switch on a rusty old kettle.

"Not much work on by the looks of things."

Germaine grunted. "Small town but they seem prepared to pay higher prices at the agents."

There was no Lada agency nearby and looking at the state of the workshop and lack of work, Yorkie wondered how they made it pay.

"Have you got any vehicles in the other unit waiting for work?"

It was a polite enquiry, but Germaine seemed agitated by it. Yorkie could see him searching for a reply. "Just one vehicle for a bit of paintwork."

At that point the Lada appeared, and Charles drove it straight onto the ramp as Germaine guided him leaving the kettle to boil. Charles was straight into action talking to Germaine, "Just check that offside calliper, I will make the drink, tea or coffee, Yorkie?"

"Tea." Then he noticed it was not Yorkshire. "No, make it a coffee, one sugar thanks."

Yorkie waited for his coffee but had time to ask Charles a simple question. "Have you got a colour chart; my Lada needs a re-spray after this winter?"

"Sorry we do not do much paintwork, bad for the lungs and takes up too much of our time."

Yorkie acknowledged the comment and wondered how much damage the smoking was doing. As Germaine came in Yorkie did not bring up the paintwork requirement but asked, "Find anything?"

"Yes, the calliper was sticking so it is released now, do not forget those discs will need replacing next time as well. Why not change it for a French car?"

Yorker smiled and sipped his coffee while Germaine slurped his tea. "No charge for that seeing as we have done your pads recently." Charles was clearly alert to the fact that Yorkie had produced a twenty euro note as a thank you anyway. "No need for an invoice." Yorkie left as soon as the Lada was removed from the ramp. He went straight back to the station to see Lisa.

"Lisa, I need your help to follow up a hunch."

"What had you in mind?"

"That garage on the outskirts?"

"Charles Lacoste?"

"Yes, they have a second unit and I want to see what is in it."

"Why did you not look while you were there? I think the garage has second-hand spares as that is where I got those cheap used tyres for the Spanish van."

"I was going to ask but it was padlocked, and I just had that gut feeling they would find a way to avoid that scenario. I did not have a warrant either."

"They are not liked by the locals as they seem like cowboys and are known for their smoking and drinking habits. I take my car to the agents." She gave him her lingering stare, "So what do you think is inside this unit, they only have drunk and disorderly convictions and both of them have done community work on court orders. Not too serious."

"Is Rene around?"

"No, he's gone to the police station at Laruns and will visit his mother in a home. She is not in the best of health and her memory is fading."

"Just trust me on this. Let me come with you and get an emergency court order to search any local unit/garage as Pau Police believe some stolen cars are being hidden in this area."

"Wow, that is a bit much, why the hurry?"

"You know that speed can be of an essence. I asked the other mechanic, Germaine, what was in the unit. He said a vehicle for some paintwork. While he did some work on my car, I asked Charles for a colour match to do my Lada. He said they did not do paintwork. I am hoping they do not discuss my conversations, but they have no work so the conversation could uncover my inquisitive questions."

"I suppose a bit of meddling with a few local garages is good police work. They might even respect us for actually doing some investigative work. I will get that order as an emergency, and we ought to do them as our second call to show they have not been singled out."

"Good idea, Lisa, we will use the official police car for this one."

It only took Lisa nearly an hour to get the search warrant. Yorkie had got the police car checked over for the basics. In particular the lights and sirens. He had half the village looking outside by the time they

189

stopped at their first house less than half a mile away. They even took in an extra stop with the siren on they entered the small industrial estate that Yorkie had been in two hours earlier. It was almost lunch time, but Yorkie straddled the entrance, so it was difficult for anyone to get in or out. Lisa deliberately checked another unit before Yorkie left the car with the blue light on to stroll over with Lisa to the garage. The owners of the only other unit now watching in anticipation of a visit after the garage.

Charles was outside first. "What the hell is this all about?"

Lisa explained as though it was her case. "It is my job to check if any stolen cars are hidden in the Arudy area, just routine, but we do have a warrant."

She showed it off and Charles relaxed as Germaine now appeared with a glass of red wine which he left on the window sill.

The main garage was empty of work, but she moved over to the padlocked unit. "Hope we do not need to use the cutters to gain access?"

Charles was quick to react. "Of course not, we just have our own spare car in there."

He duly unlocked the padlock and all four of them walked in. The car was covered over but Charles lifted the front up to show the French number plate. Just check that on your computer it is registered to me. It is the only vehicle in here we do not deal in stolen ones. Confidently he put the cover back over as Lisa checked on her iPad. Germaine now had a more confident look and moved back towards the exit intimating for all to do the same. Lisa gave Yorkie a disgruntled look and moved in the same direction. Charles tried to guide Yorkie in the same direction as Lisa confirmed all okay with the vehicle.

Yorkie acted in agreeance with everyone but then turned back to the car startling them. "Just want to see what that paintwork is like Germaine told me about?" He removed the cover with swish, as if he was a toreador, but the vehicle looked in good condition. The blackened windows alarmed Lisa and Yorkie. Yorkie was in full flow now. "Keys, please, I need to check inside."

"Why?" asked Charles as Germaine picked up a large ratchet.

There was panic in Germaine's eyes, he put some WD40 over the ratchet looking and moving towards Yorkie.

Yorkie was no fool. "You see, Germaine, I was caught pinching cars around my town in North Yorkshire and we put false plates on our main car, so it seemed they came from South Yorkshire: a poorer area."

Lisa had now grasped what Yorkie was thinking, but she had left her gun behind. Charles looked like a man waiting his jail sentence, but Germaine was raising his ratchet and walking towards Yorkie.

Yorkie remained cool. "Do you want ten years or more in jail, I was just like you, this is my call and Lisa will agree. I have a way out for you both if you both listen."

Germaine was mad with rage and moved with intent, but Charles moved even quicker and pincered his arm with the ratchet in and the two of them fell to the ground. Charles was the businessman. "Let him speak, just listen we have been caught."

It took a while for Germaine to sit quietly with Charles and await Yorkie's verdict.

"I bet you have either a revolving number plate or one to fix with Spanish plates. It is a straightforward deal. The garage closes for the rest of the day. Lisa will take you both for two hours at the houses of Pauline Poure and Christine Balfour the two ladies whom you stole, frightened and caused injuries to when unlawfully taking their handbags. They could be your mother or grandmother. You will talk to them, apologise and listen to their stories. You will not smoke or drink alcohol here again. I will clear this garage of drink and the mess. You will employ a local cleaning lady.

You will not use second-hand spares and charge for new. You will earn the respect of your fellow citizens and perhaps you will see your business prosper. The alternative is you will be booked immediately and charged accordingly. Jail is definite and a fine and your business is finished."

Germaine was seeing the offer in a better light as the words from Yorkie settled and his friend in tears, shaking with guilt of the actions they had done to support themselves in monetary terms.

People were congregating near the unmanned police car. Vehicles waiting to get in. Yorkie went outside and moved the car. If Lisa was in a state of shock, she did not show it. She guided the two miscreants to the police car and left Yorkie to clear out the garage. The two ladies gave them both forgiveness, drinks and food. Lisa simply watched in amazement at the transformation of two naughty men who had strayed. To see them so repentant was a surprise to her. They listened to the stories the ladies were keen to share. The two hours turned in over three at each home. She wondered how Rene would view Yorkie's actions as he would have to be told. This sort of news would be out of date by the time the weekly newsletter arrived in people's letterboxes.

Chapter 29   Monday, January 9th, 2017

It was 9 am at Arudy Police Station on another snowy Monday morning. Rene was in his chair, Lisa had made the teas, *again*. Yorkie arrived in five minutes, late *again*. Rene started the informal meeting.

"So are you all set for the journey, it could be a long drive. I expect you'll be staying overnight somewhere."

"Don't think we're sharing a bed," Lisa said, "I'll book two rooms going, we might make it back in one go when we return." Lisa was adamant about the booking arrangements, but Rene was in a jovial mood.

"Now, Lisa, do you think he wants to climb over you when he has got the Pyrenees to keep him healthy and fit?"

Lisa was equally as quick. "At least he will not run out of breath like you would."

"What vehicle shall we take, daft question, my Lada, weather still bad. Are we still doing narcotics?"

"Yes, do not forget your guns, I am still worried where this might lead. Trafficking is big money, and some do not take prisoners, be careful. What is all this about not reporting these mechanics and charging them? It would be brownie points for us."

Lisa was quickly on the front foot glaring at Rene in her rare demanding almost domineering manner that caught Rene and Yorkie totally by surprise. "All men make mistakes," she said, looking straight at Rene but keeping whatever information she had on him to herself. "You see it was Yorkie who guessed what was going on."

Rene was in retreat and looked at Yorkie with an air of admiration and inquisitiveness, wanting to know more. Lisa continued. "You see, Rene, it takes a thief to catch a thief."

Lisa explained how Yorkie had stolen cars in his younger days before concluding "Would you like to lose your new bobby now?"

Rene sat motionless understanding that if they went to jail, they would simply try to re-educate them. Yorkie and Lisa had done all that without the red tape and anxiety that might result in a close-knit community. It was time for Rene the station commander to make his verdict.

"You two had better get ready for your trip to Spain. Case closed no need to record the incidents."

They finished the meeting and drinks. Lisa finished off some other paperwork as Yorkie prepared his Lada. It was 11 am when they drove out of Arudy for Spain.

It was a slow journey in the Lada across the mountain roads, stopping off at addresses on their list, but so far, no luck. They found a cheap hotel where they managed a restless night and reached the empty farmhouse at 10 am the following morning. Out front was a for sale sign, an estate agent in Mojacar. They rang, explained they were from Narcotics, it was important. Could someone bring the keys.

It wasn't certain anyone would.

But another hour and a car – turned up. A woman in a crisp grey suit. Hair cut into a blonde bob climbed out, face stoic, clearly not happy. They had wandered around and found old bikes and an empty pigeon hutch. The woman seemed uncertain, reluctant as they flashed their identity badges and finally they followed her inside.

It was cleaner than they expected. The agent said they had it cleaned to help the sale. A cousin who lived nearby was the only relative. Lisa took photos inside and out. They could see nothing obvious to help them. But then again, what were they looking for?

"Where did any paperwork go, diaries, notes, files, books, was there another car here?" Yorkie was on the ball.

"Everything went to this address." The lady from the agency gave Yorkie a piece of paper with the local address on. "Thought you might want this."

They thanked her for coming so quickly and in ten minutes were at the other address. The elderly couple found some papers and diaries and offered them a drink. They had tea and went through the paperwork. Lisa found Juan's address but nothing else.

"What were her hobbies, and did she have a vehicle?"

"She loved cycling and going on the tours. Travelled all over. Her car never came back, she died in a motorway crash near Limoges. They said the car was a write-off. We have no idea why she was near Limoges; did you say drugs? Did not think she was involved with that. She never left Spain except for those tour holidays. She did like to go to the north to get wine. We could never work out why she went so far. Then the pigeons, she had a few of them. Said they could fly from North Africa quicker than the planes, because the message was door to door."

Yorkie took more interest. "Why North Africa?"

"She never said, I think she found it fascinating. The last two pigeons came from France and Spain as we had to ring Limoges Police Station, according to the message. We then found out what had happened to her. They sent us some ashes in an urn."

"Do you have the other message?"

"I believe we do, my wife told me to keep it as it was her final words."

He pottered about but it was his wife that found it in a disused teapot, "Juan killed in accident, M at SH in B on way back. P & P have 1 left Nov 19."

Yorkie asked to keep it, but they refused, so Lisa wrote the message down. Yorkie again made a good point. "That message was meant for someone else because it came here. So, when she returned, it would be sent on via another of her pigeons. What happened to the pigeons?"

They looked at a tureen and smiled.

"You see we do not like them and did not know what to do with them. A friend took four, he said one never came back. She was always sending them from her tours with notes in. Usually, which rider had yellow or green, sometimes taking all twenty-four of them. Car must have smelt rotten. The notes became her diary. We went once a week to check on them and take the notes off."

Yorkie enquired, "Have you got any from years ago 2014 Tour De France started in Yorkshire for example." They went to a back room and brought a large box. "All in here."

Lisa went to work on the box as Yorkie asked more questions. "How did she get her pigeons to or from North Africa?"

"Sorry do not know, I think it was only a few times a year March and November mainly and—"

"Got it, S to join us from W Jul 5" then another "Lost S to P Jul 12 sad." It was Lisa who'd interrupted.

It was getting to lunchtime and he offered some wine. Lisa refused but said Yorkie could have one as she would drive the first bit. He brought a nice bottle of St Emilion. Yorkie had one large glass. They both noticed Juan's stamp on the label.

They left in the afternoon, so booked a stop with two rooms at a cheap chain near the motorway. They ate in the restaurant nearby. They could solve the Yorkshire clues Sarah to join us from Whitby and the one a week later lost Sarah to Philip. The other M at SH in B on way back they struggled, perhaps Rene would solve it.

"The wine bottles with Juan's stamp. Find those wherever would be a positive result," Lisa pointed out.

"Especially near the service station in Bergerac," concluded Yorkie. "That is where we hit a dead end, and he is so far out of his route. Perhaps that is where he drops off the girl and the four cases of rioja. He goes to Bordeaux next, stays overnight then to St Emilion and bingo – 120 cases. If he was dropping off wine in Bergerac, he would have done Bordeaux first, because St Emilion is nearer to Bergerac. Of course, he offloads the girl first because he unloads all his wine in Bordeaux. Why am I so stupid? Remember the wine merchant in St Emilion buys nothing off him. The person would be discovered when unloading."

Lisa tried to work it out. "I am tired tell me tomorrow."

The next day Lisa who was normally brilliant at working things out was lost with maps and Yorkie's enthusiasm. Just tell Rene and I will see if I get it. Yorkie had phoned Rene and asked for a 4 pm meeting due to the distance and timings driving back. He repeated his assessment.

"Let me make it simple. If you had a person in that van, would you offload all your wine with that person in the van? Of course not. The ticket time of his fill up was the morning at Rue D'Airport, Bergerac. He arrived at the Bordeaux wine merchant in the late afternoon."

Lisa got it this time. Rene was impressed. "I should have seen that I am losing it."

"As well as your hair," Lisa pointed out. "What about this riddle M at SH in B on way back?"

Rene was trying his best. "Bordeaux or Bergerac or what?"

Yorkie's turn to add his opinion. "If a person is delivered from southern Spain to France via Juan, when does the money transfer take place and who gets that money?"

"Juan delivers and he gets paid. Paula wants her share so calls on the Saturday 19th as per the note but Juan is dead. For some reason they are going to a chateau in Limoges so need to collect their share on the way back." Rene was on fire. "I have cracked it, and you helped Yorkie, M is for Money SH is for Safe House and B most likely Bergerac where he filled up. Could be anywhere in Bergerac."

"There was no money in Juan's van except his pocket money. What has happened to that girl and where is the money and those cases of wine?" said Yorkie.

Rene pondered. "You need to go to Bergerac Police Station as Narcotics, do some digging and go back to the service station again, see what you come up with, well done you two. Suggest drugs are being trafficked by youngsters, it is more common than people realise."

Yorkie and Lisa concurred. "We are a team, sir. We need your back-up here in case you get more phone calls."

"One last thing," Lisa asked, "can I do a map of Juan's eight pigeons on the board please?"

Rene and Yorkie looked puzzled but agreed. She did a simple chalk map. No. 1 halfway to Bergerac, 2. from Bergerac, 3. Bordeaux 4. Evening b/b 5. Morning before leaving b/b 6. St Emilion 7. North of Pau at service station.

Rene and Yorkie together, "And?"

"Both wine merchants and the b/b said he released the pigeons before he left."

They still looked puzzled; Lisa continued. "Juan's mother said she heard the bell ring at about 8 pm, which is the pigeon he released at the Pau service station. The note said back in four hours."

Now Rene and Yorkie were concentrating and still wondering what was coming next.

"So, Juan intended to release pigeon number eight after his last stop, our layby. The van was facing the way out and was leaving, it was in second gear, then went down the ravine. The pigeon was still in the van. He was dead before he drove off."

They were gobsmacked; it was Rene who spoke. "Pretty good for a secretary recently-turned-policewoman, I should give you a rise, but it proves pigeons do talk."

In WW1 a pigeon called Cher Ami was shot in the chest and leg where the message was. The pigeon again got the message delivered despite shrapnel and gas saving many French lives. Cher Ami was awarded the French "Croix de Guerre" medal for heroic bravery

Chapter 30   Monday, January 9th

The committee met in a Mole room to discuss general events. There was an air of uncertainty and general suspicion leaving a cloud over the village. It was the American who saw an opportunity.

"We need an internal security commander with carte blanche authority to investigate anything or matters we consider worth looking at."

The people at the table looked at each other. The silence and general expressions implied this was an interesting idea. A rare, good comment from the American.

Doc responded. "Had you anyone in mind that we could possibly agree on?"

"Yes, but no point in putting a name forward unless we agree on the proposal."

The beauty about this committee was anyone could put a proposal on the table without a seconder. It simply went to the vote. They all agreed 5–0 in favour; which was a surprise to the American. Now he had to put a name forward.

"I think we can placate Mr Trump here and get an extension of his money by introducing our own Metis."

Most on the committee did not know Metis. He worked in the American booth, kept very much to himself. A man of few words.

The American continued. "He moved from Quebec to Montana, you gave him the nickname, Metis, because in French it translates as 'mixed blood between the Cree Indian tribe and Europeans'. He is excellent at tracking on the ground and on computers. He has a hereditary instinct for discovering. A natural investigator, an ideal candidate to be our own internal security commander. In these uncertain and strange times, it is time we looked after ourselves better. If Mr Trump thinks he has his own spy at RAID in a powerful position, do you think he will pull out immediately?"

This unexpected proposal had them all looking at the American with agreeable smiles. The idea and person recommended ticked many boxes.

The Englishman had his say. "We should interview him as a committee and explain his position should we agree."

Jean then added, after checking Metis's history on her computer, "We normally advertise for anyone suitable, but in this case, I think as a committee, should we agree, it is a logical appointment."

"Perhaps he needs an assistant?" Doc said.

Discussions followed and after many suggestions it was decided a loner could work better to begin with. They interviewed Metis who gleefully accepted his new position subject to Trump's approval. The American had booked the flight to be at the inauguration and to confirm at the next committee meeting on February 6th that Trump would not pull the plug on RAID just yet.

* * *

Tariq was thrilled to receive a note from his outpost – via pigeon. *Three 'ladies' will arrive in five hours.* He then ordered two of his young warriors to take three pigeons back and relieve those on sentry duty for four nights. Tariq was equally as good as Danielle at organising rotas even for his pigeons. It was time for his ladies to prepare food for when they arrived. It had been a long and tiring journey for Elena the daughter of the deceased Aqbal. Tariq let the ladies eat, drink and rest first. He would see Elena in the morning. but now he wanted to discuss the detail with his two lady warriors who had brought her to his HQ. After supper they reported to Tariq. Tariq began his interrogation. "Tell me in detail where you went, who you saw and exactly what you achieved."

One of the warriors became the spokeswoman.

"We went first to the home of Mohammed Aqbal to meet the grieving widow before Elena finished school as instructed. She was distraught. We explained how we had been sent by you, and the only way to get revenge was to plant someone at the establishment in France to gather information. She was happy with this idea but less so when we explained her daughter would be an ideal candidate. She knew her husband sent messages to you with the pigeons but became worried when we said Elena would need a new identity as they would not allow the daughter of a known ISIL supporter into their premises. As we spoke, she wailed incessantly. We showed her a large wad of money and told her we would find her a new daughter if the plan was successful. We had drinks and all this took longer than expected. We told her during the school holidays Elena would come for training and she might never see her again. More wailing and we thought we were failing in our task."

Tariq interrupted. "Had Elena arrived back yet?"

"On cue, Commander, she arrived at that moment when she fully understood what we had in mind for her daughter. She welcomed her with open arms, crying but telling her we were going to take her for a special holiday when school term finished in a few days. We were surprised by her sudden change in temperament and even more surprised Elena did not question her."

Tariq smiled. "You women understand what is best for you. The mother and daughter would have heard how I deal with people who do not follow my orders. They would recognise you both as my warriors. Then what?"

"We went to the births' registry office and found over three hundred females born within a year of Elena's birthday. We then contacted your source, Omar, in the police force. He is very loyal to you as he wished us to tell you. He remembers how you were on duty protecting and advising Geoffrey and Cherie Houston when they first arrived seventeen years ago. He sends his commiserations. More importantly he scoured the computer for us and came up with only ten possibilities. We trailed, spotted and analysed a few but they were too small, too big, different in small ways, so we never even went to see any parents. This kept us clean till we found Miss Hiba Lazaar. We spoke to her parents who did not like her boyfriend at all. Omar did well as they are keen supporters of our cause. It did not take them long to agree for their daughter to be given a new identity. They were pleased to receive the reward."

"Well done, did you give Omar my instructions?"

"Yes. He did see Elena and her mother before we left with her. He is going to check all the videos of the airport and any near the Aqbal's home. He says it could take months so as not to arouse suspicion. He did ask questions at the café where the meeting took place before he died. The only information is the bartender remembers a tall eastern European-sounding lady, very attractive asking for Mohammed Aqbal. Elena never saw her as this woman left while she was ordering some food. There are no cameras near this café."

Tariq was in deep thought. "Thank you, my trusted warriors. If we have any spare slaves, you may choose, for your pleasure and entertainment."

Tariq knew he was in no rush to get more information from his contact in the police force. It would be many months before Elena was re-educated and ready for her new role. Tariq now had to convince her. Tariq retired to his bed alone, it would be after breakfast that Elena duly arrived in Tariq's room. Knocking first and waiting for the summons she stood in front of the formidable commander.

"Thank you for agreeing to come here, did you sleep well?"

"Yes, thank you, Sir."

"This is your new identity: Miss Hiba Lazaar." Tariq waited for a reaction, but there was none. "You are here because I want to find the person who authorised the killing of your father. We are suspicious that they knew he was an informer for ISIL. Therefore, if you applied for a job as your maiden name, the daughter of Mohammad Aqbal, you would have no chance of getting the job. Going in as Miss Hiba Lazaar you will have the opportunity for revenge."

She stood motionless. "The authorisation came from this Horticultural College in Clermont Ferrand, France. It is a base for hostage negotiations by whatever means they consider acceptable. I have lost my contacts, and some of my warriors. This is a dangerous mission. Your father, Mohammad, was murdered, and the hard drive stolen. We do not know why."

"I saw my father in the café; never saw the face of the woman he was talking to, never thought more about it."

She remained calm.

"An operative was blown to pieces and I lost my hostages and another soldier. I need a contact in the Tunisian team."

"I am a primary school teacher, my name is Elena Aqbal," she said.

"I lost twenty warriors here and in France."

"I am a primary school teacher, my name is Elena Aqbal."

Tariq continued. "Your mother is a widow."

"I am a primary school teacher, my name is Elena Aqbal."

"You have no father."

"I am a primary school teacher, my name is Elena Aqbal."

"The woman that organised this might be alive."

"I am a primary school teacher, my name is Elena Aqbal."

"She has taken my daughter and I want her back."

"I am a warrior, I am a warrior, I am Hiba Lazaar, I will avenge for you and for my family." Raising her arms. "Tariq, Tariq, Tariq." Hiba kissed his feet, then with both hands saluted as per the tradition in prayer and humbleness.

"Welcome to my family, you have a lot to learn first before you start work in Tunis at the embassy. From there you will apply for the vacancy at YMCA as a Tunisian operative. For the next two months you will learn how to shoot, detonate explosives, how to fly a helicopter, how to keep pigeons and how to seduce people of either sex to gain information carefully. This is not a sprint. We will not make the same mistakes as before. It took many years to get one on the committee, he died on a mission to Somalia. That is a lie. There are four men left who know something. With your helicopter training, you will be a natural applicant. You will have a mobile phone, so it seems tracking you is not an issue. You are now proficient with computers. Be careful with emails as you will have your own iPad and everything you send will be tracked/viewed. Let them decide where you should sleep. You might not come back. This is a tough assignment; do you still want to do it?"

"I am a warrior, I am Hiba Lazaar, I am your servant, oh master."

"Good, work starts today."

"What about my dental and health records?"

"They have been taken care of, even your fingerprints and eye recognition will match. You are officially Hiba Lazaar with a new passport for you when you return to Tunis. It might be you never see your real mother again."

"I am Hiba Lazaar, my new mother is alive, and I will see her."

Tariq smiled. "I hope your new mother does not mind the lessons I will teach you."

"I am your servant, oh master, your wish is my command."

* * *

In Tunis Mrs Aqbal opened her door. "Oh, Elena, it is so good to see you, we must go to the café as usual and talk."

They went to the café that her husband had used. No one recognised the slight difference. The veils hid her face but even the way she spoke was similar. If anyone was watching, it was mother and daughter. At the primary school, the headmistress had only to change the cleaner and the cook. It was a small school with new children. The headmistress was rewarded by Tariq's ladies who saw her. She would never let on as a Tariq supporter. The mother knew she might never see her real daughter again but had gained another.

* * *

Hiba Lazaar's parents were middle class and supporters of Tariq's cause. It was lucky for them that their daughter had finished a degree at university in human resources. She had decided to take a two-month break with friends in Algeria before starting her new job in March at the Embassy as a junior clerk, linked to the French embassy. She had finished with her boyfriend which was genuine and fortuitous as the parents saw the switch as a brilliant opportunity to do that. They had an extra amount of cash and were planning a summer holiday. The return of this new daughter in March intrigued them for such a devious operation. They would never enquire. If anyone else did, they would say their daughter was seeking to travel and experience a more active life. She was even taking helicopter lessons as her urge for excitement and exploration of life was growing. She might have been a year older, but being the same height and build was perfect. A year's difference at that age was insignificant. Tariq's ladies had done a first-class job.

* * *

The New Year at YMCA had brought some changes. A new hall was built behind the apartments. It was used for schooling for all children living in the village. They allowed others from nearby to make up the numbers. It could be used for other activities like whist drives or bridge, bingo and theatre. The hamlet with the four houses was now the homes of Jack and family, the Swede and the two cleaners with their families. Those that had to move out were not too pleased. It was a pleasant spot with the single-road access, near the woods and streams, with walks along the old volcanoes. The four of them met for a surveillance discussion. It was agreed to have joint alarms so if they were all at home, they could become a unit within two minutes. That was the target; with practice it was four minutes. They identified areas and chopped some trees down for better viewing, telling their children it would be stored for firewood, which it was, but might last fifteen years. The Swede that came up with an escape route. "We tell no one and we do a tunnel from the houses."

They all agreed a great idea but how to do it and where should it finish. The cleaners wanted it house to house as it would link everyone. Jack suggested the wood. The Swede thought down to the stream. The children need to know, and it would become common knowledge via school and loose tongues. They agreed to tell the wives and see what they thought and have another meeting. It was an extremely difficult place to suddenly do a surprise attack, given the location. As it turned out the main committee decided to mothball Maggie due to her age. She was to be hidden in the forest, in a hangar, with a roof that would open. Apart from them – no one else would know. Ready for duty in case of a surprise attack. Records would show of course Maggie had been officially scrapped.

The main entrances now had two rather than one on duty at each point twenty-four/seven, all year long. The new committee member had been deferred until Trump signed to pull out, rather than gesticulating he was going to. If the American left, that made three, so decisions could be made. Jean was efficient, caring and popular. The Swede apologised for thinking she was the traitor after overhearing the end of her conversation on the phone during the round-up. Jean, even though happily married, imagined a bit of entente cordial with the Swede would not go amiss. The Swede was too busy on active duty.

Jack was off missions due to his shoulder injury. It would be a month before his next assessment. He was happy to conduct operations from his desk in the hangar. The trauma counselling was important for Suzette. They were amazed how quickly his daughter got over it. The village nicknamed her 'Rubber Ball' because she was so active, and she bounced back so quickly from the kidnapping. She loved her nickname, and even Jack started to call her that. Because they now lived at the hamlet as part of the village, Rubber Ball found the energy and atmosphere in the hangar spellbinding as helicopters burst into life and armed men went off on a journey. She would watch and ask her daddy, "I want to fly one day and be able to shoot like Mari, please teach me."

Jack knew this was not what Suzette wanted but Rubber Ball had made her mind up. She was a daddy's girl, a tom boy with all the girlie attributes. Jack wondered is it time to move and seek a different occupation.

* * *

Mari lived alone in a secluded property near a small hamlet called Villeneuve. In a valley with land for her helicopter it had many plus points. It was close to Lalinde and Tremolat where the Vieux Logis was her local favourite eating place. The security around her house was high. A fob allowed the solid gates to open, and her Porsche purred the short distance to Tremolat. She parked in the car park next to the Vieux Logis, opposite the field that she often used for clients from Bergerac Airport. She loved to dine there and seduce any rich men available. The staff were used to her. Sometimes if rooms were available, she would stay, especially if she saw a possible conquest. Only wealthy people stayed here so when she told them her bottle of champagne cost 300 euros, they knew exactly what she meant. The problem was when the rooms were all taken so she decided to look around the village. A small property called "Lou Cantou" would be available when the English owners returned from a winter's cruise. The son keeping watch while they were away. This was fun for her and now with less work, she was going to enjoy herself. She was looking forward to the summer months when she could offer the champagne in this rented accommodation just off the square, behind a pizzeria. If you can get away on your own for a walk you know where I will be, the line she had in her mind. The money not the reason, just like her helicopter, Mari needed to be serviced on a regular basis.

The events at the chateau pleased her. When she helped Jack, she thought how nice it would be to tender his wounds for a week at Le Vieux Logis or at her home. She knew that was not going to happen, but Jack was the solid type which she would ride with relish. Her trips to St Agatha were frequent and well rewarded. Life was good, her next trip was scheduled for the Saturday and Sunday January 21st and 22nd.

* * *

Lisa had a letter from her sister, it read: *I still take Rufus out for his walks around the chateau, the church and the woods. Thanks for the Christmas presents, still got a few bottles left. We also had a lot of activity on December 22nd. A helicopter came again and there seemed to be fireworks and a flare. That was just before the procession for the local wedding. She looked beautiful. Before that, maybe I was mistaken, but I thought I saw a man in just his pants and socks in the chateau grounds, but the bushes spoilt my view. Must have been a dare as it was so cold. Then later a little girl was running and nearly fell over. Another helicopter came later, but the wedding had finished by then. Two helicopters left and low and behold much later another one landed, but it was too dark to see. The next day I talked to a gorgeous Swede who was walking near the chateau. He told me the company he worked for were considering making an offer if it came on the market and were renting it to test the suitability. I gave him one of my cakes. They stayed a few days and flew off. It has been quiet here since then. See you soon I hope, love Jennifer xx.*

Chapter 31

Thursday, January 12th

Lisa drove this time; to Bergerac Police Station to arrive at 1 pm. Travelling on a Thursday was better than a Friday. They booked two rooms at a cheap B&B on the outskirts of Bergerac, near Rue D'Airport and were expected back for 4 pm Friday for a debrief with Rene. They had not booked an appointment with the station in case it gave them time to delve into the validity of this new narcotics section. It would be more difficult to pass the test with an existing force. They went to reception and showed their identity cards and swiftly back into their pockets. They waited fifteen minutes before they were ushered into a room. They accepted an offer for coffees. A policewoman who had a solid and tough-looking frame was joined by another male officer. The lady asked, "How can we help you?"

Yorkie had the same photographs he had shown at the Horticultural College. "This man we think was murdered in a layby. We believe he had drugs in his van from North Africa. They arrived via southern Spain from this lady with the rings on. We have a photo of her here from her cousin's house. We also think young children were involved in helping distribute those drugs. Our enquiries come to a dead end here. The last fuel receipt was here in Bergerac Rue de L'Airport Friday morning November 18th last year. Do you have any contacts of drug activity in this town, or have you seen this man and his van before for any reason?"

"Can I see your identity badges please, I have never heard of a narcotics team from Arudy, especially when Pau is so close."

"We are not officially in bed with Pau, we prefer to be low key. You can check with our station commander, Rene, if you like. He felt we were wasting Pau's time and we are doing routine enquiries. If there is anything we will pass on to Pau." Yorkie acted as the spokesman.

"I will go and get the files on drug activity."

She returned shortly afterwards with two files and a computer. She booted up the computer and eventually found the information she was looking for.

"We have more drug problems than people think, the hotel near the station and streets close to it are full of this problem. From here it filters out to the countryside. We try and keep it in check and manage it rather than prevent it with arrests. They always reoffend so it is about control. Here you are I will type in Rue D'Airport. Number 64 is under surveillance. We never get a problem at the ecole on that street. Schools yes they are all listed, and everyone has one or two families with history." Lisa was taking notes. "We go into the schools now and do talks about it, rewarding and successful. We now have a large database including Bordeaux. Too much wine is a bigger problem!"

"When we called at that petrol station to check the area, is there more than one ecole on that street?" said Lisa.

She checked her database "No."

"Well, it was padlocked and did not seem to be in use."

"Maybe that is why we do not get any complaints or calls."

"So, you do not do any talks there. Who owns the ecole?"

She went back to the reception. "I will let you know they are ringing the Marie. Is there anything else you want to know?"

"No, this drugs problem has a familiar pattern, need to stop it at the schools, well done you seem to be doing a good job." Yorkie's turn to contribute.

They prepared to leave and waited near the reception. The receptionist answered the phone and wrote down two names.

"Are you wanting the owners of the ecole on Rue D'Airport?"

"Yes."

"They are Edith Tavare, same address and Cecilia Jabut who lives in Marmande."

As she handed them the addresses, another policewoman, who had come through the main entrance had overheard the conversation. As Yorkie and Lisa left, she asked the receptionist what they had wanted. She said who they had been talking to. She seemed agitated and went outside, took the car number plate and made a phone call.

They filled up then parked up in a bay at the service station. It was late afternoon and they went to number 64 first. It was a large house with covered windows, empty beer bottles against the bins that were full. Yorkie opened the bin and saw several used syringes, while Lisa took some photos. The door opened and a man with lots of tattoos told them to piss off as they were on private property. It seemed a good idea to avoid any confrontation as others in the house were asking if anything was wrong. They retreated and walked casually down to the ecole. It was still padlocked and looked empty. It was Yorkie who noticed a car with someone in taking photos of them, but also had no. 64 in view. Lisa went in the service station and asked the same girl as before. "What time does the postman come in the morning?"

"Between 10.30 and 11 normally; he does the town end first. He parks his van and walks around for about twenty minutes."

Time was getting on. They could not see the postman till the next day so decided to return to the hotel and decide where to eat. They agreed to try a restaurant on Rue de L'Ancien Pont. They chose one next to the tobacco museum called La Villa Laetitia. It was a good choice, mainly fish on the menu which they both ordered, washed down with a bottle of local white wine. It was quiet enough in the restaurant for them to discuss the day's events.

"Did you see the man in the car taking photos, but probably watching no. 64?" Yorkie said.

"No, what were you thinking?"

"It must have been the surveillance team they mentioned. I hope we did not spoil it for them. I think we need to get into that school and have a look round. Did those owners mean anything to you?"

Lisa thought for a while. "No, and you are right we need to have a look round, or simply knock on the door. I think an early night and then go and see the postman first, they will know a lot about the area."

"Good thinking, Lisa."

The next morning after breakfast they parked up at the service station. Yorkie saw a different vehicle still with someone with a camera with a view of no. 64. This time it was a lady. It was 11:15 when they showed their badges to the postman. He was all too pleased to help. He mentioned no. 64 and some houses near the station were suspicious, but it was not his job.

"I have a job to do, can I go?"

"Just a few questions, how often do you deliver to the ecole, it's padlocked every time we come, it doesn't look like a real school?"

"There are sometimes about five people in there. I am told it is a specialist school so used occasionally. Not much to deliver, it used to be a P.O Box number but not now."

"We are investigating a death near our village, and there is a link around here, can you remember the names on the envelopes or any letters from Spain by any chance?"

"Let me think, names. I have no mail today and my memory is not so good."

Lisa produced a twenty euro note. "Sorry to have taken up your time, have a drink on us."

"Just remembered, she had the same first name as my mother: Edith someone, I think it began with a T. Now the Spanish letters I will ask at the depot, three of us do this run and if I get any information, I will contact you."

Yorkie gave him his card. "There will be another drink if your colleague remembers anything."

They went back to Bergerac station to double check they were not spoiling the surveillance. They saw the policewoman who had previously enquired about them as they left. She was clearly not happy with them. Lisa apologised and then suggested to Yorkie they might stay one more night.

"Where are you staying? I can recommend some nice restaurants. That ecole is used by a nun for scripture work; so is not attended very often. Because of the local drug problem, it is padlocked. We have surveillance teams in there sometimes so please keep away. They can get very touchy with people interfering. I am on that team, so can you leave it to us. You can see we often work in plain clothes."

They left and rang Rene. "It seems you are not wanted and just the same dead end, give me those names again was it Edith Tavare and Cecilia Jabut from Marmande."

"Yes. I will ring back soon."

Twenty minutes later Rene rang them back.

"Edith Tavare occupation nun, no criminal record. Cecilia Jabut owns an agency in Bordeaux for ladies only. Just been fined for assaulting a member of staff and in the same paper one of her ladies died in a boat accident last year off the coast of Tunisia. We can do a debrief when you come back."

"I just want to see if there are any wine bottles or other clues in that ecole. If we can break into a chateau and not get caught, I am sure we can sneak in that ecole, quick check and out. Best to do it at night."

"You guys be careful, looks like Monday morning debrief."

"We will go back to the service station and see which postman is on."

They booked another night at reception and left for the service station. It was a different postman, but all he could say was he thought he had delivered mail with Spanish stamps. Later they went sightseeing in Bergerac and saw Cyrano's statue. They had lunch and talked quietly about how to get in the ecole. They drove out to St Emilion for afternoon tea and back to the hotel for a rest. It was 1 am when they walked out, luckily no one on reception at that time. Any late arrivals had codes to get in and boxes with keys in. It took twenty minutes to walk to Rue D'Airport. There was a surveillance vehicle, and the service station was open. Only three cars in the forecourt. No cars in the front driveway of the ecole. They walked down an alleyway to the rear of the ecole away from the main road. The wall was too high for Lisa and nothing to gain height except her folded hands to give Yorkie a lift.

He whispered, "You stay here, I will find something to get back over, look around here for anything you might be able to throw over or use yourself. It is quiet so best I go now. I have my torch, Swiss knife, a cutter, some keys, your camera and my gun. Ten minutes maximum."

Yorkie landed safely. He was used to circumnavigating pools. The lights from the main road a help but not good if someone spotted him. He raced on tip toe to the back door. He could see no lights on in the ecole and there were no vehicles at the back. He found his knife and keys. He thought he should be a locksmith, the ease in which he opened the back door. Just like before – no alarm. He moved slowly from room to room, making sweeps with his torch; taking only a few pictures. There were desks and blackboards and books. It was certainly like an ecole. There was a hat stand with canes in another classroom with four desks. He went up the narrow stairs. Bedrooms clean and tidy, taking the occasional photo. Nothing out of the ordinary, so he came down. He was heading out, when there it was what he was looking for: a cellar door. It was behind the back door so when he had come in, the door swinging to the left had hidden it. As he pulled the cellar door, it happened.

A strike to the back of his head.

Shit.

Yorkie stumbled, instinctively raising his hands to cover his face as glass severed his arm. He screamed out as he felt a kick in his groin and another thud to the side of his head. He remembered nothing else till he awoke Monday morning in Bergerac Hospital.

* * *

Yorkie could not see at first, finally picking the fuzzy outlines of Lisa and Rene. His arm was bandaged, and his head ached. He saw the drip attached to his hand. He saw their lips moving but he could hear nothing. He felt Lisa hands on his and the softness of a warm kiss on his aching cheeks. Rene was sat just watching but smiling. Yorkie then had some pills put in his mouth and Lisa put a mug to his mouth to help him drink it. Yorkie felt his ears popping and the faces had voices. He recognised them. He felt a prick on his arm, he saw a woman in a nurse's outfit move away and he fell into a deep sleep.

* * *

"Funny place to hold a 9 am Monday morning meeting. At least we have not lost him. It must have been a nasty attack." Rene looked at Lisa as he spoke.

"Not half, it was a bottle of wine. They caught the druggy from no. 64 and arrested him. That woman we saw was on surveillance. Good thing she was. I heard the screaming but had to find something to get over the wall. I got there just before she did. The ambulance came quickly, they said I saved his life. He was losing so much blood I just slowed it down till they got there. My clothes were covered in blood. They were brilliant. I was upset as I felt I should have been with him. I cried all day yesterday, cannot sleep either. The doctor said the camera around his neck took one of the blows, otherwise that might have killed him."

"It was not your fault. You need to come back with me. I have brought an extra driver. Yorkie needs to rest. I will get the driver to bring you back on Wednesday. He should be a lot better by then according to the doctors."

"Thanks, do you mind if I stay, I need to mother him."

There were real tears in Lisa's eyes now and Rene held them back as he left to get back to the station. Yorkie just lay there; really not knowing how lucky he was to be alive. Rene phoned an old female friend. She was a trauma counsellor. Rene loved his little team. He did not need to drive back now he had the driver. Instead, he looked to the horizon, no words were spoken all the way back to Arudy. His driver did not mind Rene using his handkerchief to wipe away the tears as his heaving torso of sadness muttered, "At least they got the bastard."

Chapter 32

Lisa had spent some time back at the service station as an excuse to get fresh air. At the ecole there were two cars parked in the driveway; one of them a police car. She had introduced herself as 'Narcotics' and after the attack on Yorkie it did not make sense to go in and antagonise the local police force.

On the Tuesday morning, Yorkie was able to sit up and have the drip removed. The nurses were impressed by his recovery rate, being young and fit. While Lisa sat with him at the hospital, she rang Rene to say Yorkie was being allowed home the next day after the doctor's rounds.

"Only thing I remember was those tattoos on his arm, when I turned around," Yorke said, Lisa pulling the chair up closer to the bed.

"He has been arrested, the one we saw that came out to tell us to piss off. Your memory is good then, excellent."

"I was looking to see if one of Juan's stamps were on any of the bottles. I found the cellar door but never went down the stairs."

"The policewoman we met helped me, she gave me her number, I'll ask her; will ring later."

"No, do it now, you might as well, I am not out till tomorrow."

Lisa rang her and explained about the label on the bottles "Have you kept the bottle?"

"No, I will check with the station."

It was a good fifteen minutes later when Lisa received her reply. "Sorry, all the mess has been cleared up, I am at the ecole now, why not come down and have a look?"

Lisa saw Yorkie looking at her, nodding enthusiastically. "Yes, I will come now, it is a good walk."

As she stepped outside a few minutes later Lisa welcomed the crisp cold air and the brisk walk to the ecole. As she approached the entrance a car came out of was pulling off the driveway, but the police car was still there. The same woman.

"The cleaner has just left, you may have seen her."

"I saw a car, yes."

"Have a good look round then I will lock up and get back to surveillance of no. 64."

Lisa made her way down the steps into the cellar and its dampness. There was no wine. She checked all the rooms. The cleaner had done a good job, considering how much blood and wine there had been. Lisa felt for her camera, but Rene had taken it back to the station. He thought it might be safer there.

"Thanks for letting me look, I'll get back to the hospital, Yorkie wants fruit and chocolate. Should be out tomorrow, so pleased you were on surveillance that night, between us we saved him."

* * *

The policewoman made her way to the rear after making sure Lisa was well out of sight, slipping her mobile from the pocket of her coat.

"Hi, Cecilia, that should take twelve hours off your community service. She has left and they are going back tomorrow. If she had not have told me about Juan's stamp, they would get the connection. Good thing you took most of the wine. I have six bottles in the boot of my car. I will put them back in the cellar for you. The druggy wants paying next week, we should get him off the charge as they were entering illegally, and I saw him attack first. I was close to make sure he did not kill him, just as well I was and his associate. They will not be coming back. I will need paying as well. You did say your money was due soon."

"Thanks, good tip-off, I will give you extra next week, I take it the girl I arranged for you is doing fine."

"Yes, I am pleased. I will be having some wine with her tonight."

* * *

It was late Wednesday afternoon when Lisa helped Yorkie into Arudy station. Rene and his patrol men were waiting. "Thank God," he said in relief.

"I think all the local villages have sent a get-well card. A nice one here of a Lada about to be squashed at a scrap metal company. It just says thanks for helping us and putting us in the right direction Charles Lacoste and Germaine, do you want a new car yet?"

They all laughed. There were nearly a hundred cards, lots of chocolates and flowers.

"Bloody hell, but I have only just started here."

"You have done holidays here," Rene said. "You have saved people on the mountains. You are polite and attentive. We all love you."

There was clapping and more hugs from Lisa. Villagers had seen Lisa's car pulling out and they were appearing at the door and window with smiles of relief, thumbs-up signs. The two patrol men on duty at the door now. The old lady who had come from the bar offered to look after him. She was given directions back to where she had just come from.

223

Rene tried to make Yorkie take a week off, but he agreed on one condition.

"I am fit enough to walk here every morning. At least let me share in the debrief, then I will take the rest of the day off to recuperate."

It was agreed; and at least that way they could keep an eye on him.

"9 am tomorrow for us and 9.05 am for you, Yorkie."

They all smiled, and Yorkie shared out the flowers and chocolates before going home to take his tablets and rest. "Oh and you still need to tell me about your New Year climb."

* * *

Sister Edith was in a happy mood that Wednesday evening. She had decided tonight with some help it was time for Sister Helen's initiation. At the weekend it was over to the ecole and the week after Rochine would report to her. She reported first after dinner to Danielle.

"I have decided tonight to deal with Sister Helen. Have you any special requests you would like me to perform on her or you before we go to Bergerac on Saturday?"

"Yes," Danielle said, "we need to know which girls enjoy the same traits as you. It is important as some of our buyers like that. I suggest you choose two, but not Rochine, it is a bit early for her. Make sure Helen is not aware who they are that beat her. I need reports on Helen and the two girls for future reference. Do not forget it is you who is doing this. I am not aware of this. You are simply doing your standard initiation. You have taken matters in your own hands. Am I clear?"

"Yes, Mother Superior."

"Good, you need to take enough clothes to the ecole for a week. Some girls from the prep school will be sent to you during the week for special lessons. You can have Rochine the week after. I have received a letter via Mari that the ecole needs to be more active."

"No problem, anything special for you Thursday or Friday before we go?"

"Yes, I will let you know tomorrow after lunch."

Edith left to choose two to help her with Helen's initiation. One was tall and strong looking. Both had been at St Agatha for over two years and knew better than to disobey Sister Edith.

Evening mass was held before they all retired, Edith paid particular attention to Helen deciding what she would do, admiring her body. Candles had been put out in most rooms when the three of them walked into Helen's room. She had a lacy pink nightie on with white socks. Helen was taken by surprise as the two girls moved to each side of the bed. Edith stood there, she had changed into a reverend's outfit, crop in her hand.

"Now then, Sister Helen, you have been here over a year and you have not had your initiation from me. Everyone has it sometime. Are you going to come with me to the special room or do we have to take you by force?"

Helen froze; clearly uncertain what to say, the two girls poised. "Has the mother superior authorised this?"

"This is my initiation; any more questions and I will make it more painful for you."

Helen sighed. The two girls pulled back the sheets. Helen struggled. They held her while Edith put a tape over her mouth, then a hood and they dragged her. No doors were locked, they went along a corridor to the end of the wing and into the special room. The two girls strapped Helen onto a bench made from the forest. It was like an inverted Y so anyone could stand behind her legs apart. Her hands were secured, and her bottom arched up waiting for attention. Another strap across her waist, the hood still in place, her nightie and socks still intact. Helen was helpless, the two girls waiting for further instructions. Edith gave her first command. "Remove the tape and open the door to the corridor."

Edith stroked Helen's hair, pulling back her head and whispering into her ear over the hood. "It is *yes, Reverend*, every time I talk to you and you only speak when you are spoken to, do you understand? Now then I will start with ten while the girls fetch two of my flock to help me."

She moved over to the girls and told them to report back in ten minutes, so Helen had no idea it was the same two girls. Edith continued stroking her back, head and neck telling her what a naughty sister she had been. The first ten left the nightie flopping near her ankles. Helen was shaking now but Edith had just started.

"Good girl, now remember you can scream and cry as much as you like but if you speak out of turn, you will wish you had not been born."

Edith moved round her; hands moving over her breasts, then gently squeezing her nipples and kissing over the hood into her ear. The nipples were aroused as Edith told her to say, "I am a naughty girl and I deserve to be thrashed."

Helen's nipples hardened. Helen was begging already, "Please let me go, I will sleep with you, Reverend."

Edith was not impressed. "You spoke without permission." She moved round the bench and lifted the nightie to over her shoulders. Her hands moved up one leg up to the edge of her vagina, gently touching and almost entering, then with the other leg, leaving the crop over her naked bottom. She picked the crop up and gave her six more till her legs were shaking like an electric shock. She was screaming now. The two girls were waiting outside, they had brought some ice. She put some on her bottom and as it got smaller pushed it deep into her vagina. Helen was groaning as Edith bent over her and tongued her wet vagina, fingering her at the same time. She whispered to the two girls. They moved around the front and started stroking a nipple each, then sucking.

"Come here, girls." They obeyed. Edith went to a drawer and found a small vibrator. "You are not allowed to talk, or you will be flogged at dinner tomorrow."

They did not need telling twice. Edith inspected both girls. One girl put the small vibrator inside Helen's vagina, the other one gave her six with the crop. The red marks were becoming more severe. Helen was groaning and screaming at the same time. The second taller girl gave Helen six but much harder than the first, the vibrator left inside. This time her hands clenching at her bounds, her legs twitching uncontrollably. Edith moved round to the front and played with Helen's nipples, enjoying her control. Helen told the two girls to stand next to each other. Edith inspected them sensually. The tall girl that had washed Rochine, and who had slept with her was dripping with excitement. The other was not so receptive. She sent her to her bed. She ordered the tall girl to put a chair next to the bench and bend over it. She did as she was told. The tall girl would take the dildo that Edith had strapped around herself next to the helpless Helen. She removed the vibrator from Helen's vagina, it had been left on low and Helen's groans could be heard. She could now finger Helen at the same time and put the rest of the ice over her bruised bottom. The tall girl who had been placed over the chair was being ridden by the dildo around Edith. The tall girl came with an explosion that surprised her as Edith tasted Helen's juices. Edith sent her to bed.

Edith was now alone with Helen. She removed her headgear so she could see. She lent down and kissed her in her ears, talking gently her moist vagina near Helen's mouth.

"I have not finished with you." She took some scissors to the top of her nightie and cut it open, so her breasts hung down in the open. She squeezed them and then sucked her nipples till they were erect again. Once they had responded she moved to the back and found a softer leather strap to punish her already welted bottom. Her screams continued as she changed to a cane for the backs of her legs strapped in for Edith's sadistic attention. Helen was not enjoying it now. "Mercy, mercy, mercy please, please release me, mercy."

Edith moved around to the front again. She made Helen put her tongue and kiss her on any part of her body she desired. "This is your initiation, Sister Helen, tell me what you enjoyed most, or I will give you another twelve with the cane."

"I enjoyed the vibrator and listening to whoever it was that came next to me. Please have mercy on me. I do not like the punishment."

"I like to hear your screams and you begging for mercy, I am in charge here, not Mother Superior. Tell me you will serve me and repent your sins and I will finish soon."

Helen muttered her response. "I will serve you and I repent my sins." Edith made her repeat it. "Good girl, Reverend is pleased with you, he is going to fuck you before he leaves."

Edith moved around the back. She had to put some lubricant in both holes. She put some beads inside her tight anus and then Helen took the full force of her dildo. It did not take long for Helen's orgasm to come as Edith pulled the beads out slowly, then spanking at the same time. Her legs and hands pulling at her straps, the feeling of pain and ecstasy she had never experienced before. She dismounted and came round the front. Helen was still helpless.

"You did like that didn't you. I always go over the top to discover your inner self. Now say *thank you, Reverend*, I have learnt my lesson."

"Thank you, Reverend. I have learnt my lesson."

Edith unstrapped her, now wondering what Danielle had in mind for her.

Chapter 33   Thursday, January 20th

Rene was sat in his chair as Lisa stirred sugar into the tea.

"So one of these days, you'll make the tea, eh…?"

"Well you are a sec—"

"Don't you dare," she said plonking the cup down and sending slops of tea across his notepad. "I am not a secretary as well you know. And if Yorkie actually arrived on time, it wouldn't hurt him to make one once in a while. What does he think? It appears on his desk by magic?"

Rene laughed, but before he could respond, right on cue, in walked Yorkie with a sheepish grin. It was 9:05 am.

When he finally sat down it was 9.09 and he reached for his tea while they looked on. "What?"

"Nothing," they said together.

"How is the young warrior this morning?" Rene said as he drained the last of the tea.

"Arm is bad, no mountaineering for a while, sorry."

"What exactly happened that night?" Rene said.

"The wall was too big for Lisa to get over. We could not see an obvious solution, so I went on my own. It seemed quiet. I got in easily, took a few photos as I went around. It was just like a school, not many desks, bedrooms not used. I saw nothing till I spotted the cellar door in the kitchen where I had come in. If the door had opened the other way, I would have seen it straight away."

"Lisa went back and saw no wine at all, is that right?"

"Yes, the woman was helpful, and they got the place cleaned up very quickly, broken glass and blood. Efficient lot the Bergerac Police," Lisa added.

"Well, any more thoughts you, guys?"

"Yes, can I have my camera back?"

Rene stood, dragging his feet over to the locked cupboard and carefully removing the camera. "Better here than in that hospital or that cheap hotel you used near those druggies."

Lisa looked at the few pictures Yorkie had taken. "Difficult to see as you were using your helmet torch. You got three pictures when you walked in the kitchen from the back door. If I am not mistaken that is a bottle of wine on the table."

"It will be the one they hit me with," observed Yorkie.

"We ought to get it blown up; the label is at the front and there looks like a stamp on it."

Rene got his magnifying glass out and concurred. "Lisa, take it to the specialists and get it done now, urgent. Meet back here at 4 pm."

Yorkie rested till 1 pm before he ate his usual soup and sandwich at the bar. Though the undue attention was enough for him to wish he'd not come; everyone wanted to ask him questions about his ordeal. He kept thinking about the days in Bergerac and if they had missed something else. He concluded they had not and rested till the alarm went at 3.30 pm.

"There it is, clear as day Juan's stamp on that bottle of rioja that nearly killed you, Yorkie. What does that mean?" Rene was still pondering the significance of the find. "Did the druggy have it with him and he was already in the house or was the bottle there all the time?"

"We have trod on their toes and they are fed up with us. They thought we were a narcotics team and now do we go in as detectives?" Lisa said.

"If we go back," said Rene, "we need to search that ecole ourselves with no interference from anyone. You said they had a surveillance team on number 64."

"Yes," said Lisa

"Can we get in from the front if we pick the padlock without them seeing us, how far is that surveillance team from the ecole?"

Lisa looked at Yorkie then both agreed it was about 500 yards, depending which way they are facing.

"It is rare for surveillance teams to work before 10 am, these people do not get up till after midday normally, but they do work nights, so it was lucky that woman was there. That all fits in."

Yorkie fidgeted. "I disagree."

"Why?" said Lisa and Rene together.

"Let me ask Lisa a question. How far was it from the wall to the back door?"

"About sixty yards."

"How long did it take you to get over the wall and to me?"

"Blimey, your screams terrified me, I had found an empty oil barrel, I jumped on that and just held onto the wall and literally fell over. I landed on my feet, luckily scrambled back up when I realised I was okay and ran to help you."

"Do me a favour and walk down the road, you see that wall over there about eighty yards away, run back here when Rene gives the signal, and I will time you."

Rene was losing his patience "What is the point of this?"

Yorkie gave him his best pitiful look, gesturing to his plastered-up arm so Rene agreed. It was timed at fifteen seconds allowing for a wall say twenty seconds if you were fit. They agreed on the time.

"This surveillance woman arrived just after you?" Yorkie asked.

"Yes, maybe as little as fifteen seconds."

"She is not super fit is she. This woman got out of a car ran 500 yards, climbed or negotiated a gate, then ran to the back door, a further eighty yards minimum in forty seconds. I think she might make the Olympics. She was the one we saw at the police station. She was always around. Lisa, you rang her from the hospital and told her about Juan's stamp because you trusted her. When you get there, the place is clean. Remember how you told me the chateau was too clean. Something is not right."

With that Rene picked up the phone. "Our patrol car will be away on Monday. Can you cover the Pyrenees for us? Okay ring back when you can, you owe us a favour."

He looked at Lisa and Yorkie's puzzled expressions. "That was Pau Police Station, if they ring back and have cover, we are going in Monday morning, surveillance team or no team. We will tear that place apart. If we find nothing, we will investigate and check that woman. We need to be careful, the three of us."

"Which three is that?" asked Lisa

"My two patrol men and me."

"Make that four, Yorkie can hold the fort here. I trusted her; I want to leave a banana skin for her if we are all thinking the same."

"Well done, team, that is why debriefs are important, never forget that, and well spotted, Yorkie."

The phone rang a moment later – Pau Police Station confirming they were happy to help. Rene radioed his patrol car "6 am here, out all day Monday, details when you get back. Full gear and armed."

Chapter 34   Saturday, January 21st

Cecilia had finished her court order community service, ironically cleaning her own home being a major part of that. It would take about an hour from Marmande to get to the ecole at Rue D'Airport, Bergerac for 2 pm. She was looking forward to receiving her large share of the four sales. Staying overnight was not a problem and she knew there was some red wine in the cellar. She decided to put in two bottles of champagne as well as food for the one night. Her phone call to the policewoman a relief that the coast was clear. She had not seen Danielle for a long time, and after recent events she felt ready for whatever was in store for her, especially as she knew Sister Edith would be present. She simply told her live-in young partner she was away on business and would be back Sunday afternoon. She had never told anyone of St Agatha. She needed the cash as her business had suffered and she needed to pay the fine. She felt in a happier mood as she left her secluded home at 1 pm. She checked her glove compartment; her gun was still there. In the business she was in and single it was just insurance. She had never fired it except occasionally at the practice range.

* * *

Danielle had dressed as a headmaster. The short hair and suit with a tie she wore with black shoes would fool anybody from a distance. Mari was due at St Agatha at 11 am. Sister Edith had two travel bags as she reported to Danielle's office at just before eleven.

"I have decided to give you both a bonus at the ecole. I intend to be in charge this weekend."

Edith did not mind at all. Her share of the bonus was much less, but the thought of teaching a few from the prep school was music to her ears for the week ahead.

"Thank you, Mother Superior or is it Headmaster now?"

"As soon as we get to the ecole it is, Headmaster. Now go and wait near the helicopter."

Edith left with a spring in her step.

Fifteen minutes later Danielle arrived as the helicopter came into view above the mountain. Mari landed on the spot as usual, she did not turn the engine off as it was wintry and easier to load and go. She dropped off several bags of supplies including tampons and batteries with flour and other useful items. Danielle and Edith managed the steps and luggage, two bags each. Mari closed the doors and left for Bergerac Airport.

They landed near the hangars as usual and went through the service area to exit the airport. No need for any checks. Mari went to the hire car that was open and paid them fifty euros in cash. She made her way to the car-hire parking area and they exited the airport without anyone noticing. It was less than ten minutes to the ecole. Danielle instructed Mari to park before the padlocked entrance. It was in the same spot the surveillance teams used but it was empty. Edith exited the car and walked the short distance with one bag and opened the gate. She walked round the back and opened the back door, which backed onto the cellar door. A minute later

Mari drove in and round the back of the ecole out of sight of the main road and the service station. Danielle took the cases out, paid Mari a large amount of money, then gave her a time to meet her on Sunday morning. Mari drove out the ecole; it was 1.45 pm and lunchtime in France. The street was deserted, and she parked up the hire car and returned the keys all within thirty minutes.

Forty minutes later Mari was home but not going out as she had to work the next day. She rang Le Vieux Logis and booked a table for one at 6 pm with a room for the Sunday night. She was in the mood to see what talent might be available. It was out of season and she got special rates. The manager was hoping she would be out of luck and need his company. When she rang, he teased her by saying he would put a bottle of champagne in the fridge in her room. She teased him back: "Peut etre tu assiste moi avec le cork."

* * *

When Danielle got out of the car she had put on her special gloves. They added to her attire and she could use them with purpose. Cecilia came, but parked at the front, not caring if anyone saw her car. This was her property and the ecole needed to be seen to be active. She got her overnight case out and rang the front doorbell, hoping people would see her. Edith answered the door. "I am not locking the gate we need to be more visible," she announced.

Danielle was not to be gazumped. "Give her a big kiss before you come in, let everyone know this place is lived in and do it slowly."

They did just that and again on the driveway when Cecilia went back for the two champagne bottles. Nobody was walking by, so they went in and Danielle invited them to the kitchen at the back. She opened her red case; it was full of money. Edith and Cecilia were silenced by Danielle's move, but not when she then closed it and moved the combination lock that only she knew. Danielle moved her gloved hands over Cecilia's face looking straight into her eyes. "I have a nice fat bonus for you and Edith, but from now on it is *Yes, Headmaster.* You will only get that extra 2000 euros each if you obey me and play by my rules." Danielle stood back her gloves withdrawn ominously from her cheeks, waiting for a reply. It did not take Cecilia long to reply, "Yes, Headmaster." Her early entrance now squashed, the power of money and her compliant nature fully exposed by the dominant Danielle. Edith just sat nearby on a stool a 2000 bonus much more than she expected. Cecilia could easily count four x refugees x 2000 plus the extra 2000 and she felt like champagne now but would have to wait. Danielle continued. "Now, you girls, you will share a room and bed tonight if you behave and do as you are told. If not, you will be locked in the cellar. Take your bags to your room, I will check what food you have brought. There are uniforms in the usual place. Change into those school uniforms and report in twenty minutes for your first lesson."

Danielle was waiting in one of the classrooms. The curtains were closed. Now what do you say. In unison "Good afternoon, Headmaster."

She put up the word DOLLAR. "As new pupils you must understand the meaning of this Discipline-Obedience-Learning-Love Absolution and Reward. You will write one story now on Obedience."

They did as they were told, Danielle moving around, looking over their shoulders making comments. "Neatly and no talking."

After forty minutes, she said, "Come here, Cecilia." She obeyed. "Turn around and read out your story."

She read it out; Danielle was not impressed. "You have used a dog as a comparison, get on your fours and kiss my feet like a dog. Now stand up. Your next essay had better be better on learning. Write what lessons you have learnt recently."

Edith did the same, reading out her effort, but Danielle praised her and told her to write another on learning. Danielle picked up a cane from the coat stand and told them that they did not want to be punished if they were good girls. Time was getting on. Danielle inspected the second and made them read out again. She was pleased and asked Edith to wipe the board. "Go and get changed and report to the gym in fifteen minutes." They returned and Danielle was waiting. She watched them do press-ups, running on the spot. Arm and legs exercises. She watched them sweat wondering what was next. The cane not far from them all the time. Danielle decided it was time to inspect them. Cecilia was first. "Put your hands on the bars above your head. Edith, come. If she moves her hands use this flogger."

Danielle slowly moved her gloved fingers up her gym skirt and began exploring her while Edith watched. Danielle was expert enough to make her drip but stopped after a while. "More gym work then we will have champagne with those cakes you brought. Edith will wash you after gym in the bath."

Danielle watched them as Cecilia lay in the bath and was washed keenly by Edith. "Now, Cecilia, your turn to wash Edith."

Danielle had given them a particularly gruelling gym session. "Report to the kitchen at 6 pm."

At 6 pm, Cecilia and Edith reported to the kitchen where Danielle was waiting. "Fetch the champagne out of the fridge and open it, Cecilia. Edith, you get two glasses and put them on the table. Fill them both and drink two glasses each before you eat." They did not question the headmaster. They ate some cakes, and both burped loudly. Danielle had not finished with her instructions. "Prepare the food for dinner and place settings for you two. I will eat elsewhere. Put a bottle of red to warm near the cooker, opened, please."

They did as they were told. "Now girls have a small glass of red to taste first, is it okay?"

"Yes," they both agreed; feeling much better and slightly tipsy after the champagne. "Good it is time for your final lesson on Love before dinner. Open the other bottle of champagne and bring a glass in each to your desks."

They sat at the desks. Danielle stood in front of them. "You must write with passion and vigour. Edith, you are an angel, and you want to take Cecilia to heaven with you. You Cecilia are already in heaven and wanting Edith to join you."

They giggled and drank more champagne as instructed. The winner gets an extra one hundred euros as I have had a good year. Their voices and actions influenced by drinking too quickly and only a little to eat. Edith wrote hers. "My darling, Cecilia I am waiting for you here in this heavenly place, it is time we were joined, our futures together away from the mad world you are in. Love and kisses."

Cecilia wrote, "I have sinned in this world and I shall go on the great last journey to join you, Edith, in heaven, the promise of love and eternity with you I crave, kisses and hugs."

Danielle inspected the writings, one eye on the girls. Her carefully thought-out plan was coming together. She needed to ensure no one was left who knew anything about her role with the girls – except of course for Mari, she trusted her.

"Have some more champagne, it is so good I will give you both a hundred euros bonus and I will open the red case before dinner and pay you some now. She then aimed the cane at them both in turn. "Now sign your masterpiece."

They obliged and after a short discussion they all went to the kitchen. Danielle opened the case. They looked eagerly as Danielle counted out 5000 euros for Cecilia and 3000 for Edith. They did not care that Danielle did not join in the toast with some more champagne. Danielle proposed the toast. "To a bright future and hope for our refugees." They sat until Cecilia now things were a bit more informal asked, "Are you going to join in the fun?" She looked at Danielle as she spoke.

"I have a bad stomach and taking tablets for my headache, I simply want to watch you two. Take your money to your room and come back changed for dinner."

They obeyed in a buoyant mood. They cooked their own dinner, finishing the second bottle of champagne and back on to the red rioja. Danielle kept out of the way and went upstairs to check her bag, when she came down, they were ending dinner, putting the sets of dirty plates on the side to be washed. "I will wash up later for you as a reward." Danielle pleased but conscious they had drunk too much and did not want any breakages. Danielle insisted they finished the bottle before retiring to bed as the evening dragged on and Cecilia and Edith were getting the urge to retire and enjoy each other before sleeping. Danielle made her way down to the cellar. When she returned, she said, "There are four bottles of rioja left, I will give two to Cecilia and leave two for you Edith as you are staying here. I will put yours in the car for you, Cecilia."

Cecilia fetched her car keys. It was cold and quiet outside, she noticed a few at the service station. Danielle came back and they were ready for bed. "Sleep well, girls, do not forget to say your prayers first. I will come and check on you soon."

Fifteen minutes later Danielle checked her girls. They were just awake having had some fun in their inebriated state. Danielle still had her gloves on, but she just stood and watched them fall into a deep sleep, singing a soft lullaby as if they were young children. She went downstairs and fetched the two signed declarations of love in heaven. She put them in one of their hands. Edith was snoring and Cecilia a hand over Edith. Danielle prepared herself. Mari was not due till 7 am. She waited till they were close together, heads facing each other, she had to adjust the two notes, she placed a gun in each of their hands. This was it.

Danielle had practised shooting with both hands, so she could do this. Pulling the trigger on both at the same time was an art but hitting the brains and watching the splurge of gunge, blood and debris from their heads was even more miraculous. As quick as Danielle could move, some blood got on her clothing but one bullet for each was all it took. A dog barked at the back. Danielle spied out and only saw a curtain flicker then retract. She did nothing to her clothes, she did not even take the money. She only had the red case downstairs to take back. She had taken Cecilia's gun out of the glove compartment. The other bag she had put all Edith's clothes in as well as Edith's gun from St Agatha. She had done this while Edith had waited for the helicopter. Danielle had put the extra clothes in cupboards when she had gone upstairs, so it now looked as though she was living at the ecole.

Danielle had never taken her gloves off. The kitchen looked like a dinner for two. Danielle had never sat down. She had not had any drink or food. She had been the headmaster on duty, the adrenalin of her plan enough to satisfy her. She stood in the kitchen, her red case with the remainder of the money next to her. She walked around the rooms and double checked she had left nothing. This was a masterclass of a performance, she refused to wilt, but stood getting very weary until 6 am. Danielle had accomplished her mission to leave no threads

240

of her hideaway at St Agatha. Sister Edith and Cecilia Jabut would no longer be under investigation which might've lead to her being discovered alive. They had become dispensable to safeguard herself as well as being the undisputable 'boss' of St Agatha.

The front door was locked, Danielle simply took her case, dropped the latch on the back door so it would lock. She had no keys to get back in, a forty-minute walk to the airport. She still looked like a headmaster, but she could not hide the blood on her suit and gloves. It was dark and just a few streetlights as she walked out the open entrance that Cecilia had insisted on. This made it easier for Danielle. She turned right past the service station almost opposite. She walked past number 64 head down. She walked briskly to the deserted airport. It was too early for domestic flights, but the reliable Mari would surely be on her way.

Danielle waited near the hangar maintenance entrance before 7 am. She saw Mari's helicopter land and just after 7 the door opened. It was Mari and the nightman keeping an eye on things. Danielle brushed past him and headed straight for the helicopter. Mari was not far behind but wanted her say. "Weather is bad at St Agatha, may have to wait till the fog and possible thunder has gone past, weather has gone crazy."

Danielle's heart hitched up a notch, she had to get to St Agatha as soon as possible. She could not stay at Bergerac Airport in her state.

"Just take me to your place down the road and then go when possible."

Mari did not mind, she had never had anyone at her home except delivery vans, mainly for St Agatha. They landed fifteen minutes later. Danielle fell on the floor as she exited the helicopter. The dirt and grime from the field hiding the blood enough not to be noticeable. She had taken her gloves off now and put them in her red case. They had coffees,

Danielle trying to keep awake, she told her no more newspapers for three months. Mari said she wanted to practise her shooting in the wind. She had a 600-yard garden with a human target at one end. Danielle watched near her cabin, where she kept a few rifles and ammunition. They went down to inspect the target.

"Now you see I have to adjust more if the wind speed is like this," Mari said, her measurement tool in her hand, most only two inches out but not good enough by her standards.

They went into the small cabin. Danielle looked at the list from one to ten. At the top was Chateau Dec 2016 3 kills. 2nd Sicily June 2015 1 kill. 3rd Zagreb Oct 1992 5 kills. It listed seven more. Mari saw her looking. "My best shot ever, close to 500 yards to save Jack, but I am not so good now over seven hundred. My practice here is limited to under six hundred and I have stopped using the one at YMCA for bigger distances. "That number 3, Zagreb Oct 1992 5 kills. That was during the civil war?"

"Come into the house and I will show you before the weather improves."

They moved over the now sodden grass from the firing range and the hut. They took their boots off at the entrance as Mari continued the conversation. "You are the only one to set foot in here since I moved all those years ago. My father taught me this so please understand the situation back in 1992."

Mari guided her to her bedroom and put a light on as it was still dark outside with the storm. "You see those ropes on the bed and at the back two bars to tie them too?"

"Yes," Danielle said, intrigued by the obvious use they could be put to. Mari lay on the bed her hands sprawled behind.

"Well just tie me to the bars so I am helpless then go and put the kettle on in the kitchen and make two coffees, one sugar for me."

Danielle obeyed and went into the kitchen leaving Mari helpless. She perused the large number of speeding fines on her notice board, as she

242

waited for the kettle to boil. She made two coffees. As she approached the bedroom door Mari had a gun aiming at her and a hand grenade in the other hand.

"Now I will show you how to get rid of unwanted company."

Danielle trembled, spilling some coffee at this sudden surprise. It was only when Mari smiled and put the gun down and came to take a cup of coffee from her that she relaxed. They moved back into the bedroom to show a rope cut and two opened sections of the wood panelling behind the bed. Mari continued, "My father made me practise; you see next to the bars are two secret panels that open when you touch it like so." She demonstrated the contraption, each one revealing a knife and one with a gun and a grenade that she had left in.

"I did cut myself a few times before I mastered the knife. When my father never came back these five renegades dressed in our uniforms tricked me and took advantage. They were drinking beer from my fridge and hot drinks in the kitchen debating who would go next. Two grenades and one gun ended that debate. I fled the country with a plan devised by my father. Switzerland then France. It took a while to prove to the Swiss bank my father was dead. I knew he was dead as one of the soldiers had a photo of me and his wallet. I had the codes to eventually take the money and invest here."

"Wow."

"Let us check the weather. I think we can risk it soon. Say 11:15 am. We will take the rope in case I have to drop you with it."

"What do I have to do?" Danielle a little worried now.

Mari explained. "Just hook this onto the rope, which is 100 metres long. You hold tight and let yourself drop down naturally. I know what height I am, you either unhook your end or I can let the rope go when you are close to the ground. If I let you go, I will pick it up another time.

Normally there is a net or hands up to your chest and roll over the same as a parachute drop."

Danielle had done parachute drops so knew that procedure. She only wanted now to be at St Agatha. They set off but the wind and rain had not abated as the forecasters had predicted. They were buffeted most of the way. It was too dangerous to try and land. Sister Helen and the girls had heard the strains of the engine earlier and had prepared the nets quickly as they had done before. Mari's skills were tested as Danielle dropped the supplies, including her red case. Sister Helen and her flock gathered in the supplies. There were oohs and sighs as they saw Danielle preparing to leave the rocking helicopter with a rope. She grabbed the rope and lowered herself like a monkey. More oohs and sighs. The wind got up and the rope drifted over the side of the mountain, Danielle clinging on, her body hitting the side of the mountain as Mari lost control.

The engines were now at full throttle as Mari battled to get the helicopter higher. Danielle hanging on for dear life. The tiredness of the previous twelve hours taking its toll. Danielle took one last look at the bottom of the mountain, the rain in her eyes the howling wind, her arms aching, she was losing the battle. The helicopter seemed to tilt one way then the other, some expecting it to crash. Mari was praying and swearing in her native Croatian tongue as she thought her end was near. The wind just died enough to allow the helicopter to rise level with St Agatha then higher. Mari had this one chance. She guessed and pressed the release on the rope. Mari was too busy saving her helicopter and herself to see that Danielle had fallen. Danielle could see small figures and nothing else as she hit some sort of net, her hands up against her face as instructed. Her legs crumbled and she felt the hardness of the terrain. The thud and pain over her whole body but alive. Many hands were now lifting her up and gathering the rope. Those that could watched the helicopter fighting the elements and heading away from St Agatha, no one fancied a ride today.

Once inside the monastery, exhaustion hit and Danielle wanted her bed. Two girls helped, as Sister Helen insisted on a hot bath and oils, then a warm drink before bed. Some had noticed the blood. Sister Helen brought her red case to her room.

"Tell all the girls I will make a speech at dinner when I am rested, Sister Helen, thank you, is my nose still bleeding?" Danielle was still the thinker and planner. She knew she was without doubt one of the bravest and cleverest women that France had produced. She was still the "BOSS" of St Agatha and the old regime at the monastery no longer existed. Such had been her ordeal Danielle would not wake up till Monday late morning, which gave her time to prepare for her speech at dinner and who would sit where. The corridors of St Agatha were alive with gossip, prayer, thankfulness, learning, love and absolution. They wondered what the speech would entail and if Discipline, Obedience and Rewards were to change. Sunday evening dinner was without Danielle, but she would never miss another.

* * *

Mari made it back to Villeneuve. She swore to herself for agreeing to make the journey. She showered, changed with all the trimmings plus Chanel no5. Her Porsche at her mercy as would be any suitable victim of her alluring beauty at Le Vieux Logis. Parking up opposite the field where she often landed, her table was waiting as per the booking. This Michelin star hotel and restaurant did not disappoint. She checked in and put her bags in her room. She noticed the log fire in a snug room with panelled walls ideal for a pre or après drink. Plush and roomy bedroom, Mari was hungry and ready for a drink. Two couples and a single lady were already sat and eating a starter. Another couple came in just after her. Mari studied her menu noticing admiring glances from one man. He got up later and hobbled as though he needed a hip replacement, so was crossed off the list. Wine and dinner completed, conversation was difficult on one's own, so Mari retired to the snug room for a brandy with a coffee. She was alone when Pierre the manager appeared at reception which was twenty-four-hour. The receptionist was surprised. "Not often you come on a Sunday night." The receptionist smiled at him as he walked into the snug room.

"Good evening, Mari, everything to your satisfaction?"

"No, I have had a scary day and no suitable talent for me to entice."

He went back to the receptionist and ordered two more brandies. She smiled. "So what did you tell your wife?"

"Just keeping my new clients happy, unexpected visit today so back late."

As the manager at the most upmarket hotel for many a mile, all staff understood that many clients added to their wages via tips for excellent silent service. His attention to detail and pleasant attitude to his staff did not go unnoticed. They accepted his rare indiscretions with Mari that was common knowledge to the staff only. An opportunity with Mari would be the envy of many a man. The two brandies arrived very quickly.

Mari was not a shy person. "Thank you, I take it you want to check if my fridge is working."

"Of course, I have two hours to fix it."

Pierre returned to see the receptionist. "The fridge is broken, bill half price please."

"Such an important guest, if your wife rings I will tell her you did a good job."

He gave her a fifty euro note and went home with a skip, a jump and a big smile on his face. By the time he got home he would have to change his smile and say that work must come first.

Chapter 35   Monday, January 23rd

Rene was waiting for Lisa and his patrol men. He had been at the station since 5 am. He had his full uniform on and bullet-proof vest. He had checked his guns. Coffee had been made by the time they arrived. It was debrief at 5.45 am.

"Now then, Lisa, a vest for you as well, we will take two cars. Lisa can drive her car with me and you two in your normal patrol car. We will stop just before we arrive at Bergerac. Lisa will drive past the ecole, come to us and advise. Yorkie has shown me what I need to get in the back door. We can always fill up and park at the service station if we want to. Remember we are going inside no matter what."

It was an easy journey at that time of the morning. They parked on an industrial estate on the ring road. Rene waited in the patrol car while Lisa drove to the ecole and back. She reported to them, "Gates are open, no lights on but a car in the driveway. Traffic starting to pick up and some in the service station."

She gave Rene the car registration number in the driveway. He rang Yorkie who was now at the station. Yorkie checked and informed him the car belonged to Cecilia Jabut of the 'girls only' agency. Rene told them his plan. Lisa drove to the service station. The lady on the tills was surprised to see a policeman in full regalia get out and stride across the street with a familiar-looking lady just behind. They marched behind the ecole and waited at the back door. They heard the sirens of their own patrol car getting louder as they approached the entrance to the ecole, and pulled up at the front. Then the slamming of the doors and the front doorbell followed by hard knocking of the front door. No lights came on, there was no noises from inside. The doorbell went again and more knocking. Rene knocked as well. He ran out of patience and opened the back door. He saw empty champagne bottles and unwashed plates on the sink. He shouted. "Police... anyone in?" Lisa was just behind putting the lights on and taking her first photos. Rene shouted again and went to the front door, unlocking it and letting his men in. They had their guns at the ready, except Lisa who went from room to room taking photos.

They started in the downstairs rooms first, but Rene knew someone must be asleep upstairs. He nodded to them and they moved with purpose up the stairs. One door at a time was pushed open until Rene heard, "You had better come up here, boss, do not let Lisa up."

He saw the expressions on his trusted men and Rene knew something was wrong. "Lisa, stay downstairs, get your gun out and stop taking photos, guard our backs."

Rene went to the room and in all his years of service he had never seen such a mess. Two nearly headless bodies covered in dried blood, hair and gunge; a gun close to each of their hands. The bedclothes gave them some decency, but the top of their nighties bloodstained as well. He could see two pieces of headed notepaper also with blood on. The bodies looked serene and totally lifeless; they had been dead for some time.

Rene felt sick and the two police officers were white with shock. They went downstairs to the kitchen. Rene tried to compose himself. "We have a problem, Lisa, give me your camera and mobile."

She gave them to him and could see there was sadness in his eyes. "We have two dead bodies upstairs and we should not be here. This is a crime scene, it is a good thing we all have gloves on, I will report this to the Bergerac station. The police car will have been noticed by now at the front. You three check downstairs for any addresses, clues. Lisa, write down anything you think might be useful and use your mobile for photos when I come back down. I will then phone the station. We have fifteen minutes maximum to get whatever information we can find. They will be livid with us. It will be their case we have to come clean with them."

Outside, Rene told Lisa to put the camera in the car at the service station and come back to the police car in the entrance before the Bergerac officers came. Soon after the sound of sirens again, people at the service station looking over as were passers-by and people living in houses nearby. Rene showed an officer his badge.

"We came here on a tip-off, there are two dead bodies upstairs in bed."

"Forensics will be here soon; we will need to interview you all at our station."

Rene nodded as another police car parked on the pavement. Lisa recognised her immediately as the one that helped her with Yorkie. She was soon on the attack as she saw Lisa. "What the hell are you all doing here, have you made a mess of things again?"

There were now four from Bergerac Police Station.

The woman in charge made her way inside. When she emerged ten minutes later her face was pink and blotchy and as soon as she saw her colleague she broke down; sobbing into his arms.

Lisa did not know what to say; she had not been upstairs. She did not know who had died but guessed one was this Cecilia that owned the ecole, but she also knew she lived at Marmande, so was it her?

Rene was pensive, they agreed to meet at Bergerac station to go over everything they knew and why they had come from Arudy. It was 9 am and forensics were in the building now. They took the police car to the station.

"We tell them what we know," said Rene. "We all came in this car, okay? We will go back and fill up when we leave and decide then what next."

Before they got to the station, Rene rang Yorkie to tell him what had happened. He was gobsmacked and knew the next morning's debrief would be a long one. They were ushered into a large interrogation room. The station commander was there with two others including the policewoman. He started. "You had better explain why you are here and did not inform us before."

Rene looked right at him. "We have been investigating a death near us. It led us to a chateau near Limoges and back to this ecole in Bergerac. We believe there has been trafficking by the Spanish man that died near us. We came originally as narcotics mainly because we wanted to get information from a place of work that belonged to the owner of the chateau. We felt it a better ruse to try and assimilate information. The Spanish man was a wine merchant and did business in Bordeaux and St Emilion. However, his fuel receipts led us to the garage on Rue D'Airport. We regret not coming here last time as normal detectives to see what link, if any, near the said service station. We have discovered at his home in Spain a place where he had his victims. We believe he dropped that person or persons off in Bergerac before going to unload his wine in Bordeaux. He had his own label on his wine bottles. If we found the said wine bottles in a property, it was a chance there could be a link. We were looking for that link and anything else in the ecole when we discovered the dead bodies. I rang you straight away. It is also the same house where our man was brutally attacked and because of

250

certain anomalies from that attack we decided to act. We would like to hear from the lady next to you."

The station commander looked over to Audrey Gauthier, the policewoman. "Have you anything to say?"

"Yes, what is it you want to know, it was lucky I was on hand last time."

Rene nodded. "According to Lisa here, you were helping within fifteen seconds, how did you get there so quickly from your car six hundred yards away?"

"I resent your attitude. I am a serving police officer. I was on surveillance duty and I saw a man from number 64 leave and go towards the ecole. I had seen figures go down the side alleyway, so I followed him. He must have seen someone entering and thought they were up to no good. I thought I saw your man attack him but was too far away to see properly. By the time I got there Lisa was helping her colleague. I thought it more important to help him than go after the man as I had a good idea who he was."

"Did you know the deceased?"

"Why yes one was Cecilia Jabut. I rang her recently to ask about using the ecole for surveillance, an upstairs window looks over the main door of number 64 and garden."

"You told us last time it was already used for surveillance," Lisa said.

"We sometimes used the grounds but not the house, I am not sure exactly what I said to you, did you record the conversation?"

"I rang you from the hospital to come over and check if any such labels were on any wine bottles. I found none, but there are some now, how do you explain that?"

"They must have brought them. I do believe there are two bottles in her car."

Rene realised they were losing this battle. "Commander, can we work together, have you any records or information of suspicious activities concerning trafficking?"

"We have none, Bordeaux might have some as it is a port. May I suggest you leave this to us now. If we find anything of interest, we will pass it on to you."

Audrey Gauthier was not finished with them. "Problems seem to follow you guys. You have questioned my integrity and I will lodge a complaint unless you apologise for those insinuations and do not bother us again. You were told before and now we have two dead bodies, and you were first on the scene. Did you guys have anything to do with these deaths? You have already made an illegal entry that almost cost him his life. If you took any photographs, we need them as well as you were first on the scene."

Rene was prepared. "Lisa, please hand over your phone. We want it back by Wednesday recorded delivery. There are a few photographs on there, including those empty bottles with Juan's label on."

The station commander knew Rene from before. "There is no need for us all to fall out, we need to cooperate. However, she does have a point, will you leave now, and we will handle this investigation. We hope you have a safe journey back."

They all left, the patrol officers had little to offer, but it was important they had been there to confirm the events at the ecole. They drove to the service station. Rene told his patrol men to go back to Arudy, thanking them for their assistance. Rene rang Yorkie. "Cecilia Jabut, she had a house in Marmande, text me her address, we will call on the way back."

He sat in the car and asked Lisa to make enquiries at the service station about any activities in the last twenty-four hours. He filled the car up while Lisa was busy. He could see them making phone calls. "Well did you find anything out?"

"The shifts are 6 am to 2 pm then every eight hours. On Saturday, one of the staff saw two women kissing near the car. The gates were open all the time from 2 pm Saturday till a police car came this morning. The Sunday morning shift said it was dark, but a man walked past as he started the shift. The reason he noticed was the streetlight showed up a red case. He did not see where he had come from. He was heading towards number 64, very well dressed in a suit. He thought a bit early for church but thought no more as it might have had drugs in it. They all know about number 64. He went out of view very quickly."

Rene had received the address. He entered it in his Sat Nav and let Lisa drive to Marmande.

They arrived at a detached house with rows of vines and a circular driveway, with a gate that was easily opened. They both got out and rang the doorbell, Rene his police identification open. A young lady opened the door nervously asking, "Are you from Bergerac?"

Rene was on his guard they had rung her and were on the way. "No, we are on the way back to our police station near the Pyrenees. The Bergerac Police do not want us to help you because we believe there is trafficking and Cecilia Jabut is involved, this is her house?"

"Yes, what's happened? Bergerac police station rang earlier, they are coming to see me as well."

Lisa decided to join the conversation as a supportive female. "We are here to help you. They will explain to you. We just want to know your relationship with Cecilia Jabut, and how you met her."

"Cecilia is my partner and I love her. I met her through her business, and she kindly sponsored my schooling."

"That may be so, we cannot stay now we just want to ask you one question and we will leave. Please see what information the Bergerac Police give you and then decide if you want to contact us. It would be best for you to sleep on this predicament and say we have not called."

She looked very worried now. "Is it bad news?"

"The only question I want to ask is where did you go to school before you came here?"

"Is Cecilia okay?" The girl was now shaking.

"We are not at liberty to say, Bergerac Police will arrive soon, I just need that one answer for now and we will go, remember we have not called."

"It was St Julien de Crempse, north of Bergerac, a private school."

Lisa wrote it down and spoke kindly to her. "You must be strong, I am a woman, I feel for you and we will help you, please for your own good do not tell them we have called, we must go. Look up Arudy Police Station to contact us. If we give you a card it proves we have called. It may be unbelievable but do not trust all these people from Bergerac. Listen, think and decide tomorrow."

As they left, they wondered if she would stick to that story. Why would she believe them? Lisa pulled up in a layby. Rene checked the map. "I will drive, it will be a long day, we have to investigate this school."

As they pulled away, Rene removed his uniform top and put an old cap on. They were on the D933 towards Eymet when a Bergerac Police car with four in the car including Audrey Gauthier sped past on the opposite side. Rene put his foot down, the Sat Nav said arrive at 5 pm.

The school was tucked away with a large wall around it. An old manor-type house with a wooden solid gate like an old monastery. They had to ring an outside bell on a rope. A lady opened a hatch. "Can we help you?"

Rene showed his badge, and the door was opened. They walked past two cars and were escorted through a door to an office. The lady behind a desk waiting for Rene to speak.

"Are you the principal of this school?"

"Yes, I am the headmistress, why are you here?"

"We have reason to believe pupils here are being groomed for slavery, can you tell me where they go from here?"

"We educate our girls here on the basis of teaching the DOLLAR method, have you heard of it?"

"No."

"It is Discipline, Obedience, Learning, Love, Absolution and Reward. We have companies and individuals who sponsor us. They are all refugees or single ladies with no hope that are rescued and then guided by us. I am proud they then go on for a better future than their previous existence."

"So what age group are they here and what happens afterwards?"

"Ten to fifteen years old and then Sister Edith takes them. I never get involved afterwards."

"Have you heard of the ecole at Rue D'Airport in Bergerac?"

"Yes, we sometimes send pupils there for lessons with Sister Edith. She lives there. I have to collect the mail from the ecole every two weeks."

"So, this Sister Edith is not always there?"

"I am not sure, she prefers me to travel, but her car is outside. She says it is safer here as there is a drug problem near her."

"This school, is it all girls?"

"Yes."

"I need to speak to a few of them, in fact Lisa can help me, do you mind?"

"Of course not, why are you asking these questions, is everything all right with Sister Edith?"

"We are investigating the death of a Spanish wine merchant. He sold bottles of wine with his own label on, some were found in the ecole, do you keep wine here?"

"No, I have had some on the few occasions I have been to the ecole."

Lisa nodded. "One question from me, are there any male teachers?"

"No."

Rene and Lisa selected a few of the girls to talk to in one of the classrooms. An African girl came forward. "I am Bolanle and came in a van full of wine. I saw Sister Edith and came in her car here with Matron. Ladies leave here, we are not allowed computers, mobile phones so we cannot contact anyone after they leave. We are happier looking after our pigeons than seeing Sister Edith."

They went back to the office. "We need the keys to Sister Edith's car?"

A few minutes later they opened the dirty boot and the glove compartment. They found an empty flask and a parking ticket dated November 18th, expiry time 6 pm in Lourdes. They took a photo of it. There was not much else in the car. They took the keys back to the office.

Rene and Lisa asked more questions to the headmistress. "Does anyone else contact you, anything unusual happened around November 9th onwards?"

"Not that I can think of." The headmistress was sticking to her story. "The other person we see rarely is Cecilia Jabut from the agency in Bordeaux."

They were about to leave when a lady appeared, she was dressed in a matron's uniform. "I am Constant the new matron, I understand you have been enquiring about Sister Edith. She interviewed me at the ecole, and I came from the agency in Bordeaux run by Cecilia Jabut, if that is any help. She did have a dominant streak, but I did want this job, so I agreed to role play for her. She had come back from Lourdes when she interviewed me. The next morning, I dropped her at the airport and drove here with her car on the Monday."

"Where was she going from the airport?"

"She did not say. She may not have been flying, it is a popular meeting place. She did not have much luggage."

"Thank you, Constant, you have been very helpful," Rene said, but Lisa had one final question. "Why are the girls happy in this environment?"

Constant smiled. "We educate them here and use mainly the LL and R in DOLLAR, then we hardly use the D, O and A. Love and learning with reward seems powerful enough. Edith had other ideas that did not go down well with the girls."

Rene took the keys out of his pocket. "Lisa, your turn to drive must think how we tell Bergerac about our visit."

Chapter 36

Tuesday, January 24th

Rene was sat in his chair as Lisa put the kettle on. 9.05 am. Yorkie arrived; his mug of Yorkshire tea ready for him. They started there informal meeting Lisa with pen and paper ready. Rene went over the previous day's events cumulating with the revelations by Constant at the prep school. Yorkie summarised as best he could.

"You were blown out by Bergerac Police after finding two dead ladies in bed together. Suicide notes according to these photographs you managed to get. Lots of money in those bags. Wine bottles with Juan's labels on, plates and glasses for two waiting to be washed. Lisa's mobile coming back tomorrow. This Audrey Gauthier has all the answers to put you on the spot. You call at Cecilia's Jabut house and hope she tells Bergerac Police department you never went. You go to the prep school and it is a dead end. They have no idea where these girls go after they leave. They use the ecole and the only people they have met are these two dead lesbians. Wow that takes some organising. We are waiting on tenterhooks for phone calls from either Bergerac Police or this girl at Cecilia's house. You only think it is her that is one of the two dead bodies. We might get a forensics report and more information from Bergerac."

Lisa saw how frustrated her boss was. "Any phone call would be better than none. They did promise to keep us informed and we said we would cooperate."

Rene moved into action, he picked the phone up and rang Bergerac Police Station.

"Put me through to the station commander, it is Rene from Arudy." He waited a short time. "I would like to report that when we filled up at the service station, we were told the ecole used a prep school at St Julien de Crempse. We want to report that we found nothing except they confirmed they used the ecole, had no idea what happened to the girls when they left. Sister Edith Tavare was the main contact and they saw Cecilia Jabut rarely. We regret the circumstances of our visit and apologise for any inconvenience. Once we have received confirmation from you of the two dead bodies and the forensics report we can close the case. Everything seems to tie in that Sister Edith Tavare was trafficking young girls. Cecilia Jabut was also involved, reference her agency. Have you any further news for us?"

The commander listened and replied. "No further news I will have the reports sent to you within fourteen days, we feel the case is self-explanatory. The suicide notes look genuine, the solicitors are looking for any relatives of the deceased, confirmed as the two previously mentioned. They had equal shares in the ecole. We do not think anyone else is involved."

"Many thanks I will wait for your reports, all the best." He put the phone down. "Lisa, do you want to add anything to Yorkie's summary?"

"No, I think we have to wait for those reports. Everything seems to fit."

Yorkie added, "The day the van went into the ravine was the same day Sister Edith had that parking ticket in Lourdes. She left herself time to meet Juan and get back to the ecole. She had that interview with Constant on the day after. I bet she killed Juan, they did find his bottles at the ecole, it sure does fit now and all that money in the bags."

Rene with a wicked smile and blatantly laughing at his own words concluded, "A nun with bad habits."

Chapter 37   Monday, January 23rd

Danielle sat at the head table for dinner. She had recovered from her ordeal with the helicopter and was ready to address her flock. Sister Helen and Ruslana next to her.

"Ladies, I am pleased to say I have had no further nose bleeds." Danielle looked around and the nods and smiling faces accepting her version of events that led to her having blood on her suit. "You might be glad to hear that Sister Edith, after the tragic death of the mother superior, her friend, has decided to retire." She watched a few sighs and even bigger smiles. Her flock now very attentive waiting for more news with eager anticipation.

"She has moved to near Lourdes and asks if anyone here would like to serve her? Do not be shy, ladies, hands up for any volunteers." The room went quiet, "I thought not, and I cannot blame you. The DOLLAR regime will continue but not with the same methods. I heard rumours of her sadistic nature, that will not happen from now on. Ruslana will help with discipline with mine and Sister Helen's guidance. Obedience I expect through our love to help each other. Learning from Sister Helen and myself. Talent here will be nurtured to learn amongst us, knitters, cooks, laundry, pigeon fanciers, beekeepers and woodworkers. They make easels for painting. I will allow a guitar as I hear some of you can play them. Yoga classes will start soon. There will be singing lessons and more readings. Absolution as and when necessary. Rewards will be variable for what we can offer in this sanctuary. You may ask for that reward on your birthdays and one other day of the year. Only two will be leaving us in the spring. I will be asking Ruslana if she prefers to stay here longer. I am of the faith so I will be your new mother superior. We three will be your guiding angels of love and learning our two main aims. New rules and rotas will be arranged. The fires in our monastery must keep us all warm. We need to be strong and loyal. I ask you all one by one to come up to this table and kiss the three of us in turn and pledge your allegiance to St Agatha and our standing among you. For me it is Mother Superior, then Sister Helen but for Ruslana you will call her "Loving Lioness." For those that do not know that is the meaning of her name in her native tongue."

Danielle surveyed her flock at dinner. She addressed them all. "Have you heard of the Chinese philosophy of the four stages of life?"

They all looked bemused and a chorus of "No."

"Let me educate you all. Number one is happiness followed by pleasure then sorrow and finally love. Every creature on this planet kills to survive or is killed for someone else to survive. There is pleasure and pain for everyone. The rule of DOLLAR will help you all understand the meaning of life. The word normal should be eradicated from languages. Life for every creature is a repetitive process that becomes acceptable."

Danielle looked around the room and intensely at Rochine. "Some of you were not meant to be here. Some will leave and find variations of DOLLAR. It is not the principles of DOLLAR that will determine your lives – it is the teacher who interprets and guides you. For now, I, as your mother superior, and with the help of Sister Helen and Ruslana we will be your guiding figureheads."

Danielle raised her glass of wine to her lips and drank. The girls had no idea what she was talking about. Sister Helen clapped and everyone followed. Ruslana stood up as Danielle sat down. "As your lioness I have my own beliefs. I do not tolerate jealousy, obsession and greed. My motto is JOG. I do not want to see that in any of you. JOG will destroy our world but if we are all to survive, we must understand DOLLAR."

Sister Helen and Danielle were in shock at Ruslana's sudden awakening at such a young age. The room erupted with more clapping and stamping of the feet. Sister Helen felt she had to say something. She stood up as Ruslana sat. There was an eerie silence as Helen surveyed the tables. Finally, she spoke. "I have no motto as DOLLAR is the answer. I will give you love, learning and rewards in abundance. You must then ask yourselves do *I* need discipline or absolution and have *I* been obedient?"

Sister Helen sat down to emotional clapping as all the girls stood in awe of this new regime.

Danielle smiled and her mind flashed to the events of the last few months and wondered about the irony of life. With love in their eyes they all walked up in turn and ritually kissed the three, acknowledging their titles. When they sat down one lady stood up, hand in the air. Danielle looked at her. "Yes, you wish to speak?"

"Mother Superior, what if no one wants to leave St Agatha now?"

Danielle stood and pointed to the roof. They all looked up.

"My child, our destiny is written in the stars, we were brought together for a reason. We will only know that reason when we ascend into heaven."

They lowered their gazes and Danielle said grace. Wine was allowed with the meal. There were happy faces and muttering. At the end of dinner, Rochine was the envy of the flock when she was chosen by the official new mother superior to bathe and massage her aching body before sleeping with her. As in Noah's ark the remainder did their chores or slept together to keep warm two by two. The new regime was now operational at St Agatha with Danielle the undisputed "BOSS."

Chapter 38

It was Monday late afternoon when Kari opened the door. Facing her were two policemen and two women, one in uniform. The news was too much for her when one police lady told her Cecilia had died, looking like suicide. She swore and went down on her knees sobbing, her hands over her face. Two policemen immediately went from room to room, gathering any letters, information and simply checking for anything odd. Kari felt the woman's arms around her. Kari got up screaming, "She loved me, she loved me she would not do this to me!"

Kari heard the police lady ring her partner and told her to get the train to Marmande. A car would pick her up and she could stay. The other lady with her arms around Kari whispered, "I will stay as well and make sure you are okay."

Kari reeled with the news of her death. She was even more mortified when the policewoman told her there were two of them together.

Kari felt the woman's arms tighten around her and asking the policewoman to make a drink. She could hear the two men searching and looking in places she did not expect them too. She felt her world and privacy she was used to disappearing in front of her eyes. She heard them smirking and making lewd comments when they found items in the bedroom. She wanted to scream at them, but the other police lady stood in front of her. "Where is your mobile, I need it for the investigation?"

Kari instinctively pointed to a socket where it was charging behind the sofa and she picked it up. Kari was crying but asked politely, "I want it, surely I am not a suspect? I hardly ever rang Cecilia, she is a busy Lady. I wait for her to contact me."

"Was, and just for the record, anything you say may be taken down in evidence, but at this stage we are merely gathering evidence. Are you happy with that?"

Kari felt her lip quiver, bunching her fists together. What was this? They had not even asked her name, why was she being treated like a criminal? She felt the other woman's uneasiness, at last she asked, "What is your name, we should have asked you that when we came in. I understand from the police you are a refugee, and Cecilia was your partner. I am a qualified counsellor sent by the station commander I will stay one night as well."

Kari felt her warmth and kindness, a handkerchief over her eyes. "Thank you, I have no idea what to say or do, my name is Kari."

The policewoman continued. "That is why I have sent for Sofia, she is Portuguese and will be good company for you, about your age. I will stay as well, and we can return to Bergerac by train in the morning. Sofia will stay till I return after I have seen the station commander."

Kari looked into the counsellor's eyes pitifully.

"I will return when Sofia leaves and check on you, do not worry."

Kari heard the two policemen return to the room. They had bundles of papers, bank statements, anything they fancied picking up. Kari felt helpless, trapped and worried when the policewoman asked her the next question. "Where were you this weekend when Cecilia left and stayed at the ecole?"

"I was alone all weekend, I never left."

"Any witnesses?"

"No, I have no car, I do not drive, I did not need to walk into town."

"There is a train to Bergerac, did you know Cecilia had other lovers?"

Kari was screaming, "We loved each other, we were planning a holiday soon. She had to collect some money. It was business. I want her back!"

Kari again felt the counsellor's arms. "That is enough for now, you cannot interrogate a girl when she has just received such information, it is a shock. We need to order a takeaway and pick up Sofia from the station later. It will be best to ask more questions in a few days when you check all this paperwork and your forensic evidence."

Kari watched the policewoman and thought of the words the elderly police duo from Arudy had warned her about not trusting Bergerac Police.

Her sixth sense was telling her to contact them, but how? She was now a prisoner under suspicion.

Kari liked Sofia as soon as she saw her. Like her she was dark skinned, similar age and something about her demeanour made her feel better. The policewoman mellowed during the evening as they said little. Kari could not eat but the others enjoyed the Chinese meal. The counsellor slept in the bed next to Kari and the other two found a spare room. Kari never slept, wondering what the hell had happened and what her future held. She was a refugee and according to the policewoman she would have to move out soon. She was told that a fair amount of cash would be given her to help with her next journey. Kari cried again, she had no plans and was trapped.

The next morning, they had breakfast, and she saw the policewoman talking to Sofia before she left with the counsellor. They were going to catch the 9.14 am train to Bergerac. It was cold but she walked with Sofia around the large garden and vines. Near the vines was an open expanse which had been used by helicopters. They talked about life in Iceland and then Portugal. They had both arrived on boats to

Bordeaux and were guided to Cecilia's agency. Kari saw Sofia take a phone call on her mobile. When she finished Kari asked, "Can I borrow your mobile to make a few phone calls?"

"No, I am not allowed they will be back on Friday so we can have a couple of days together. They will check all the evidence before you are eliminated from their enquiries. You are not allowed to leave these premises. Will you cooperate or I am instructed to call Marmande Police Station for extra help."

"No need, shall we talk about music next. It might help if we play some and help me meditate."

Kari put some music on in the lounge. She could see no point in trying to do anything, after all she was totally innocent of whatever had happened at the ecole. Having another refugee in the house was a pleasant surprise given her shocking news. Kari wandered aimlessly through the house, every step, every breath painful. She did not officially exist – Cecilia was dead. What now?

* * *

The station commander at Bergerac Police Station was having his debrief with Audrey Gauthier. "It seems they have a different version of events which is worrying. However, you were on duty watching number 64, what do you know about these two dead bodies?"

"Edith Tavare is a nun who lives at the ecole, but spends some time away, not sure where, and she goes to the prep school north of here. She gives specialist lessons at the ecole for miscreants at the prep school. They are all refugees or ladies on the run from various countries. Cecilia Jabut at her agency helps young ladies sent to her, often from the ships and either finds work or if too young sends them to the ecole. I must admit, Sir, that I employ one such lady at my house provided by Cecilia Jabut. If you want me to resign, I will do so. I am shocked at her death. I did not know she was involved with Edith Tavare. The problem with refugees is a national and European problem, we are just helping."

"Mmm, I find it hard to believe that as a country we have got into such a mess. Where do all these people go? I have two dead bodies to account for and suicide looks obvious with all the facts, how do you see it, Audrey?"

"I am baffled, Cecilia has a lovely lady at her home in Marmande. I went to see her yesterday with the others you recommended. We found nothing to suggest Cecilia was about to commit suicide. I tried to console and counsel Cecilia's partner. She is called Kari from Iceland. She was distraught. She tends the vines and does all the work in the house and garden. I stayed with her and got my partner to come down and take over from me. Her mobile phone is here for examination. I fear for her and ask permission to go back soon to check on her."

"Take the specialist paper trail team to Bordeaux. Find the Notaire they use, and who benefits by their death. Is your partner alright to stay with her a few days?"

"Yes, Commander, she gets on well with her as they are a similar age."

"Check the ecole here first, see if anything has been missed. Rene just rang to say the service station gave him some information, you had better have a word with them as well. They went to the prep school but found a dead end. That was annoying as I told them to go home. They are now waiting for the forensic report. They agree it looks like suicide and have left it to us. Did Kari say if any other police had turned up?"

"She said no one had been. She was on her own all weekend and could have gone to Bergerac by train and back without anyone knowing."

"Interesting theory but stick with the plan I have given you for now. This is our patch and you have been honest with me. The refugee crisis is not our problem, I need good officers so off you go. I doubt a girl with such a good home and life would do that."

"Thank you, Sir."

Audrey rang her partner. "Will make it Friday, do not let her out of your sight. She must not be allowed to contact anyone she is a suspect. Any problems contact Marmande Police."

Chapter 39   Thursday, January 26th

Rene was sat in his chair as Lisa put the kettle on. Yorkie came in and took his mug of Yorkshire tea. Yorkie started with a question "Has the forensic report come yet?"

"No," was Lisa's blunt reply, "and no news from Marmande either."

"Busy on the mountains, how long are you having that sling on for?" Rene said.

"Another week, sorry."

The phone rang; Lisa answered it. "Yes, this is Arudy Police Station. You say you are a milkman from Marmande, and you have a message."

The phone crackled and it was put onto speakerphone. "Yes, I got this message on Tuesday morning. Forgot about it as it was on an order form for milk. Went back this morning and another girl picked the milk up. I did not see Kari, the nice Icelandic girl always comes out to say hello and take the milk in. I was unsure about wasting a phone call to you guys. Anyway, I have rung just to let you know, sorry I did not ring before if it is important."

"What is the message?"

"Oh yes, just says ring Arudy Police Station."

"Any cars there this morning?"

"No."

"Thanks, we have your mobile number now if we need you."

Rene looked at Yorkie and Lisa. "You two had better go over this afternoon. Lisa, you have reports to do this morning. Yorkie can go as I am doing his jobs. Be careful, take your gun, Lisa, Yorkie cannot use one with that sling. Park the car south of the property and proceed with caution. Bergerac Police Station is to the north. This is a Marmande Police number if you need support. Best to simply knock on the door if only two in the house. See if you can look around first. There is plenty of land and it is a private residence. She needs our help. Lisa, you can borrow the social worker's badge, I think that sounds a better ploy to get in. If the other girl opens the door and resists, force your way in. Both of you go dressed casual for this."

They left and used Lisa's car as Yorkie could not drive yet. It was 4 pm when Lisa parked away from the house. Yorkie went into the grounds, passing the vines at the back while Lisa boldly went to the front door. Yorkie could see Kari sat in the lounge calmly reading a book. He walked round to the front as Lisa rang the doorbell. The Portuguese girl opened the door but still on the chain. Lisa made the first move, flashing a social worker's badge.

"Been sent round from the social services, the commandant at Bergerac Police Station asked us to check if she is coping." Lisa waited as the girl thought what to do. The doorbell alerted Kari as well and she appeared. "Please let them in it will only take a minute to tell them I am okay." She smiled at her friend. Yorkie also had to make a comment to Lisa. "My arm is bad, and I am due at the surgery in fifteen minutes, just go and check so we can get off."

Lisa was thinking on her feet at Yorkie's sudden comment, "I have this for you to sign, all I have to do is look inside and make sure all is well."

It was so convincing she took the chain off and let them in. Yorkie then produced his police badge, as Lisa held her gun in her pocket. "I am Yorkie, and this is Lisa from Arudy Police Station. Can we take your names please?"

"I am Kari, and this is Sofia." Kari said it with relief as she recognised Lisa.

Sofia was edgy. "Do you mind if I ring someone."

Yorkie took over. "Yes, we do, we just want to ask a few questions and then we will leave." The two refugees sat next to each other. Yorkie continued. "Sofia, tell us who you are and why you are here."

"I live with Audrey Gauthier who is a policewoman at Bergerac. She asked me to keep an eye on Kari as she is a suspect in two deaths. She is due here tomorrow with another counsellor."

"You look Spanish, how did you meet her?"

"Portuguese, I ran away and got a boat to Bordeaux. The captain gave me an address. I went to an agency run by Cecilia Jabut who introduced me to the ecole and then Audrey."

"We have been told it is a suicide pact. Lisa has some interesting information for you both." Lisa put her notepad down.

"I have been on the phone for two days trying to establish who the Notaire might be that has the wills for these dead ladies. Edith Tavare died intestate we think, and with no known relatives the money goes to the state. Cecilia Jabut has left this house to you Kari with a small amount of cash. She stated that in the event of your death, it would be split 50/50 between Edith Tavare and Audrey Gauthier."

The two girls looked at each other, Yorkie took over. "You see, girls, we think Audrey will attempt to kill Kari for her gain. We think but cannot prove that she was responsible for my injuries. We do not know how she will achieve this, but she has already implied to you Sofia that Kari is a suspect. She has stopped Kari her right for legal representation. As refugees you have no standing in society, but you have a right to inherit and defence

273

for any crime. If Audrey believes it best to get rid of you both, there are plenty more refugees to choose from."

The two girls sat silently then Sofia cried. "I do not think Kari could kill anyone. She loves life and the countryside, what are you going to do?"

Yorkie and Lisa shrugged, then Yorkie said, "We eat and wait to see what happens, then we decide."

It was 6 pm when Sofia's phone went. They all kept quiet as she listened. Eventually the call finished. "It was Audrey, she is coming here by 9 pm. She says they have found proof that Kari was at the ecole and she is dangerous. She says there will be drugs in this house, and she could be suicidal. She asked me to prepare the bed in case she needs to be restrained for her own good till the counsellor comes. She told me to tell no one she was coming."

Yorkie and Lisa devised a plan. "Sofia, we have to record everything in the bedroom. Without that proof of her intentions, we have no case against her. She has told you to tell no one so she can say she was never here. Your life might be in danger as well. My guess is she will try to get rid of her. She is a policewoman and trained. She is dangerous you must play along with her and agree with her."

They inspected the bed that Kari used. The bed sheets and covers went over the bed down to the floor. "Can you crawl under, Lisa?" She managed it and they checked if her feet were visible. They were not but they found a bag and put it at the front. Yorkie looked outside. "I will go in the shed near the vines. All this food and drink wants putting in the bin and clearing. I am sorry, Kari, but you will have to act accordingly, or we will never get an admission and her to jail. If we are wrong about her then we are all fools, so be it."

274

Kari spoke. "I am Icelandic, I will be as cool as possible, I trust you. I am scared though." Sofia held her hand, Kari spoke again, "The truth will be out soon."

Sofia prepared the bed as Kari went with Yorkie to the shed. "This is a key to the patio door for an emergency. That is my room with the light on. It is difficult to see anything from inside the house as the curtains will be closed."

"The problem is I cannot see what is going on inside. I might have to creep out earlier."

Lisa prepared herself, she would have to stay still under the bed with a gun cocked. She prepared the recorder to start when Audrey arrived. Kari sat in the lounge with the music on as Sofia waited in the kitchen near the door Audrey would use.

It was 9.20 pm when the doorbell rang. Lisa froze and put the recorder on. She was not the young agile chicken. She closed her eyes to calm her nerves racing away with her. Sofia let her in "Where is your car?"

"Left it in a layby about a kilometre away. Is Kari in the lounge listening to the music?"

"Yes. I am really worried about her after what you said."

"Good, she and Cecilia have been providing drugs to a house near the ecole. Do you see these opiates? I am going to ram them down her throat. I want you to make a phone call soon to the counsellor and tell her Kari is getting high on drugs she has found, and you need help. You think she might do something stupid. You did not see how she got them. Now it is time for a nightcap, you make it as my gloves make it awkward, and we will pounce on her when she goes into her bedroom. The bed is prepared as I asked?"

"Yes."

In the lounge they sipped hot chocolate. Audrey waited in the kitchen first, before making her way to the bedroom "Why is this case here? I will put it back." She moved the bag as Lisa instinctively moved her legs towards herself. The covers at the end moved but did not reveal her. Lisa's heart felt like hooves at full gallop inside her chest, surely Audrey could hear it? Straightening, pulling herself together, she went into the lounge. "Sofia can sleep next to you, she has prepared your bed, I will sleep in the other room, the counsellor is coming tomorrow morning."

Kari moved towards her bedroom, having turned the music off. Audrey stopped. Did you hear that?" She opened the lounge curtains and saw the shed door open. "When Kari is in bed, Sofia, you need to close the shed door, it has been left open."

What was Yorkie doing?

The thud of the bed as Kari landed on it, the springs catching her breasts as she tried to lie flat. Kari's screams coincided with her own muffled howl of pain. Lisa could hear screams from Kari as she heard Sofia and Audrey cuff her to the top of the bed. Lisa could see the end of the bed where Kari's legs were bouncing away, springs going up and down. Then her shouts of panic were gagged, and her legs stopped moving. She knew her legs had been tied down. Kari had been immobilized. Lisa's breathing intensified but she did not make a move as Audrey had said nothing yet. Then she heard screams from Sofia and Audrey talking at last. "You see, Sofia, you will take a beating from Kari, because she wants that tramadol to kill herself." Lisa heard more thuds into Sofia as she fell to the floor. She was so low, their eyes met, and Lisa gave her the sign of silence. She was dragged up onto her toes, another punch. "When they arrive tomorrow, they need to see you were attacked by her. I will tie you up before I leave as though Kari had done it." She struck her again. "Now fetch some water."

Audrey approached the bed as the water arrived. "Now, you rich bitch, I am going to ram these opiates down your pretty Icelandic throat. This will teach you to beat my Sofia."

Lisa could hear gurgling noises as the tape was ripped from Kari's mouth. Kari's legs were twitching, the springs moving again. She heard Kari scream as the bed creaked where her stomach would be as she heard another thumping noise. Audrey now shrieking at Kari, "I will keep thumping you in the stomach until you take the water and these pills."

Lisa could tell Kari was trying in vain to move her hands and legs to escape. She had got the evidence. She had never shot anyone before. She had now, the bullet went straight into Audrey's ankle. It was too close not to miss. She saw pills falling on the floor, a glass fell breaking into pieces, some water splashing on the floor. Blood and tissue, ankle bones distorted hanging by a thread as Audrey fell crashing onto the floorboards. Lisa saw a bandaged arm, but the other striking the back of Audrey's head, then a foot crashing into Audrey's gut. Lisa pulled herself from under the bed, thought about another bullet in the other leg, instead she used her foot to smash into her mouth, the sound of teeth creaking like an old boat at sea. Sofia walked over her, hitting her once. It was over. Yorkie had a knife and found the keys for the cuffs. Kari had been helpless. She got off the bed and stepped on Audrey's bad ankle, leaving her weight on it to hear the deafening agonising yells from her. Audrey could not stand, helpless and in pain beyond the norm. They played back the recording once, so everyone heard and then rang the local police station's emergency number.

Chapter 40

RAID, Monday, February 13th

The four committee members located a spare Mole room for the meeting. Doc, the Englishman, Jean and the American who was particularly full of himself sat at the table. Volvic water and notepads, spare pens with an agenda in front of all of them with two spare sets and two vacant chairs. A secretary joined them on one of the spare seats with a laptop.

They had all heard from the American; who had extended his stay in America after his successful visit to see Trump and have a two-month extension of funds. It did nothing to hide the anxiety in so much as a long-term deal would have been better. Jean started the meeting by going over the minutes of the previous meeting. They all agreed, and they were duly signed and given to the secretary who was busy typing. Her job was to record/note the meeting. Being German, she was extremely good at her job with a poker face to match. Doc was pleased to have got her the prestigious work. Jean began the meeting… "Item 1 Selection of a fifth committee member."

They all looked at the German secretary for any news. She remained poker faced. "The French government have emailed to say they prefer someone from inside the organisation. It would then not need to be funded as an extra. Local knowledge for such an appointment preferred given the disastrous appointment of the previous ISIL infiltrator from their own recommendation."

The four of them looked for someone to comment, so the American as ever was quickly into action. "Given Trump's two-month deferral, maybe it is best we wait as we might need two if I have to go."

Doc joined in. "Then we have to think of two more to join us as three is simply not enough diversity to make decisions of high magnitude."

"With just the four of us we have no natural majority," concluded the Englishman.

Jean added her thoughts. "Just one female is also an uneven balance." The German secretary almost smiled but continued to input the comments. Jean continued. "Can anyone put forward a sensible proposal?"

The American suddenly smirked. "We have to confirm with Metis his new role soon. As an internal security commander, I think we should enrol him onto the committee. This could be relayed back to Mr Trump at his requested two-month report. Should little have happened over that period it might give us more time, and he needs to know the inner workings of RAID."

Heads again moved as they all took in that idea. No one spoke for a while. The room went eerily quiet as the secretary stopped typing on her laptop, waiting for the next comment. They had to be careful as the minutes would go back to the French government. The Englishman, forever the American ally. "Sounds a logical move. Why don't we do the interview and job description now and then decide."

The proposal was tabled and passed 4-0.

They went through other items on the agenda. Greek homes and more refugees still a problem. The Somalian pirates had been less of a worry after several successful raids. Knife culture and many deaths in the UK and other European countries from this weapon was noted but not their concern. A different food supplier was added to the list after a few complaints about another. State of the hangars/helicopters was reviewed.

They voted unanimously to use some of the funds for six more Anti-Missiles from the Barnes Wallis institute. The one that failed was checked to have had a loose release wire only. The Russian and a Latvian along with two other reserve pilots coining it from selling weapons supposedly used on sorties were asked to leave. The evidence from the secret camera gave them the authority to dismiss them but no further action to be taken. The decision to invest in a new helicopter and select a crew was to be reviewed in two months' time.

They called the meeting to a temporary halt while the secretary arranged to fetch Metis to the Mole room. They used the time for a toilet and drinks break with a few biscuits. The German secretary arrived and Metis sat down next to her as she readied herself to use the laptop. The four committee members in place Jean started the final point on the agenda. "Item 8, the official recognition for our new internal security commander to be Metis from the American booth. Before we vote on that we need to clarify with Metis a) his role and b) his acceptance."

They all looked at Metis, including the secretary. He sat motionless and said nothing. It was Doc that decided to read out his role. "You will be responsible, as well as fulfilling any work required for the Americans in your booth, duties on this complex known as YMCA.

a) Advising on and improving general security here in view of recent ISIL infiltrations causing danger to personnel living in and out of this village.

b) You will have access to all committee members private RAID information to assist with your job. You may interview anyone in the village but must have another committee member present. There will be no records of any interviews or such information unless we as a committee agree it should be added to the notes by our secretary.

c) You will have access to any part of this complex including homes/bedsits/hangar/stores etc. If you need to check any homes/bedsits you must have one other from the committee and the said person or persons whose home it is, with you as well.

d) You will be voted onto this said committee with immediate effect.

e) You will report to this committee with your findings, recommendations, and information for all five of us to make decisions from such findings.

f) Your new official title will be Internal Security Commander. You will work alone to begin with. The job includes membership of our committee. Should you be replaced then so does your entitlement to be on this committee. You are bound by the secrets act and have to sign here accordingly."

Metis looked around the room very slowly and spoke. "There will be the two of us."

Bemused faces looked back at him quizzically.

"My German Shepherd, Bronson. He likes expensive meat, what is the extra pay?"

Jean checked her notes. "Three thousand euros a month, plus any expenses should you have to travel. We expect reports from you. We have no problem you working in the American booth as normal. We expect there to be some computer work to be done, and your role is not regarded as full time. The reports will give us a good indication of the work you have achieved. Your role and income will be reviewed in six months' time unless Trump pulls out earlier. We appreciate that you have to impress him as well as us."

Metis responded after a thoughtful pause. "I am not really interested in the workings of your committee, especially for the ransom demands and decisions. I understand that if one of you is not available for a Mole meeting then you simply take another from your country's team on duty at the time. Is that correct?"

"Yes." Jean was quick to answer as the secretary entered the information on her laptop. "Then if I am not available for any reason you can do the same from our American team."

There was a quick nod of heads and they agreed to accept this so that the number on a committee would be five now.

"I will need a computer for this use only." Metis was quick as he saw it as a necessary addition for his eyes only. "I will not be allowed access to other countries' computers as they all have diplomatic immunity. I take it I will only have access to the committee's findings and decisions, which should be adequate as that usually relates to all the incidents."

The Doc was on the ball. "Yes, I am sure that will be arranged but we want all passwords and access as well should any member of this main committee demand."

There were nods of approval and everyone seemed happy with the outcome. The American had his say directly to Metis. "As you are now working part time for me your pay will be reduced a small amount, but the extra from the central fund will give you a larger extra income."

Metis smiled. "How much less?"

"We will discuss that privately if you accept these terms."

"Okay, I accept the terms and will start immediately."

The meeting duly closed with all accepting the proposals as outlined. The American was left alone in the Mole room with Metis as Jean asked the secretary to get a laptop for Metis from the stores. "Your pay will be reduced by 1500 euros per month, leaving you 1500 better off for your new role. Your first job is to follow up on Tariq. Trump needs information on him and we have to find a way of taking him out. Losing all those men at the beach and two more on a boat was not good news. There was one man that survived, and Trump is keen to send a small squad to Northern Algeria and get his revenge. Good luck. Your first report to the full committee is due Monday March 13th. You must keep me informed every week. Any questions?"

Metis had a habit of silence before responding as though he had nothing to say. "Yes, the first thing I want is all the information from your committee leading up to the disastrous meeting at the beach. I need times and dates and the contacts that made all that possible. That is all for now."

Religious groups in India believe in death their souls assume the form of a bird (normally a pigeon). By feeding them they are caring for the souls of their ancestors

Chapter 41   Monday, March 6th

Tariq summoned Hiba Lazaar to his room. His plan for a replacement inside RAID now fully worked out.

"You are to leave tomorrow. You have done well. You know how to handle a gun, set off explosives. You start next Monday at the French Embassy in Tunisia. You will apply for the helicopter course at the training camp in Tunis. You have a basic knowledge of flying helicopters, but you need to practise more. Your hidden beauty will be your biggest asset. In the western world at YMCA, you will be able to dress as you like. Do not worry, liberate yourself, remember the information I am after. I intend to set up a cell nearby. That plan is ongoing, so no need to worry."

"Thank you, Master, I hope to be a successful warrior."

"You will be. We are expecting you to be interviewed in June/July. Keep your ears and eyes on the American booth. They will seek revenge. I need to know anything you come across. I will have my own contacts in place by the time you start. Any urgent information simply email your parents for some clothing to be sent. That package will have to be signed for by you. Be outside in the open when he or she will call you Miss Tariq by accident. Simply sign and let the courier keep the pen with your message hidden inside. A pigeon will do the rest. This will be the standard form of communication. Girls like presents from their mothers so is natural and above suspicion. Try and arrange a visit back home before Christmas. Keep your head down initially. Good luck."

"I understand my job."

"Good, I need to check one more time, you will eat and then sleep with me tonight as an honour for your hard work."

Hiba's eyes smiled; that of a lady who had to surrender to a man of passion and strength that made her wish she could stay in his arms longer.

* * *

Early March at St Agatha and Danielle was at dinner giving her monthly long speech.

"Ladies of St Agatha. Winter is behind us and I have ordered more protective clothing for you bee workers. Mari will be bringing the East African honeybee and we will start new hives at the far end of the forest. They survive better at high altitude and in colder climates. There will be cloth and wool for sewers. Some new tools for you woodworkers. I am also going to let Rochine show those who want to learn how to climb/mountaineer. I have ordered several of these items, belay devices, carabiners, crampons, crevasse rescue equipment and harnesses. There will be dynamic rope and helmets so you can learn in safety. There is a steep drop to a small plateau near the new helicopter landing site we made. That is a good start to learn. Here we rely on helicopters but one day you might want to try and navigate the treacherous route to the valley. We are not experienced or skilful enough to do that. One day someone might be able to achieve that. Without the right equipment and practice it is an impossible task. Rochine learnt how to climb in her original home in Algeria. Rochine is looking forward to her challenge to help, including me. I will be her first pupil. Kitchen utensils as well. Larger bowls for you chefs and oven gloves. A new pizza shovel to use in the ovens. I think the latest love juice magazine to share and Cadbury's hot chocolate."

There were giggles and laughter. Danielle continued. "Only one of us is leaving at the end of this month, but two will arrive. I think that there comes a time when you will know if it is time to leave. You are all not naturally born to be in this environment, and I accept that. We have rules and tasks and erotically-motivated acts of discipline, love, obedience which equals learning to discover your desires. We are all friends, and you must obey the command that is still DOLLAR. You must accept the roles and rotas. That way we become better people to face whatever the future holds. God bless you all. I will now ask Ruslana to say grace."

The people inside without their knowledge were becoming institutionalised through teamwork and love. The pigeons the innocent communication tool and the two helicopter pilots the lifeblood of St Agatha. This had become a proper sanctuary, an operational masterclass by one of France's cleverest women, the officially deceased Danielle Bousquet.

Chapter 42

Monday, March 13th

It was the long-awaited meeting of the committee, time for Metis's first report.

Items on the agenda also included Jack's scheduled six-month recuperation exit from the village. They were all in attendance with the German secretary taking notes on her laptop. The committee agreed to accept Jack's letter asking to leave. They decided to keep him on the books and reward him and his family a six-month stay at a private villa on the Isle De Re.

Next was the report from Metis. He duly opened his own computer and began his first report to the committee. "I have done a survey of the grounds of this complex. The security is of low level. The reason being is that all countries have access to the information and demands by hostages and so it is in the interests of the countries not to disrupt that information. You have allowed families into the new school from nearby villages. We have delivery drivers from many companies. We place orders individually and as a company we order food and equipment as we like. There is no real check on goods entering and leaving. It is accepted what is ordered or sent is as listed. Should an organisation want to disrupt us we are an easy target."

Metis waited for a reaction. The Englishman started the comments. "We have nothing to hide and why would someone want to disrupt us?"

Doc continued. "We are tucked away from any town, so our horticultural façade seems to work for those that wander here by accident."

Jean added, "We have had no problems for over forty years."

The American continued the argument. "It is good to be able to come and go as we like."

Metis was quiet for a while. "The entrance to the main building has no security apart from the doors. No weapons checks like at an airport. I like taking Bronson for walks and the children love to play hide and seek with him. He is very popular for birthday games. If we can walk out easily anyone else can walk in easily."

Once again, he faced the same arguments. Metis felt the committee was not impressed with his start, but he had not finished. "I have checked the timelines and information surrounding the death of Cas, the hostages and Danielle Bousquet. Then we had the incident of three dead ISIL men at the chateau. I asked for all the items that were taken from the chateau belonging to Danielle Bousquet. It transpired it was all in Paris. I travelled to Paris and discovered nothing unusual on her computer or phone. It was all business with occasional private phone calls to her chateau. Danielle Bousquet had been noted by reception leaving and re-entering on many occasions. We do have reports of her using a phone in her car. I believe she had a second phone which was never found. We know from your records that Cas was an ISIL infiltrator and sent information to Tariq. We got Tariq's name from the now dead Henri, the other ISIL contact. We know the dead ISIL men were after information. They killed the glazier and then tried to get whatever information they were after from Jack. The pigeon gave us a lead to the outpost in Northern Algeria. I can pass this onto Trump, he will be very grateful for that information. I need to interview Jack and ask him more about his ordeal."

The other committee members listened but where not sure what it all meant. Doc asked the question. "So, what are you trying to tell us?"

"The pigeon told us that Tariq had sent these men to get information, but why? He had a helicopter and some money. The hostages were dead and so was Danielle Bousquet. Jack was the only person at the chateau when he killed three ISIL men. He was also responsible for killing Greco and the other ISIL team at the chateau. You see Jack is the key and he might not be safe wherever he is. I need to look around the chateau and report again. I need to ask more questions in the French and Tunisian booth."

The Mole room fell silent at the conclusions of their new security commander. Jean made the decision for them all. "Okay, you can have the chateau keys and given the information I think we should meet in two weeks' time for this specialist report, do we all agree?"

The motion was passed.

Metis had his final word. "Which one of you wants to be with me when I interview Jack?"

The American raised his hand. Nobody else did as they would get the report in due course.

Chapter 43

Monday, March 13th

Monday morning and Rene was sat behind his desk, Lisa had put the kettle on and five minutes later Yorkie walked in. He grabbed his mug of Yorkshire tea that Lisa had ready for him and sat down. Lisa joined him with her drink as Rene already had his. The debrief was more interesting today as Rene started it, he had the morning paper and Audrey Gauthier was the headline. "She got what she deserved sixteen years minimum for attempted murder, perverting the course of justice and dealing in drugs."

Lisa nodded. "Will have difficulty walking again for the rest of her life, might need a prosthetic lower leg."

"And new teeth," said Yorkie.

"Did you break her collarbone as well, Yorkie?"

Yorkie smiled, his sling long gone and showed how he had healed by standing up and doing a few exercises. "I left the hut a bit early to try and listen, I saw the curtain opening and dived behind a tree. I left the door open, luckily, she asked Sofia to close it. When I heard the gun go off, I was already at the patio with the key in. I dashed in and saw her on the ground, I just wanted my own back for what they did to me. Best bit was when Kari got off the bed straight onto that ankle and she just stopped, full weight on it. That is the sort of girl I like. I can still hear those screams."

Rene continued. "Bergerac Police were very apologetic to us all. We are on better terms with them now. They did say the two girls Kari and Sofia are living together at Marmande. Apparently bought some more fields and starting a wine business. Yorkie you have missed out there, that Kari is an attractive girl."

"Yes, it just the way the cookie crumbles."

"You are on mountain duty now. Lisa has to summarise the Bergerac case as we call it now."

Lisa took her folder out. "I know the case is closed. Forensics said it was just those two in the house and the letters were genuine handwriting. Suicide the verdict as we all expected. Five points I want to make from my notes. 1) The man walking with a red case was never identified at 6 am on Rue D'Airport. 2) When we took those pictures previously Edith's wardrobe was empty. When she died the wardrobes were full. The postmen all said the ecole was not used much and few letters delivered. Where did Edith go when she was not at the ecole? She did not stay at the prep school. 3) What happens to these girls after they leave the prep school, Edith and or Cecilia the only contact, very odd. 4) We have not found out why the car went all the way to the chateau near Limoges and the owner committed suicide with her maid. 5) Very odd two x two suicides."

Rene was quick to acknowledge. "Very good observations but we have nothing to go on for any of those points. Any views, Yorkie?"

"No, there were pigeons at the prep school so not needed at the ecole. Good point about the girls, not allowed mobiles, computers. Whoever organised this must be either very clever or we are over thinking."

Lisa turned a page. "I think the only point of interest now is the prep school. If we were to continue the case, I think the headmistress knows more and is not saying."

Rene drank his tea. "For what gain, even if we find out more, we are not looking for an ongoing offence."

"I agree," Lisa said, "I am only making notes in case we come across a possible connection in the future. My sister says the chateau is empty. We are planning a summer holiday with Rufus to the Ile De Re in August."

Yorke had plans as well. "I might be going climbing in the Auvergne or the Alps with our local club."

The phone went. Lisa answered it, her hand over the mouthpiece. "Talk of the devil, it is the headmistress." She put it onto speakerphone.

"The government will give us half of the value of the ecole plus twenty thousand euros to continue our good work. The ecole is to be used by the council as a rehabilitation centre for drug addicts. We were worried about what to do with the girls that were due to leave. Edith used to pick them up so now they are going to senior schools in the area. All good news. I did forget to tell you that Edith sometimes brought a pigeon. All she said was to release it when a girl or two were ready to leave. She had not brought pigeons for a long time. I had a mobile to ring in emergencies, but the Bergerac Police said it was a pay-as-you go phone, and it was not in use. I think it belonged to Edith. I never spoke to anyone on that phone. That is all."

Lisa looked at Rene and Yorkie both nodded, "Thanks for ringing, all the best."

"Why not go and interview the pigeons, they might tell you where their friends flew to."

Yorkie looked at Lisa and rolled his eyes at Rene's comment.

"It is a waste of time we have got nothing from that headmistress and those bloody pigeons," Rene said.

"That is where you are wrong, Rene," Yorkie said. "The pigeons have told us they have not been to the ecole or Juan's house. That dead phone was not Edith's as she knew her and would have freely talked. She knew Cecilia so it was not hers either."

"Who owned that phone and where did you go to my lovely?" Yorkie imitating a pigeon by cooing.

"Are you talking about pigeons or Lisa?" Rene enquired with a smirk on his face.

Yorkie thought for a while until he retorted, "Wouldn't you like to know?" He paused for a moment looking at Lisa then Rene. "Well, they do have many similar attributes. Both take notes. Both return to their own nests after flying off to do their duties. Both are cuddly and beautiful creatures. But there is one big difference.

"What's that?" Lisa said, looking at Rene and then smiling at Yorkie.

Yorkie gently set his cup down on the table, "Well," he said, "only one makes the best tea in the world."

A homing pigeon must love her home;
otherwise, she will not return
– Meir Shalev

Chapter 44

Late March – April 2nd
Jack's Departure

Jack and Suzette were busy packing; resigned to their new stay on the Isle De Re when the doorbell rang. The American and Metis with Bronson wagging his tail were at the door.

The American enquired, "Is Rubber Ball at school?"

"Yes, it is her last week before we move out."

"This is Metis who you know. He has a new role as our own security commander. He wants to pick your brains and ask a few questions. Can we talk for a while?"

Jack showed them in as Suzette offered them a drink and a bowl for Bronson. She was much happier at the thought of moving to a more peaceful area. They all sat down and Metis pointed out the lack of general security on the complex. It got very little response from Jack or Suzette. Metis did point out the guard on duty was alert when they walked down the track. Eventually Metis came to the crunch. "Just a couple of final questions before we leave. You must understand that with my new role, safety of members of this village is paramount. I also believe that you and your family's safety is paramount as well." Metis had one of his long pauses deliberately looking at Jack's wife. "The abduction ordeal must have been frightening beyond words."

Suzette concurred. "Yes, lucky to be alive."

"Of course, but in my investigation so far, I am perturbed for the reason Tariq sent another hit squad to kill the glazier then abduct you and your daughter. You see he already had a helicopter, a large amount of money and Danielle Bousquet was dead, who he possibly believed had some of his money or was somehow involved in the death of his hostages and some of his men."

Jack moved uneasily in his chair. "Interesting, sorry I cannot help you."

Metis relaxed in his chair stroking Bronson. "One final question. How did you take out three ISIL operatives on your own?"

Jack looked over at Suzette, who remained amazingly calm. "I survived because I do not give information away. My wife sent me a coded message to tell me there were only three abductors. Two I took out easily but the third injured me and luckily I managed to kill him."

Metis was unmoved and said nothing. He was not going to antagonise the situation by asking how powerful bullets had penetrated the three abductors, instead he finished the meeting to allow them time to consider his next words. "Fine, but I will want to see all three of you before you leave, I think that wherever you go you will be in danger."

He and the American left with Bronson obediently following without a lead. Suzette was shaking after they left. "Why did you not tell them about Mari?"

"I did not want her involved and felt it was not important. While I have her as my ally, I feel more secure."

"Why, could we be in danger?"

"Nonsense, Metis has a new job to do and no doubt he will report to Trump. He needs to create problems to safeguard his new role. Let us wait and see what he says to the three of us before we leave."

Suzette left the room, the tension taking its toll, her hysterical words hanging in the air: "All I want is a quiet life, somewhere safe, the sooner we go the better."

The tears of despair wet her face, she came back in attacking Jack aimlessly with her hands, but he just held them and kissed her saying, "Do not worry, I am here to keep us all safe." They fell onto the sofa, Jack's shoulder painful enough for her to say sorry and kiss him. They sat motionless for several minutes before they continued to pack.

Jack's leaving do was well attended. His wife and daughter appeared for part of the time but left early for him to enjoy a few more drinks mainly with helicopter pilots, the Swede and maintenance men of all nationalities. The next day Metis and his German Shepherd appeared much to Jack's annoyance. He did not want Suzette going into panic mode again. It was Sunday March 12th when Metis simply announced at the door, with all three listening, "Just popped by as promised to wish you a safe journey and all the best."

"Thanks," Jack said putting a few items into the car.

"They have decided to let me use the house from now on, so anything you want to tell me about the house, for example where is the stopcock etc."

Jack was relieved there were no more intrusive questions. He duly gave him a quick tour and came out the back door. Metis was pleased he now had walks for Bronson on his doorstep. Jack looked at Metis. "If you are staying here perhaps it is in your best interest to know we have Maggie about one thousand yards away in a well-hidden building as our secret escape only known by the men living here for security reasons."

"So, you have made precautions." Metis smiled. "I will be talking to the Swede and the two cleaners. Before I go, I need to check we have your mobile numbers. I need all three. You might not think it, but I am on your side. I have some more research to do, and I will keep you informed. I know your wife does not want to come back here. I think it is in your best interests you know what is happening here. The committee secretly hope you will come back. May I suggest you rent another villa as everyone here knows where you are going. Security is slack. I do not trust my boss either. You know him as the American, but he is a Trump man. They want Tariq eliminated by whatever means. I am only interested in any information when you are ready to give it to me. This is my number. If ISIL failed in the mission at the chateau, do you think they will stop? They are fanatics, suicide bombers, killers of the innocents. I wish you all the luck. I have to go."

With that bombshell of support and warnings, Jack felt he had another ally. He pondered a while and decided to tell his family nothing. He would wait for more information or questioning from Metis. He knew that would happen, it was just a question of when, not if. He went back into the house. The hired furniture removal company would arrive at the new villa on Isle De Re on Monday. Sunday was a good day for travelling. The Swede, the two cleaners and family waved them goodbye in the hamlet. They dropped the house keys off at reception for Metis to pick up in his own time. A few from the hangar and the main building appeared and those from the security gate. Rubber Ball smiled as most were saluting Jack.

They were approaching the barrier and about to leave, Suzette and Rubber Ball looking to the right at the security guards saluting as well.

Jack peered to the left and saw Bronson near a tree. There he was, Metis his right-hand saluting, but his left hand the sign of a V pointing at his eyes. The Indian warning of *be observant, keep your eyes open*. Jack sighed as Suzette drove past the barrier, oblivious of the eye contact between Jack and Metis.

* * *

Tears were on her face, tissues handy to wipe them away, Suzette wondered how long she could keep Jack away. Somehow, she knew he would return – just like a homing pigeon.

Chapter 45   The Summer of 2017

Kousair Amdouni was found face down in the Mejerda river on the outskirts of Tunis on June 18th. The policeman on duty was Omar who found his throat cut after a dog walker had rung in. Kousair had no known enemies. Theft was a possible motive as nothing was found on his body except his works badge on the inside of his coat. Omar reported to his superiors that an investigation, given no evidence or motives, the matter could be put into a pending more information file. They took his advice.

They were shocked at the news at the embassy but held an emergency meeting. He had been shortlisted as a single intelligent qualified helicopter pilot for the new position at RAID HQ near Clermont Ferrand. Hiba Lazaar was duly informed she would start her new job on Monday July 10th.

* * *

Tariq was pleased to hear the news of Hiba's new job and convened a meeting of his inner circle. They had received information where Jack was living. They agreed that taking a hit squad to the Isle De Re to confront Jack and try and glean any information was not necessary. One being the risk too high as there was only one way road/bridge in and out and now there was time to give Hiba her chance. Tariq learnt his new cell near Clermont Ferrand was now in place under the guise of a local delivery service and subcontracted with Amazon.

* * *

At St Agatha the summer season had brought a few ladies for weekend convent experiences. Only two had moved on. Spirits were high, mountaineering lessons going well even if on a limited scale. Danielle gave instructions for a small tunnel to be dug from the monastery to the new helicopter landing site adjacent to where they did the mountaineering. It was accepted as a different workout than tree chopping.

* * *

At YMCA work was as normal. Metis had done enough to convince Trump to extend monies till the end of the year. That was a huge relief to many, but Metis still met huge resistance to making the site a fortress with tighter controls and regulations. They now viewed his role as superfluous. Metis had delayed his report till the end of July as he had travelled to Tunisia and was meticulously prepared. Silence for several seconds before he began his verbal onslaught on the unsuspecting committee.

He told the committee that he had come across several anomalies. On interviewing the French team, he had asked everyone if anything unusual had happened before the demand came for the hostages. A young man said Danielle swore "fucking hell my dog has died." He then said she asked him to get her a jumper from her apartment and a sandwich. I checked the computer and found an eight-minute gap and no spare hard drive. I

308

need to go back to the chateau and ask if there was ever a dog there. I went to Tunis and discovered Mohammad Aqbal died the day before the disaster in Northern Algeria at the beach. I believe he was the ISIL contact that only the committee knew about. I went to the Tunis police HQ. I went through the files and found a certain Tariq was sent to assist them when the Houstons first moved to the house over seventeen years ago. A policeman called Omar was particularly interested in me and why I had come to Tunis. I went to the Houston house where they were abducted. I was followed all the time and felt my life was in danger but avoided any confrontation. No one has any photos or recognition of what the girl known as Rochine looks like. On my return to Bordeaux, I checked any emails from/to the governess from the agency computer where the previous owner committed suicide Cecilia Jabut. The only item of interest was that Rochine broke her arm when twelve mountaineering down from the cliffs. They went private to a Mr Sharma for the operation. The secretary at the agency also said that Bergerac Police had been as well as someone called Lisa ringing up from Arudy Police Station after information. The coincidence is that a young man came here to see if we had drugs and he was from Arudy Police Station."

Metis gave one of his long pauses eyeing the committee. "You see I have to contact this Mr Sharma, go back to the chateau and go to Arudy. It is for these reasons we still have Trump on our side and questions need to be answered."

The committee had been snookered. Much information and unsolved answers intrigued them all. He was given permission to pursue his lines of enquiry regarding incidents at the chateau, dog or no dog and contact Arudy Police Station as well as Mr Sharma.

* * *

Hiba had blended into her role with the Tunisian team. A natural and open agreeable enthusiasm made her popular. Keeping to herself and allowing her mobile and computer to search and email occasionally. She managed a couple of helicopter trips to areas of disturbance that were low key. She deliberately did not show her qualities in the shooting range by scoring average marks. The pilot who was due to retire in August felt Hiba had just enough flying experience to leave as planned. She engaged with the nurses and small hospital unit, especially after a minor injury on one of her excursions. She learnt it was used as an emergency outlet for Clermont Ferrand main hospital. She enjoyed a part-time role at the school teaching them some languages. She enjoyed the pool and local walks bumping into Metis and Bronson and others stationed at YMCA. She kept her distance and refused several invites for dinner and walks. Metis checked her mobile/computer activities but could see no alarm bells. Hiba had heard that the famous Jack and family were due to return in early October and the non-too pleased Metis was moving out to a different location on the complex. She remembered her remit to keep a very low profile and book the first week in December to return to her family home. She would be required to work over the festive season, so this action was popular with the others in the Tunisian team.

Hiba ordered some winter clothes for delivery at the end of October. She knew some information would be expected in her pen.

Chapter 46　　Monday, September 11th

It was 9.30 am when Metis and his German Shepherd walked into Arudy Police Station under the suspicious gaze of two uniformed men and a woman. They were expecting him. The meeting had been arranged for after the customary French August holiday period.

"Morning all, I am only staying one more night, just had breakfast so not thirsty." He eyed the empty tea cups. "I will not take up much of your time. My name is Metis, and this is Bronson."

They formally introduced themselves.

"I remember you calling us back in the summer?" the one called Rene said.

"I am the security commander at RAID and I am investigating the whereabouts of an ISIL man called Tariq. I believe he was after information from one of our pilots, Jack. Jack was injured at this chateau where a certain Danielle Bousquet and her maid committed suicide." Looking at the younger of the men, he continued. "I believe you came to RAID to see if we had any drugs links?"

Metis turned to Lisa. "My investigations took me to a ladies only agency in Bordeaux. The governess for the abducted Houstons who tragically died in a disastrous pay-off deal came from that agency. You rang them after information about Cecilia Jabut. The secretary told me she had also committed suicide in a house in Bergerac last December. Certain anomalies in the work patterns and events surrounding Danielle Bousquet have brought me here as well as the coincidence of your involvement. I recently contacted a Mr Sharma about Rochine Houston. He did a private operation on her broken arm. He remembers her as a fit young lady with lovely olive skin and brown eyes. That is the only description we have of her. No photos and no official registry in either Tunisia or France. Why? I checked the photos of the carnage a bomb caused at the site of the failed hostage release. We had photos from a helicopter and Jack's own camera. There were white and dark skin remnants on the beach but no olive skin."

The room went silent. Lisa spoke. "I was only enquiring if Cecilia had any relations and where she went on her holidays or visited."

"We were investigating the death of a Spanish wine merchant. That led us to the same chateau owned by Danielle Bousquet. It seems there was trafficking of young girls. There was no connection to the chateau, but it did lead us to Bergerac. The suicides of Cecilia and a nun with a written note closed that case as the nun was discovered as the one that killed the wine merchant. A school north of Bergerac was used. The nun collected the girls for further education/placements, but no one has any idea what happened afterwards," Rene said.

"The Spanish trafficking connection then led us to North Africa via a pigeon link, but we are not sure where," added Yorkie.

"The girls were not allowed phones or computers. Rene used the guise of drugs to try and find out more at RAID. I discovered Danielle Bousquet was responsible for the failed mission in North Africa," said Lisa

Metis listened to the new information. There was a feeling of mutual cooperation and friendliness as they realised they were all on the same side. Lisa put the kettle back on and washed the mugs. A bowl of water for Bronson. Yorkie made polite conversation about his mountaineering hobby and rescue work. "Lisa, you made some notes about the conclusion of the case, can you find them?" said Rene

Drinks were served as Lisa went to a back room and brought out a file. To summarise "Five points. 1) The man walking with a red case was never identified at 6 am on Rue D'Airport. 2)When we took those pictures previously Edith's wardrobe was empty. When she died the wardrobes were full. Few letters and where did she go to when not at the ecole? 3) Where do the girls go to from the prep school Edith and Cecilia the only contacts and both dead? 4) Why did the car go all the way to the chateau? 5) very odd 2 x double suicides. I have pictures of the two suicide notes. My darling Cecilia. I am waiting for you in this heavenly place. It is time we were joined, our futures together away from the mad world you are in. Love and kisses. The other reads, I have sinned in this world, and I shall go on the last great journey to join you, Edith, in heaven, the promise of love and eternity with you I crave, kisses and hugs. Both genuine signatures." Lisa sighed deeply.

Metis viewed the photos and nodded his acceptance of the facts. He spoke after one of his long pauses "I can clear up points four and five. The car had ISIL killers in. They were killed in the chateau, and we did not want the public knowing ISIL terrorists had been in the area. The most interesting point is the man on the street with a red case. Red cases are used for money deals with abductors/terrorists from the chateau/RAID. Coincidence. Also Rue D'Airport, perhaps using the airport?"

Rene butted in. "I checked the airport it was not open till 10 am."

"That might be so," said Metis. "We use all airports with our helicopters for refuelling. They are usually manned twenty-four hours for emergencies, even if closed to the public."

Yorkie, checking his own computer then added a small comment that excited Metis "Yes Kari, Cecilia Jabut's partner remembers a helicopter landing on Wednesday November 16th at Marmande. She saw a lady pilot and a girl being loaded into the helicopter. It took off straight

313

away. She got only a glimpse as it was evening and looking through a window."

Metis had his computer open. "Blimey, that was the day before the exchange was due in Northern Algeria."

They all knew the significance of their joint efforts. Danielle was more than likely the lady pilot but why was she taking a girl back? Cas was dead and could not be interviewed. Metis sat sipping Yorkshire tea for the first time.

"The new matron dropped Edith off at the airport before driving to the prep school." Lisa smiling at her contribution. Metis was in deep thought as his feet massaged Bronson.

"There is one common denominator in all this and that is Danielle Bousquet. She must have been the lady pilot at Marmande. It is on the route to North Africa as I have Cas's refilling stops as well. The times match up when leaving RAID. She owns the chateau. She went to North Africa. She handled the red cases. She was on the committee and had access to helicopters. She was in Immigration before her new job. There is an eight-minute gap on her computer. She never had a dog. Her contact in Tunis is murdered. Of course, the one person I have not seen is her friend who resigned the day before she committed suicide, Mari. Another helicopter pilot."

He stopped talking as the Arudy team could not follow all his comments. Metis closed his computer. "You have been a great help. Here is my private email if you think of anything else. The only people who know what happened I think will be Jack, his family and perhaps Mari. I have my own plans now."

"Do you think Danielle actually died at the chateau? Cremated within a few days?" Rene said.

Metis smiled at him. "I will find out."

314

Chapter 47   Monday, October 2nd

Jack's return to RAID in October was a boost to the flagging helicopter crews. Metis immediately arranged a meeting with him at the house, which he now had to vacate. Metis had moved onto a ground-floor apartment on the complex as he had a dog. Hiba was in the same apartment but on the top floor.

Suzette had gone to town to shop and Rubber Ball was at school where Hiba was doing a lesson. Life at YMCA was normal, a haven, with hidden fire power and diplomatic excellence for the purpose it was created.

Jack was keen to start the conversation. "You were right. I kept my eyes open. There was an apartment overlooking my villa. I had monitored it for a few weeks before I took them by surprise. They were a hit unit from America. I frightened them with my revolver but just said thanks, watch out for any terrorists. Someone had leaked I was at the villa, so I managed to acquire the one adjoining mine. That would be enough to confuse anyone, and I still had the Americans watching me."

"Mr America on the main committee is not to be trusted. I am sure he deliberately leaked out where you were. They want Tariq to come out of hiding and then take him out. They did not take the bait for whatever reason."

315

Jack was pensive as Metis continued. "I need Mari's mobile number to ask her a few questions. I could have got it from administration, but I need you to know. Have you anything to say before I see her?"

Jack could sense that eventually Metis would discover that Danielle was not dead. This was not the time to give him that information. Jack's sixth sense said that until Tariq was taken out, his family were in danger. They would soon know he was back at RAID. Jack wrote down her mobile number. "She is a very good pilot and first class with a rifle. Treat her well, she is one of us."

Metis acknowledged his comments and left to go back to his apartment with his trusted German Shepherd. Hiba had finished her lesson and approached the apartment at the same time. "Hi, can I take out Bronson?"

"Of course, it will give me time to do some computer work and tidy up."

Hiba quickly changed and then went for a walk with Bronson around the volcanoes near the rifle ranges where a few were practising. On returning to the apartment, she noticed Metis had still not emptied his many boxes as he had to pack up and move. Hiba was an engaging and pretty lady. "Come on, Metis, let me help unpack these boxes, you single men are all the same, they could be like this till next year."

Metis smiled, he admired her beautiful body. "I will put the kettle on, why not go up and change then help me?"

Hiba did not need asking twice. Removing her walking clothes and changing into a smart casual top and tight jeans. She thought too early for a skirt. This was not a sprint. She knew exactly how to entice the lucky Metis. His background she had discovered from his friends that he was a loner. No chance of marrying he went from lady to lady on short term romances or conquests. Metis did not engage with married women. The lady had to like him first due to his background and colour and his rugged look. Above all she had to like Bronson. Hiba had been at YMCA since

316

July and shown no interest in Metis. Metis was probably thinking all his birthdays had come at once. She had taken Bronson out and now she was volunteering to help him get his flat in order. When she reappeared, Hiba took her time unloading and bending over in her tight jeans at suitable moments. She smiled at Metis and Bronson a lot. Her lips and eyes with her voluptuous breasts hidden from view induced Metis to mischievous thoughts. They had coffees and spoke little, but Hiba deliberately left several boxes untouched. "Shall I come back in a couple of days and help with those?"

Metis was in a trance. "How about one evening and I can get some food in?"

"Sounds great, I am a bit lonely here. Is good to help you. I do not drink alcohol but do not mind if you do."

It was two nights later that Hiba returned in a beautiful dress and showing some cleavage that would not have been allowed in her own country. She duly helped unpack the remaining boxes. The takeaway from a local restaurant was washed down by a couple of beers for Metis, and Volvic water for Hiba. Bronson cuddled up on the sofa dividing Metis and Hiba. They both stroked Bronson till their hands met. Gently touching each other and fingers clasping together. Slowly he moved his head and lips across to plant a long and energetic kiss on Hiba's cheek then her mouth responding to this sudden demand. Bronson was sent to his own corner. Metis could see her heaving breasts and her defences melting like the ice in the Arctic circle. He had been seduced to the point of no return. Hiba tried to stop him with faint cries of "no, no, no" but his hands were probing, and her resistance was over. She moved her hand to stop his hands exploring her more intimately, but then slowly spread her legs just enough for Metis to know he had conquered her. He had no idea that Hiba had conquered him and the consequences this would eventually bring for YMCA.

* * *

Mari was at home when her mobile went. She did not recognise the number so ignored it. Then a text arrived to say Jack had returned and a new security man wanted some help. The phone went again and this time she answered.

It was a few days later they met at the Tremolat square at 11 am for a coffee outside the pizzeria. Metis introduced himself as Mari waited rather nervously. Bronson lay down near a bowl of water.

"You resigned from active duty the day before Danielle Bousquet committed suicide with her maid."

The direct comment surprised Mari. "Yes."

"I see from the records and from Jack that you are a first-class marksman or should I say lady and worked for RAID for several years."

"Yes."

"Do you know a nun called Edith Tavare or a businesswoman called Cecilia Jabut?"

He showed her pictures of the two. He waited several seconds then showed her the two as dead lesbians. Mari instinctively got up and went to the toilet. She was under scrutiny and had no idea what to say or do. She felt sick but having washed herself and calmed down a little she returned to the table.

"I have never seen them before; you must understand that seeing such pictures disturbs me."

Metis did one of his long pauses. "Did you ever fly in your helicopter to Bergerac Airport or take Danielle Bousquet to other airports or sites?"

Mari was now very much on the defensive "I often go to Bergerac Airport to collect or take clients from the Vieux Logis around the corner here in Tremolat. I never took Danielle Bousquet anywhere except from her chateau to YMCA or here."

Metis eyed her up. A tall attractive eastern European and single. He would love to add to his hit list. Business must come first. "Your helicopter is quite old now. I checked it out at RAID it has the same rotor blades as Mitter and Maggie. You might not know but Mitter has gone on an exchange and Maggie has been scrapped."

"Why do you tell me that?"

"Before they both left service three new higher quality blades were ordered. They are slightly heavier than the old type and can withstand stronger winds. They are scrap value now as they have stopped manufacturing these, as only suitable for older type helicopters."

Mari's ears and brain were in tune now. Her helicopter had not been serviced for some time. The high winds at St Agatha a constant problem. "What deal can you offer me?"

Metis again looked at Mari with his penetrating eyes. "What can you give me back?"

Mari knew he was after more information. Jack was back and she wondered how long before Danielle was discovered. The questions being asked and the death of those two ladies who she knew frightened her. Her answer came from a sudden rush of blood. "I do charge 300 euros for a bottle of champagne at the Vieux Logis."

Metis smiled and rang the stores at RAID. "Hi, this is Metis. Those rotor blades that are scrap value. What sort of cash price will the committee accept? OK get back to me as soon as possible."

Metis did not hesitate. "I will reduce the cost as well as a service to include the 300 euros."

Metis could not believe his recent good fortune. He had gone a long time without sex and suddenly two buses come at the same time.

"Rotor blades and services are expensive. It would have to be done at RAID. I would have to fly over and would be a full day's job..

"Plenty of good walks, you could take Bronson out. Might let you use my apartment."

They drank the coffees and ordered two more and pizzas. The phone eventually rang and Metis got his prices. "Including an extra 300 euros off," she smiled, "and a service with three new rotor blades 5800 euros, earliest date Monday November 6th."

"5500 cash and you have a deal. I will want to practise on the rifle range and buy some more ammunition."

Metis rang his contact back and after twenty more minutes the deal was done. Metis had never been to the Vieux Logis. He left Bronson in the car. An hour and a half later he started the journey back to YMCA.

The next day he reported to the American. "Now then, Metis, how are you doing?"

"All starting to take shape, just need more time."

"They are sending three to Northern Tunisia to try and infiltrate Tariq's HQ and take him out. The misty mornings and darker days might give them an edge. The one that survived the original ambush, and two navy seals will be landed at the same beach under cover of darkness. They think a small task force has a better chance."

"I could be redundant soon?"

"I hope so, you will inform the committee. Then your job is secure until we get the results of this sortie."

Metis acknowledged and left. He wondered how three could succeed given they only knew where the pigeons flew to. A dangerous mission in unchartered territory. An away match against a wily leader. His meeting with the committee was very familiar territory. He told them Mari was having her helicopter serviced and the new rotor blades fitted. He updated his findings, but they were inconclusive. They were pleased the extra cash could be used for the festivities especially the New Year. His idea of having two guards who went from one entry post to another and then relieved one at a time allowed them all to get some walking exercise. This was proving popular, less boring than stuck on sentry duty all the time, plus extra surveillance on the whole campus. He had not seen Hiba for a while and was looking forward to his next dalliance with her.

Chapter 48

Tuesday, December 5th

Hiba arrived safely at her parent's home on Monday December 4th. Little use of her phone and internet meant she had not aroused any suspicions. During one of her unnoticed nights sleeping with Metis, she had been disturbed by him waking up and begging Mr America not to send the three men to certain death. Bolt upright and obviously oblivious to his own nightmare Hiba had to find out more. Mr America lived on the married quarters in another area of the complex. Pretending to want to discuss a nativity play with his wife, Hiba knew she was away for the day on a shopping trip. Spiking his drink with just enough to let him sleep a short while and spend time on the toilet, she could not crack the password for his mobile or his computer. She avoided Mr America after this excursion and kept a low profile as per her brief. The note in her pen warned Tariq of a possible three-man invasion.

It was Tuesday December the 5th when Hiba walked into the back room of her new family home after dinner.

"Good evening, Hiba." Tariq spoke quietly with an air of authority and intent.

Hiba fell to the floor and humbly kissed his feet. "Have I pleased or annoyed you, oh master?"

"You have done fine work. I am ready to implement my plan to get my daughter back. Please confirm if you know any tall eastern European ladies who work on the complex? My contact in the police here has a poor picture of a lady with a red case entering through a dignitary door from the airport the same day as someone met your father in the café."

He showed the picture to her. Hiba looked intently as the head was down and not in view.

"I think that is Mari. She recently brought her helicopter in for a service. She used to work sometimes for YMCA. I took Jack's daughter; they all call her *Rubber Ball* and their dog Bronson for a walk to the volcano and the shooting range. I had booked a practice session. Mari was also there. She was brilliant up to six hundred yards but poorer at longer distances. I did not show my true ability. When we walked back, I told Rubber Ball how good Mari was at shooting. She then said she was the best and had saved the family. She suddenly stopped and said it was just a dream. I kept quiet in case she told her parents."

"Well done, Hiba, it all fits now. I need to know the weaknesses of this complex and Mari's house. Wherever Mari has flown to on a regular basis is where they are no doubt hiding. If Danielle is alive with my daughter it will be somewhere remote. My plan is to take Mari and then check her flight paths. They will show an unusual place. A team will take her helicopter to that rendezvous. They will inform me from a pay-as-you go phone. I will take the YMCA and destroy all their helicopters except one. I will fly that to the given point, take my daughter back by force and Danielle as my prisoner. I am convinced she is alive."

"The defence is virtually nothing. Metis is the new internal security commander but the lacklustre committee will not allow massive security expense. They have new lights at the entrances and two more security men walking the complex. Security booths have hidden machine guns and the weapons room is manned 24/7. A trained outfit could overhaul in minutes.

Helicopter crews are on standby but average eight minutes in case of an emergency so one helicopter is always fully armed on standby. Jack and a few others are in a hamlet at least ten minutes away by foot."

Tariq brushed his chin and was in deep thought. "How would you infiltrate this complex, Hiba?"

"Oh, that is simple. The ambulance is on reserve especially for south of the city. It is next to the hangar. A false call about an accident and it would be an easy target. You then use the same ambulance to return in with no suspicion. You can take out the service entrance guardroom which is quieter and get straight to the hangars. I could take the storeroom and you have a clear entry."

"Brilliant. You will hear from me. New Year's Day early morning is my planned attack. I will be at a secret location south of the city and my cell armies will be prepared. I now need details of Mari's house when you return."

Chapter 49

Hiba returned to YMCA with clear instructions from Tariq. She observed Mari's house at Villeneuve near Lalinde. She ordered some winter clothes and sent details of the property to Tariq via the delivery company he had set up as a cell. Hiba took life and work in her stride, enjoying the company of Metis on a few occasions. They spent most nights in their own apartments keeping the workforce guessing if they were having an affair. The Christmas festivities came and went. The nativity play she was in went down well with many guests from the villages enjoying the performances of a mixed group of adults and children. Mr America's wife watched but had not agreed to join the cast. That was a relief for Hiba who was concentrating on New Year's Eve. She had agreed to work the 10 pm to 6 am shift much to the relief of her team. An email from home wishing her a happy and healthy New Year arrived on December 29th. Hiba felt a lump in her throat as she now had to implement Tariq's orders.

Tariq meanwhile had got his armed cells ready for action. His aim was simply to take over Mari's home on New Year's Eve. His delivery team were poised waiting for the go ahead. They received the orders the same day as Hiba. Tariq himself had decided that it was time for him to take command. He ventured via a well-disguised route to join a specialist team near Clermont Ferrand. They had taken over a large house for rent south of the city from December 30th for a week.

Metis meanwhile had his own plans. The servicing of Mari's helicopter had allowed him unbeknown to her to put trackers on the new rotor blades. He was convinced that Mari was the key to where Danielle Bousquet, if alive, was hiding out. He thought she might be a link to the possible trafficking of these girls. He refused to comply with the committee about his thoughts as this was his own operation. He could use his computer or mobile to track Mari. He contacted Yorkie at Arudy and begged him to do the New Year's Mountain climb in the Auvergne at this location. He wanted a report from Yorkie. His standing as a police officer his only hope of information.

At St Agatha the helicopter brought supplies for the festive season as well as a letter from the Marie. It confirmed they had given the Arudy climbing club permission to climb up to the monastery on New Year's Day. It said they would picnic for a short time and descend to get down before nightfall. Danielle announced the surprise visit to her flock over dinner. It was agreed to provide some mead and snacks if the weather allowed them to climb to the area where Rochine had begun her lessons. It was next to the new landing site. The monastery was a hub of excitement for a rare visit. Danielle gave clear instructions that the refreshments would be left near the end of the ascent on tables. There would be no contact with the climbers and they could view the climb in small numbers but must retreat to the monastery when they were close.

Danielle was concerned when Mari told her of Metis's interest in her and now a climbing club were to encroach on her land. She was knowledgeable and experienced to worry about such coincidences. Instinct made her check her small armoury. One gun with three rounds of ammunition and two hand grenades. She sent two pigeons back with Mari. If one returned with no message that was to be a warning. Mari accepted her instructions. She devised a pull-down chord behind her bed to allow a pigeon from St Agatha to be released from the loft in an emergency. Her history from war-torn Yugoslavia etched in her for ever. She knew Danielle was on the run, they were colleagues against whatever was against them. Danielle had large planks of wood made from the forest. Several doors could be strengthened to stop entry by slotting them into wooden supports at each side of the solid doors. She encouraged more work on the tunnel to the woods. Trying to be calm and authoritative a trait she was good at. Her actions did not worry her flock. It was Ruslana who questioned her and sensed danger. Danielle dismissed her and said it was just to keep them busy. The main door a worry if a hurricane swept up the mountain and battered the main door. She had two planks made for that one. The ones for the dining room and her private room purely for practice.

* * *

Tariq assembled his two cells at his rented property. He had to synchronise his battle plan. He instructed seven of his men to travel to Mari's house at Villeneuve. "You will have one delivery vehicle and a spare car. Only five can go on her helicopter. Find out the flight plan where she goes. She always has her helicopter full of fuel at the ready. Make haste at exactly 7 am for that destination. Let me know immediately you find out from her charts. You do not have to torture her to find out. Come armed ready for any battle. I will be in front of you, simply follow me to that destination. The two left behind must take the two vehicles to Spain to our new safe house. Mari must be killed before you leave.

The rest of us will go to La Roche Blanc junction where an accident will have been reported. An ambulance will arrive at 5 am. We will take that ambulance back to RAID HQ. I have an agent inside. We go in the tradesman's entrance as normal for the ambulance as it is the nearest point to the on-site hospital which is next to the hangars. As we pass the entrance four of you will take over the sentry post. You will wait in case two more on patrol appear. The rest of us kill anyone at the hangars and prepare to blow up all the helicopters and the tracking rooms and any communication rooms. Four of you will go to the main entrance to the auditorium and Mole rooms and hold off/kill anyone who appears. I need time to take four of you on the helicopter prepared for an emergency. It will be well armed and that is how I escape with four of you. You that remain will probably die for Allah. Create carnage and destruction while I complete my mission."

They all nodded and shouted with enthusiasm not caring whether they lived or died.

* * *

Hiba had finished her shift and gone to the hospital to wish those on duty a Happy New Year. Her mission was simply to answer the phone when Tariq rang to send them to an accident at La Roche Blanc as if the hospital had asked them, which was usual as it was south of the city. Hiba then had to take over the armoury and secure that. Then check how many were in the hangars and wait for Tariq and his men to arrive. To help Tariq, her job was, once he was airborne, to stay behind and remain his contact at RAID. Her other orders were, if necessary, take out any of his own men to help safeguard her position in the camp.

The sound of the ambulance siren approaching the tradesman's entrance made Hiba's heart beat even faster. She had stationed herself next to the armoury and was allowed entry. She shot dead the Latvian guard as soon as she entered. She left the door open and watched two of Tariq's men jump from the slowing-down ambulance to easily engage and kill the two guardsmen in the booth. They remained there for a short time as the ambulance sped towards the small hospital next to the hangars. She circumnavigated the booth to avoid detection, watching events unfolding. Two more went in the open armoury. She then saw the two from the booth moving and taking up a position opposite the main building and the outside Mole room, where some steps lead to it. They avoided a couple, obviously drunk returning to the bedsits. Hiba went into the booth, avoiding the dead bodies and retrieved a machine gun. Taking spare ammunition and waiting until explosions beckoned inside the hangar and the sound of a helicopter fired up. The still cold morning air was now resplendent with the sounds of burning structures creaking and collapsing with the inferno of a war like zone. Alarms sounding all over the village but no one to stop the attack. Hiba watched a helicopter rise in front of her Tariq clearly visible with four of his men aboard. She watched him circle and fire one of the rockets which resulted in another explosion from behind the hangar where the last helicopter was ready for action. Then she saw in the distance two figures approaching from the hamlet. It had to be Jack and the Swede. The two from the armoury were waiting for them as that also exploded with a huge bang that shook the area and forced Hiba to the ground. It lit up the area as Jack and the Swede dived for cover as a hail of bullets came their way from the two armed men. Hiba did not hesitate; she let fire at them as she got up and dashed towards them killing them and acknowledging Jack and the Swede. She heard the sound of machine gun and hand grenades being thrown at the outside steps to the Mole room where three who had tried to venture out from the auditorium were lying dead. The main entrance also under fire from the other gunman. She noticed Metis and Bronson running from behind the complex where she lived. Hiba saw the helicopter leaving. Jack and the Swede arrived in total disbelief at what they saw.

"There are two left, good thing I was not at home yet. Got the machine gun from the tradesman's entrance." Hiba quick to point out her action.

"Great work, what the hell is happening?" Jack said.

"They have taken a helicopter, I wonder why?" the Swede added.

All three tried to find a spot to take out the last two gunmen holding the main auditorium at bay. Then they saw a huge explosion at the new metal doors Metis had managed to have done were shredded in front of them. The mangled sound of metal and the open entrance spelt danger for all inside. They could see the two gunmen advancing and they had no chance of stopping their intended suicide mission. The two men were feet from entering when a hail of bullets stopped them as they arched backwards then sideways another explosion from their hidden belts of explosives sent them to heaven or hell in a thousand pieces.

They saw Bronson first, then Metis, machine gun just used, at the ready as they all met near the now extinct entrance. Doing 360 degrees checks around the complex in case of more attacks. Inside the sound of wailing, disbelief, and shock. Hiba quietly convinced Tariq had a clear run to his objective, wherever that might be.

The whole village, despite the celebrations, were awake to the destruction. Hiba saw the total devastation of the armoury; the hangars and the communication rooms a godsend as her involvement now impossible to prove. Hiba watched Jack rip off a hood of one of the dead attackers, "ISIS." Hiba listened with sudden apprehension as Jack gave orders as he tried a mobile number.

"No reply from Mari, come on Metis, what the hell is happening."

They were all making their way back to the hangars – rabbits caught in the glare of headlights. Metis busy on his phone, "Mari is okay; she is in the air, I have been tracking her."

"At 7 am, she is never up this early, why the hell are you tracking her?"

"Just doing my job," Metis responded.

"Come on team we have Maggie, we are going to Mari's first, where does it normally go to?"

Hiba thought Maggie had been scrapped and now realised it had not been. She hid her dismay at her lack of this knowledge and wondered what to do.

Metis continued to reply to Jack's enquiries, "We have had her tailed, the helicopter is on her usual flightpath to St Agatha."

Hiba heard those words. Her heart sank a little, she wondered if she should take them out now with her machine gun, but the speed they were going now into the forest to get to Maggie took her by surprise. She followed as if by instinct rather than wanting to.

"Follow me and we need to be airborne in minutes." Jack issued the order to the three of them. The Swede checking the armoury. "We only have those decoys, no time to put on missiles. Machine guns, smoke bombs, grenades and flares are all we have."

"That will do I will pilot you three in the back, we go straight to Mari's first, I owe her that. Then to St Agatha."

Rubber Ball had come out with Suzette. They took Bronson. Metis, the Swede and Hiba found a seat, as Jack expertly brought Maggie to life the whine of the blades and Suzette worrying if this was the last time she would see him.

"Hold on." Jack's final command as he lifted the ageing Maggie into the cold blue skies and headed away at high speed.

Hiba sat there, her machine gun nestled on her lap wondering when she could use it to cover Tariq's back. Mari had saved him and his family and as Jack approached, Hiba was conscious of no movement at Mari's house. She expected to be shot at by the ones left behind unless they were already heading for Spain and Mari was dead. She knew Tariq's plan. They all scoured the landing spot and the house as they circled once then Jack landed with clinical expertise. They saw a parked delivery van and a car. Metis and the Swede jumped out first guns ready with Hiba close behind. She wondered who to kill first or wait and see. They all approached the house, Jack a little behind which made Hiba's task difficult if she were to shoot them all. Hiba raised her machine gun but slowly lowered it as Mari appeared, dishevelled but cool as a cucumber, her trusty rifle and an assortment of hand grenades and extra cartridges around her body.

"Glad to see you guys." Hiba could see smoke and dust from the house. The air of a battle, she wondered how she had survived. "They took my baby and left two to keep me company."

The smile said it all; as did two dead bodies inside the house in view through the open door. Jack was quick to register the events. Hiba was in a quandary as he gave instant orders.

"Mari takes the sniper role, Hiba in the middle, Metis and the Swede take each side, let's go to St Agatha."

"There is another landing spot at St Agatha, from the other side," said Mari.

Metis was on his phone. "My tracker says they are about fifty minutes ahead but not going too fast, we can gain time and hope they do not use the radar."

"Bastard," Mari said, knowing now he'd put trackers on her baby. She got into her sniper spot as they all took their positions.

Jack was alert checking the map.

"We will set a route for Rodez so they think we are going there. At high speed, by the time they land, we will be on course, and they should not know we are coming."

Mari was about to be hemmed in. "Managed to get a pigeon out with no message to the monastery to warn Danielle. It was our agreed signal of a problem. She is an experienced lady I hope she can buy us some time."

Hiba listened, her machine gun on her lap still biding her time as Jack took off, pleased his instinct was right. Mari never flew so early, and he guessed ISIS were after her helicopter for the same reason they demolished all except one at RAID. His mind in a whirl as to why they had not taken two from RAID. Then it dawned on him. His private intercom to Mari, "Did they want your helicopter to find out where Danielle was hiding?"

"Yes, they could easily check my timetables and routes." They left two to drive back the delivery vehicle after they had me. Luckily, they outstayed their welcome. I am armed ready and waiting skipper."

"Clever girl, I hope the pigeon got there."

In WW2 G.I. Joe saved 1000 British troops who had taken an Italian town. G.I. Joe flew the twenty miles in less than twenty minutes as bombers were taxiing on the runway ready to blast the Italian town, unaware the British had taken it. Five minutes from a disaster G.I. Joe was awarded the Dickin medal for bravery

Chapter 50   St Agatha
Monday, January 1st, 2018

Danielle was awoken by the night shift at 6 am. They entered her room and told her a pigeon had arrived but with no message. Danielle sighed and told her to awake the whole monastery and meet in the big breakfast hall. The sound of the bell in the morning mist alarmed Helen and Ruslana as well as all the nuns. They washed and changed into their uniforms for morning prayer before breakfast. They talked quietly wondering why this early meeting had been called. Danielle checked her armoury. She arrived in the great hall, and all were present as Danielle sat at the top table as usual. Ruslana and Helen beside her. With a lump in her throat, she addressed her flock. "I am not sure of the danger approaching us. I have sinned in my past and I believe someone is coming to take me away. You are all innocent, but you might also be in danger. The men who might arrive soon will try and force me to leave. You will pray for only ten minutes now and return here. You will barricade this great hall and I will face them alone. The escape route should you feel endangered is the tunnel and prepare for the descent. You might have no choice; some men are animals they might want to kill you or rape you. Should I fail to repel this danger you must decide your own fate. There are mountaineers climbing up that could be your salvation. I wish to see Ruslana and Helen in my office first. Go and pray."

Ruslana responded, "Mother Superior, I think I speak for all here, we want to help you, what can we do?"

"Come to my office with Helen, the rest of you pray and be back here in ten minutes."

The meeting in the office was quick and to the point. Helen asked, "Surely the danger is not from the mountain, they can be easily sent to their deaths, so where is this danger coming from?"

Danielle was surprised by the choice of words, but Ruslana was quick to point out, "By helicopter is the normal way in here, we have several good binoculars, perhaps the first thing is to observe and see who approaches."

Danielle decided now was the time to show off two smoke bombs, two hand grenades and the gun with a few bullets and three spare magazines. "This is all I have against a possible army."

Ruslana was now in her lioness mood. "Give me a smoke bomb and one hand grenade. We know our terrain, we can set traps. What we do not know is how well they are armed and how many we are up against."

Danielle felt shocked at her intuitiveness and returned with them to the great hall. Danielle watched Ruslana in her innocent way not aware of the real danger, trying to compose herself to help her. Danielle allowed Ruslana to give out the same orders she had considered. Three nuns were sent to high points with powerful binoculars Mari had brought some time before, normally used innocently to watch for birds and animals. The mission now to see if any helicopters were approaching. They took drinks and sandwiches and put warm clothing on, as did all the nuns. Danielle was speechless with apprehension, her voice croaky with anxiety and breathing heavily as Ruslana continued her authoritative manner. "Prepare to barricade the main doors and here to the great hall, in case we are threatened. All of you grab our local knife. Rochine, take three of you and go through the tunnel to the new landing site. See if the mountaineers are on the way up."

Danielle had her grenade and gun hidden under her clothing by a special belt. Helen was looking perplexed at what might be happening. Ruslana gave her orders, "Take the netting we use for helicopter drops in high winds and place it above the second door to our monastery. Have it so that if we cut it from above it will float down and fall over anyone near that entrance. There is a wooden bar for that one as well. We must defend our monastery if we are to help Danielle."

Danielle felt she had one idea Ruslana had not thought of. "The rest of you prepare as quickly as possible small bonfires on the normal landing site. It just might deter them."

The flock were about to leave the great hall having rushed to their rooms to put warm clothes on and sturdier boots with long socks in case mountaineering was required. Under their nun's outfits they were much more prepared for the cold outdoors. Ruslana produced the hand grenade and the smoke bomb. Panic gripped a few of the girls but Helen and Ruslana with the help of a quick slap across two faces brought them to their senses.

Ruslana took control. "The last two of you with no jobs will turn this great hall into our hospital and food hall. Be prepared for injuries, hot water, and all medicines, first aid in here now, get moving. We are all in danger, now get a grip, you two provide food and drink and prepare hot water in a bucket. Find dressings and ointments and slings in case of injuries. This great hall is our last line of defence. This is the new hospital and our tunnel escape from that corner. Last one out puts the small table back in place."

Danielle looked in admiration at Ruslana. Lean and fit with no hint of panic a natural leader and thinker. Ruslana continued, "Mother Superior will check any sightings and then she will decide our course of action. Two of you prepare bonfires on the landing areas. Time is limited."

Everyone now had a job. Danielle could not think of what to say she knew that if it was Tariq or his men, they had no chance. Danielle went to the pigeon loft and sent a message back to Mari as she checked her gun yet again. A belt under her garment hid the last smoke bomb and grenade. It did not take Ruslana long to know how to use them as Danielle explained the workings. Danielle went over to the landing site where Rochine was organising the gear for a mass exodus. Her binoculars picked up about six to eight bodies ascending the mountain towards her. Like ants in the distance. Danielle kissed the three girls as if it was her last goodbye and ran back to see more of her flock putting bushes and branches over the other landing sites. She was gambling whoever was coming would use the main visible landing spot and not the one out of view unless you came from the opposite direction. Then she checked the barricades were ready for extra protection. Finally, she took up a position as the light improved to view the horizon next to one of her nuns.

"Look in the distance above the treeline at 1 pm!" a shout from one lookout.

Danielle turned her binocular to the timeline that was in front of her. She could see a helicopter coming straight for the monastery. Her heart bounced back from the floor engulfing her with fear. She did not show it. Her trembling hands tried to keep the binoculars steady. She had a relay of nuns to tell those at the makeshift bonfires to wait for orders. She knew that to light them and get them back to the safety of the monastery would be a tricky calculation.

"Get Rochine and her girls back to the monastery, tell them to come back through the tunnel." Danielle barked out the order. Ruslana and Helen suddenly appeared next to her as if commanders waiting for a general's order. "We do not use any weapons unless forced, they may be friendly."

Slowly through the backdrop of a blue clear cold sky the sound of an advancing helicopter approached. A lookout then cried out, "Another helicopter about a mile behind, also heading this way."

Danielle gave out hope to her flock. "Surely one is a friend."

Binoculars focussed on the first one the three lookouts in unison, "Armed with balaclavas on."

Danielle could see Tariq piloting the helicopter she shouted down "lite the fires and get back."

They had been seen and machine gun fire peppered around them as they struggled to light the fires and cause any problems in the time given to prepare them. The cold and damp frustrating their efforts, a waste of time. They all retreated to the safety of the monastery, the last two placing two wooden supports that surely made it impenetrable. They raced to the next door and did the same to that. The only way in/out except the new tunnel which finished well short of the forest. The mountain had proved the tunnel to be a chore of slow progress and much toil.

Danielle now reassessed the situation. "Helen, you take over I will be out of view. We need to buy time. When they land, they will be after me, they will give us time for me to appear."

The drone of the helicopter subsided as it landed, and the blades whined to a halt. Danielle went out of sight down the steps but near enough to hear. Danielle froze and started to sweat as she heard that familiar voice of Tariq, "I want Danielle and Rochine, and we will leave immediately."

Danielle heard Helen's response. "Why do you come with such weapons when we are a peaceful monastery?"

"Danielle and Rochine please." The tone hardening as Danielle listened for Helen's delaying tactics. "Please repeat your request the wind makes it difficult to hear." Danielle could sense Tariq had moved closer to the monastery doors and heard him deliver the same request with a note of finality. She then heard Helen's reply: "We do not have anyone here by the name of Rochine."

Danielle knew she had lied to give her time to consider. Time and the impatient Tariq had had enough. "You may not have but Danielle will know who she is. You have ten minutes for both to appear or I will blow these doors open and tear this place apart. My men will enjoy the spoils of victory."

Danielle could hear the lookouts talking to Helen all in unison "another helicopter approaching. It is Mari's but no sign of her just more armed men with balaclavas."

Danielle saw Helen shouting to one of the lookouts. "Go and tell Danielle to come here with someone called Rochine."

Danielle still out of sight whispered to her, "Go and warn the girls to use all barricades and then we will go together up the stairs. Bring Rochine only. I will talk to Tariq then."

Danielle spotted relief on her face as the other lookouts came down and went to the great hall murmuring, "They look well armed."

The silence of those ten minutes were broken by the arrival of Rochine and Ruslana. Danielle could see Helen peering down then announcing to the army outside, "They are here."

Danielle was annoyed Ruslana had turned up, "I only asked for Rochine."

Ruslana ignored her comment and walked up first to see the situation and be next to Helen.

Danielle made Rochine face the wrong way as she could now see over the parapet with Helen and Ruslana. Danielle took over the conversation. "We need to get some clothes and we will come out in fifteen minutes on one condition."

"You are in no position to offer conditions, but what is it you want?"

"We will come outside, you back off fifty paces so the doors can be closed, and you do not enter this monastery."

Tariq was impressed by her attention to detail. He sensed victory. "No more than ten minutes, I am not bothered if you come with nothing. No red cases no tricks."

Only Danielle knew what he meant. She had a final question. "That is Mari's helicopter, where is she? RAID will be here soon from Clermont, you have no chance."

"I destroyed all their helicopters and took this one and as for Mari." One of his men interrupted him with a hideous remark, "Last time we saw her she was tied to a bed. We left two men to guard over her, those two seats are for you two. We might find room for another."

The men all laughed with anticipation. They knew Tariq would reward them. Tariq quick to confirm his intentions, "Your position is hopeless. Ten minutes or we blast the doors. My men can do as they like, they have their own helicopter and can stay longer."

Danielle remembered been shown Mari's bed of tricks. Surely some hope. Her instinct was now the safety of her flock. "We will come down." Helen was now holding the frightened Rochine who was hysterical "Why me, why me?"

Helen was guiding her down the stairs as Danielle prepared to follow. They had lost and in ten minutes they would be both at the mercy of their abductors. Danielle turned instinctively as she heard an explosion outside an attacker blown up by Ruslana's well thrown hand grenade, another wounded. Within seconds bullets rained close to them aimed at Ruslana, who sensibly had ducked below the wall and was coming down the stairs. "One down and only seven left!" she exclaimed. "I have one smoke bomb left."

"One grenade and a few rounds of ammunition for one gun, with one more smoke bomb will not stop these ISIS assassins, you stupid fool, I should never have given you a hand grenade."

Danielle now realised it was a fight for survival. She gave out orders "Rochine, go to the great hall and start getting them through the tunnel. Get to the mountain and start the descent with as many as possible. The ledge will hold at least ten bodies. Just leave two medics behind who will leave at the last moment with Helen and Ruslana. We will wait above the second door and try and delay them. They will soon have the main door blasted open. You have no idea what we are up against."

Danielle went back up the stairs and sent three shots at some figures before running back to be above the second line of defence. It was several minutes later when a blast sent the oak door that had been there for centuries was ripped apart. Through came Tariq's men machine gun firing aimlessly to allow them to get to the second door. Danielle instructed them to cut the net. She watched it drop slowly down and entangled one of the soldiers. Three more rounds from her gun and another magazine quickly replaced the empty one. She hit one but had to retreat as machine gun fire came her way, Tariq's men ignoring the instructions of wanting them alive.

"Hold your fire," Tariq shouted, as more dynamite was placed against the second door.

Danielle told Helen and Ruslana to go to the great hall and all go to the tunnel. I will hold them off and retreat to my room. That will give you more time to escape. The mountain is your only hope."

The narrow corridor was ideal for Danielle to hold them at bay. She saw Helen running to the great hall. Ruslana stayed by her side. "I have one smoke bomb left to help you."

Bullets now raining down the corridor as they sought shelter in the doorways running from the corridor. They retreated to be almost level with the great hall in a door opposite after Danielle had rolled over on

344

the floor sending three more bullets into the darkness. Hearing one soldier being hit a bonus as the advance stalled. "Ruslana, get into the hall now and barricade it and all go via the tunnel. Give me your smoke bomb and go. You have to cross over on the count of three you roll and go in the hall, I will follow and send three more bullets and retreat to my room."

Ruslana did not disobey; the situation was hopeless as more bullets came from the advancing soldiers and then a smoke bomb from them. "One two three." Ruslana went first followed by Danielle this time three more shots and then running backwards at high speed to her room. To her dismay she saw Ruslana on the floor wounded but so close to the hall. Six bullets left; tears were now streaming down Danielle's face as she let off three more in anger. Coughing in the dust and retreating further she saw hands grappling with Ruslana and dragging her into the great hall. She heard the barricades being put into place to stop them entering immediately. Her mind conscious she had to give them three or four minutes to get into the tunnel, those that were left. The coughing a sign for the attackers to send more bullets knee high at her. She winced as two grazed her legs and sent her to the floor. Her bedroom still twenty metres away. It was the last throw of the dice. Dragging herself along the floor she sent her final smoke bomb down the corridor near the great hall. Then with two bullets only sent in the direction of the attackers she covered the twenty metres in quick time. Once inside she barricaded the door. Isolated now and one bullet left she awaited her fate. She put the bed on the floor to protect her from the blast that would surely follow. She crouched behind it. She hoped Tariq would appear and the final bullet she would implant in his head.

Counting in her head, Danielle heard footsteps and words being spoken. She guesstimated three minutes before she heard them retreat down the corridor. The blast sent her door off its hinges. She waited as she heard footsteps approaching on either side. The two soldiers a gun each pointing at her. As she stood up another great explosion was heard down the corridor. The great hall doors she thought instinctively. She stood up and there he was Tariq in front of her staring at her. Her mind confused now as to what to do with the final bullet. Herself or one go at Tariq. It was too late, she felt the full force of the butt of the two rifles, her gun falling to the floor. Danielle saw Tariq's arms waving at the soldiers. She saw his fist crashing into the left cheek, her teeth creaking and her head moving sideways. A soldier stopped her falling as his fist then hit her right cheek. Her mouth filling with blood as his boot kicked her on the legs, then his fist in her abdomen. Danielle felt the pain and only the two soldiers stopped her falling. She wanted it to end. A fist hit her near her eyes Danielle felt her vision impaired. She heard two more soldiers arriving and saying, "No one in the hall, no lights."

Danielle felt her legs dragging along the floor, the two soldiers taking her away from the smoke-filled corridor. She could see the great hall and nobody in it. She smiled to herself despite the pain and hoped some would get to safety. She saw Tariq go into the hall, his torch scouring the room. The two soldiers stopped waiting for further orders. It was another minute before she heard Tariq: "Blood on the floor, move the table." There was silence for a few seconds then, "You four go down the tunnel and send a report to me at the helicopter. If you find Rochine, bring her to my helicopter."

Danielle could see from the doors the four-armed men scurrying off like rats with intent.

The dragging continued till the fresh air hit her beleaguered body. She felt strong hands strapping her to a seat unable and not wanting to move. One eye out of order and feeling sick. She felt a sense of a small victory as one of his wounded soldiers was next to her. She wanted a drink, her dry mouth and body in need of comfort. There was none around. It seemed far too quick when she half saw one of his soldiers return. Danielle's

346

heart sank when she heard him report, "We caught six of them near the mountain edge, the others have got to a ledge about sixty metres lower. We asked where is Rochine? Or we kill one of you. All six said they were Rochine as if prepared to die for her. We do not know what she looks like."

Danielle was so pleased to hear that. She had deliberately not let Rochine in view of the raiders just in case this scenario happened. Her years of hostage negotiating and once picking up someone who was not the real person, a lesson for her she had kept up her sleeve. She listened carefully in spite of her pain and being trapped.

The soldier continued, "Then we saw some mountaineers coming up the mountain a good distance away. One had the word Police on his helmet. There is another helicopter landing site as well. We wait for your instructions."

Tariq was quick to act. "Go back and kill the mountaineers coming up. I know who Rochine is, she has olive skin and big brown eyes like mine. Remove their head gear. I will bring this helicopter to the other landing site; in case you need more armoury to help take out the climbers. We need to get out of here fast. Two of you take up position near the monastery garden walls. I can see them from here. They have a good vantage point over the landing site and where you say the nuns are. I will reconnoitre from above before landing. There is room for five in this helicopter."

Danielle felt another soldier close to her, machine gun at the ready. Just one seat left for Rochine. She watched the other soldier running back to join the other three. She saw the triumph in Tariq's face as he started the engine. The whining of the rotor blades a familiar noise. There was nothing she could do except pray for a miracle. She heard Tariq shout out as being in the middle seat Danielle saw the radar and an aircraft approaching from the other side. Tariq was airborne and travelling around the monastery. Danielle had heard him tell them he was coming round.

They both knew that whatever that helicopter was they would think it was Tariq.

Tariq checked his instruments. Danielle had noticed one rocket left when she was dragged into her seat. It was instinct and now she wondered what she could do. The state-of-the-art helicopter easily manoeuvred around the monastery. It approached the other helicopter from behind. As it the turned the corner Danielle saw it was Maggie, she could clearly see Jack and three others. She could not tell if anyone was in the sniper hold. She could see that it had no rockets and knew it was too low and too close to save them from Tariq's rocket of destruction even if the decoys were on. She watched hopelessly as she saw Tariq's grin and his fingers hovering over the red button to send Maggie to its final resting place.

Danielle wanted to see the outcome but the syringe a soldier had pushed into her sent her eyes and body into a coma. Tariq wanted to make sure she had no tricks up her sleeve.

Chapter 51

Jack expertly brought Maggie towards the landing zone with the wind against him. The lie of the land and woods meant the noise was not obvious till he was very close. He appeared as Mari saw a gun held at a nun's head and another stepping forward. All with heads open to the world in the cold. She saw another pointing a machine gun down the mountain near a rope. The sound of Maggie now the attention of all at the monastery was enough for Mari to deliver her task. The man with the gun at the nun's head reeled backwards with the impact of her shot, no longer a menace to anyone. The other near the mountain edge about to cut the rope and shoot, the receiver of her second bullet and a third to be on the safe side. That body disappeared over the edge of the mountain as startled nuns ran to the hut.

"Bandit behind!" the Swede announced.

"Too low and not enough time for those decoys to work." Jack had no answer as he saw Hiba shuffling in her seat to see it was Tariq behind clearly visible with bodies behind him in the helicopter. Metis looked resigned to their fate. The one guided missile now in line and about to be released by Tariq as Maggie hovered near the landing zone. Bullets hit Maggie from behind the garden walls as Metis pathetically sent some back from his machine gun not knowing exactly where they were hiding.

"It has been a privilege, we are doomed," said Jack as they awaited their fate.

The sound of a massive explosion and the helicopter behind dropping in slow motion at first and then cascading down the mountain was the most joyous sight they had ever witnessed. How the hell did that happen? They were still under attack from gunmen. Jack as he landed had instinctively shut off engines. "Get out, dive and head for cover, I will let Mari out. Hiba, Metis, Swede give cover. We will be out shortly, use the smoke bombs now, we are all kitted up, go go go!"

They dropped out of the helicopter rolling, the Swede and Metis throwing smoke bombs and shooting in the vague direction of where they were being fired from. Hiba followed and ran towards the woods as Jack helped Mari out. Metis followed Hiba as Jack, the Swede and Mari ran to the logs and hut where the nuns were hiding. There were screams from the side of the mountain where several nuns had been waiting and could only hear the explosions and gun noises, no idea what was happening above them. The mountaineers now close to the ledge on the lookout for danger, one with a gun handy.

Hiba was ahead of Metis and the smoke bombs did not give them cover as they neared the forest. A hail of bullets rained down on them as branches, tree trunks and eventually they were both struck and wounded falling onto some leaves in a safer part of the forest.

"I thought you were here to save us," muttered Helen, being left with some first aid to help her and Ruslana who was hidden nearby. They could both use their guns, but Helen attended quickly as best she could to their wounds in shoulders/arms/legs. They could see Jack, Mari and the Swede with the nun's safe but pinned down. Binoculars were used by the nuns, and they showed Jack who recognised small rocket launchers about to be deployed. More smoke bombs sent as they all ran from the hut to behind the logs. Twenty seconds later the hut was obliterated.

"You need to get back into the monastery and take them out from the ramparts," Rochine said, "Those men are not the ones that came out of the tunnel and captured us. The tunnel ends over there in the middle of nowhere near that big stone. You can lift the wooden cover. I know the monastery. If we can get there undercover, we can use the tunnel and get behind them. They have no idea where it ends."

Jack was impressed with the plan and her observation. Binoculars showed that perhaps another rocket was to be launched as well as where the tunnel was. They could see Metis and Hiba with Helen in the woods. Jack gave the signal for cover. "I only have two smoke bombs left, Mari/Swede you go with Rochine and see what you can do. I will cover from here as well. Speed is important, they are well armed."

Without more thought, the smoke bombs were thrown as far as possible. Two of the nuns picked up spare guns and joined in with Jack as well as firepower from the woods. Rochine led Mari and the Swede successfully to the tunnel entrance. It was more difficult for the Swede as he was tall. Mari and Rochine crawled to the great hall. They waited for the Swede then they followed Rochine to the ramparts at the back of the monastery. Jack meanwhile had ordered all the nuns to back away from the pile of logs to be close to the mountain edge. They all lay flat on the ground. It was not long before another explosion sent the logs in all directions, some rolling towards them. "To the woods – now!" They all did as they were told; Jack was to one side of them firing at the walled garden. They assembled as one unit. The nuns attending to and kissing Ruslana, trying to keep her alive and awake.

Jack and the nuns with binoculars trained on the walled garden prayed for Rochine and her little army to be in place. They saw the armoury about to be launched at them. Rockets and a mortar redirected to the forest.

Suddenly there was silence at the monastery for a minute or more. They heard from behind men approaching them, one with the word "Police" on his helmet.

"Hi, Metis, you look rough. A war zone round here, what the hell is going on?"

"Am I glad to see you, Yorkie. Get down, there are still some terrorists over there."

"You call a nun a terrorist?"

There she was a beautiful nun, looking ragged, dirty with another lady carrying her trusty rifle. Then there was a blond man, machine gun used, he spoke, "It is all over, we took the last ones out, just need to do a final check."

Nuns started crying in shock and disbelief of what had occurred. "Where is Danielle our mother superior?"

It was Hiba who spoke. "I saw Tariq in the other helicopter with a woman in the back with a soldier."

"Yes it was Tariq, we have been waiting for him to come out of his hideaway in Algeria. It was lucky I sent a message to Mr America that a drone was needed to take him out. I just gave him details of which helicopter he had taken and where he was going. Must admit I thought it was D Day for us."

Jack took control. "I will check the monastery with the Swede now. Then find shelter in your monastery and get some drinks and food prepared. That girl needs attention. I think too ill to move far. I will get a medical helicopter here within the hour."

"She is Ruslana and she caused this mayhem," one of the nuns commented.

"You have no idea what she has saved you all from." Mari was philosophical. "Why was that gunman pointing a gun at one of you?"

"He was going to shoot her unless the girl with olive skin showed herself to be Rochine. As you can see there are a few of us with that colour," one of the nuns replied and then continued, "but why you, Rochine?"

Rochine did not reply, she walked away as Yorkie approached her and took her hand. They walked hand in hand all the way to the monastery. They passed the broken doors, spent cartridges some dead attackers still lying around. Yorkie looked into her eyes as she went to help get food and drink. Yorkie's heartbeat rocketed. He followed her to the kitchen and helped, gazing at her beauty. Rochine felt his firm hands and his vibrant persona engulfing her with feelings she had never experienced before. She could not help but smile back at him.

* * *

The medical team that arrived at the monastery had more work than they anticipated. They managed to stabilise Ruslana's injuries. They also attended Metis, Helen, and Hiba and some of the nuns were in shock and minor injuries from the escape; some shrapnel from the exploded logs and knocks descending the mountain to the ledge. Then having to climb back up with the help of the Arudy climbing rescue team. Mari was able to fly home with the Swede and help move the dead bodies she had left behind. Jack came the next day in Maggie which was worse for wear having been peppered with bullets. Mari gave him the last message Danielle had sent. It had four rows of six numbers and simply said, "Jack will know what to do with these red cases if I have not contacted you."

Jack duly flew back to the monastery and discovered her red cases. He decided to go to the local Marie. Explaining to the Marie would be difficult so with the help of his trusted ally the Swede they came up with a solution. "Those girls at St Agathe need to move on. Some might want to stay. They were sent here for trafficking, but many are not wanting their own life. They are victims of misfortune. However, we have some ISIS money that needs to be distributed. Before we discuss your share, we will pay for some ski lifts to be installed to/from St Agatha. This will give them more security. They need love and education and be accepted for who they are."

The Marie fell silent, not really understanding what he could do. He nodded finally commenting, "They are out of the way and never been a problem to us. If anyone stays, we will keep an eye on them and charge them the normal rates. You say they need electricity. Perhaps that can be done at the same time as the ski lifts. They need workmen to repair doors and phones to contact people."

Jack opened two cases full of money. "These are for all that. There is over two million euros. Send me the quotes and there is 100,000 for your own distribution. I will pay the quotation as instructed. The nuns have very little money, they will all receive some money so they can choose their own future."

Jack and the Swede visited St Agatha with the news, and they were in good spirits as Ruslana had returned from the hospital. They had tidied up as best they could. In the great hall with no main doors Jack spoke to them all. "You are all not naturally nuns. This is a forced existence. You now have the opportunity because of Danielle to go it alone or with anyone you like. Ski lifts and electricity will be supplied here at no cost to you. The money has come from Danielle which may have been why Tariq was after her. We do not know why he wanted Rochine."

The promise of money to go it alone in the world attracted a few to leave. Helen said she would like to stay as did Ruslana and six other girls. It was going to be a new dynasty at St Agatha. Mari will still be your contact and look after those pigeons. A pigeon saved you all. Danielle may not have been what you thought she was, but she was a great leader. A thinker and strategist. She received a message to say danger was coming here. She and your Ruslana bought valuable time for us to arrive. Luck took its course and you will all find that is normal in life. Good luck to you all, I leave in peace and love to you all."

Chapter 52 Monday, January 8th

Rene was sat in his chair while Lisa put the kettle on. It was 9:10am.

"Where the hell is Yorkie?"

Lisa smiled. "Oh, give the boy a break, you were young once." Lisa poured out the tea and still they waited.

"No point in starting a meeting without him. 9:20 now, better dock his wages."

Suddenly the door opened. "Sorry I am late, oh just brought someone to help with the meeting."

Rene stood up and he beamed with amazement in his eyes, a beautiful olive-skinned lady with brown eyes appeared behind Yorkie awaiting introductions.

"Come on in, my dear, can we get you both a drink?" Rene in flirting mood.

"The 'we' means me, I am Lisa. He is Rene our station commander and you are?"

"I am Rochine Houston."

"We rescued her from St Agatha, and we are here to tell you the details of the trip to the monastery."

They sat down at the table as teas were poured out. It took two hours and then a lunch in the village as Rene put all other duties on hold. When he was alone with Yorkie he muttered, "Do not let this one go."

Yorkie smiled. Rochine was now the love of his life. He held her hand as they walked to the restaurant. Bush news meant by the time they had finished lunch most of the village had been to see them. The attention from the locals, and the surrounding countryside with the mountains in view made Rochine feel warm inside. She looked at Yorkie and kissed him as they left the restaurant. In her heart she had found her hero and her home. As for Yorkie he was totally besotted and now knew the meaning of love.

* * *

Jack called a meeting with his associates who went on the mission to St Agatha. They were all due to report to the committee to discuss the attack and subsequent events. Jack told the Swede, Metis, Mari, and Hiba that there would be no mention of Danielle Bousquet, only that a mother superior had died in the attack. It was Metis that had worked out from the photographs and his journey to Tunisia that it was probable Tariq had an affair with Mrs Houston and somehow his daughter was at this monastery.

At the committee meeting Metis was the main spokesman. "Tariq needed a helicopter or two to get to St Agatha and attacking here and getting Mari's helicopter which had regularly gone there was a logical answer. Destroying our helicopters here meant he could not be followed instantly from here. Luckily they did not know about Maggie."

Doc the German enquired "How did he know to get in via our own ambulance and get all this knowledge?"

Jack entered the discussion, "He would have known about the ambulance from my brother who died as he was an ISIS informer and the arrangement with the local hospital has been in place for many years. He has many cells and spies in areas we are not aware of. The good news now he is dead with his local army, that threat is now over."

358

Hiba remained calm and said nothing but made her point, "It was lucky I had just finished my shift and was able to take out two of the attackers here on the base."

Jack and the Swede concurred. Hiba looked around the table to see no suspicious gazes at her. Jean continued, "I do think there are more important issues at RAID. America is pulling out and the exodus has started. We have lost aircraft and our capabilities for several months. By the time any smaller agreement is reached we must accept looking for alternative employment is the order of the day. The good times here are over."

There was a sombre mood. The Englishman had thoughts: "We are starting a group to try and buy this defunct village to be. We can still use the leisure facilities and buy the accommodation. The commune could thrive if some people stay. It would simply be our own village."

Several nods liked that idea. It would take some organising and arguments at meetings. In principle a good idea. Operating and all being happy with the outcome another matter.

Jean ended the informal meeting, no secretary taking notes. "Countries are not putting more money into here, I have twenty-seven listed here who have given three months' notice. Ladies and gentlemen, I wish you all well and good luck. We only have Maggie in need of repair and the other helicopter that was on duty. With limited firepower all operations will cease in three months. We will only go out one serious mission at a time as of now. The main committee can stay behind, but in real terms you all have three months' wages before we officially close. Goodbye."

Jack, the Swede, Hiba, Metis and Mari agreed to take a taxi to a restaurant. They wanted their final goodbyes as Mari was not going to return to YMCA again. Mari had a bed for the night in the accommodation block before flying back the next day. The seven-seater taxi duly arrived, and they went into Clermont Ferrand. They took their seats and ordered drinks. They had to go up to the bar area to order food independently. The girls went first, Mari following Hiba. As Hiba ordered she started scratching the back of her right ear. Mari felt a shock wave through her body. She questioned herself silently "where have I seen that before?." She could not remember. Hiba did not have alcohol, but the rest had plenty of beer and wine. Jack raised a glass. "To our last supper together and to Danielle Bousquet, a saint and a sinner, God rest her soul."

The evening progressed with conversations often returning to their missions and the monastery. Hiba was aware of Mari's interest in the Swede as she had at first flirted with Metis until he held Hiba's hand and kissed her. They returned in good spirits despite the imminent closure of the operations at YMCA. Mari retired on her own, annoyed the Swede had resisted her charms. She lay in bed thinking, until she sat upright as though hit by a bolt of lightening. "The daughter of Mohammad Aqbal in the café when she had gone to Tunisia. It was her that scratched the back of her right ear and her father told her it was only when she ordered in public."

Speaking to herself was not the same as the next morning she met Metis before flying back to her pad. She explained that Hiba Lazaar was likely to be the daughter of Mohammad Aqbal. Metis was straight onto the main committee's computer. He still had authority and access. He traced the timelines and when Hiba arrived. How was this possible? He did not want to believe it. She had killed the attackers and helped at the monastery. He then remembered her comment about Tariq in the helicopter, the nights she had slept with him, the visit to the American's wife when she was not in to join a play. The threads of possibilities mounted when he contacted the Tunisian Embassy in Tunis. The secretary said the only thing she could remember was the original guy due to have the job was found dead in the local river. Hiba was working there at the time. Metis was dumbfounded but contacted Jack and the Swede. They agreed to meet up with Bronson near the volcano where they often went.

Hiba was pleased to get some fresh air. She was wondering about her future. The sight of Jack and the Swede surprised her. Bronson went off with Rubber Ball, Jack's daughter who was happy to see such a gathering left them to talk. Jack was straight to the point.

"Hiba, we believe you are Elena Aqbal and that you were planted here by Tariq."

"I am Hiba Lazaar, I am a warrior and I serve you all here."

Metis continued, "I believe you killed the man who was to have the new job and left him in the river."

"I am Hiba Lazaar, I am a warrior and I serve you all here."

The Swede drew a gun out. "I believe you let in the attackers on this site, then killed two of them to maintain your role here if Tariq's mission was successful."

"I am Hiba Lazaar, I am a warrior and I serve you all here."

Jack's turn. "I believe you are Elena Aqbal, that you were forced into this to save your family and help Tariq. You were a primary school teacher and have done good work here."

The Swede as he put the silencer on the gun spoke sternly. "Your actions cost the death of several members of this community; you are an ISIS spy."

"I am Hiba Lazaar, I am a warrior and I serve you all here."

Metis was increasingly agitated by all this. "There is no future now Tariq is dead, admit who you are and the truth, then we will decide your fate."

"I am Hiba Lazaar, I am a warrior and I serve you all here." Tears started to roll down her cheeks and her legs were going wobbly as the Swede moved her to the edge of the volcano, a gun to her head.

Jack moved closer to her. "You have been a warrior. You know the truth. You can save yourself."

"I am Hiba Lazaar, I am a warrior, I serve you all here." Now she was shaking, waiting for the bullet to end her life.

Metis jumped up to join Jack staring straight at Hiba. "Tell us the truth, reform, marry me, let us buy a house here, go back to primary school teaching, the past has gone forever, we have a future just like those nuns."

The Swede was now sweating with indecision, Jack wondering what to say next as Hiba burst out, "I am Elena Aqbal, I was forced to come here, Rochine was Tariq's daughter, I was a warrior, please, please spare me, I will marry you, Metis. I have nowhere to go, I want to teach again, I want to be here."

The Swede withdrew his gun as Hiba fell into Metis's arms rather than into the depths of the volcano. The uneasy silence followed as Jack decided to solve the problem. "We tell no one. You will be Hiba Lazaar. There has been enough killing. I see no gain by turning you in. Metis is a kind man. We must never tell Rochine the truth either. Some facts of life are best not told."

Bronson came bounding up as Metis and Hiba stroked him, tears still rolling down her cheeks. Rubber Ball asking, "What is wrong with Hiba?"

"She is crying with happiness, Metis proposed to her, and she has agreed. She is going to continue teaching and they will live here even when RAID ends its operations." The Swede happy to put his gun out of sight as he gave his verdict.

Pigeon racing started in Belgium where in December 2020 a racing pigeon called New Kim was sold for a world record $1.9 Million to a Chinese breeder. The previous record was $1.3 Million

Chapter 53

Monday, April 2nd

RAID HQ was now officially closed and the base looking like a ghost town. Repairs had been done where possible and many had bought apartments or houses on the complex. Some had found new jobs nearby. Hiba was teaching at the school which had depleted numbers. The barriers had been taken down. People accepted that a new way of life was now in operation. Jack's wife Suzette was in a much happier state of mind now that Jack had found a safer job.

* * *

At St Agatha Helen and Ruslana were at the head of the table. There was a buzz of excitement as word had got to them that work on the ski lifts was to start in the Autumn but would take a year to complete. Helen addressed her small flock, "We have bills to pay and a small business to run here. We have some capital but that does not last forever. We have a school near Portes off the D906 in the Gard department of France of the Occitaine region. You will be aware a second helicopter sometimes came here with new ladies. This was a source for us. Ladies who may have a better life with us than where they had been before. The rule of DOLLAR has to exist. It will be a much different order. Ladies will not be sold on unless it is their wish to serve another. You will be encouraged to go and learn new trades or leisure activities. Anyone is free to leave anytime. This is not a prison anymore. We may have ladies here for experiences of our life if we agree now. Any comments?"

One of the girls: "It is fun to see different ladies and exciting for us to share our love and way of life."

Another: "We can be more open, but we do need protection. While we have Helen and Ruslana that is good, should we allow men here?"

The room then had a hum of disbelief at such a comment. Helen asked for a quick vote and the motion was defeated. Helen continued, "Let us decide to advertise experiences at our monastery for ladies and find local businesses for support. In return we can do placements and support their staff, if needed."

The motion received a majority vote. Ruslana made her point. "Here is your month's rota, we have to keep the fires burning, feed the pigeons, prepare food and drink, pray. This is our home we need each other."

Some went hand in hand to work. Life at St Agatha would abide by DOLLAR.

* * *

It was 9:20 am at Arudy Police Station where Yorkie had just arrived. Rene had put back his meetings to 9:15 but Yorkie still arrived five minutes late. Tea was brewing as they all sat down. Lisa brought a notepad and pen to the table.

"Anything to report?" Rene enquired as Lisa went to fill the mugs of tea and bring them to the table.

"Spring is in the air," Yorkie commented.

"I have a letter from my sister at Brandiol."

"Why is that important?" muttered Rene as he sipped his tea.

"It will be important for Yorkie as you will see."

"Okay."

"Let me read it out to you. Dear Sis. Just to let you know a lovely young couple arrived at the chateau last week. They have come from Yorkshire to live here. Two gorgeous children play in the fountain and the garden. Lovely to see them all smiling. They do local cycle rides/routes and have turned the big barn into a repair shop with new bikes for sale and she does food and drink in the tearoom. The long-lost son has returned much to our relief. The helicopter pads have grown over with grass and used as a car park for visitors. That Swede I met ages ago came with one that used to fly helicopters. I think he was called Jack. I saw them go into the barn with a red case but never came out with it. Must have been a welcome present or whatever. I even went on a bike myself. Rufus followed and we had a lovely picnic in the countryside near a small lake. When you come, we will hire bikes and have a day out. Just a hint but I want a year's membership for my birthday present so I can lose more weight, Love Jennifer."

Yorkie smiled. "I wondered if my hunch was right. It was only when Lisa went through all the notes, I noticed his name was Phillip and his grandma was from Marseille. He did say he lived in Paris for a while. I contacted the North Yorkshire Police two months ago."

"Blimey, Yorkie, you and Lisa make a formidable pair. Someday you might be on my side of the desk. It is about time you brewed some more tea lad. I have got you a pair of pigeons for your engagement present. Might be useful one day."

As they looked at the two pigeons, the postman appeared. Before their raucous laughter rang out, the room filled up with the sounds of everyone cooing.

Contents

Chapter 1 1

Chapter 2 5

Chapter 3 13

Chapter 4 19

Chapter 5 31

Chapter 6 39

Chapter 7 45

Chapter 8 51

Chapter 9 53

Chapter 10 57

Chapter 11 67

Chapter 12 79

Chapter 13 87

Chapter 14 91

Chapter 15 99

Chapter 16 107

Chapter 17 113

Chapter 18 115

Chapter 19 123

Chapter 20 131

Chapter 21 135

Chapter 22 145

Chapter 23 153

Chapter 24 157

Chapter 25 163

Chapter 26 169

Chapter 27 173

Chapter 28 185

Chapter 29 193

Chapter 30 201

Chapter 31 213

Chapter 32 221

Chapter 33 229

Chapter 34 233

Chapter 35 247

Chapter 36 259

Chapter 37 261

Chapter 38 ....**265**

Chapter 39 271

Chapter 40 279

Chapter 41 287

Chapter 42 291

Chapter 43 295

Chapter 44 301

Chapter 45 307

Chapter 46 311

Chapter 47 316

Chapter 48 323

Chapter 49 ....**327**

Chapter 50 337

Chapter 51 349

Chapter 52 357

Chapter 53 365

Printed in Great Britain
by Amazon

87215525R00222